Solc

They had caught up! I dashed after the others, slipping and tripping on the wet ground and low brush snags. I knew we weren't far from gaining shelter. But I couldn't imagine what we would do there, and we wouldn't have much time to figure it out. Regardless, I ran as hard as I could.

Behind us, I heard the shouts of captains and the tearing of brush as they advanced at a run. Another ill aimed volley of arrows glanced off the trees around us and slid to the ground at our heels. There, just ahead, I could see the shadow of the degraded Post Neth.

As we got closer I began to pick out discouraging details. It slouched dejectedly, its walls bowing with age. Ivy and other climbing plants overran the outer walls, making it look more like a giant mass of greenery than a building. Half the roof was gone, and there were no doors to speak of.

I wished I had looked closer before I ran with the others into the small clearing near the front of the old outpost. But by the time I saw and registered movement in the shadows of its walls, it was too late.

The
Slayer Amongst Us

A. S. Evon

A huge thanks to my great friend Elijah. If it wasn't for you, this book wouldn't have even been started. Thanks for being an encourager when things got rough, a reminder to include depth in more aspects than one, and most of all, a fellow slave to all the joys and anguishes of writing.

Thanks a million.

Contents

To the King on the Throne

Part 1

Chapter 1
The Hope of the Hopeless

If it was up to me, I would be sitting before a blazing fire in the vast hearth, a cup of evening tea in my hands along with a good book. I would just be looking at the time and considering getting ready for bed. I would have called Sari, my maid, to request a cup of warm milk and to turn down my covers. I would have been enjoying the prospect of a comfortable night's sleep filled with pleasant dreams.

But no. It was not up to me.

Instead, I was shivering with cold and feeling rather miserable in the cramped entryway of a deplorable house in desperate need of remodeling. The old house was damp and filled with drafts that swept right up your skirts and chilled you to the bone. Or, at least they did to me. My stomach was howling with hunger, and my legs were about to give out from under me from pure exhaustion. Not to mention that my hem was six or seven inches deep with the latest, wettest, grossest muck this miserable settlement had to offer. But that was the least of my worries.

The biggest thing that rest on my mind was that my life was in imminent danger of either being taken or destroyed by this whole plagued ordeal.

And it was all my brother, Nollem's, fault.

I had been drug from my very home streets halfway across the mountain range, being pursued by city officials—whom I hold in the highest regard for protecting our city streets—and fleeing for my life because I, *me,* was accused of being a Radical. A *Radical!* Me! Have you ever heard of such a preposterous idea?

For the past three days, I have been abused because of my association with my brother. To spell it out clearly, I am not a Radical and have always been a loyal citizen of the Kingdom. I have forever served my duty as a citizen of Monare Pelm and am proud to wear the emblem of the Crown. And now to be roped into this all because *he* was one of *them!*

I can't do justice to my outrage on paper.

But no one cared. Our minds were preoccupied with more important matters—our lives. The soldiers were still after us and, at any moment, could burst through the door and arrest us all. By the next day we could be dead, as the law says is the just punishment for being a Radical. The king was of the opinion that the religion they embrace (which is very much different than ours) would infest and throw the entire city into upheaval. I wholly agreed. The only down side was now I was in danger of the very law that I supported. How's that for ironic?

Regardless, my life was in danger. Currently, we had been thrown into the laps of a homely old couple who didn't seem of much use in our situation. They bustled about trying to get everyone inside and somewhat comfortable, which to me seemed nearly impossible and highly improbable that they would succeed. There were five of us total. Of whom, I will get around to describing further when this current episode is completed.

I had just been admitted into a dim smokey room, which I assumed to be their single room for the preparation of victuals and everything else that might go on in such a poor family as this. The first thing I spotted was the fireplace, and I made a beeline for it. I spread my stiff fingers to better catch the welcomed heat. Mrs. Kelvin (she was the mistress of the house, though I never saw any kind of servants) busied herself with preparing something to eat and was bustling about her kitchen in a flurry. Her husband, Mr. Kelvin was taking coats and offering seats by the fire. One of my five companions, Bilham, who had led our motley group thus far, was passionately discussing what was to be done to secure our safety with Mr. Kelvin. I tuned out the heated conversation, too exhausted to care at the moment.

I could just begin to feel the tips of my fingers again when the door burst open. We all froze, our minds jumping to the the same awful thing. But it wasn't the soldiers. A young boy dashed in, his face with a wild look in it. He shouted, "Soldiers! They just came to the edge of the village!" Then he ducked out the door and disappeared.

Mr. Kelvin jumped into action. In a whirlwind, he distributed our coats again and ushered us down a narrow passage and up a small flight of stairs. Then another onto the second floor. Then another that led into the attic. Just as I reached the top and scrambled onto the hard, cold floor, I heard the front door open with a crash and many boots clump around.

They had come.

We stood crammed in the attic, anxious and uptight. It was then that I noticed two others were in the small space. At a first glance I thought they were just old bundles. But I was corrected when they moved to get up. It was a boy and girl, a little older than myself. The boy was tall and seemingly well built, but it was hard to tell between the lack of light and the amount of wraps he had. The girl was quiet and a whole head shorter than he was. Both held grave expressions.

Mr. Kelvin elbowed his way through with a candle in hand. He and the strangers exchanged a nod while he passed to the other side of the room. Like magic, he pounded on a section of paneling, and it popped open to reveal a hidden passage. Well, it wasn't so much a passage as it was a stairwell leading down into the basement. I thought this was odd too, but it was explained to me later the reason why. No one would ever suspect it. Why would you put your access to the basement in the attic?

Anyway, we squeezed down the narrow spiral stair all the way to a damp, freezing, pitch black basement. By now the warmth in my fingers was long gone. I shivered again. Great, now where? I somehow doubted that we would end in a cozy room filled with firelight and cinnamon smells.

Mr. Kelvin stood in the center of the room with the two strangers. The rest of us were only a few steps behind. The light of the candle illuminated several tunnels branching from this large room.

Now I could definitely hear the soldier's hard boots pounding just above us. Nervous and uneasy, I glanced up as if I could see the bottoms of their boots, then turned back to Mr. Kelvin. He was passing the candle to one of the strangers. He quickly introduced us to them. "This is Dwin," he pointed to the tall boy, "he knows the tunnels and will guide you to the forest." He motioned to the girl who had shrunk beside Dwin shoulder, "This is Kattim." Then he addressed all of us. "Have a safe journey. Elohim be with you all. Farewell, my friends."

With that he scrambled back up the stairs, leaving us in the scary cellar alone with two strangers.

Stepping forward, Bilham inquired with a hiss, "Where will you take us?"

"Somewhere safe," was the brief answer. Dwin wasted no time. He spun on his heel and marched, nearly trotted, down a yawning tunnel. His candle cast distorted shadows which leapt across the walls.

My brother Nollem kept right behind me, with Bilham, Kattim and Dwin ahead. I could hear everyone else behind me. All I could think of was where they were leading us. Were they trustworthy? Would they hand us over? Which emblem did they bear?

My thoughts were interrupted when I just about ran into Bilham. We had stopped. I saw Dwin climb a short ladder, with the candle in hand. He reached up and I heard a muffled thud. A cold gust of night air swept down and blasted our faces. The candle blew out, leaving us in the dark. I heard faint mutterings behind me, but didn't notice them. I gazed curiously up at the opening through which Dwin had now disappeared. I could see a perfect square of the night sky. The distant stars were framed by the edge of the trapdoor. Kattim's, and then Bilham's, silhouette blocked out most of it.

Then it was my turn. I studied the old ladder a moment then reached up and placed my foot on the bottom rung. The wood was slick with moss and frozen moisture, and my hands wanted to slip away. I planted each hand and boot with firm resolution and made it up into the frigid night.

I had emerged into a narrow alley, squeezed between two slouching houses. I could see the main street that passed through the small village of Divel. It was the only street. But I would hardly call it a street since all the cobblestones were buried under at least a foot of local muck. With each step there was the threat of your boot disappearing and being sucked down by the mud.

The small village itself was nestled between two mountains which held snow most of the year. It rests halfway along one of the few roads that passes over the Slaggar Mountains. Therefore, it was seen as a good place to put a town, seeing how it would get travelers. But the crops never grew well there, so the town was reduced to a village full of struggling people.

But back to the alleyway. It too contained the smelly, snow, mud, and manure muck that clung to your boots. It was like a death wish to your nose.

I shivered again and wondered how it wasn't snowing.

The others had finally all climbed out of the tunnel. Closing the trapdoor, Dwin motioned for us all to be silent as he led us around to the back of the house. We filed around the back of it, clinging to the siding as if we could blend in with it if we pressed against it hard enough. We halted. The sounds of soldiers shouting and cursing drew closer. They passed down the street, their boots squishing.

Dwin dashed across the narrow gap between this house and the next. Likewise we stole from building to building, keeping always on the back side of them. I began to pick out a dark shape ahead. We seemed to be heading for it. As we got closer, I saw the jagged lines of tree tops scar the night sky.

We finally made it to the edge where the village of Divel and the forest met. The main road was just to the left of us, zig-zagging further down the mountain like a dark ribbon. We dove to the right, into the old forest. We didn't have much lead on our pursuers. And we were all still exhausted from our run up the mountain. Now Dwin was pressing us down the other side at a quickening pace. Neither him nor Kattim seemed tired.

The descent was long and steep, with many boulders and stumps to trip over. We all knew the soldiers wouldn't be far behind us. It was only that thought that kept us going.

I only hoped that we could lose them in the forest, without losing ourselves at the same time.

Chapter 2
An Introduction

Now I will pause in my narrative to introduce you to those in our small company. Please keep in mind that all, except myself, are considered to be Radicals according to the officials in the city of Monare Pelm. I haven't actually seen it with my own eyes, but I'm assuming that they all bear the emblem of the Radical.

You're probably wondering what all the talk about "emblems" mean. Let me explain. Everyone's true allegiance, where their heart and life is dedicated to, is shown by a symbol engraved a few inches above their heart. We're all born with one and can never get rid of it. Each symbol is about an inch in height and width. These are called emblems. The emblem of the Kingdom is a Crown surrounded by a curly circle. That's the one I have. It signifies true citizenship in the Kingdom.

And then there's the emblem of everyone else who is not in the Kingdom, whether they call themselves Radicals or by any other name, it doesn't matter. They always said it was a dark symbol, etched in the blackest of ink and forming some unspeakable shape of horror. No one ever spoke of it directly. There were no pictures of it, and I had never even seen it on someone either.

Until Nollem showed me his emblem.

When I was little I saw a skull with a crown on its brow painted in bright red on a wall in the rougher parts of Monare Pelm. It was quickly painted over by city officials. I had always thought that it would look like that, but no. Nollem's was like a dead bush. It had one big twisted vine, with several branches that swarmed out from it. He called it a tree. I remember a tingling feeling that shivered through me, and I remember being very confused. It didn't look very scary at all. He used to have a Crown emblem, then it changed when he did.

Now that we have that cleared up, I can start the introduction by telling a little about myself. My name is Limira of Rose House, which is located in uptown of Monare Pelm. I'm moderately attractive with dirty blonde hair and grey eyes. I'm a fantastic spy, seemingly gifted at overhearing conversations and putting together tidbits of information. And I would like to say that I'm nice to socialize with, but I'm not sure. I never had many friends back home, and never did anything noteworthy to gain special attention.

I grew up in a fairly influential family; my parents did everything special. We're moderately rich, though I prefer to call it wealthy. My family, which consists of only my parents, myself and Nollem, were always pure loyalists to King Hobbel IV. But most importantly, we were dedicated to obeying the commands of Elohim. Our lives were committed to doing good things. Our life after this one depends on it. If we do good things, we will be rewarded. If not, punished.

Those who believe this are citizens of the Kingdom and, as mentioned above, the Crown emblem testifies to it. Monare

Pelm is full of such citizens, and likewise, we have the lowest crime rate in all the region of Fairlend. Everyone is nice and helps however they can.

But sometimes I get the feeling that the "good work" thing is a little overdone. I never bothered too much with it. It was always exhausting and inconvenient. Besides, I went to hear the priest every seventh day, and I'd never done anything really bad, like stolen or killed someone.

Lately, there's been a craze in Monare Pelm about following someone called Shalom, not just following Elohim's commands. They've been labeled Radicals by King Hobbel IV. They believe that doing nice things isn't enough to save us from punishment, and instead you need to see that you can't be good enough and believe in someone called Shalom, who lived a perfect life and died to take the punishment we deserved and transfer His perfection to us. Apparently He did all that years and years ago.

It's ridiculous, I know.

These Radicals have been cropping up everywhere. You can't imagine my horror when my brother became one. My parents were as shocked and displeased as myself. I personally blame them for his turning against us. It was their fault that they didn't instruct him better. But my parents weren't very involved with us anyway. So I guess it's only fair that we have to "find our own way," so to speak.

Now for my fellow fleeing group.

First, there's Nollem, my brother. He's tall-ish with the same dirty blonde hair and grey eyes. He's two years older than myself, which places him at nineteen. He used to be the most dedicated citizen of the Kingdom I ever saw. He was always rushing out to help others and do good things, and he was constantly in search of something that would fill the hole in his heart, as he would tell me. I guess he found it. Ever since he became a Radical something's changed. And I hate to say it, but it's changed for the better. There's something about him... A new light, or a glow in his face that wasn't there before. It's almost desirable, but yet... not for me. I'm fine as I am.

The second in our group is Chimel. He's jolly, always cracking a joke at something, and is liked by everyone. He's thin, nearly wiry, and trips over everything. His sandy hair is wiry too, and his expression is always comical. I think he's around Nollem's age.

Bilham is the exact opposite. Middle aged, his dark hair and trim goatee are flecked with sliver. Yet his broad shoulders, commanding presence and chiseled features declare he is still well in his prime. His fitted jacket adorned with gold trim and glimmering buttons denoted his high position of authority within the city of Monare Pelm. He appeared to be a natural leader and seemed to be well aware of that fact.

Then there's Alletta. She is rather pleasant to look at, seemingly kind and compassionate. She always has this innocent, child-like simplistic look on her face. I rather like her, she's always ready to sympathize with me. We understand each other well enough. I often feel what she expresses. Whenever there is any sign of trouble she always turns pale and looks like she could just crumple under the weight of anxiety. And that's how I start to feel. My stomach gets into knots and I feel just the way she looks.

Finally, there's the two strangers who joined us. Dwin and Kattim. I suppose Dwin's in his late twenties or so, and Kattim's around my age. But it's hard to tell. And no, I would never ask them.

Dwin has dark hair and deep blue eyes. As I said before, he's tall and muscular. He hasn't made much of a favorable impression on me yet. He's always stalking about three yards in front of everyone else, and he's always grim, well, solemn. Yet there's something about his eyes. I don't know. I'll try to determine what it is about him. He's a strong leader, I'll give him that, but I'm not so sure that he has any emotion beyond that.

Then there's Kattim. Can you say weird? Well, not so much weird by herself but her devotion, and I mean *devotion*, to Dwin *is* weird. She is inseparable from him, always at his elbow. I haven't heard her utter a phrase, no, not even a word. Not only that, she seems scared, perpetually in fear of... something. She shrinks if I even look at her. My guess is she's had some awful social experience when she was little, or something along those lines.

Well, that's us at present. There's one thing that is common to all: we're all exhausted and most of us are confused as to why we're even in this mess.

It just occurred to me that you don't know how our band got together. Well, as it was, Nollem and I were out in the streets, wandering about and talking. We were just about to head back for home when a group of ten or so soldiers rounded the corner. They shouted for us to stop, approaching with their swords drawn. I had no idea what they would want with us, and only followed Nollem's lead because I wasn't sure what else to do.

As soon as Nollem saw them, he shouted, "Run!" and we raced in the opposite direction. We were skidding around corners and down streets, disrupting things all over. Very soon, quite by accident, we ran into another patrol as we turned a corner. These soldiers had prisoners with them already. We gave them such a start, that everything was thrown into confusion, and we as well as a few of the other prisoners got away. That was when Chimel, Bilham and Alletta joined our numbers. We all flew through the streets like wanted criminals, bucking it towards the mountains.

Only then did I remember that that was the first day King Hobbel IV's decree for the round up of all Radicals went into effect. In an effort to suppress and crush the new religion cropping up, he had ordered that all suspected Radicals be hunted down, brought to the Monare Pelm Tower—the courthouse and jail of our city—given a fair trial, and executed in anyway the judge chose shortly afterwards.

So we ran for three days, came to the little shack of a house owned by the Kelvin's, met Dwin and Kattim, and ran down the other side of the Slaggar Mountains.

Now we'll resume at the bottom of the mountains, at the edge of Slaggar Forest.

Chapter 3
The Fateful Decision

The sun was just ascending over the horizon, spilling its welcoming rays over the forest. We had finally stopped for a breather in a small clearing. I heard Bilham mutter something about the poor navigational skills in young minds these days, how could there be anywhere safe within this forest? Maybe they should have reconsidered who they were allowing to lead the group.

Not caring in the slightest, I sank gratefully against a boulder and stared at the pinks and oranges painting the sky with soft streaks. Nollem sat down beside me and smiled as he joined me in staring.

We enjoyed the sight. The pinks and oranges blossoming into dark and brilliant hues as it hit the dreamy clouds. It was breathtaking. But luckily for me, I was already out of breath, so I didn't notice that much of a difference. Regardless, it was the most lovely and enjoyable sunrise I had ever seen.

Nollem's grin widened and he said, "Just think of it, Limira, if you were back home you would have missed all this." He motioned gracefully with his hand toward the colored sky.

That ruined it. I glared my appreciation of reminding me of my dreary situation. I replied rather testily, "I'd rather be home, in a nice warm bed, still sleeping restfully. I hope *you're* happy, because I'm certainly not."

Nollem's grin dropped to an apologetic smile, and his tone dropped with sincerity, "I'm sorry you got roped into all this mess." He paused for a moment to think then added with a thoughtful air, "You know, life with with Shalom isn't promised to be all roses. In fact, there's bound to be more thorns than pretty flowers. But that's what makes the roses all the more special. Even through all this, I've never felt more at peace."

I stared at him incredulously. How could he be like that? How could he be at peace right now? Look at him! There was a certain smile and shine in his eyes as he stared at the sky. How annoying was that?

I was just about to say something in return when Bilham demanded in a laud voice, "Wherever do you plan to take us in this blasted forest?" He leaned against a tree, his arms crossed and his expression hard.

The question was obviously directed to Dwin. All eyes turned on him with the same question in them. Some inquiring looks were more friendly than others. Reposed against a tree, Dwin stared back at us, not offering to say anything.

Sitting on the ground, Kattim inched even closer to Dwin's feet, shrank back, and turned pale.

Chimel's merry laugh rang through the small clearing, severing the icy atmosphere. "Give the man a break! I'm sure he hasn't any more clue than we."

Bilham returned Chimel's comment with a withering glare. "If we were in the city, I could have you flogged for such insolence!"

That's when Dwin finally spoke. His voice was low which made us all hold our breaths to hear him, "But we are not in the city. Which is why you all need me. I have a few ideas, if you all are agreeable to them. But one fact remains the same. The solders are still after us, and they aren't far behind either. We have maybe a six hour lead, so we have to act fast. We can either hide out in the woods and wait for the storm to blow over, or we can try backtracking and confusing our trail. Ambush is obviously not an option, seeing our lack of weapons and resources."

There was a general silence for a few moments. It was broken by the soft voice of Alletta. "Why don't we go to Post Neth? It has been long abandoned, everyone knows that. It would give us some shelter, and since we very clearly can't go to any other post, it seems a good option. Besides, it's far out of the way and doubtful that the soldiers would track us that far."

I, not being interested in geography, had not idea where this Post Neth was, but it sounded agreeable. And I was willing to trust Alletta's judgement. And she was right, it was certainly a better option than just living in the open woods.

There are three Posts scattered through Slaggar Forest, all manned and supplied from Monare Pelm. The one closest to Monare Pelm, being just at the edge of the mountain range and to the south, was called Post Dagget. The second and largest Post, Baldar, was closest to the enemy lines separating Deceiver's land from ours'. It gets the most attacks and raids. They are also the most suspicious of anyone, Crown emblem or not. Then finally there was Post Neth, long abandoned and generally forgotten.

Everyone else thought that it sounded better than staying in the woods, and it was quickly agreed upon.

We set out again.

I wasn't sure how long I would be able to keep up at the pace we were going. My feet ached so much it felt like one big blister covering the whole sole. I was so hungry that my stomach had stopped growling hours ago. I guess it knew it wasn't going to be satisfied any time soon, so it just stopped protesting. And I had barely any sleep the last four days. But there I was, plodding along as before, with Dwin in the lead.

By now we were fully immersed in Slaggar Forest. It was not a very friendly looking forest. The canopy of foliage was so thick that the air and greenery below was dark and gloomy. The sunlight hardly ever made it down to illuminate the underworld. The forest floor was one dense hedge of brush with a few animal trails snaking through. Despite its looks, I didn't have any foreboding thoughts when I entered it. It just felt like one old forest.

But if I had known what would happen in its depths, I would have turned around right then and there.

Chapter 4
Out to get Us

Nothing new or exciting happened all day. The entire day we were all conscious of our pursuers, but we never saw or heard them. The real action began with the sun disappearing. We settled in a spot where the trees weren't so thick and we could see the sky. I'm not sure what the advantage of this was, except perhaps to see the stars. But, to my disappointment, the night sky was cloudy with not a star in sight.

Against Dwin's cautioning, a fire was built and we gathered around it. We weren't in the mood for talking, and I think we were all a bit on edge because we felt so miserable. We had nothing to eat except what we found in the woods, and we hadn't come across any sort of stream so we were all parched. To sum it up, all we wanted was a night's sleep, uninterrupted.

But of course, that's not the way it went.

The fire had reduced to embers when I woke suddenly. It was strange because usually when I woke up during the night, I would still be sleepy. But not this time. I was wide awake in just seconds. I stared up at the sky. It was a blank slate of grey, and night sounds were nonexistent. I hadn't been on many night outings, but it seemed odd to me. I searched my surroundings; the darkness greatly limited my field of view. But I saw nothing out of place.

I settled my mind on it being just a freak thing—oh for the days when my mind was so easily consoled!—and snuggled back into my cloak for sleep.

That was when I heard it. A low growl sounded just behind me. Startled, my eyelids snapped open. Rolling on my stomach quickly, I attempted to see what it was, but only tangled myself further in the the cloak. I got my elbows under me and finally scoured the darkness. There it was! A chill raced down my spine, and I inwardly wanted to dismiss it as a horrible dream. But I knew it wasn't.

A single pair of blood red eyes, void of pupils, were suspended in the black surroundings. They narrowed with a simultaneous growl. The villainous pair of eyes stared directly into mine.

I sat up abruptly and searched around our camp. More pairs of glowing eyes appeared, encircling us. Light from the embers didn't need to reflect on their retinas, they glowed on their own. I wanted to scream, or at least say something, but my mouth went dry with fear. I never imagined that I would meet any of these creatures in person. I had heard of them from travelers, but never actually saw one. But frankly, I never wanted to either. They're known as Weavels. Cute and fuzzy during the day and no larger than a bobcat, they become the fiercest predator at night. They were renowned for haunting these woods. Many innocent travelers had met their end by these creatures. But maybe they weren't so innocent after all, because it's said, and well believed, that Weavels can only be called by a servant of Deceiver. Do I believe it? Yes, I do.

I could feel my mouth moving but no sound came out. Finally I croaked out a sound which was loud enough to wake the whole camp. In an instant everyone was reaching for any weapon they had. Unfortunately for us, it was mainly daggers. Not much use against the cat-like razor claws of Weavels. The Weavels began their approach, slowly at first. The men of our company dashed to the edge of the ring of dim light our embers produced, ready for the first onset.

In the blink of an eye, the Weavels charged into our camp, attacking the first thing they ran into. Their claws slashed through the air, fully extended and deadly. They always went for the throat. Snarls and grunts combined in the din. I could barely see the dark figures of Dwin and Nollem on one side of us, and Chimel and Bilham on the other. Kattim and Alletta had fled to near the fire. In a desperate attempt to help, I grabbed the nearest stone and chucked it into the night. A satisfactory yelp came in reply. I seized another and threw it. Perhaps my aim wasn't so good, but it didn't seem to matter. Before I knew it, I was snatching up anything at hand. Pine cones, sticks and even handfuls of dust were hurled into the night. I knew that I had my five inch boot knife on me, but it wouldn't do much good unless I physically engaged them. And to be honest, I was too scared to do that.

Somewhere in the brawl, a Weavel raced through our embers, scattering them in a dozen different directions. Our small light was completely extinguished. Kattim and Alletta screamed as the Weavel knocked them down in its dash.

The confusion amplified as we could not see what we were fighting. I paused in my missile throwing and took a quick stock of my surroundings. The central amount of ruckus was coming from my far right, where Nollem and Dwin had set themselves. I could barely see their silhouettes surrounded by a furry mass that came up to their knees. Occasionally a dagger blade would flash.

There were so many darting creatures all about us. I was certain that we would be overrun before the hour was up. But on we fought against the increasing numbers of the Weavels.

Just when I thought we were goners for sure, a chilling, inhuman scream rang through the darkness.

Both Weavels and people alike paused. It was a signal to the creatures. The signal to leave. As quick as they appeared, the Weavels darted away.

I stared into the blackness, thinking it was just a trick. They had to be back, why would they just leave? A few moments passed until I was fully convinced that they were gone. By then our group had congregated closer to where our fire was. Someone gathered together tinder and some old coals and struck a match. The brief flare of light illuminated Chimel's face. He was sweaty and dusty, and he had a bruise on his forehead. But the thing that caught my eye was his expression. It was mix of horror and shock.

He coaxed a larger flame from the tinder and piled it with twigs and sticks. Bilham joined him by the fire, and Chimel muttered to him, "I think a rock or something hit me. I'm not sure how..."

I covered a snicker with a cough. It may, or may not, have been me, but let's keep that between just the two of us.

Bilham inspected a slight scratch on his hand in the light. Kattim had been knocked to the ground when the Weavel rushed through, but she was fine.

The worst of us all were Nollem and Dwin. I gasped when they hobbled into the firelight. Dwin had an arm wrapped over Nollem's neck. Both were limping. Nollem had a gash on his leg and his shoulder had been grazed. Dwin's lower leg had three deep claw slashes. Blood was seeping through his pant leg, leaving a dark, wet stain. He also had a cut across his left eye, leaving a red trail down his cheek. They hobbled a little closer then collapsed to the ground. It was then that I noticed another cut across Dwin's collar bone. It was just inches from his throat... and a death stroke.

Never shying from the sight of blood I moved over to Nollem. I bent to look at his leg, but he brushed me off, insisting that I look at Dwin first. I consented rather reluctantly and was relieved when Kattim rushed over to Dwin's side and started dabbing at his forehead. I was surprised that she was so calm.

Leaning down, I inspected his leg. Not seeing much with the pant leg in the way, I tore it open to reveal the wound. Three distinct claw marks ran down the majority of his lower leg. I grimaced at the sight. I reached under my skirt and tore the hem of my petticoat—it was never much use anyway. I used the strip to carefully wrap his leg, then added another strip from my cloak over the top since a red stain was already showing through first strip.

While I was working I heard Dwin muttering to Kattim, "Weavels. Someone had to call them."

It was directed to Kattim, who nodded, but I heard and wholly agreed. I stood up, and noticed that Kattim was tending to the cut over his collarbone. I couldn't help but notice the emblem above his heart. It was the bush symbol, like my brother Nollem's. It merely confirmed my suspicions, but I felt a strange tingling in the pit of my stomach when I saw it.

I moved toward Nollem, but Chimel and Alletta were already with him. I wasn't needed so I sat down with my back to the fire. I scanned the blackness for any movement. I knew they were out there. I could feel it. They were called by someone near us, but they hadn't completed what they were called to do. I glanced at Dwin. They were out for him. But they hadn't succeeded, and now they were awaiting their next opportunity with restless anxiety.

We passed an uneasy night. I don't think any of us got much sleep. The night slowly faded into a grey morning. In an effort to give more rest to Nollem and Dwin, we didn't move out till about noon. We made sure to always have one fully capable person with them. And as a precaution, we had one scout watch the trail we had just traversed for any sign of the soldiers. The rest of us went foraging for berries and roots.

Kattim had found a certain kind of berry, called Delbriars, that are famous for their healing properties, as well as for the enormous thorns that surround the medicinal berries. Alletta explained their history and properties to me.

I haven't heard of anything like this in your land, but you might have them. Kattim had braved the sharp thorns and retrieved some berries for the injured. I also picked just a few extra berries and stashed them in my pocket for a later time.

It was around midday when Bilham came crashing into the camp, shouting like one would shout fire. "They're coming! They're combing the brush, not fifteen minutes from finding us!"

At first I was too shocked to do anything. I could hardly think till Alletta took action. She jumped up and gathered up her cloak.

I snatched mine and hurried over to offer Nollem my shoulder for support. He accepted and leaned heavily on me. I noticed Chimel and Kattim position themselves on either side of Dwin. Between the two of them they could support him well enough.

Alletta took the lead, with myself and Nollem next, and Dwin, Chimel, and Kattim hobbling behind. Bilham took up the rear.

I awkwardly stumbled with Nollem. Already he was heavy, making my shoulders droop and ache under his weight. Progress seemed slow, and we couldn't help but trip over roots and snags protruding into our path. I tried keeping an eye out for obstacles in Nollem's path, but there wasn't much I could do. He was definitely in pain, I could tell. He was breathing heavily through his nose with his lips tightly clamped shut.

I couldn't hear anything other than the four of our group behind us. But that didn't mean anything. Realistically, there was no way I could hear over the crashing and ruckus they were making. Regardless, my suspicious side wondered if there actually was anything behind us.

By now, I had fully resigned myself to being stuck on this adventure, whether or not I wanted to be. But right then, I was asking myself, did it have to be so miserable? The adventures in stories never expounded on the true hardship of being hunted down, stuck out in the woods to survive, or having to deal with actual wounds. And I know that this may seem just like those types of stories to you, but let me tell you, I can't describe the half of it.

We were all tired, and I mean drained of energy. Our tongues stuck to the top of our mouths for lack of water. Our stomaches had given way to constant aching. Nothing to eat besides earthy, foul tasting plants scavenged from the brush and briars of the forest floor. No baths, sleeping on the cold hard ground with biting bugs and dew dampened clothes. The forest was eerily silent in the night hours. Every snapping twig resounded through the deafening quiet like a crashing log. Sleep seemed to be the only thing to relieve this nightmarish state. But even sleep alluded me. There was no refuge from this wretchedness. And it only made it more miserable for me that Nollem's spirit seemed unaltered. It was like he refused to admit that this was the worst thing that could happen. I wasn't sure where the others stood on their morale. But one thing I did know, we were all in this miserable ordeal together.

It was about an hour before we stopped for a break. We heaved to the ground, closing our eyes and trying to wet our mouths with our dry tongues. It was useless, but we tried anyway. After I let Nollem down gently, I chose a tree across from him and fell against it. He leaned his head back and closed his eyes, grimacing against pain. He eased his leg slowly so his knee was slightly elevated. His sides were pumping up and down, even though I could tell he was trying to take controlled breaths.

I glanced over at Dwin. His face was drawn and grim. His head hung lower the longer he sat there. I glanced at his leg and thought I caught a glimpse of a growing dark stain.

I couldn't help but think that he wasn't going to make it. Maybe that's why the Weavels left, they knew he wouldn't survive and it would be more miserable for him to die in slow agony than anything quick. I wasn't sure how I felt about this. It wasn't like I particularly liked him. In fact, I didn't. He didn't seem to have any feelings. He certainly wasn't enjoyable to be around, always solemn and studying you with those dark blue eyes.

I almost felt bad for Kattim. She would be crushed if he died. They were inseparable. I don't think that she had talked to anyone but him. What would she do if her only friend wasn't here? But maybe he wouldn't die, and they could just move on like normal.

Normal.

I almost laughed. Was there even such a thing anymore? Everything was getting turned upside down. First I get the news that father's been promoted to the High Council, and would be around that much less. Mum's days became "unexpectedly" busy with helping what poor beggars we get through the city. Then Nollem, the only one who was not changing, decided to up and leave our entire beliefs and adopt the latest new one. Our very lives were shaped by our faith, and he went and messed it up. And now because of that, I got wrapped up in this mess.

All I wanted was to go home and live life as it was—normal, peaceful, routine. Nothing to drag you out of your comfort zone. But no. That's not how things played out at all. Instead I was here, and it wouldn't do me any good to wish I was elsewhere. That's what I told myself, but I only half believed it.

Chapter 5
"Someone had to call them."

We started again and only stopped about an hour later when we found a meandering stream. Immediately, we all knelt and slurped the cool, sweet liquid. I cupped my hands and let the water slip over the edge. Then I raised it to my parched lips and drank heartily. I felt it slide down my throat with refreshing ease. Water never tasted so good. Nor was I ever more grateful to have it. I splashed some on my face and drank more. I didn't think I could ever get enough.

Kattim produced some water skins from their small bundles and filled them. Soon, some roots and berries were passed around. We settled against some trees and boulders and sighed with contentment. My stomach full and my thirst quenched, it was the best moment since that miserable journey had begun.

Chimel sat down next to me with a sigh of ease. He smiled and wiped his mouth, collecting the water drops off his chin. "You know, Limira," he began, "nothing could be more satisfying than full bellies and good company. But, of course, the most satisfying of all is a wet mouth."

I laughed slightly. His jolly face beamed brighter and he continued, "Well, only one thing could make this better. Music. It might brighten things up a little, and of course we'd all love to see Dwin do a jig for us."

I smiled as I thought of the picture; grim old Dwin dancing a jig with his bad leg. "I'm sure that would improve our spirits greatly. Only, I don't think that Dwin would oblige us."

"Even if we pleaded?" he asked, his face the very picture of teasing.

"Even so."

"Then we'd have to pester Bilham."

We both laughed at the idea. Bilham, who overheard, scowled dangerously at Chimel. He spat back, "Frivolities! I was always far too busy making sure Monare Pelm remained well defended and its armies prepared for any assaults."

Chimel replied, merry and mirthful, "Never thought you'd be chased out like a common thief by the very men you trained, did you?"

We both laughed all the more as Bilham's face acquired a deep shade of red. Then Alletta came over and joined us. She smiled and asked, "What are you laughing about over here?"

"Why?" Chimel returned, "Are the people next door complaining that we're too loud?"

Alletta and I laughed and she said between laughs, "No, it just sounded like fun so I came over to see what it was all about."

"Oh. It was just Limira and I, uh..."

"Goofing off," I interjected. "So how far are we from Post Neth?"

"Maybe three or four days away. It depends on how fast we travel. Especially with a certain problem," she gave a slight nod of her head towards Dwin.

I nodded looking over at Dwin. Chimel and Alletta continued talking, but I didn't hear. My attention was grabbed by the picture of Nollem and Dwin talking together. Kattim was sitting, more like cowering, at Dwin's elbow. She's seemed to be listening, but not participating. I was surprised to see them conversing. And somehow, I still don't know how Nollem managed it, he coaxed a smile out of Dwin. And later, a slight laugh. They seemed to be getting along rather well. I was immediately curious what they were talking about. I couldn't hear them distinctly, since they were rather quiet about it. I was interrupted by Chimel asking, "...Don't you think Limira?"

I startled back into our conversation to find Chimel grinning expectantly at me. "Uh, sorry, what was that?"

"I was just saying that it would be funny if we found a banquet table all ready and warm for us when we reach Post Neth."

"Though it's highly improbable," Alletta added.

My smile returned and I replied, "Yes, it would be most pleasant. But as Alletta says, it's highly improbable."

As I lay awake that night, my thoughts bounced from one thing to another. I wondered how Dwin would be feeling in the morning, and how well of friends he and Nollem would turn out to be. A sudden thought hit me, it was strange that Dwin seemed to be improving as the day went on. Those Delbriars must be helping him in some way.

Chimel may have made my day. No, he did make my day. I felt much better after our little jokes. It wasn't much, but even a little laugher was good for my spirits.

Now it was night again. Last night was horrible. Would it repeat?

I immediately tried to stop this line of thinking by insisting that I should go to sleep. I was quite tired, and it had been a taxing day. Yet regardless, I couldn't sleep. I watched the small patches of sky through the many branches and the firelight scatter strange shadows on the tree tops.

My thoughts turned yet again to what Dwin had said last night, *"Someone had to call them."* I shivered to think that someone, it could have been any of us, had called those beasts to attack us. I couldn't begin to imagine who. It couldn't have been Dwin, because they were obviously out for him. Nollem would never do anything like that. Chimel was too light hearted and nice to intentionally harm anyone. Alletta had no quarrel with anyone, and she was too sweet anyway. Bilham, well, he didn't like that Dwin was more in charge than he was, but I doubted that he would do anything so drastic as that. Lastly there was Kattim. I paused in my thinking. It could be her. She's so silent, and I never heard her profess to be a Radical. But on the other hand, she was so devoted to Dwin she wouldn't have called them to harm him. Or maybe she did. Maybe all this loyalty was a play, and she had been out to kill him from the beginning!

I cut myself off there, almost laughing at my silly suppositions. This was ridiculous! What was I doing? Throwing suspicions on those who least deserved it. It was probably someone on the outside who called them to go after us.

But then, the idea that Weavels had to be called had never been proven. So I was probably just working off a myth. And since there was no real suspect, reason or evidence, I would just have to go with the idea that they attacked us because they wanted to. Or maybe they were attracted to the light.

I glanced over at the fire. A shiver ran up my spine. If they were attracted to light, then they could attack now.

On second thought, I liked the the idea that someone called them. Because then they wouldn't come back. Unless that someone called them again. But who would do that?

And round and round I went in my mind, tossing the ideas back and forth, debating within myself, trying to find out the truth of the matter.

Maybe after about an hour of thinking, my eyelids began to feel heavy and droop. I must have dozed off because the next thing I heard was a blood curdling scream ring through the wood.

Chapter 6
By the Cover of Darkness

MY eyelids snapping open, I sat up abruptly, half out of my wits with fear. Everyone was awake in seconds. The scream was filled with horror and pain. It seemed to be coming from everywhere around us. Just when I thought it would never end, it was suddenly cut short.

It was happening again! Another attack! I could hardly think of anything else. My eye strayed over the company counting numbers. Nollem, Dwin, Kattim, Chimel— No! He wasn't there!

I threw off my cloak and stood up, quickly heading in the direction I thought it might have come from. From behind, Nollem caught my arm with his hand.

"Wait a minute, Limira. Get some light first." We scratched up a make-shift torch and the others did the same. Within minutes, we fanned out searching between the trees and under brush. Time and my movements were agonizingly slow, as if I was running in a dream. I vaguely recognized that Kattim and Dwin were hobbling behind me. I didn't slacken my pace for them. In the distance of my mind I heard Nollem and Bilham over to my left.

Soon I was a sizable distance from my followers and fully focused on the ground. I searched intently for signs of recent passage. I never had any experience at tracking, but they always made it sound easy in books. Really I was just looking for anything to lead me on, something to give me the slightest bit of hope. I could hardly dare to hope that he could still be alive, and my mind screamed against the reality of his probable death.

He had to still be alive.

I swept the torch back and forth, trying to widen my range of sight. My heart was pounding rapidly in my chest. Fear and tension filled me. Every snapping twig made me jump. Every rustling leaf a beady-eyed predator lying low, ready to attack. Every flickering shadow a slinking beast stealing away.

Wait, what was that? I stopped completely, staring. The toe of a boot caught in the light. I took a step closer, my breath held in anticipation. I halted mid stride. I felt the color drain from my cheeks, and I had the sudden urge to throw up. I reached a hand up to cover my mouth and stifle a small cry.

Laying on his back on the cold forest floor was the still body of Chimel. His eyes stared distantly at the sky. They caught the light of the torch and glimmered dully. There, on his throat, was a ghastly red slit contrasting with his deathly pale skin. It glistened wetly.

My mind went blank as I stared. I felt numb all over, my stomach in churning knots. I almost dropped the torch. He was gone. I vaguely heard Dwin sigh as he drew closer. I couldn't think about anything else, my mind was filled with the images. I had never seen a dead body before. Much less the dead body of someone I knew. My hands began to shake uncontrollably, and my chin was quivering. I couldn't brush away the tears that begin to glide down my cheeks. I didn't care. Chimel, my friend Chimel, was dead.

A hand on my shoulder roused me and I turned slightly to see who it was. Nollem had come up behind me. He gently pulled me around to face him, taking the torch in his hand. I dimly remember seeing everyone crowd around as Nollem led me away. After a trip that I remember little of, I was back at camp and nestled under my cloak.

Everyone slowly filed back to camp. All were solemn and lost in their own thoughts.

I tried to go back to sleep but every time I closed my eyes images of his still form flashed back. I couldn't stop thinking about it. I concluded that the Weavels must have gotten him. But who called them? Who would want Chimel dead? Why was he out there alone? What had he done that anyone would desire his death?

❦

No one felt like moving on in the morning. The whole atmosphere was heavy and downcast. It would have fit the mood perfectly if it had been raining. Even Bilham seemed subdued. His usual fiery comments dowsed by a forehead clouded with despair.

Kattim was on edge, even more than usual. But that was probably due to Dwin seeming to look all the more spent from the activity and unrest of last night. Nollem was gravely remorseful, and was discouraged at the loss of our companion. Alletta was visibly grieved and had a vacant look in her eyes. I was totally distraught. I couldn't think of anything else. All I kept asking myself was what could have justified his death? Had he ever done anything to deserve it? Was it Weavels? Or someone amongst us? Or was it someone on the outside? It was

Dwin the first time, why now Chimel? But the biggest question of all was, who would be next?

❦

It was about noon when Dwin felt ready enough to start again. Nollem's leg was nearly healed except for a slight limp. We decided to set out again.

Before we left, we spread out to find roots and herbs and berries. We even found a few more Delbriars and sacrificed our fingers to get the healing berries. But we all consciously avoided the place where Chimel was found. It was then that we were struck with the idea of getting staffs for Dwin and Nollem, seeing how it would help them with traveling. Accordingly, we found some sizable branches and stripped them of their bark with our daggers. Keeping our hands busy seemed to distract our thoughts from Chimel. We returned to camp triumphantly bearing our prize. While we were gone, I suppose Nollem and Dwin had a lengthy conversation because it seemed we interrupted it when we returned.

But they seemed sociable enough, and in noticeably better spirits. This yet again roused my curiosity as to what they were conversing.

Readily enough, they caught on to the idea of using staffs, and we were off as I said before. The going was a little slower, but it was a better alternative than supporting them ourselves. That way less people were continually being worn out.

On our trek Alletta found some nuts, which we gathered and stowed in our pockets. Shortly after we came across a lone stream, from which we drank our fill. Kattim filled the skins again. The nuts made for a delicious supper that night. When we lit the fire, we produced them from our pockets and toasted them over the flame. I felt like I had never tasted anything quite so good. Finally, for the first time in days, our stomachs were completely satisfied.

Night had fallen with occasional clouds sailing on the ocean of the sky. The night air was cool, but not cold. It made for a very pleasant temperature. Sleep quickly overtook our exhausted limbs and full stomachs.

When I woke, the sun was up and birds were singing gloriously in its light. It filtered through the trees casting a lacy light on the patches of fog, leaving delicate patterns on the leaves of underbrush. All seemed to be happily living this morning.

It was strangely reviving to see and hear everything so alive. It reminded me that I had lived through another night. I smiled slightly just to be alive. I sat up and noted that Bilham and Alletta were still sleeping. The fire was nothing but a cold pile of grey ashes. I heard quiet voices behind me and recognized them as Nollem and Dwin. In her usual place, Kattim sat nearby, listening. I noticed that Dwin looked significantly better. His color had returned as well as the light in his eyes.

I stood up, curious as to what they were talking about. And this time, I thought it wouldn't be rude to join them, since we were the only ones up. I approached them, and Dwin stopped talking. His sentence trailed unfinished. He looked awkwardly at Nollem who gave a slight nod with a reassuring expression as if to say "she's trustworthy." Nollem turned to face me, and I could immediately tell he wanted to say something to me, but he wasn't sure how I would take it. I could tell that it was important, and he looked slightly dismayed.

"Limira," he started then hesitated, obviously unsure of how to phrase whatever it was he wanted to tell me. "Limira, I'm not sure how to tell you any other way, so I'll give it to you plain. Bilham's been killed."

That was an unexpected blow. Glancing over at where Bilham lay, I stared for a couple seconds in shock at the cloaked figure. He looked as though he was just sleeping. I nearly exploded with shock, "What?! Why? What do you—?"

"Keep it down!" Nollem hissed at me. "Limira, now listen closely. This is important. Both Chimel and Bilham had the emblem of the Kingdom. We checked. Dwin looked at Chimel's, and we both saw Bilham's emblem. You have the same emblem."

"Are you saying..." I couldn't finish my sentence, my mouth went dry and a hard lump sprung into the back of my throat.

Dwin added, seeing I was having a hard time swallowing this information, "We're only concerned for you."

"Exactly," Nollem reiterated. "Be careful. Especially at night. Okay? Dwin says we'll arrive at Post Neth tomorrow night or the morning after. When we get there you should be in less danger."

Barely hearing the last part about Post Neth, I asked vaguely, "How did he die?"

Dwin and Nollem exchanged glances neither wanting to reveal the details.

"Tell me!" I insisted. I needed to hear so that could I know what to expect.

After a few seconds of silent tension, Dwin finally said quietly and calmly, "Smothered in his sleep. As soon as Alletta awakes, we'll move on. Unfortunately, we don't have time to bury him."

Alletta stirred as we spoke. Our talk immediately disbanded. Nollem and I had the same thought to gather up our cloaks. He whispered as we walked, "Remember what we talked about."

I barely nodded, just enough for him to see. How could I not remember? A flooding wave of new thoughts came to torment me. Both Chimel and Bilham had the symbol of the Crown. Where was the King that we serve now? The emblem meant that they were perfectly good people. Just like me. They did all the right things, said all the right things. And if they died like that, no one was safe.

I was next.

A terror that I had never known consumed me. It was the terror of death. Could I be certain of my citizenship in Elohim's eternal Kingdom? I hadn't been into the "good works" stuff, but I was a good person. I never killed anyone, nor stole from anyone. But, regardless, I was next on this death list. Unless Alletta bore the Kingdom's emblem as well. Then I had a chance to live one more night. I can't describe how much I wanted to live just one more night. Just one would be enough. That's all I was asking for. Just one more night.

It all rested on whether or not Alletta had the emblem. But come to think of it, I had never see hers. Her dress collar was high, concealing her mark.

I tried to put it out of my mind by thinking I only had to worry when nightfall came. Till then I had nothing to worry about. It wasn't very effective, but I tried anyway.

The terror was still there. And it would never leave.

Chapter 7
I was Next

It was a clear night sky, filled with starry constellations. There were thousands of the winking lights dotted over the deep blueish black expanse. There was a quarter moon casting its silver beams, illuminating the forest with a strange, magical light. There was a distant red moon, about half the size of your regular one, as well as a few planets visible.

All this beauty and wonder, and my mind was still wandering back to that haunting thought. I'm next.

I laid awake long after the others drifted into sweet sleep. My thoughts strayed to the day's events, or lack thereof. It had been an overall silent day. There was no Chimel to lighten the air by a random joke. There was no Bilham to add a heated opinion. And no grumbling about peculiar things. I missed them. I missed both of them.

The Crown mark.

I was next.

I purposefully diverged from this line of thought, and instead thought of... Dwin. He was looking much better today.

Strangely. So was Nollem. Both hardly had to use their staffs. It was curious to see them so much better. And it certainly wasn't just the Delbriars. There had to be something else. It was odd to see them talking so much together. How much of that talk was about me?

Speaking of talking, Kattim was *so* quiet, and... protective over Dwin. Now *that* was weird. I also noticed that she was just as devoted as before, yet she seemed less fearful than before. What was the cause of her being more comfortable? Was it because Dwin was getting better? Was it because we, as a group, had been together longer? Or because it was getting smaller? Regardless she had become more brave and bold. Unflinching at —

Wait! What was that?

I heard the distinct sound of a twig snapping. It was close.

Just some animal, I guess, I told myself, consciously trying to keep my mind from racing. It probably sounded a lot closer than it actually was. Just like everything else at night.

I closed my eyes, determined to sleep. I couldn't lay awake all night, I told myself. But part of me wanted to.

I woke with a jolt. Something touched me. My eyelids snapped open, and I looked quickly around.

Wait, what? How did I get here?

I was standing in the middle of the forest. Moon beams, bright and silvery, filtered through the the trees, faintly illuminating the forest floor. To my sleepy eyes, the bright spots were much brighter than what they actually were, and the shadows were much darker, more ominous looking.

I must have been sleep walking. To this day, I can't explain it in any other way. I had to get back to camp. In my search for it, I turned around, looking for the glow of embers.

Thwack!

A solid object flew through the air and struck me square on the shoulder. The force of the blow sent me careening to the forest floor. My head hit something hard, probably a fallen log or rock. My vision blurred and I looked around but couldn't get my bearings, nor my feet under me. Suddenly a creature jumped on my back, its arm finding my neck. It began squeezing as hard as it could.

Choking, I roused myself into action. I grabbed at the creature but got nothing except a fist full of cloth. I yanked at it, but the creature only tightened its hold around my neck. I rolled onto my back, smashing it between me and ground. It wriggled out and rolled away from me. I caught a glimpse of it just as a cloud drifted over the moon, shading the light.

It was a small person, female. She had pale staring eyes. More importantly, I caught the glimmer of a knife in her hand. Before I thought to get up, it was on me, her empty hand reaching for my throat. She squeezed again with all her might.

Panic was beyond me. I began to fight for my life. I seized her wrist and wrenched her hand from my throat. Gasping for air, I coughed, holding her wrist in midair. Her other hand, the one with the knife, flew down towards my neck. I caught her wrist; now I had both of them. That knife was dangerously close to my throat. She was much smaller than myself. I shifted my weight and threw her to the ground. I leapt up, determined to be ready this time.

She rolled a small distance from me then spun, landing upright on all fours. Her agility amazed me. Now I could see more clearly its features. It had death-like white skin, wrinkled and spotted with green, glistening slime. Her stringy, thin hair also glistened as if it was wet in the moonlight. When she snarled, she revealed a mouth full of rotting, pointed teeth.

It was a monster. And it was charging right at me.

Ramming full force into my legs, she gained the advantage again. I toppled to the ground, taking her with me. She pounced on my chest and raised her knife, bringing it down. I threw a punch just in time and hooked her right on the jaw. Her head jerked back, and the knife caught my chin. Warm blood oozed out.

The creature righted itself, and glared at me with fierce eyes. She pinned one of my arms and brought the knife down full at my face. I screamed and raised my arm to hopefully block the blow and protect my face.

Before the knife came, I felt the creature flung off me. It landed a few feet away with a thud.

A strong hand grabbed my arm and lift me up. I stumbled, trying to get my feet under me. I instinctively hid behind him and peered over his shoulder. It was Dwin! He had his dagger drawn and waiting for the creature to charge at us. He moved to shield me as he stared her down.

She seemed uncertain of what to do, then after studying Dwin and seeing his knife blazing in the moonbeams, she looked defeated. Turning away, it seemed to shrink in size and slink away through the underbrush. We were frozen in time as we watched its retreat.

After a few moments of watching it, Dwin relaxed, satisfied that it had gone. I was still wide eyed and shaking like a leaf in a cold winter wind. Dwin turned slightly to his right, and dragged me the rest of the way in front of him. He looked squarely into my eyes then studied the rest of me with concern written over his face. He reached slowly up to my chin and tenderly wiped the blood with his thumb. It smeared and he dabbed at it again.

I dropped my gaze. All I wanted to do was cry. I bit my lips together and my shoulders began to shake. Before I knew it, a tear or two were sliding down my cheeks. I barely whispered a, "Thank you," before he wrapped an arm around my shoulder, drawing me close.

I couldn't help but break down sobbing on his shoulder. He just held me there. I'm not sure if he was saying anything or if he was just silent, but either way, he was a comfort. I couldn't believe that I had been so close to death. After a few more moments, noticing my tears to be somewhat subsiding, he led me back to camp with an arm still around my shoulders.

I couldn't believe I was still alive, that I didn't die.

By then, I collected my thoughts enough to think of asking some questions, and I asked him how he knew I was out there.

He whispered his explanation, "Nollem and I took shifts to watch you tonight. It was Nollem's idea. I followed you when you wandered off. You were very brave back there. Try to get some sleep, Limira," he added.

I didn't think I ever could.

I woke to find a grey morning. The wood was completely fogged in with the misty, heavy grey. But my first thought was I had survived another night! I lived! But somehow, I didn't feel any different on the inside. Another day hadn't given me much. Yes, I was grateful that I lived, but I didn't feel any more alive because of it.

It was then that I remembered Dwin. He had been so kind, and he was so... Oh, no. I blushed slightly at my behavior with him. He had hugged me, and I cried on his shoulder. *I* cried on *his* shoulder! Then I remembered my cut and how he wiped the blood with his own thumb. I was embarrassed that he had seen me in such a vulnerable state. If only it had been Nollem who had been looking after me when it happened.

I tried justifying it—and to help me feel better about the whole physical contact—as that is what Nollem would have done if he were there.

I intentionally turned my thoughts to the creature I saw, trying to recall the details.. It was small, it was female, and it looked nothing like anyone here. The facial appearances were *totally* different. Not to mention behavioral patterns. Besides it was much smaller in stature than Kattim and Alletta, so it couldn't have been either of them. So it was definitely someone from the outside doing the killings. It was someone who was sick in the brain and went about killing people for the fun of it. That had to be it. Nothing else fit.

By now, Nollem had noticed that I was awake and he came over. I could hear Alletta and Dwin talking in the background. Apparently I was the the last one up.

Nollem took a seat by me on the ground. I sat up, and tucked my knees against my chest, still wrapped up in my cloak.

"When Dwin told us about what happened last night, we were all shocked. To imagine, you could have died at the hands of that beast and none of us would have ever known the struggle behind it. I was pretty sure that if Alletta's eyes had gotten any bigger they would have turned into saucers right there." He laughed a little. But I just smiled, feeling tired and a bit sheepish. Nollem continued after a pause, the serious note back in his voice, "Are you alright, Limira? I mean, really, truly alright?"

I frowned and replied as best I could, trying to keep a brave face through it all, "Yes, and no. I'm alright in that I survived, but I don't think I'm alright now. And I don't know if I'll be alright again."

"You want to talk about it?" he asked gently.

"That creature." I relived the moment when I saw the beast. "It was so horrifying. But at the same time, I found it fascinating. It gave me the chills of fear and the tingles of wonder at the same time. I'm just glad it's gone and out there. It's not here with us. Nothing so despicable could be amongst us and not be found out. It was a person, I think. A female. She was so disgusting to look at. And she had a cold, pale light in her eyes. It was like she was death itself. All she seemed to care about was killing me. All it wanted was death. It was the most terrifying thing I ever knew. But I was curious about it. It's like I didn't see it as death then like I do now.

"It was strange. And I keep thinking about Chimel who had to fight that thing by himself, with no one to save him. And Bilham who had the life smothered out of him by this evil thing. I can't help but wonder if they were just as fascinated with it as I was. If they were as fearful and curious of it as I was. It had the sole intent of killing me. I only hope that it won't return. You don't think that it will come back and try again, do you?"

Nollem looked puzzled and he replied after a moment of thought, "I'm not sure. It might have given up on you, but there's no way to tell for sure. But one thing is for certain, it's still out there. Dwin may have only frightened it away temporarily."

"That was the other strange thing," I cut in. "It, the creature, was afraid of Dwin. It left without even challenging. As soon as Dwin came, it seemed to shrink in size, and it slunk off into the night. Instead of being feared, it was afraid. I don't understand. It was like it knew it was defeated before it even started fighting. It was strange," I summarized, still not completely sure what to think about the night's events. The more I thought about it the more I grew confused.

I didn't realized it until afterwards that my hands were shaking through the entire conversation.

Chapter 8
Post Neth & the Surprise There

It was about noon later that day. My hands still shook when I thought of the previous night.

But we had quite a different problem now. It had been raining all morning and into the afternoon. Everything was wet and miserable. To add to matters a breeze had kicked up just enough to chill us thoroughly. To make matters worse, there wasn't a dry place of refuge to shelter us. And there wasn't a chance that we would have that for a long time. We were all downcast with our hoods pulled low to cover our faces, and each drowned in our own thoughts. Mine were mainly about the mystifying events from last night. I still couldn't make sense of the entire matter.

The rain did not stop until after dark. And we didn't stop until after dark either. We barely got a small fire going before we hunkered down for the night. Being too petrified to sleep, I got hardly a wink that night. The dark terrified me. I was trembling with fear—or was it cold?—all night. Even if the ground had not been soaked and cold, I'm sure I wouldn't have gotten a better night's sleep.

To sum it up, I laid awake far into the night.

Alletta must have been dreaming. She kept making these grunting and low guttural sounds. It held a striking resemblance to the creature's sounds. My imagination was running away with me.

❦

Nothing else happened all night. I could sense we were all relieved, though no one said anything. I personally think that Dwin scared the thing away, but its memory was enough to send chills down my spine.

Dwin informed us that Post Neth was about an hour's walk from here. So we set out after a quick breakfast of the same roots and edible plants.

I wasn't sure what we were going to do once we got there, but I wasn't going the mention it. Thinking back, I realized that we never had a plan beyond Post Neth. We certainly hadn't been very strategic about losing the soldiers by meandering our path. Dwin's and Nollem's injuries had eliminated that idea. How could we know that we had fully lost our pursuers? We couldn't. And that was a problem. If they were still back there, once we got to Post Neth we'd be trapped and easily exposed. Either way, I told myself, I didn't have much say in the matter. We were all going to die sooner or later. All we were doing was prolonging the inevitable.

No! What was I thinking? If I really thought that way then why did I fight that creature so hard? I willed to survive. I had to survive. But what for? So I could be "good" for the rest of my days? That already felt empty. It was exhausting thinking of being "good enough" all the time.

Wait, was I starting to think like a Radical? No, I'm a citizen of the Kingdom. Which means I fight death till I've got nothing left, till I can fight no more.

My thoughts were untimely interrupted by a distant shout, which I barely took heed of. But I noticed when everyone but me shouted, "Run!" just as a volley of arrows whizzed through the trees.

Soldiers! They had caught up! I dashed after the others, slipping and tripping on the wet ground and low brush snags. I knew we weren't far from gaining shelter. But I couldn't imagine what we would do there, and we wouldn't have much time to figure it out. Regardless, I ran as hard as I could.

Behind us, I heard the shouts of captains and the tearing of brush as they advanced at a run. Another ill aimed volley of arrows bounced and glanced off the trees around us and slid to the ground at our heels. There, just ahead, I could see the shadow of the degraded Post Neth. As we got closer I began to pick out discouraging details. It slouched dejectedly, its walls bowing with age. Ivy and other climbing plants overran the outer walls, making it look more like a giant mass of greenery than a building. If parts weren't covered in leaves, the grey stones had disappeared under an inch of moss. Half the roof was gone, and there were no doors to speak of. The windows had long been without glass in them. Stones had fallen out of their places, leaving empty gaps. Trees had grown up all around it, choking any sunlight that might have had any chance of reaching it.

I couldn't believe that *this* was what we had trekked all through Slaggar Forest to get to. It was a dump, and we would have been better off under the trees. At least there we wouldn't have the worry of the roof caving in on us and burying us alive under its rubble.

I wished I had looked closer before I ran with the others into the small space that was unoccupied by trees near the front of the building. But by the time I saw and registered the movement in the shadows of the building, it was too late.

Burly, mean looking brutes filed hastily out the wide door, two at a time. The one in the lead was a Vaudian, most of the others were Vaudians as well, though there appeared to be a few Between mixed in. The Between looked young, far too young to be doing things like this. They each shadowed a Vaudian.

I had only ever heard of these creatures before, but I immediately recognized them. Between bear the other emblem that was never talked about in Monare Pelm, which I could only assume would be the bush symbol. In the daylight, they look like normal people, but at night they reflect what is in their hearts. That's the worst time to meet one. They are nasty with evil intents, and usually drunk, which doesn't help matters.

Vaudians are worse than Between. They're always living as though it's night, always fulfilling their own desires. They become deformed and scarred, larger and stronger than their former creatures. Their skin is thick and dark, with splotches of slimy brown spots. Their eyes become dark, glinting dangerously. What was written on their hearts became their fixed appearance.

And we were at the mercy of these beasts.

The Vaudians and the Between filed out the door, and spilt around us, forming a "V." The Kingdom soldiers from Monare Pelm had by now caught up. From a distance they fired a volley at our new assailants. The varied creatures closed their formation, creating a rough diamond shape with us caught in the middle. Dwin and Nollem drew their long daggers. Kattim produced a dagger as well. I seized a stone, knowing that my boot knife would, yet again, not be of any use in this situation. I hurled it at the closed wall of bodies.

More offenders poured out of the "abandoned" outpost. They advanced towards the King's soldiers with their assortment of wicked blades drawn. Dwin, Nollem, and Kattim rushed against the the nearest, hoping to break the lines. They were met with cold steel. Dwin and Nollem, fighting side by side, slashed at the armored beasts. Kattim had engaged two rascally looking fellows a small distance from the men. She caught a descending stroke with her blade and raised it diverting the sword from its course. For just a moment, it left her lower torso exposed. A moment was all it took. The second attacker took the shot and plunged his sword through her middle. Kattim screamed in pain, doubling over. Her dagger fell from her hand to the ground.

I screamed and ran forward, nearly feeling the same pain that she did as my gut wrenched inside. I only took a few steps before a strong arm caught me up from behind. The lead Vaudian pinned me against his foul smelling body with both his arms. I fought him, kicking and squirming to get out of his hold. Cold, blackened steel slid to my throat, raising my chin to avoid being sliced. I stopped struggling in a heartbeat.

I saw Dwin and Nollem had been overpowered. Four brutes were rough handling them into line. Dwin and Nollem were fighting hard against them; they were fighting for their lives.

The one holding me barked in a guttural voice, thick with a heavy accent, "Struggle and she dies now!"

As he spoke, he dug his knife into my throat just enough to make a bleeding cut. I stood as still as I possibly could, willing myself to stay calm. I knew that if I made one wrong move, I would be dead before I knew what had happened. I swallowed hard, feeling it lump against the blade. I pleaded with my eyes for them to do as he asked.

Dwin and Nollem scowled, furiously throwing down their weapons. The Between vagabonds surged forward and shoved them towards the door of the building. I was pushed from behind to follow them. Just as I passed Kattim, two wiry Between in dark clothing grabbed one of her arms and roughly yanked her upright. A cry of pain escaped her lips.

I half yelled, half begged, "Don't hurt her!" But my pleads fell on deaf, uncaring ears. We passed through the doorway, and immediately I was surrounded by pressing bodies. The Vaudian who held me forced my arms in front of me and tightly tied a leather cord around my wrists. I lost sight of Nollem. Dwin was to my right, and Kattim behind me slightly to the left. Then I suddenly remembered Alletta. Where was she?

The leader flung me into the arms of another tall Vaudian with a wild look in his eyes and sandy hair that matched it. His grin grew larger as he pulled me close against him, holding me securely in his arms. I nearly gagged from the stench that filled my nostrils. Scars and lumps patched his face and arms.

The lead Vaudian, who had just passed me off, yelled above the noise. I couldn't understand what he said but it sounded like orders of sorts. About a score of them pealed out from the group. Snatching up Dwin, Kattim and myself, they moved to the door again. Just as I passed out the door, I caught a glimpse of Nollem. He was being held from behind with his chest pinned against the wall. He had a bleeding cut across his cheek, and he was grimacing in pain as the brute who held him there dug a calloused elbow into his back with a vile smile.

No! Nollem! I struggled against the arms that shoved me out the door. There was no way I could win that battle.

I was being taken some where, and Nollem was being left behind.

The Vaudian that held me clamped a firm hand around my arm and dragged me along beside him. Kattim had been scooped up in one brute's arms.

I was crying by now. And our awful journey just began. Only after the old Post had disappeared in the trees I realized Alletta was standing by Nollem.

She was unguarded and smiling.

❦

The sun set to our backs, so we were traveling east. If I had studied maps like I was supposed to, I would have known that we were headed toward the border. It marked the line where our land stopped and Deceiver's conquered territory began.

The company of assorted Vaudians and Between ran straight through the night, dragging us along with them. Just when I thought it couldn't get worse, darkness fell and the young Between took on their other forms. I thought they seemed scary before. Most of them grew several feet in height and considerably in strength. Some shrank and became thin wiry creatures. Words slurred with growls and snarls.

I was exhausted. My constant tripping and stumbling was testament to that. Eventually, the Vaudian who held me, just picked me up in his arms. I supposed that he grew weary of having to haul me upright again. My arm was bruised and aching from where my captor held me. The cut on my neck from the lead Vaudian's knife had crusted over with dried blood. It didn't hurt unless I stretched the skin around it. Occasionally, I got passed off to a different creature. It seemed like every few hours I would be given to another of the strongest in the company. The same happened to Kattim.

Only once did I get a glimpse at her. She had passed out, from loss of blood was my guess. Her head hung cocked in a funny position and her limp arms dangled. Blood had fully seeped through her dress. It created a growing dark wet splotch right over her stomach. Illuminated by the pale moonlight, her face was deathly white. Her scarlet lips contrasted with the rest of her face, making them look like they were of blood.

I might have fallen asleep at some point in time, but I don't remember. It all seemed like a dream. All the events mushed together, and are foggily stuck in my mind. It's like waking up after having a dream then trying to remember it. Some pieces weren't there, or they were jumbled together and didn't make sense. Exhaustion and lack of food dulled my mind.

Though there was one incident that I do remember. I think the stress and uncertainty impressed it into my memory. We had been traveling for a few days I think. I couldn't keep track of time very well either. But it felt like we had been on the move for some time.

The company had stopped for a rest. They hadn't given us food or water. I faintly remember that it was a cold night so we huddled together in an attempt to stay warmer. I had Kattim's head cradled on my lap. She was still unconscious, and I was stroking her hair back gently. This was the first real affection I had felt for the girl. I was actually afraid that she might die. I think it's because I didn't want anyone else in our company to die. There had been enough death, that I was holding onto whatever life we had left.

Dwin was beside me, he had his cloak wrapped around Kattim. We had wrapped her own around her snugly, but she was still so cold to the touch. Dwin had been selfless enough to give up his. He sat shivering beside me, and I think that I offered to share my cloak with him. But I'm not sure. All I know was that when the incident went down, Dwin and I were shoulder to shoulder under my cloak.

We were sitting miserably in the wet grass when the fight broke out. The villainous creatures had gotten in some disagreement and were drawing swords and yelling over it. I caught only a few words in English, the rest was in some other harsh speech.

Here's the general meaning of what I got:

The whole company was tired and complaining against the leader of their group. There didn't appear to be much respect or fear of the Vaudian leader.

The brutes were against carrying us, because they got tired faster. And it was a bare to support something that was all limp, because it was hard to grip and even harder to carry.

I knew they were talking about Kattim.

So they had devised a solution to their pains. Leave the sick one—meaning Kattim—and the strong annoying one—I assumed they meant Dwin—behind, bound and left to die.

I was horrified to hear this, and even more so to find that the majority of the group wanted this. I could only hope that they wouldn't separate us further. We were the only ones left together.

Much discussion, or more than likely threats, were passed back and forth. I couldn't help but notice a word that kept reappearing in their speech: *sullase.*

I could never begin to imagine what it meant. But I kept hearing that they thought they only needed one *sulla*, not *sullase.* Something about payment was mentioned too. The riot was put to an end when the lead Vaudian screamed above the rest in the most threatening, hate-filled voice I had ever heard, "No *sullase,* no you!"

It meant, as far I could tell, that if we didn't survive, they wouldn't either. That put an end to the whole mess immediately. Though there was still a great deal of angry mutterings.

Only after things simmered down, did they give us some old hard crusts of bread, and half a bottle of water.

Dwin and I ravenously ate and drank first. Then we both thought of Kattim. Neither of us said anything, but we had the same idea. We attempted to get some water down her throat, but we spilled more down her neck than in her mouth.

She looked more dead than alive.

Dwin was taking it hard, I could tell. He looked haggard, with no fight left in him. Defeated. It was difficult for me to see him like this. If he had no hope, then I definitely had no reason to hope. It was in his darkest hour that he told me more about Kattim, and how they met. With much sighing and pauses he recounted their history, which I shall try to hit the highlights of. I find it amazing that I can even remember most of their tale, but there's something about it that gained my attention. And I could never put my finger on it.

It was about two and a half years ago that they had met. She was a slave, being sold in Birset, a city deep in Deceiver's land. She was sick, half starved, and half out of her mind. Out of compassion, Dwin bought her and nursed her back to health. Through that he slowly gained her trust. The more she opened up to him the more he realized that she was a slave in more ways than one. (I thought that was an odd thing to say about a person, but he said it.) He shared the love of Elohim with her, and they became united in their faith. She was a fighter, but he realized now, that she never truly opened up to him. She still held scars from her days as a slave. She had never told him who her parents were, where she was born, or any childhood events. He sometimes doubted if she even knew. He wished she could have gotten more time to heal from those things.

I had never heard a more heartfelt or sincere story of perseverance and friendship. And he hadn't even known her. I think that is why he told it to me then. To keep our courage up. But he might have told it to me because he was reminiscing the days he had spent with her. To this day, I still don't know for sure, and I never bothered to ask him. We don't talk much about those days.

Then, I couldn't have imagined ever having such a devoted friend.

Chapter 9
Deeper into the Land of Deceiver

A few days after, we were nearing the border, which was pretty easy to pick out. The distinctive thing about Deceiver's land is that it's in perpetual darkness. A continuous bank of black, grey cloud cover the land, blocking out most light from the sun, stars or moons. Just along the border, the cloud bank lowers so it looks like a wall of swirling grey mist that rises into the sky. No green things grow near or in the grey mass, so the tree line breaks off about a hundred and fifty feet from the border.

Not only could I plainly see the border, but I was beginning to *feel* it drawing closer. A dark, ominous dread rose in my heart, and I grew troubled, but had no idea about what. I could see Dwin felt it too.

We were just about to clear the scattering forest, when the most unexpected thing happened. A shout rang out through the woods and two volleys of arrows arched through the air, one from either side of us. A handful of Vaudians fell to the ground, though only wounded. One was right in front of me. As the angry brute yanked the arrow out of his shoulder, he snapped it and threw it to the ground. I recognized the fletching as the same on the arrows that had been shot at me only a week or so ago.

The soldiers from Monare Pelm had set an ambush! That meant that there was hope of being rescued! Well, rescued from the hands of one enemy into another. And the officials of Monare Pelm would certainly send us to our executions. Unless I could be saved during trial by the testimony of my parents. Surely my rank and birth gave me some advantage?

There was more hope of survival with the soldiers of Monare Pelm than with the servants of Deceiver. I really did hope that the soldiers would overcome these beastly creatures.

The first round of arrows threw the entire company into confusion. Angry and surprised yells and shouts irrupted. The ones on the outside edges of the company drew their swords and charged into the brush. A few produced bows and returned a few arrows. Most took the fight to a personal level by forcing the soldiers to engage in hand to hand combat. I heard yells and screams from both conflicting sides. Those who remained in the center of the group, myself, Dwin and Kattim among them, broke out into a full sprint for the border.

I screamed and kicked, trying to make him stop, or drop me so I could run to the soldiers. The Vaudian held me tighter. A large fist swung down and hit me just above my temple. My skull rammed against his vambrace, hitting hard. My vision went out of focus, and a splitting pain shot down my neck and spine. I felt my stomach turn into knots. I almost went limp in his arms, fighting against passing out. My head slipped back over his forearm, giving me a view of the darkening sky. The treetops disappeared and a pale blue sky gazed impartially at me. Then I watched, through dazed eyes, as the blue turned to a more dusty grey, then darker and darker until we passed the border. Greyish black dominated over the light of day.

I felt a sharp pain in my chest as we entered. I gasped for air, only sucking in dirty, smoky smog which burned in my lungs. I could smell nothing but smoke, foul, rotten things and old blood. My head ached all the more, and I felt like I couldn't breathe. I took one more ragged breath, feeling a darkness slip over me.

An inky splotch grew from the corners of my eyes, shrouding over my vision. Then everything was black.

❦

I didn't awaken till we were already in the city of Moneth. It is located just a few miles from the border, so the air had not cleared any. It was just as dark as earlier, though maybe a bit darker since night had fallen. The city itself was poorly lit by street lamps and shreds of light that spilled out of open doors and windows. The streets were alive and crawling with rats and any other kind of pestilence you could think of. They reeked of human and animal waste and rotting dead things. The boots of our captors were caked with it, sinking inches deep in mud.

The cobblestone sidewalks were not much better. Though they were elevated above the street, muck was still transported by hastening feet from street to sidewalk. Not many were on the street at this time of night, but those who were quickly made way for the company of ominous vagabonds.

There were, however, many people on the sidewalks. Many wore ragged and dirty clothing, had unkept, scraggly hair and had evil looks on their faces. Many sneered at us with dirty looks and curses. Some even spat and threw stones at us. They all had the same haunting look in their eyes and expressions. They each had their own varying degree of evil about them.

Some *looked* like they belonged there, while others almost seemed out of place. But it was night, and the Between were running rampant.

As we passed by the different crammed together buildings, I could distinctly tell which ones were the popular places in town. There was a general noise of voices, and women in skimpy dresses draped on knees and in arms. Drinks and mugs were constantly raised to something or other, and sometimes snatches of songs would rise above the muddle of voices.

Much to my relief, we passed by all these popular night places. Instead, we halted in front of a large brick building. It was nothing spectacular, dirty and stained just as all the fronts of the houses in Moneth. The Vaudians marched right in without a moment's hesitation. As I learned later, this was the Vaudian headquarters in the city. They all lived there when they weren't on any missions.

We were taken to a room vacant of windows and thrown against the dirty wall. They threw in some scraps of food before they closed and locked the door behind them. The floor was filthy with grime and muck from the streets. The walls were no better with their candle smoke smudges and dark brown stains dotted along the lower half. I didn't want to think about what made those. All I will say is that they closely resembled old blood, but I really didn't want to know.

Occasionally I heard raised voices in another part of the house. Rats roamed the cell floor, feeding on the piles of refuse in the corners of the room.

Dwin and I snatched up the food scraps before the rats got to it. We ate them, not complaining. Any food after having none for days was welcome. We again tried giving Kattim some water. But it didn't go well.

I heard Dwin mutter something under his breath.

"What was that?" I asked in a voice that was much different sounding than I thought. It sounded harsh and cracked from want of use.

He raised his head to look at me and repeated, with a lighter tone in his voice, "It's out of my hands."

I couldn't help but give him a strange look because I had no idea what he was talking about. It didn't make any sense to me. What was out of his hands?

He continued after a pause, a clear sense of relief appearing in his facial expression and voice, "It's out of my hands. It doesn't matter. I can't stop things anymore by worrying. She's not in my hands." He almost smiled after he finished.

I stared at him. Was he losing his mind? What was he talking about? I determined that the pressures of the last few weeks had finally caved his mind. There was nothing I could do with him except bear it. He kept mumbling the same thing over and over, "It's out of my hands."

It was almost like he was saying, "It's okay, Limira. If she dies, I know that there was nothing you could do." Was he attempting to comfort me with that?

Trying to ignore his mutterings, I curled against a filthy wall and resolved to sleep. Despite the condition of the room, I slept like I was home on my warm, downy mattress.

I awoke with a rough hand on my arm pulling me to my feet. I was scuttled out of the room we spent the night in, and can I tell you, I was glad to get out of there. Before I knew it, I was settled on the back of a Vaudian who smelled strongly of rum. My tied hands were forced over his head and held by his rough, scarred hands. That was the new arrangement for traveling they had thought of during the night. They, of course gave themselves a pat on the back and declared themselves to be "clever" because of it. That way they could hang onto the prisoner, but not have the inconvenience of having to support their entire body weight with their arms.

In this fashion, we left the brick building and turned into the streets. We marched down the same muddy road, passed the same degraded houses, and were stared at by the same hollow, empty looking faces. When we reached the end of the miserable city, the company broke into a full run. I was bounced around like a sack of potatoes.

It was a painful, foggy journey. For most of it my memory has gone blank. I know we passed through a bog area, I remember the foul odor. But other than that, I couldn't be sure of anything concerning our surroundings.

Kattim faded more as we traveled deeper into Deceiver's land. Dwin said less and less. But I could nearly always hear him saying that phrase over and over again: "It's not in my hands." Sometimes he would look directly at me and nearly shout it. I grew frightened whenever he did this. I couldn't be sure what he would do when we were alone. It was certain now that he had lost it. I was the only normal person left of the company.

There's that word again, "normal." I wasn't really normal, nor was I in a normal situation. But what could I do about it? Maybe Dwin's phrase was fitting, "It was out of my hands."

Maybe that's what he meant. He was giving up ever being able to change any of this. He had stopped fighting.

He had given up.

But I wasn't about to. I was a citizen of the Kingdom and had vowed never to give up. I had to survive, I had to live. I had to get through this. I was on my own, I couldn't expect any back up, but I would make it through.

I would survive.

These were the things that I kept telling myself through that trip. It was only my will that kept me pressing on. I had no other support.

As the sky got lighter, I knew we were going away from the border. Day and night strung together, I hadn't learned to make any distinctions between them.

After what felt like an eternity, we arrived at the edge of some dilapidated, worn city. It started with meager and squat shacks for houses, then grew into multi-storied buildings at the heart. Smoke and mists were always rising from this city and it was illuminated in a grey light. It reflected strangely off the eternal cloud and smoke that filled the sky. This city, called Birset as I found out later, was much larger than Moneth and was filled with much more sinister people.

There were plenty of glares and sneers from hollow people with dark eyes. Once, even a crowd mobbed against the company of vagabonds in an attempt to reach us. I saw murder in their eyes. But I also saw misery, pain, emptiness and hatred.

Slaves, drudges, prostitutes, and drug lords sat on every corner and door step. There were screams, shouts and definite sounds of brawls. A continual stench rose into the air and the city reeked of it. If death had a particular scent, this would be it. All the eye could see was destruction, misery and emptiness. Yet if you asked anyone, they would say they would never choose to be anywhere else. They loved the very thing that was their torment.

It seemed all too familiar. I had seen the exact looks on the faces of those who lived back home, in Monare Pelm. It was only the surrounding and outward look that had changed. The heart of everything was still the same.

I had felt the same emptiness as these people did. The drained feeling of being too exhausted of just living. They weren't really living at all. Were we all doomed to this fate of inward death?

I suddenly thought of Nollem. How I missed him. I never realized how much he impacted my soul, till he was gone. But there was something in particular that he had said. He mentioned being full. That was what had changed about him.

He was full. And I wanted to be. But it was too late for me now. He wasn't here to tell me how to get it.

My heart ached to know where Nollem was. It ached for Chimel, Bilham and soon Kattim who would join them among the list of the dead.

The evil glares that people shot in our direction gave me the same suffocating feeling as when I was attacked by the creature that night in the forest. Fear and death lingered on every street and around every corner. It was just waiting for you to walk by unsuspectingly, so it could snatch you up and consume you, body and soul.

At the time, I didn't know how close to death I truly was.

We were taken to a massive building in the center of the dark city. It was a stately looking mansion. Made of brick, it rose three whole stories above the street in a straight, formal manner. Glass window panes were orderly placed across the front of the building to make it appear more symmetrical. It was a monster of a house, looming so high. Its dark stained, double doors only added to the look with the black face of a mutant fox for a door knocker. The Vaudian leader mounted the steps which led to the front door. The brick steps fanned out from the door with ornate, cast iron railings that edged the brick and matched the snarling door knocker.

Seizing the ring that the mutant fox held firm in its barred teeth, the leader struck it against the metal plate. Almost immediately, a large, solemn fellow opened the double doors and admitted us into a wide hall. The floor was of white marble with large pillars of the same, reaching to the vaulted ceilings. Cast iron candle holders of ornate shapes lined the walls between the pillars, casting their dark smoke stains in contrast with the white marble. The grim splendor of it all I took in with an open mouth. Unfortunately, I noted that the elegant flooring was spoiled by the muck of the streets. And no amount of scrubbing could keep on top of the sticky mud tracked in by stomping boots. No rugs had been placed in the entryway probably for the sake of them being spoiled in a matter of days.

I noticed that over half of our menacing escort stayed outside on the street. I couldn't help but assume that they weren't allowed to come in. But it occurred to me that we might be dropped off so quickly that there was absolutely no need even to come in. It might have been for a completely different reason too, but I would never know.

When we first got through the double doors, the Vaudian who was carrying me, hoisted me off his back and set me on the floor in front of him. It felt strange to be on my own two feet again, and I almost had to remind myself how to walk. He gave me a gruff cuff on the side of my head and a growl as a warning to behave myself.

At one point during our unpleasant journey, I *may* have thrown a fuss in a futile attempt to break free. And during that fuss I *may* have bitten his hand and kicked him in the shin a few times. And he *may* still have the scar from my teeth, and I *might* have gotten a few deep bruises in return. But I'm not confirming or denying any of this.

The solemn and brutish fellow who opened the door, escorted us down the hall and to the right. At the end of this hall—it was much like the entry hall in style and decor—were two daunting, angry doors. If a door could have any facial expression, this one would have been raging mad and scowling like you wouldn't believe. It was through these doors that we were shown, our escort narrowing even more. By now it was only the lead Vaudian and three others who were there to hold us. One literally held Kattim in his arms, but Dwin and I were forced to stand.

We entered a grand chamber with vaulted ceilings and a beautiful window arrangement on the wall just opposite to us. Squarely below the window, exactly centered between the two side walls, sat an oversized desk. Along the wall to our right was an elegant table set with the finest silver and china the country could offer. The table was laden with the most bountiful amount of rare foods I had ever seen. My mouth watered at the sight of it.

Movement behind the oversized desk caught my attention. A tall man turned around to face us, his cloak sweeping and rippling behind him. His black leather armor gleamed and creaked as he moved. His face was proud and sinister. His skin was milk white, and his hair jet black, slicked back from his forehead to the top of his head. He was the very picture of authority. And I mean, if you were to look up the word "authority" in a dictionary, you would find a picture of his face next to the definition. Or at least, you would in one of our dictionaries.

As we drew closer, I began to smell the air around him. It stank of the most odious, repulsive stench. It was the smell of the city, what I call the smell of death.

His ominous form leaned over the desk and looked expectantly at the leader of the Vaudians. The large Vaudian, who I thought was the toughest of them all, quailed under his gaze. He shifted from one foot to the other and nervously said in a gruff voice, "We have brought the *sullase* that you requested from Post Neth. There are three of them."

"I can count!" the man snapped. Then his voice changed to a more commanding, or business like tone, "Good." He produced a sizable leather pouch that clinked metallically as he set it on the desk and slid it towards the Vaudian. "Your payment, as promised. You may leave us. Your services are no longer required."

Approaching the desk, the Vaudian snatched the pouch and bowed his respects as he retreated back towards us. He turned on his heels and marched out the door. The other Vaudians followed suit, dumping Kattim on Dwin and I. I was pretty sure that they were breathing huge sighs of relief outside the chamber, doing cartwheels out the front door into the streets, and definitely dividing the spoils.

The man in black said nothing for a moment as he studied us. Meanwhile, Dwin and I were awkwardly supporting Kattim's limp form. We were about to drop to the floor ourselves when he motioned, with the flick of a hand, to a chair along the wall behind us and to the right of the door. We shuffled over to it and dropped her in it, trying to arrange her in the most natural, comfortable position we could manage under the circumstances. After we got her settled, the man in black motioned, with another flick of a hand, for us to come stand before his vast desk. We walked over, our shoes clumping over the marble floor.

There was a short silence, then he began in a smooth, slick voice that reminded me much of his hair, "I do apologize for your long journey and mode of transportation. It's only the brutes that we can hire to go beyond the border nowadays. But of course, you must understand that there was no harm intended, nor is this anything against you personally. Regardless, I would be a perfect beast if I did not apologize for any mistreatment."

I nearly snickered, thinking that he was making a joke. Looking at Kattim's condition, I could hardly say that no harm was intended. But he continued uninterrupted, "Now, you are probably wondering who I am. You may call me Lord Hirabith. I am quite sure that you have heard of me before so this will only be a face to go with the name. (I had never heard of him before, but didn't dare, nor really care, to contradict him.) I am the ruler of this city and only take orders from Deceiver himself. But before we get down to business, I must entreat you to help yourself to my dinner spread. I have had it prepared just for you, you see. Surely you are hungry after such a journey, no?"

Dwin and I exchanged glances, uncertain of his offer. It could have been a trap to poison us. But as I looked more carefully at what was on the table, I was more inclined to think that the food was alright for us to eat. There were large grapes, white breads, cheeses of all sorts, various minced meats, citrus fruits, and rich red wines poured in crystal glasses. My hunger got the best of me, and I helped myself to his offer. I couldn't help but send quick glances at him between mouthfuls. He was smiling. It was a twisted grin that made me think twice about taking another bite. But another I took, if only to sustain my appetite and delight my tastebuds.

Dwin took the seat across from me, at the other end of the table, and helped himself as well. We exchanged a few knowing glances, and between those, we determined to stand our ground and be as honest as we could. Especially since we didn't know what we were here for.

After some time, during which Lord Hirabith busied himself with some papers on his desk, we were done with our meal. Our shrunken stomachs finally felt full, and perhaps a little overstuffed.

Lord Hirabith made another motion with a flick of his wrist, permitting us to bring over our chairs from the table before his desk. As I was dragging it over, I was beginning to wonder how much he actually talked and how much he just nodded his head or twitched a finger.

He stood up as we drew near—I suppose to make us feel smaller, which he succeeded in doing. He struck a gallant, threatening pose by turning just slightly so that his left shoulder was towards us, and he had to look over his shoulder to gaze down at us. He kept his chin and eyebrows raised as he peered condescendingly. He folded his left arm behind his back and picked up a cup of tea with his right. His pose was quite impressive. After taking a painstakingly long slurp of tea, during which Dwin and I sat there waiting for him to say something, he spoke. "I am," he began, his voice haughty and self assured, "quite certain that you are aware of why you are here. So we can get straight to the point." He didn't seem to notice our confused and surprised expressions and continued after a slight pause for affect, "I am determined to be as straight forward and plain with you so that I do not overwhelm you with the elegance of superior class. So this I ask of you plainly, would you like to say anything before we begin? Or shall we jump right to it?"

I took the opportunity and spilled out hastily before he could continue, "Sir! I swear that neither of us have any pretense as to why we are here. What have we done to offend you?"

By now I was completely exasperated and I wasn't afraid to show it. Dwin glanced over at me, and I wasn't sure if he approved of me saying anything or not. I couldn't tell from the face he was making. Quite on the contrary, I understood Lord Hirabith's expression well. It was something of shock mixed with indignity, and yet, at the same time, he was struggling to keep an air of indifference.

A few seconds passed before he did anything. Then Lord Hirabith gave a quaint little laugh and a smile as if he were talking to a young child, "Yes, of course you don't *know anything*," he mocked. "Come then," he coaxed in his smooth, understanding voice, "tell me what you do know. Why were you sent to Post Neth with a company of little Kingdom guards?"

My mouth dropped open with rage and confusion, "Again, I have no idea of what you are talking about! Sir," I added as an afterthought.

"Enough with the games!" he snapped. Turning upon us he threw his fists against the desk and leaned forward on them. He smoothly slid his face towards mine till it was inches away. His expression was contorted with rage, "Now tell me, why were you sent there? What was your mission? I'm not going to ask again!"

I indignantly snapped my mouth closed and tilted my head with a look of defiance in my eyes. His hand flew to my throat just below my chin. His hand turned white as he squeezed. I tired not to choke and to stay calm, despite the panicking feeling swelling in me. I kept eye contact with him, which infuriated him all the more. I gagged, trying to suck air in, but none came. He pulled my head towards his own. He hissed, his foul breath blowing into my face, "Speak, or I'll snap your neck."

"Alright that's enough," Dwin finally cut in. I thought he was going to let him strangle me. "I'll tell what we were doing there."

Lord Hirabith's released his death grip. Gasping for air, I fell back into my chair, carefully rubbing where his fingers encircled me. Lord Hirabith turned on Dwin urging, "Well, don't just sit there, proceed!"

Dwin shot a glance at me, then began. "You see, m'lord, we weren't leading those Monare Pelm soldiers. They were chasing us. We, a small company of seven, had been running for our lives when we came across Post Neth. We had no idea that your men were there."

"What were they after you for? The soldiers I mean," he asked almost eagerly.

"Our crime is being followers of Shalom." Dwin chose his words well.

Like an injured animal, Lord Hirabith recoiled to the safe retreats of his desk. His pale eyes grew wide with horror, and he cringed as if in pain.

I was shocked at his reaction, thinking him incapable of fear, and at a loss as to what had caused it. It was obviously something Dwin had said.

After a moment, Lord Hirabith regained his composure. His horror turned to anger and he spat back, "Oh really? that's a likely story. Tell me the truth, what were you doing there?"

We were silent, having nothing more to say. That was the truth, if he wanted anything else we would have to start making things up. But fortunately he liked to talk.

"Well then, since you have nothing further to say, let's compromise. Let's say, for the sake of working this out, that you actually are Lightbearers. (That was a term I was unfamiliar with.) And, just throwing it out there mind you, you were running from the little soldiers, when someone in your company suggested that you run to Post Neth." He was smirking wide by now and I immediately grew suspicious. He went on, "So, thinking it to be safer than hanging out in the open forest, you went along with that idea. Little did you know that a surprise greeting party would be there to receive you all. Or what was left of you. But really, none of you were very useful except this one here," he nodded to Dwin.

I spun to look at Dwin, my surprise and questioning obvious. Lord Hirabith laughed, enjoying the scene playing out before him. "So you didn't know did you, darling?"

Dwin gazed at his lap, avoiding my questioning looks and feeling rather awkward.

I finally managed to hiss at him, my voice full of shock, "Dwin! What is he talking about?"

He didn't get the chance to answer before Lord Hirabith continued, clearly enjoying his narrative, "Yes, don't be too surprised. And you're right, *you* don't know anything. All we wanted was your friend here. He's the only one who can be the least bit helpful. The rest of you were just extra baggage. But he has a history of mischief here. And maybe he might know a little information that would be helpful for our cause. You see, pretty one, we never let any wrong against us go unpunished."

He paused to let that sink in a bit. "So, *Dwin*, is that what you're going by these days? Just for the sake of being thorough, what new plans have you got from your headquarters? I know you have friends there, so let's not bang around the barrel and waste time. Because I believe your friend in the corner," he nodded his head to Kattim, "doesn't have much time left."

Dwin studied his lap and said quietly, but resolutely, "I haven't been back to headquarters. They moved and I'm not sure where they are now."

"Well, that's interesting. Isn't it? You at least know what their general plans were, right?"

"I know of no plans that you don't know of already."

Lord Hirabith sat back against his chair heavily. His hand went to his chin as he thought on what was said.

Chapter 10
Toe-Stepping, Tally Marks & Rat Taming

Retaining the silence, the man in black continued to ponder what to ask next. At last he spoke, "Well, then. You would at least know where the centrality of your men are placed?"

"No."

"Why not?" he demanded sharply, clearly getting fed up with the lack of answers he was receiving.

"We never know where they're at because it's hard to keep track of such a growing number."

Shots fired! I thought triumphantly. Dwin was pressing buttons and hitting all the right ones.

Lord Hirabith looked flustered and pressed further, the monster in him rising again, "What was your assigned mission?"

"I have not been on one in months."

"Then what were you doing in Divel?!" He was loosing it by now.

Dwin kept his cool demeanor and answered evenly every time. "It was a personal visit. I had no idea that we would be swept into this."

"You say 'we.' Who was with you and why?"

"Only Kat, there. She always goes with me. We've created a special bond through our faith in—"

"I don't care about it!" he cut Dwin off quickly.

"Shalom," Dwin finished in the same tone unaffected by our host's reactions.

Shrinking back into his chair, Lord Hirabith scratched at his ears as if trying to un-hear the Name.

A small smile appeared at the corners of Dwin's mouth. The tables had been turned and he knew it. I watched breathlessly as the verbal battle commenced.

"While we were in Divel," Dwin continued, "we were checking up on some friends. I believe you know the Kelvins. I heard in your younger days you two had quite the—"

"Enough!" He nearly sprung over his desk in his fury to stop Dwin. "You are of no use to me! Begone! Men!" he screamed.

There was a clatter in the hall outside the door and two Vaudians rushed into the room. They looked frantically around them, as if expecting some fight to be going on.

Lord Hirabith shouted at them in a high, staccato voice, "Them!" He nearly shrieked, wildly pointing a finger at us. "Out! Instantly!"

The two Vaudians jumped into action. They seized our arms as Lord Hirabith shouted orders of where to take us.

Then he calmed down enough to say before we left, his tone dripping with revenge and malice, "Oh, and don't forget to take the dying one. Make sure she gets the best of treatment. It would be a pity for her to die. I'm sure she would go for such a nice price at market. Away with you, oafs!"

We were drug out of the chamber and taken back out of the house. On the streets a cold air met us. I shivered. It was colder out here than I thought. A chilling breeze wafted up the street. It carried a strange scent, one that I couldn't identify as any one thing. It was getting dimmer. What light filtered through the constant dark shroud was disappearing. Night was coming.

We were escorted down the street and around a few corners. It wasn't long before we entered another building. It looked rather nice from the outside, but nothing like the last mansion. Upon entering, I saw that it was a decent place, but no finery to speak of. I wasn't about to complain. From the way we left Lord Hirabith, I would be happy to keep my life.

We were taken down a hall with many doors on both sides of it. I noticed that all the doors had metal flaps at the bottom. Made of a dull metal, they had hinges on the top and were about twelve inches wide and five inches high.

Halting suddenly, we stopped before a door that had a strange symbol on it. A Vaudian pulled out a massive bunch of keys and selected one. He unlocked the door with it. We were deposited into the room with a shove from behind that landed us on the floor. Without a word, the door was closed and locked behind us.

Sitting up, I absorbed my new surroundings. It was a small room with a bunk bed on one wall, a chair and small table on another, and a bucket in the corner. There was also a bench along the last wall. There was one high window which was lined with bars and had no glass in it. It let the cold air drift in. I was glad to see a heavy wool blanket on each bed.

The floor had once been rough wooden planks, smoothed by the wear of years. The walls were a dull whitewash. Well, not entirely. Many someones whom had occupied the room at some point before us, had scratched marks, numbers and what looked like names in the once blank walls. They showed themselves plainly in the grey stone of the original wall.

The place seemed comfortable enough. I stood up, and walked immediately to one of the beds. I chose the lower one and sank onto it. Even if it was hard, it was the first bed I could remember laying on for a long time. And it was welcome over the ground any day. I hadn't realized how tired I was till I closed my eyes and relaxed. I was asleep before two minutes had passed.

❦

I woke up to the sound of the Dwin's voice whispering under his breath. I could tell that he was above me on the top bunk. I stayed quiet and listened to what he was saying.

"...Seventy-eight, seventy nine, ..." he was quiet, then, "Eighty nine marks. Days? Signed Hallia. Borgon, twelve marks." A pause. "What's this?" I heard him shifting his position. "S. H. A. L. O. M. Shalom. Is. G. R. E.—"

"Dwin," I interrupted, and I think I startled him, "what are you doing up there?"

"Oh, uh, I was just reading some of the scratched in marks up here." There was a pause. "Sorry if I woke you."

"I don't think you did. What have you found?"

"Well, there's a lot, and I mean a *lot*, of names and tally marks. I'm not sure if the tally marks stand for days, weeks or what. But one girl, she scratched her name after it, put in eighty nine marks. Then on the ceiling, I think this is the most interesting, there is 'Shalom is great.' There's no dates or anything to any of these. I can't help but wonder who put them here. And where they are today."

I could easily guess where they were. Most likely in their graves. I had nothing to say in response to Dwin on the topic of marks on the wall.

"There's another fellow," Dwin went on either not minding or noticing my silence on the matter, "who wrote in big letters a phrase. It must have taken hours to scratch out. It says 'Death is near.' What do you make of that, Limira?"

"I think it's pretty close to the truth," I said honestly. "I mean, look at..." I stopped before blurting it out. Instead I chose to say, "Have you heard anything about Kattim?"

"No."

There was silence.

"It's not in my hands."

There was that phrase again! Maybe that's what all the nonsense about marks on the walls were about. He was trying to distract himself!

"Limira." He stopped as if thinking whether or not he should say it. He then continued, "Limira, have you ever felt... how do I put this? Have you ever felt as if no matter what happens, everything is against you?"

"Yes." I could emphatically agree with that.

"Have you ever felt like you don't care? Even though it feels like everything's going wrong, have you ever felt at peace?"

That was a question that went straight to my heart. I didn't reply. I couldn't.

Dwin went on, "Well, I do. Right now, I'm feeling that. It's out of my hands."

My thoughts trailed back to the interrogation the previous day. It was all so confusing. Why had they wanted us in the first place? Lord Hirabith had said something about Dwin doing something against the city. Was that right? Or had Dwin done something personally against Lord Hirabith? What was a Lightbearer? Probably a motley pack of psychopathic vagabonds, all romping about cities and countrysides terrorizing people. It would make sense if Dwin was a part of them, he was acting strange enough. What had he done that Lord Hirabith would drag him, and myself, halfway across the world just to get even with Dwin? Should I ask him about it? No, definitely not.

"Dwin," I started slowly and against my better judgement, "what was Lord Hirabith talking about back there? What's a Lightbearer and why does he hate you so much?"

Dwin sighed. "I can't really tell you about it Limira. I wish I could, but..."

He didn't finish. I was too busy being offended to notice. "Why can't you tell me?! My life has been in danger more than once because of this ordeal that *you* started. I have a right to know!"

Silence.

I blew out a breath of frustration. "Fine. At least tell me what a Lightbearer is."

He didn't reply immediately, and I was beginning to wonder if he ever would when he said, "A Lightbearer is what you call a Radical—followers of Shalom, all living for His glory. We're in constant battle against Deceiver and his cronies like Hirabith. It's both a physical and invisible war. Blood has been shed on both sides. Many souls have been lost and found. Deceiver is getting stronger, the fighting more desperate, but we have no fear. We have already won. Deceiver knows this, but he still tries to gain the upper hand, using any form he can. That is why they wanted me. They know I have been deeply involved in Lightbearer movements and they were hoping to get new information. I honestly have nothing to give. I don't know where the new headquarters are, I don't know who is in command there, I don't know where the concentrated front lines are, I don't even know if my friends are still alive." Here he paused for a moment before he continued. "But I do know that Shalom is at work in all the cities. We're fighting for His kingdom. I have done nothing that I wouldn't do all over again, but I am sorry that you got caught up in it. This battle is not yours, not yet."

Yep, I concluded, psychopathic vagabonds romping the cities and creating terror by preaching about invisible wars. How could a war be invisible, yet people get killed? It didn't make sense, and yet, there was something very real about what he was saying. Sometimes it did feel as if the world was at war. But how could there be blood shed if the war was just a feeling?

Just then the metal flap which covered the opening at the bottom of the door opened. Through the opening, a tin plate and flask of water appeared. Then the flap closed with a slam. I sat up at the sight of the food. There was fluffy mashed potatoes, some sort of meat that resembled fried ham, and scrambled eggs. All were steaming hot as if they'd just come from the pan. The delicious aromas filled our small room and tempted our noses.

Dwin's feet and legs appeared over the side of the bed and he jumped down to the floor. All other thoughts abandoned, I crawled out of my blanket as quickly as I could, banging my head on the top frame of the bed in the process.

My feet hit the smooth wood, and I clamored to my knees beside Dwin. We hovered over the food for just a second, trying to be polite and let the other person have at it first, but our hunger made us impatient and rather inclined to forget about being polite.

Finally, we both reverently reached our dirty fingers to the heavenly smelling food. We silently agreed to split everything evenly and set to work polishing off the plate.

Having just finished the last remnant of our meal, a bit of mashed potato, we settled back, looking at each other with the same thought. That didn't last long.

I was about to get up, when the metal flap opened a second time and delivered an identical plate. Our eyes grew wide with delight, and we set to that plate as well.

In total throughout the day, we got four plates of food. Two in the morning and two in the evening, both filled with marvelous warm foods.

Other than that, things were pretty quiet for the next few days. We were under the assumption that Kattim was being taken care of, but we had gotten no word concerning her. Nor any word concerning anything. We were suspicious, but then, there was absolutely nothing we could do about it. Being fed and sleeping regularly, Dwin and I were soon back in good health and good spirits.

Despite the comforts, after a few days, both Dwin and I wished that we could be out in the rough again. We were bored out of our brains. And no amount of story telling, riddle wracking, or game making could amend for the hours of endless confinement.

In a week and a half, I was dying to get out of the little room. I had memorized all the messages written on the walls. Dwin and I had made a game that one would say a name, and the other would try to guess how many tally marks went with it. By the end of a day we were masters. And could even do it backwards where one would name the number of tally marks, and the other all the names that went with it. We even made it harder by only giving the first three letters of the name, but still, by supper we were bored with our mastery.

We had paced out the width and height of the room and determined its area, perimeter, cubit space, etc. We had even made a few of the visiting rats our friends. But it was at the cost of some food scraps.

And I'm sure that when you're confined in a small space with someone for a long period of time, you would understand how we might have some disagreements. Well, more like arguments. These happened more frequently as we got to feeling stronger and more anxious to get out. I'm only going to insert one of these instances, because it has the least amount of degrading remarks and hurtful words that we now wish we had never said.

This argument started when we were in the second week or so of being confined to the cell. It was about our pet rat, whom I had affectionately named Blisha. And yes, we did have an argument of what we should name it. Unfortunately we never resolved it, so I called it Blisha, and he called it Maiva. We still can't agree on that.

Every meal we gave it some scrapes from our plate. She grew into a very fine looking, fat rat. The supper plate had just come in and she had scuttled right up to eat with us. I tore off a bit of bread and was about to give it to her when Dwin interrupted. "Wait! you can't give Maiva a piece of bread! That's what she had last night."

I cocked an eyebrow, not at all convinced and not too pleased at being told what to do. "Well, why not? I think *Blisha* will be just as grateful for a piece of bread as she would anything else. More so than you."

"Why not? Because *Maiva* needs to have a varied diet in order for her to be healthy. Therefore we must not give her the same thing every night," he finished in a crisp tone.

My mouth dropped open with rage and indignity. I exclaimed, starting to get really angry with him, "*I* don't get a varied diet! Why should Blisha?"

"*Maiva* actually has the option of a varied diet. Whereas we do not. It is our duty, as fellow cell mates, to look after—"

"Our *duty*!" I exploded. "Don't you talk to me about duty! I, being female, have the most motherly instinct of the two of us. Therefore, I should know very well what is best for our youngster here. And I say, if a non-varied diet is good enough for us, is good enough for *Blisha* as well!"

"Oh yeah, now we bring out the gender card. And by the way, I think you could really use a diet, not as trim as you could be, huh?"

That was crossing the line. I was outraged. "Oh, yeah? You're not looking so hot yourself, big shot!"

"Better than you."

"Are you calling me fat?"

"Well, I think we can both agree that sixteen days, nineteen hours, twenty-six minutes and fifty-five seconds of being fed the finest foods and confined in a small room such as this has indeed left its mark on you." Clearly he was being overdramatic, for we have absolutely no way of telling any particulars of time.

"So, yes, you are calling me fat."

"Now, I didn't say it partic—"

"*Oh sure*. Like I'm believing that!"

"Why don't we return to our original topic that we were discussing."

"You call this a discussion! I'd hate to see a conversation."

"Suddenly you're the clever one, huh?"

"Yes, I do think I rather am. Thanks for finally noticing. But let us return to Blisha's predicament of victuals. Unless you have any objection which I would refute perfectly."

"No! no objections, though I would like to see you fail epically at being perfect."

My mouth flew open in protest, but Dwin continued, "Let us say if I were a rat, take *Maiva* here for instance, I would do my best to find a different kind of food so that I wouldn't get bored with it. And if I did get bored with it, I would leave to find better, *more varied*, kinds of foods. So unless you would like her to leave, I would highly suggest that we give her a bit of whatever this meat is. I for one would hate to see her leave because she is the only sensible companion I have."

"You're right, it would be a pity if she left, then I would be deprived of the camaraderie we have formed. Such a friendship of devotion and loyalty I could never expect from *you!*"

Now, reader, it would be profitable to note that we were in fact arguing about a rat. And how silly it was that this even started, much less continued on for an hour at least. It finally ended with Blisha getting both a piece of bread and meat, and with me declaring I preferred the company of the bed post over his. He retorted by declaring he rather liked that arrangement since he would not have to talk to someone with such an inferior intellectual mind. Determined to have the last jab, I proclaimed decidedly that I was sure he had meant *superior* intellect. Thus, it was drawn out another fifteen minutes.

So, in summary, we fought a lot. We even made a pact not to fight anymore, but ended up going back on our words because we couldn't agree whether or not this pact would last just the duration of our time together in the cell, or rather would it last the entirety of our remaining lives. As you can see, it was a very serious matter that needed to be resolved one way or the other, but it never was.

One thing we did agree on was that our short tempers were due to being cooped up with no way to expend energy. So we began our own "fitness club." We would drill and challenge each other to see how many pushups, pull ups, planks, jumping jacks, and sit ups we could do.

Even with coming up with all this and more, it never damped our longing to get out.

But I never wanted what was coming next.

Chapter 11
Betrayed into Bondage

Three weeks and five days was the total of our stay. During which, I described the general events above. We kept track of the days by tally marks, which we scratched our names next to, like so many had done before us.

On the twenty-sixth day, we heard the sound of a key scraping into our lock. The door opened with a squeal and footsteps entered. It felt like so long ago since I last heard it, I was startled by the sounds. Three men came in. They were silent as they roused us from lounging on our beds. They escorted us out of the room and into the bland hall that we had seen what felt like forever ago.

Looking back, I'm sure whoever, if there was anyone, was in the rooms next to us was glad to have us out of there. If we were in any tight living quarters with neighbors, I'm quite certain that we would have been complained against, and the very least been visited by some officials.

We were marched down the hall, the men taking long hurried strides. It felt good to walk more than six strides without being interrupted by a wall or bed frame. They took us into another part of the building, and deposited us into two separate rooms. At first, I wasn't sure if this was going to be good or not, because now we had been separated. Though in the moment, I couldn't help but smile a little to be in a room, twice or three times as large as the one before, by myself.

Just as I was thinking that, a woman, dressed surprisingly fine, whisked through a door to the right and on the far side of the well lit room. Her silk dress swished as she practically floated over to me. She wore jewels around her neck that glinted magnificently, catching the light just right. Her smooth dark hair was waved back into a loose up-do.

I wasn't sure what to make of it. She seemed out of place for this city. But then I suddenly wondered what she looked like at night. Then, she more than likely fit right in with the rest of the population.

She swept right up to me, took my hand in her's and gushed airily, "It's such a pleasure of mine to meet you, Limira. My name is Rosamund. Are you ready to start looking like a lady again?"

I didn't have time to respond before she pulled me over to a wardrobe and threw it open. It revealed a nice dress, nothing in comparison to Rosamund's, but a definite upgrade from my own. By now it had stains, from blood and dirt alike, and tears to kingdom come. My formerly white petticoats were now soiled and resembled a dirty brown. I was glad now that I happened to be wearing a dark blue dress when Nollem and I were first chased by the Monare Pelm soldiers. It was a good thing that I hadn't been wearing anything finer, like my white muslin I sometimes wore out. But now my regular dark blue dress was hardly recognizable. The small cream print was nearly invisible under the layers of travel dirt on my skirt.

The dress before me now was a dark green with small black stripes and small black rose-like flowers in between the stripes. The skirt was full and to the floor. The bodice, of the same fabric, was a swiss body with a crisp white blouse for underneath. The blouse had full sleeves and buttons down the front and at the wrists.

It was quite lovely and I could not be sure why I was receiving it. It didn't make sense why they, my enemy, would want to give this to me. I was of course skeptical, but my fears melted when Rosamund giggled at my expression and practically sang in her silvery voice, "That, my dear, is yours. But first we must give you a bath and wash out your hair. I'm sure it will be rather lovely once all the grime is gone."

She grabbed up my hand again, giving it a little squeeze as she tugged me across the room towards a screen. As we crossed the room, we passed a mirror, and I caught a glimpse of myself. I stopped in my tracks and just stared at the ugly beggar looking back at me. My hair was a mess, and I looked like I hadn't gotten a bath or even changed in months. I hardly recognized myself. In my astonishment I said under my breath, "Is that really me?"

Rosamund laughed one of her tinkling laughs and exclaimed good-naturedly, "Don't you worry! You'll look your self again once we scrub a few inches of dirt off. Come, come, the bath is drawn and ready. Don't want to wait too long, or else it will be cold!"

She gave me a slight push to go behind the screen. My feet carried me behind it, and I nearly squealed with delight. There, was a tub full of lovely warm water. Steam was rising from it into the air. Rosamund was beside me in an instant. I took slow steps and gingerly ran my fingers over the edge of the tub.

Only minutes later I had undressed and was soaking peacefully in the warm water. It was the best feeling I had had in a long while. I began to feel more human again. After a short while in our journey, I had stopped caring about what I looked like. Staying alive was all that mattered.

But that was then, this was now. Now, I was thoroughly enjoying doing the very human thing of bathing. Rosamund came in to help me wash my hair.

I had been soaking about twenty minutes when Rosamund presented me with a towel and ran around the screen to fetch my dress and new under things. She draped them over the top of the screen and let me put them on in privacy, which I was grateful for.

After a moment she inquired politely if I needed any help. I said no, grabbing the blouse and buttoning it up. Then came the bodice and skirt which only took a couple of glances for me to figure out how they went together.

I was surprised to see how well the dress fit me. But it was a pleasant surprise. I suddenly felt a lot better in a fine dress, fully clean and dry. Except my hair, that was still wrapped in the towel. I rubbed my hair with the towel and then let it fall over my shoulders and most of the way down my back. The blonde shone again with its usual brightness. Throwing the wet towel over the top of the screen, I stepped around the corner for Rosamund to see.

I couldn't help but smile, and I did even more so at her reaction. Rosamund's white hand flew to her mouth, and she beamed in happy delight. She rushed over to my side dramatically, cooing in her excitement, "Oh, Limira, you look absolutely beautiful! That dress compliments you so well. Come, come see yourself in the mirror now."

I excitedly followed the giddy Rosamund over to the looking glass. I couldn't help but admire myself, making little turns to see how I looked all around.

"Now," Rosamund interrupted my gazing by pulling out the chair that sat before the mirror and table, "sit down right here and we'll see what we can do with your hair."

After a serious combing, some playing, tweaking and pulling, Rosamund had pinned my hair to the back of my head in neat ringlets, some of which cascaded down the back of my neck and brush my shoulders when I turned my head.

She had me look at it, and I fell in love with it at once. Then she rushed me up and over to the wardrobe again. She knelt and opened one of the drawers, revealing rows of black polished shoes and a stack of woolen socks. She pulled out a pair of the warm socks and handed them to me. Then she lifted my skirts slightly to reveal my bare feet. She looked them over and pulled out a pair of shoes from the drawer. "Here," she said handing them to me and motioning to the chair right beside the wardrobe, "try these on for size."

They fit perfectly. And I relished the thought of brand new boots which were shockingly comfortable. Once again, I found myself wondering why I was being treated like this. Someone must have paid for all this, and I wondered what I was expected to do next.

I stood up and Rosamund took a step back to admire me. She sighed with content, seeming satisfied with her work. "Now, my dear," she breathed, "we get to reveal you to your friend. He's out in the hall waiting for you."

I stared at her, unbelieving what she was saying. Did she mean Dwin? Must be. But how did she know? I shook off my expression, figuring it would be better if she didn't know that I was slightly doubtful. I assumed a smiling face and remembered my manners enough to take her hands in mine and say, "Thank you, Rosamund. For... for everything." A laugh escaped me and I continued, "I can't tell you how much you've done for me." And really, I felt like a new person. I couldn't say how much I enjoyed her girly attention and companionship.

She looked me straight in the eyes and replied so sincerely it almost looked like she might cry, "You are very welcome, darling." She paused, holding my gaze. "Now, go. Out the door, go on. Out you go!"

She shooed me towards the door, and I paused with my hand on the doorknob. I took a breath then opened it. I stared in front of me, until I turned into the hall. My attention was immediately drawn to Dwin. He was sitting in a chair, which was along the wall between the two rooms. When he saw me, he rose hastily from his seat and gave a slight bow.

As was proper, I bobbed a curtsy in response and looked him over. He was dressed in a fine new set of clothing consisting of a white shirt, waistcoat, necktie, pants and tall shining black boots.

"You look lovely," he rushed, with a strange smile on his face.

He looked rather dashing himself. But all I said was, "Thank you. You look fine yourself," I added with a friendly smile. He didn't say anything. I turned to nervously picking at my skirt and studying the floor. I looked up and was about to say something, but our awkward conference was interrupted.

A brisk man rounded the corner. He was carrying a cloak and heavy overcoat. He handed the cloak to me, and Dwin the overcoat. Then he bid us to follow him. I put the cloak over my shoulders, glad of it when we stepped into the chilly afternoon air.

Our guide directed us through a maze of twists and turns, landing us in a large courtyard, or market square. It was humming with the sounds of many people. A sizable crowd had gathered, pressing to see something on the far side of them.

The brisk fellow led us around the edge of the oval shaped courtyard, skirting the throng of people. I glanced over at Dwin, and my heart sank with uncertainty. His smile had long vanished, and he was staring grimly over the heads of the crowd.

Being nearly a head shorter than he, I couldn't see what he was looking at with such foreboding.

Then I heard a voice call above the all others. It was harsh and commanding. It was only then that it came together in my mind.

A slave market.

Oh no. My heart sank even deeper inside me, and I looked wildly over at Dwin. My mouth parted in shock.

They were going to sell us.

Just as I realized this, we rounded a corner of the crowd and before us was a long line of people against the wall. They were all in chains, with dismal expressions on their faces. None of them moved, or looked anyone in the eye when passerby's strolled along beside them.

We were guided over to the line. There were two spots just waiting to be filled by us. The fellow who escorted us, handed us over to a gruff, burly, giant of a man. He clapped our wrists in shackles and joined us to the line of other doomed souls.

I was so shocked that I didn't think to do anything but let him shove me in line. So many thoughts and feelings swirled through my head. I felt betrayed by Rosamund. She seemed so nice. Then to set me up like that! I immediately thought of Alletta. I had trusted her too. Then she was the one who betrayed us. She had handed us over to the hired thugs and was doing who-knows-what with Nollem.

I was too trusting. They had set me up, and I had fallen for it. Now, I had unsuspectingly walked right into their trap, laid so perfectly behind smiling faces. And now, Dwin and I were to be separated forever. We would never find each other after this unless, by some wild chance, the same person bought us both.

I knew that was never going to happen and dismissed the thought before it became a hope.

And Kattim! She was left behind. She was headed for the same fate as us, only she didn't know it yet. She was going to be sold back into slavery after being free.

But I, *me*, Limira of Rose House, was being sold on the slave market. I would never see Dwin again. Our company was scattered, and never to meet again in this world. I would never see Nollem again. I would never see Monare Pelm, my home, again.

I leaned against the brick wall, in a dazed shock.

I was roused by Dwin's hand touching my shoulder. He had poked me. He whispered, "Limira, you okay?"

What a question to be asking right now! The worst possible nightmare I could have dreamed up for my future, was about to come true. And he was asking if I was okay! I dumbly nodded my head in response. I couldn't think of what to say.

Dwin brushed his hand against my sleeve again, and this time I looked him in the eye. His ocean of blue eyes stared into my grey ones. They were startlingly calm and sincere. He said, slowly, making sure that I caught every word, "Limira, never give up hope. Everything's going to work out alright."

"But, Dwin—" I cut him off, but he placed a finger on my lips to silence them.

He continued in his steady, even voice, "Listen to me. Don't worry about me, or Kattim, or Nollem, alright? You've got to look out for yourself and be careful. Don't let that fiery tongue of yours get you into trouble. Never give up hope in Him. Remember that, don't you dare forget it."

I felt like I might faint. I heard what he said, but it wasn't much comfort right now. I returned my gaze to the cobblestones. I could hardly believe that this was happening to me!

My life would be ruined. I would be lucky if I got a position in a house. It was near impossible to get a kind master, it would never happen in this land. I would die young, prematurely and miserably. I would be starved, beaten or maybe even worse.

Oh for the days when I had no fear!

I hadn't noticed the sounds of the crowd until they grew silent. My heart wrenched inside me. The harsh voice rang above the crowd, as the first of our desolate group was led to the block. I stared in horror.

Voices called out, bidding higher until the auctioneer declared in a booming voice, "Sold! To the man with a thousand pounds!"

Each time those words rang out, I shuddered with fear. It sickened me to think I would soon be next.

I hardly paid attention to who was taken up. By now I had closed my eyes and fully leaned against the brick wall. I couldn't watch. I tried blocking out the horrifying calls and shouts of the bidders and the seller, but they rang through my head like dooming claps of thunder.

In my thoughts I stretched for shreds of hope, and my mind jumped to the biggest most unreal ideas. Lord Hirabith had said something about Dwin having connections in this city. Maybe he had friends in the crowd who would buy me and set me free. Maybe I would get a kind or careless master, and I would be set free or escape. Maybe there was someone from Monare Pelm who would buy me and take me back into the city where I could explain my family lineage and certainly gain my freedom back. Or maybe I would grow wings and fly away.

All were just as impossible.

Suddenly I felt a hand latch onto my forearm and give a yank towards the block. I whirled to face my captor, the giant of a man. He had a nasty scar running across his left eye. He unlocked me from the long chain and pulled me with him. In a shear panic, I pulled against him, fighting to get out of his grip. I twisted my arm and struck out at him with my other hand.

I heard Dwin in the background whispering frantically, "Limira! Don't fight! The nastiest like those with spirit!"

Just as Dwin's warning sank in, the burly man's hand came full down, striking my cheek. It stung with pain, and I cried out. The fight left me, and he dragged me the few yards to the block.

By now, every eye in the crowd had turned to me and the scene I created.

The big man grabbed me by both arms and lifted me effortlessly to the top of the block. A big red mark appeared on my cheek, stinging like an angry hornet. I could barely look into the crowd. I was struck numb with fear.

The auctioneer began his lively speech, "Now this here is a fine specimen, ladies and gentlemen. She's strong, she's pretty, and, the best of all, it looks like she has a temper. I'm sure she'd make a lovely wench for you men, and helpful in the kitchen for you ladies. With a bit of improvement she might even make a good field hand. So with that, we'll start the bidding at a hundred pounds. Can anyone give me a hundred pounds?"

Now I looked over the crowd, watching which people called out. There was one man, in the far right corner, who caught my eye. He was a scowling, unusually grim looking man. If looks could kill, then he'd be a serial killer. His manner and eyes were sinister, cruel and villainous. His slanting eyes were fixed upon me, a thin smirk smeared over his pursed lips.

I nearly fainted when he called out among the bidders.

He drove the price higher and higher, in his sharp cold tone. I tried not to make eye contact with him. Soon all the other bidders were driven too high.

The auctioneer's shrill voice called out, "Sold! To the man with a thousand and seventy five pounds!"

My mouth hung open in disbelief. Of all the people, I *definitely* didn't want him, but it was him I was stuck with! He wove his way through the crowd. The burly man gave me a sharp pull off the block, nearly making me fall. I stumbled to get my feet under me as my new master approached.

He was even more terrifying close up than far away. He had a high brow, and a stiff, cold manner about him. He was a full two heads higher than me, and he towered over me with a leering look. He scowled horrendously at me as he counted over the money. He barked at the big man to release me of my shackles, hissing a warning to me not to try running away. He pulled me away with a hand clamped around my upper arm.

We passed the line of soon-to-be slaves, and I gave one last despairing look at Dwin. He stared solemnly back at me and nodded his head as a farewell. I was close to tears and held his gaze till my new master jerked me to keep my head forward and down.

One tear streaked down my cheek unnoticed by him and unwanted by me.

He kept his pace quick with long strides, I had to trot to keep up with him. He stalked with me by the arm to the edge of town where we briefly stopped before an inn. The stable boy, whom I looked on as fortunate, had the grim man's horse saddled and ready for him when we arrived. He pulled a rope from a saddle bag and tied my hands in front of me, leaving a good long distance. Then he took the other end and held it in his hand. Tossing a measly coin at the boy, he mounted and started out at a walk.

It took a moment before I realized that I was attached to him and needed to keep up. To my relief, the horse was easier to keep pace with than he had been.

Once we reached the edge of town, he began to talk to me. I would say talk "with" me, but he never paused or expected me to respond. So, talk "to" me is much more accurate.

Chapter 12
Grenith

He began in his cold, impersonal tone, "You may call me Master Abburn, nothing else would be appropriate. It appears to me that you have never been a slave before. That is quite lucky for me, since I now have the opportunity to break you into my rules without any other habits getting in the way. It is also good because you are fresh and young, and therefore useful for many purposes. You shall be a field hand during planting and harvesting, since I can tell you have a strong back. During the rest of the year, you shall be under the Head Cook, whom you are to call Meddella. She gets her orders directly from me. And you shall do anything she asks of you without questioning.

"The slave you are replacing did basic, simpleminded things like scrubbing the floors or bringing up my tea tray. Perhaps you shall exceed her knowledge by learning to serve tea when expected. But it is doubtful. I do hope though that you will prove useful for something. I believe that everyone, no matter what status, is born with at least *one* thing they are especially good at. And, believe me, my standards are low when it comes to your kind."

He continued to paint a grim picture of my future life. It was only brightened a sliver by the fact that there were others of my "lower position," and in fact that there were those who would be below me. Their only gifts were their capability to work in the fields, and that was it. So, I would undoubtedly be better off than they. That's what he said anyway.

After a bit, probably to collect his thoughts again, he proceeded to say in a threatening, warning voice, "But I would have you mind yourself. We are not afraid to punish any misdemeanor. The lash is used on those who don't behave. We have other means of breaking the spirited too," he added, more than likely thinking of my outburst so rashly displayed.

I cringed, trying not to think of what he might be implying, but thoughts and images flooded into my mind unbidden.

I had never thought that life could turn so ill for me. The run for my life was a welcome discomfort compared to this. I could barely think of home without wanting to cry out for the injustice of it all. What had I done to deserve this? Was I that wicked of a person to be punished so severely? Where was Elohim in all this? Was He laughing at me from a distance? Did He even care?

Life turned out to be worse than it was described. I was living in constant fear of being beaten. I was ordered around by the sourest people I had ever seen, cuffed for no reason, and scolded for things I didn't do. During the day I was mocked and laughed at by Master Abburn. By night I was beaten and slapped. Night hours were the worst. It was like Master Abburn turned into a beast, touchy and easily infuriated. The things he would laugh at during the day, he would snap at and strike over at night. A few days after I first got there, I was told what happened to the slave who used to work my position. She had dropped an insignificant plate by accident. For punishment, Master Abburn had her locked up in the mud room for a month. No one was allowed to see or talk to her. She had starved to death.

The other slaves pitied and envied me. They envied me because I got to work in the house near Master Abburn and I was the newest of them all, but they pitied me because I had to work near Master Abburn. Their envy out weighed their pity, and in short they hated and despised me, offering no comfort or companionship.

Luckily, I was not the only target for their ill will. There was another girl, she was called Grenith, whom all the slaves mutually hated. We became close because everyone else disliked us. Their biggest complaint against her was that she was different than them, so she would never really fit in. She was strange. And I would agree, she was different than the rest of them, and she looked truly out of place among the slaves.

She was happy. Like always, never ceasing, incandescently happy. And that was strange and out of place because she had one of the hardest jobs on the entire manor. She worked out in the fields from sun up to long after sun down. But she always had a light, a twinkle in her eye. The rest of her looked awful, well... used and fully abused. She was unnaturally thin, and her skin was darkened from what sun filtered through the constant cloud cover. Her skin was pulled gauntly around her bones, of which I could almost number them all. Her clothes sagged around her shrunken frame. Her hair was light and always knotted under a dirty, hole riddled cloth.

She offered every bit of companionship one could ask for, and more. She would wait up for me to come to the slave shack every night. She would sit up, and we would talk about our day. Mostly I would talk, and she would laugh lightly at Master Abburn's antics and actions. She would sympathize at every strike he would give, every scolding from Meddella, and patiently tend to any wound I had received from either of them.

She never told me anything about her day except the remarkable and beautiful things she saw. She would delight over the rising and setting of the sun, seeing both the lightening and dimming of the fields in one day. She would tell about the pale light during the night depending on how many moons were out, the cool stillness just before the first glow of light, and the birds calling to one another through the warmer afternoon. I knew that she must have had rough days, as a field hand, but she never mentioned anything about it.

And I never asked.

For two weeks—two very long weeks—I had been ordered and bossed around. I can't even begin to describe how miserable it really was. But today was an absolute dread.

Meddella, the head cook and housekeeper, ordered, ran and slapped me like never before. I had to scrub all the floors downstairs including the double staircase, dust the parlor, dining hall, and library, sweep the porch, fetch buckets of water, and anything else that she thought of. Master Abburn wants tea, and serve it to him, wash the dishes, you missed a spot, get this, now that, Master Abburn wants this and that. Don't forget! And on and on... All. Day. Long.

It had to be around midnight before I got out of the kitchen. I was escorted to the slave shack, which is across the yard, beyond the huge barn, and sat parallel to the pastures. Just in front of the slave shack, were the fields. They went further than the eye could see. The main crops were wheat, oats and corn. There was also a large garden out of which we gathered most, if not all, of our produce. Another thing to add is that the slave shack isn't really a shack. It's a long, narrow barn with a slanted roof and straw and dirt floor. It was rickety, and not at all insulated, which made for some cold, wet, dreary nights and some sweltering, sticky nights. It eternally smelled of body odor and other repugnant things.

It was to this foul place that I was escorted to be chained in with everyone else. By then all the others were long asleep. I believe the field hands got in around ten o'clock that night. In the far corner from the entrance, where we usually slept, I could see Grenith. She was huddled up in a ball, wrapped in an old, tattered blanket. She was sleeping.

I thought that was strange. Granted, I was unusually late... but still. Something wasn't right. I frowned, beginning to get worried.

The man who was in charge of locking up the prisoners at night and letting them out in the morning, chained me next to her. The noise woke her up. She blinked a couple of times before she saw me. She sat up, slowly and stiffly with a grimace on her face, as she leaned carefully against the back wall.

By now the man had disappeared out of the shack.

Wincing she asked in a whisper, barely managing a tense smile, "How was your day, Limira?"

It was then that I knew something was definitely wrong. She was bitting her lower lip and her face was pale. I ignored her question, and drilled her anxiously, "Are you alright? What happened?"

Refusing to say, Grenith stared at her feet.

I was getting angry by now, thinking of what could have happened. "Grenith," I practically demanded, "what did they do to you?"

She didn't say anything for a moment. I was about to ask her again when she spoke, her voice quiet, "Now don't be upset, Limira. I'll be better." She paused. "I spilled a basket of corn. So I got punished. It's alright, really. I'll be fine in a few days."

I couldn't believe it. I stared at her in outrage. I repeated, "What did they do?"

Silence.

"Let me see," I insisted firmly, feeling confident in my ability to stomach anything.

I had to persist until she reluctantly leaned forward, wincing and holding back a whimper. I stared, more in disbelief than before. Her entire back was striped with dark, bloodied lash marks.

"Don't go fretting," Grenith said. "I've had worse. But don't you go saying anything or you'll get in trouble too. Maybe far worse than me. Do we have an understanding?"

I nodded, but was inwardly seething. "You get some rest," I replied in a surprisingly calm voice. My troubles of the day were long forgotten. How could they do that to her? It was just an accident! She never harmed anyone! Oh, if only I knew who had hurt her—!

"You should have seen the sunset this evening," Grenith murmured with her eyes closed. "It was just a beauty. A true reflection of the One who made it."

I stared at her incredulously, my mouth hanging open. How could she think of Elohim at a time like this?! My thoughts flew back to the time just after Master Abburn told me about what it would be like here, just after he bought me. Where was He in all this? How could she have such faith in Him, when He wasn't with her? How could He let this happen to her?

I couldn't even begin to have answers for any of these questions. Not yet.

Chapter 13
Consequences & Resolutions

MY stay at Master Abburn's manor was long and tedious. I couldn't, therefore, describe all of it to you, nor would I want to, since my purpose is not to depress you with my tale. I had been there long enough that I could now easily discern the movements of the sun, as well as distinguish day from night, despite the constant grey cloud cover.

But I would like to acquaint you with the people and surroundings with and in which I worked. And maybe a few memorable events and conversations to go along with them.

First, I will begin with the mansion belonging to Master Abburn. It was a typical mansion with a finished, noble exterior, and a polished, fancy interior. There was a sizable round yard with a drive circling about it, which led up to the house. The lawn was always green—which I wondered at, and found myself completely baffled and at a loss for any practical reason—and well trimmed and weeded.

On with the house. There was a covered porch that ran the length of the main front. In the exact middle, the double doors loomed threateningly with their dark green hue and black, scowling door knocker.

Once inside, the white and black checkered marble floor mesmerized and offended your eye at the same time. After you could ignore the floor, your gaze was suddenly attracted to the wide staircases that led up the second floor. There were two, slightly curving stairs of polished marble, one on each side of the room. Dark green paneling striped the walls and accented the vaulted, pristine white ceiling. In the entry, the ceiling reached to the top of both stories, with a domed skylight in the center.

Between the glorious staircases, was a wide arching passage that led you to a "T" leading off in either direction behind the staircases. Directly in front would be the door to the lavishly decorated parlor. That was where Master Abburn always took tea and entertained when guests came over for the afternoon. To the right of the "T," and immediately to the left, was the dining room. That door was parallel to the parlor door. There was another door that connected the parlor and dining room. If you looked to the right, you would see a wide room, off which the kitchen was located. This wide room had general small decorations such as tables with arrangements on them and a few paintings on the walls.

But if you took a left at the "T," there would be Master Abburn's office just slightly to the right. To the left there was another wide room, very similar to the one on the exact opposite side of the house. But instead of non precise decor, this room was themed to be the "Ancient" room. All down both walls you could trace the family line by portraits, group and single paintings. On tables and such that lined the walls were old family relics. To give you an idea of what those were, they mainly consisted of vases, intricately painted dishes, teacups and saucers. There were even a couple of old maps from when

Deceiver hadn't come to Fairlend yet. But that doesn't mean that he wasn't in the world then, just not our part of the world.

Anyways, back to the point. Separated by a door from the Ancient room, there was a mud room.

In the upstairs there were three rooms that spanned the back length of the house, much like the downstairs. From left to right there was the master bedroom, then the indoor water closet, and then the library or fireside. There were two doors that led to the water closet, one from Master Abburn's room and the other from the main hall. The library, or fireside, was my favorite room of the house. The walls were lined with floor to ceiling bookshelves that were simply stuffed with books. Reading had always been my favorite past time, and I found from an early age that the company of good books was more enjoyable than that of people. There were three stately, upholstered chairs arranged before a magnificent fireplace.

On either side of the stairs, there was a guest room. These rooms would be directly above the two side rooms downstairs. Judging from the rest of the house, I was slightly surprised to find that he didn't have a ballroom as well.

The kitchen, as you might expect, was large and roomy. It had a massive wood stove, plenty of counters, cupboards and drawers. In the center there sat a sizable table at which the head cook, Meddella, and the kitchen help ate. Two small rooms extended off the kitchen. One was Meddella's quarters, and the other was a store room. There was also a cellar dug under the kitchen, and it was big enough to hold a year or more worth of barrels of wines and brandies, as well as the stores of potatoes, onions and other such food stuffs.

That concludes the tour of the mansion. Now I get to tell a little of Meddella and Master Abburn.

Meddella reminds me of a toad in every respect. So much so, that if by a magic spell or something, someone turned a toad into a person, they would have made Meddella. She was quite round, had a flat face with two bulging eyes and nearly nonexistent eyebrows. Her face and hands were permanently red from the steam and hot water she constantly worked with. Or maybe her hands were red from dealing out blows so often. Either idea is likely. She had nasty warts over her face and stubby arms. Even her voice strongly resembled the croak of a toad with its strained, hoarse tone. And like a toad, she was very unpleasant to look at and be around.

Master Abburn, on the other hand, reminded me of the most stately thing I had ever seen. If I was to compare him to an animal I would have to say a race horse. Finely built, majestic to look at, with temper and passion enough for both horse and rider. As I have described his appearance already, I shall have to expound a little more on his character. His mood swings and temper were very unpredictable. I never knew what to expect of him from one moment to the next. He could have been laughing and joking, overlooking mistakes and dealing out quips. At other times, sometimes within minutes of his former mood, he lashed out physically as well as verbally. I never knew which side of this beast I was going to get. Though during the night hours, his physical manner showed up more.

But on the brighter side, Grenith was always there to see me through the hard days, especially the worst. She would often talk of Shalom along with the sunrises and sunsets like it was just normal to do so. I personally thought that was why all the other slaves hated her. They scowled and growled every time Elohim or Shalom was mentioned.

That was another strange thing about the slaves, they always complained of their life there. But if I asked where they would rather be, they could not answer beside that they would probably hate it more if they were free. None of the slaves who worked in the house with me or who worked in the fields ever made any sort of effort to be friends. And I suppose I was alright with that. The strange part was that they shunned me like they did Grenith, but we weren't alike. Grenith was so different than myself, that I almost laugh that we even got along. I guessed then that it was her glad spirit that drew me to her. But now I see that it was Elohim in her that really attracted me.

❦

Sometime after about a month of being at the manor, I had a notable incident. By then, it wasn't unusual that Master Abburn would send for me to serve his tea or read to him in the evenings. Once he had learned that I could read and write very well, he employed me for his entertainment. The same happened with serving tea, he found my manners nearly equal to that of a wealthy lady. I was, of course, glad to hear that, because it showed that I had learned it well and that my absence of high living hadn't taken its toll on my refined skills.

Around eight, the request was made for me to bring tea to the library. Meddella whisked together a tray with all the needed things. I was shooed out the door, my nerves on edge, and my ear stinging from a blow that was given because I didn't come into the kitchen fast enough to satisfy her expectation. I scuttled around to the main staircase and hopped up it, keeping the tray fairly steady. My steps were quick because I knew that Master Abburn was always impatient for his tea in the evenings. I crossed to the door of the library on the carpeted floor. Reaching out I turned the door knob and opened it, quickly entering the room. Apparently a little too quickly.

Not two steps into the room, I slammed into Master Abburn's solid frame. The tea tray, which I had been balancing with one hand while opening the door, tipped forward and

121

crashed to the floor, spilling its hot contents all over Master Abburn's expensive waistcoat. He cursed loudly at me.

I gasped with surprise and horror, remembering what had happened to the last girl who had broken a plate. Now I had broken an entire tea service *and* ruined one of his nice waistcoats. For a second, all I could do was stare and stammer over the mess I had made.

As it turned out, he was already mad because of the delayed tea. He was about to rush out the door and yell down the hall for his tea when I bustled through. So, naturally, he was beside himself with rage.

The second I had foolishly taken in shock was all he needed. With his face red and contorted in anger, he brought down his fist forcefully against my jaw. I, not thinking, didn't even brace for the blow, and toppled to the floor. The broken porcelain teapot cut into my hands and forearms. I cried out in pain, but I knew this was just the beginning.

My hands were shaking, my mind reeling at the sight of the blood smearing red over my palms. I was so absorbed with the initial shock, that I didn't see Master Abburn's foot until it was too late. His black boot came full force into my rib cage.

Instinctively I curled up, cringing and gasping for breath. I could feel the air leaving my lungs and none coming back in. I covered my head with my hands. I felt his boot dig into my back. Then glance off my spine. Then another blow, and another. The last thing I felt was where he had struck the back of my head somewhere.

Then everything went black.

❧

When my eyelids fluttered open, the next thing I knew I was in the slave shack. Light was pouring in through the cracks in the walls, and I knew that it was day. The light hurt my already throbbing head. I squinted at it, then at the surroundings just around me. In the dim light, I could see I was in my regular sleeping area, but I couldn't figure out why. It was obviously in the middle of the day. Why wasn't I working in the house?

I determined that I must have over slept, and they hadn't missed me yet. I went to sit up then fell back again with a cry of pain. My torso screamed back at me, shooting darts of pain through my entire body.

Then everything from the night before came flooding back. I started to tremble with fear. I felt a hand touch mine. I jumped, looking wildly to see who it was.

Grenith. I let out my breath in relief. I was truly glad that it was her and no one else.

She looked at me with understanding eyes and spoke softly, "They told me to watch you. They came earlier to see how you were doing. When they feel like you're well enough, you'll return like normal."

"What happened?" I asked groggily, trying to figure out how I got here.

I heard Grenith sigh, like she had been hoping that I wouldn't ask that. "He beat you unconscious. They didn't find you till after an hour or so. They thought that he might have had you read to him. But you had been gone a long time so they sent someone to check. Apparently Master Abburn went to bed, leaving you on the floor. You were carried here and I've watched you ever since."

I almost didn't want to know, but I asked anyway, "How long have I been here?"

"You've slept through the night, and it's around six by now. I was catching a little shut eye as well, till you tried sitting up. How do you feel?"

"It hurts. All over. I guess he got his fair share in for the tea service I broke and his waistcoat I ruined."

Grenith obviously hadn't heard about this part, and she asked in wonder, with a smile on her face, "What's this?"

"I opened the door and ran straight into him, spilling hot tea over his front, and the tea service shattered on the floor." I smiled slightly thinking back on it. My fear of being scolded or worse was what made me hurry. But hurrying was what got me in trouble.

I was surprised to hear Grenith actually laugh, and she exclaimed between giggles, "I'll bet he was a sight to see. Imagine it, his face getting all screwed up and real red. And the tea stain spilled over one of his fancy waistcoats! Ha! Not so elegant now, huh?"

I couldn't help smiling at the picture she painted over the real version. Her's was certainly more enjoyable than the original. Then I grew serious and asked, "How are you... so, well, so happy all the time?"

She got one of those smiles that Nollem used to get when he was about to say something about his faith. It was the same look of contended joy. "Well, I suppose it's cause my hope isn't in things that are here and now. My hope is in Shalom. And everything else, it doesn't matter so much anymore. It fades away in the light of His glory. That's why I can laugh at Master Abburn and the like, because I know that they can't take, or scare, away what truly matters. They can never get their hands on Shalom. So, I'll bear the bad things that come my way with gladness, because my true joy comes from being in Him. I know that He'll never abandon me, and even if I can't feel Him here, He still is. It's simple, really. He loved me first, and now I get to love Him back."

"But doesn't it get... lonely? I mean, everyone else hates you for it."

She shrugged a little. "It goes back to what your hope is set on. I'm not worried about what other's think of me, only the approval of Shalom. His opinion is all that matters. And yeah, there are days when I cry myself to sleep. I'm not inhuman. I still have plenty of emotions that aren't just happy. But you should try to get some rest now."

"Just one more question. If He really loves you, then why are you here?"

"What do you mean?"

I tried to rephrase it better, "If He really loves you, then why does He let you suffer like this?"

She sat back to think for a moment, then said slowly, "Who can say why specifically? But I do know that when we go through hard times, He is making us to be more like Him. Or He might be testing us, both of which in the end will turn out for the better. But either way, those rough patches draw us closer to Him. Now, get some sleep. You're not going to have much of a recovery time if you ask me."

Grenith was right. I had three days before they employed me again. I was still far from "back to normal." I had deep bruising and possibly a cracked rib or two. But never the less, I was sent back and expected to do the same. I got more boxed ears because of it, but what could I do? I eventually healed, but one thing never did: my fear of Master Abburn. The pain of the memory lasted long in my mind and left me timid and shrinking.

It wasn't long after our little episode, I determined that I wanted to get away. And there was no other way except to run. I knew they would never send me back to the market, even if I faked bumbling or sickness. They would just keep me and use me till I died. The only other option was running away.

I told Grenith of my plan, and she agreed that it would be best carried out at night. The only problem came was how to get out of our chains. I suddenly wished I still had my boot knife. I had forgotten about it when I received the new set of clothing from Rosamund. It wasn't the first time that I wished I still had my other clothes. When Grenith was whipped, and I was beaten, I wished that I still had those Delbriars that were in my pocket.

But I didn't, so I would have to steal a knife from the kitchen. If I got caught, I knew that I would be in serious trouble. But I soon devised a plan anyway and carried it out one evening.

It was the usual routine of supper time. Meddella loaded up a tray of foods, and I would carry it to the dining room. Master Abburn would be ready and waiting with a full set of dishes before him.

Master Abburn also liked meat with every meal, so there was guaranteed to be a knife for cutting it on the tray that I carried.

I got the call from Meddella to come and serve supper. I rushed into the kitchen and found that Master Abburn had requested supper in his office. So I got a tray of already loaded food with the silverware and cups ready. It was a stroke of luck. As I passed through the wide room, I swiped the dinner knife. Quickly, I stuffed it in between my bodice and blouse, holding it securely in my waistband.

I rounded the corner, passed the entry hall on my left and hurried to the far door. I turned into it, pushing the door open carefully. Looking at the floor, I approached his desk timidly. He glanced up and motioned with his hand to place the tray down. I did as he directed, bobbed a swift curtsy and walked out the room, trying to keep a steady, normal pace.

When I reached the door to the parlor, I heard Master Abburn scream my name. First off, I was surprised that he actually knew my name. Second, I was surprised that he didn't notice sooner that his knife was missing. I turned on my heel, and nearly ran to his door. I was trembling with fear that he might do something violent and then discover the knife I had hidden away. He didn't seem to notice my nervousness or he was just too mad.

When I opened the door, his stately figure was bolt upright, standing perfectly erect. His fists were rolled into white balls and he screamed a curse at me, "Where are all the knives in this house?! My staff shall hang for this! Don't just stand there! Get me one!"

I bobbed another curtsy and rushed out the door. I heard him yell something about a man can't just sit down and eat his supper without interruption, but with a string of foul language through it.

I practically ran to the kitchen and blurted out before Meddella could scream at me for rushing into the kitchen, "Master Abburn demands a second knife be brought for him!"

Meddella rushed over to the drawer to get one then paused to ask in her screechy voice, "Whatever for? He has one already."

"He didn't say, he doesn't need to say. He just demanded that I get him another." I hoped my story was convincing enough. But I knew we would have to leave tonight, before they discovered one of the knives was missing.

Meddella handed me the knife, apparently buying it. Snatching it out of her hand, I raced back to his office. Pausing before entering, I smoothed my skirt and opened the door, hoping to appear calm. It didn't take much effort to approach him timidly, and I handed the knife to him. He grabbed it without a word and signaled me to leave.

Once the door was closed, I nearly melted with relief. I felt along my waistband, as if to make sure that the knife was really there. It was.

The rest of the night seemed to take eons to pass. Master Abburn had his tea that evening in the library and went to bed a little earlier than usual. When I returned to the kitchen, I found a mass of dishes stacked along the counters, just waiting for me to do them.

Because of that, I was the last one to leave. I was escorted to the slave shack and chained in. Grenith had fallen asleep. After a few minutes, to make sure that it was all clear, I woke her up.

Rubbing the sleep from her eyes, she stared eagerly at me and asked, "Did you get it?"

"Yes," I replied, producing the knife. Moonlight shining through the cracks glinted off the well polished metal.

I set to getting us undone right away. I reached down to do my own first. After a significant amount of scraping and time, I finally did something right and it clicked open.

Once I got the shackles off, I set to work getting Grenith undone. Her's went quicker than mine. Before ten minutes passed, we were picking our way down the line of sleeping slaves with our tattered blankets in hand, towards the opening at the far end. We paused at the door frame and looked out to see if it was clear. I'm not sure why we did this, but it seemed the right thing to do then.

The yard, barn and fields were, of course, empty. We slipped out into the night and hung to our right, keeping close to the fenced-in pasture. Hoping to keep our course straight, we wanted to skirt around the fields. We were just about two thirds of the way there when the most alarming sound bellowed from the slave shack.

Someone, to this day I still don't know who, was shouting at the top of their lungs that there was an escape. The racket quickly awoke half the people in the big house, and sent them running outside.

As soon as we heard the yelling we cut straight across, dashing head long into the corn fields. We charged between two rows, crashing through, caution thrown to the wind. The green stalks were just beginning to brown and turn stiff. They crunched underfoot and the leaves cut our arms and faces. It was not unlike being cut by blades of grass.

Not that it mattered much anyway, nothing was going to stop us now. I knew we would have a small head start since the men would have to actually figure out who had left, how many, saddle their horses, get organized, and only then could they set out.

But they would quickly cover what distance we had since they were mounted.

My heart was racing inside my chest, breath gasping in and out. It felt good to run again, but I wouldn't be thinking that an hour later.

Before long, our pace slowed up. Not being accustomed to running long distances, both Grenith and I soon lagged. But Grenith more so than myself. I slowed my pace even more, determined not to leave her behind.

Suddenly, we burst out of the corn field. Open plowed flatlands stretched before us. We ran towards the horizon, hoping to get beyond it. I had no idea which direction we were going. We could have been running further into Deceiver's land or we could have been running back to the border. I had no idea. And it didn't matter to me. We were getting away from Master Abburn, that's all that I cared about.

After what felt like hours, but was probably only an hour or so, something ahead broke the flatlands. I could tell it was some sort of encampment, but I had no clue as to who might live in it.

Just as we sighted it, I glanced behind us and saw a cloud of dust rising off the plain. In front of it was a pack of horsemen galloping after us. I knew they must have seen us.

My eyes grew wide with fear, and I yelled something to Grenith, urging her to run if she valued her life. Our only hope was to reach that encampment before they caught up with us. Maybe, just maybe, we could get refuge with them. But if they did turn out to be enemies, anything would be better than Master Abburn. Right?

Willing myself to run, I sped into the lead, keeping my eyes on the encampment. As we drew nearer, I started to distinguish ornately carved and painted wagons. They were scattered in no distinct arrangement, but anywhere they pleased. Wisps of smoke curled from stove pipes that projected out the roofs and from old campfires also scattered about.

We were nearly there, and Master Abburn and his men nearly caught up to us. The pounding of the horses' hooves drowned out any other sound.

The noise must have woken up the people in the camp, because a few figures appeared. Most of them men, whom were multiplying until quite the crowd had gathered. Grenith and I ran right into the middle of the men. Two of them reached out and snatched us into their arms. They held us close, laughing at their prizes. Panting for breath, I struggled against them, but it was no use.

More men appeared from the odd wagons at a whistle from someone in the group. First they pressed around to look at Grenith and I, laughing and joking. Then their attention was drawn to the approach of Master Abburn and his five men.

At the head of the small group, Master Abburn reined in his horse, kicking up more dust. The others halted just behind him. They looked savage and mean in the moonlight. Catching sight of me in one rascal's arms, Master Abburn pointed a stern finger at me and bellowed out for all to hear, "Those are *my* slaves who foolishly tried to escape. Hand them back over to me and no harm shall come to you!"

Chapter 14
Seven Days of Bliss

There was a brief silence after Master Abburn spoke. They seemed to be thinking among themselves. My heart stopped beating. I watched tensely, waiting for someone to speak. Would they give us back? What would Master Abburn do as punishment?

Suddenly one called back out, "They came to us, ran right in here! And now we're claiming them as ours. So shove off!"

There was a chorus of agreement from the rest of them. Turning red in the face, Master Abburn shouted back at them, "I demand you release them to me! They are mine, I bought them!"

Laughter rang out, and someone called back, "What are you going to do about it? There's a score plus of us and only six of you!"

Master Abburn's face screwed up with rage, his hands quivering. His thick voice spat back, "You'll be sorry you laid a finger on even one of my slaves!"

With that he swung his horse around and galloped off with the others following.

A giant shout of applause broke out among the men. There was much back slapping and well-dones all around. Feeling extremely relieved, I smiled, still breathing heavily. I felt free from his power, and I never felt better. I let out a whoop with the rest.

The fellow who held me, picked me up and cheered, swinging me about in his arms. Then I got passed from one set of arms to the next, each man getting more possessive over me. I soon had a following of angry shouting men, reaching out to get hold of me and claim me as his own. It was then that I began to fear for my life again. I wasn't sure what they would do with me. They were, after all, gypsies. You can never be sure about gypsies.

By now, the entire camp was awake. Some women appeared among the mass of men. Quicker than I imagined, everyone knew about the two slaves that had just run into their camp.

Suddenly, a shout rang above the noise. It was a female voice, and I searched for the owner. Mine, with every other pair of eyes, turned to an old woman standing at the door of her wagon. She was raised above everyone else, and waited patiently for them to quite down. Apparently she held some seniority respect because everyone looked at her waiting for her to speak.

Her voice sounded again, warbling with age, "Now listen up! Set those girls down, and treat them with a little respect! Are we the low scum people think we are? Or are we decent human beings? Set them down I say! Look at them. Young, frightened, and uncertain, and you've gone and scared them half out of their wits with all your talk of owning them. Well, I have news for you! These nice girls shan't be owned by anyone here! Are we not gypsies? Do we not fend for ourselves, helping each other live, not forcing others into servitude? Let them alone! Nor shall any of you rouges touch them! As far as I'm concerned, they shall be treated just like any other gypsy. And they will live with me, out of harm's way. Come, come, my dears, come up here with me. There's no need to worry now."

She beckoned us up with her hands. The gypsy man had finally set me down on my own two feet. I was a little leery of going up, but it was better than standing among these men. I threaded my way through the staring people.

As I was doing so, the old woman spoke again, "All of you, go back to your homes and sleep the rest of the night in peace. It is late. Go on, back to your beds before they get cold."

The group of gypsies obeyed her orders and slowly filed back to their wagons. A general hubbub rose up as they talked quietly among themselves.

Grenith and I both went up the stairs that led to the door of her wagon. The old lady, briskly wrapping her knitted shawl closer around her shoulder, shooed us inside the wagon. We emerged in a warm space that was larger than I expected. A few oil lamps lit the room with a soft glow, even though all flame had long since disappeared. Heat still radiated from the small stove to our left.

In the far right corner there was a double bed. Both bunks were piled with round and square pillows and assorted blankets and quilts. A thick rug covered the floor. The walls were covered with paintings, pictures, fragments of pages from notable books, and dried plants.

There were two windows on either side wall that currently had thick, dark curtains drawn over them. There was an upholstered rocking chair by the stove. A cupboard that was attached to the wall, was filled with dried goods and tin plates and pewter mugs and silverware. There were a couple of stools loitering about in no particular order. In the corner with the double beds there was a trunk, which I supposed held her clothing.

Over all, it was cozy and inviting, if not a little messy. But I didn't care and it only added to the homeyness of the wagon. It was warm and safe, that's all that mattered.

The old woman rushed in after us, shut and bolted the door behind her, and turned to face us with a smile that lit up her entire countenance. Her wrinkles crinkled even more. She said warmly, "Well, then. Welcome to my home. I suppose we should begin with introductions. My name is Starlight Glimmer, but most just shorten it to Glimmer. The young ones call me Granny Glimmer, but I don't expect either of you to call me that. Glimmer will do fine. Now tell me your names."

Grenith answered first, "My name is Grenith. Pleased to make your acquaintance." She bobbed a slight curtsy.

"Limira," I said shortly, then rushed, "How can we ever thank you for—"

She held up her hands in protest. "Now, now, there's no need to mention that. You'll be helping me too, you know. First thing's first though, it is way past my bedtime, and I'm sure that you're positively exhausted from your journey. Of which," she added, "I will expect a full report of in the morning."

Glimmer bustled to the far side of the wagon to the trunk. She muttered along the way, "I'm sure that I have something for you to slip into for the night..." She dug into the trunk, and after a bit produced two rather large chemises. Holding them up for her inspection, she mumbled, "Yes, these should do for now." Then she addressed us, "Here you are. Slip into these while I get another bed settled on the floor.

Undressing, Grenith and I hesitantly changed. We were both uncomfortable with it, and Glimmer seemed to notice because she said while laying out a great deal of cushions and blankets on the floor, "No need to worry, my dears. I shall keep my back well turned to you for your sakes."

Pretty soon we were both nestled under blanket and quilts. Grenith insisted that I take the upper bed, and she the floor. Neither of us were at all accustomed to mattresses, but Grenith insisted that I sleep on the one because I had at least slept on one before.

When Glimmer heard this she gasped with shock and asked sensitively, "You have *never* slept in a bed before?"

Grenith shook her head no.

A hand when to the old lady's mouth and she gasped. "Slavery is worse than I had imagined. But surely, before you were a slave, you have slept in one?"

Grenith shook her head with a slight shrug of shoulders, "It was either the floor or cots."

That ended the conversation. Glimmer went to bed, shaking her head and muttering to herself, Grenith burrowed between quilts and cushions, and I climbed up to the second bunk. I covered myself with the blankets and went to lay back but it felt like I was just going to keep sinking lower and lower into the mattress. I sat bolt upright, smacking my head against the top of the wagon. I groaned slightly and put a hand to the top of my head. Then I slowly tried again, but got the same feeling of melting.

I never before would have thought that I would have that problem. But I did and it took me quite some time before I could get to sleep.

❦

When I woke, daylight was streaming under the still drawn curtains. I heard birds singing outside and muffled voices. I lay still for a while, just resting, waking up, and stretching a little. I stared at the smooth wood ceiling, following the grain of the stained wood. Once I had fallen asleep, I slept like a bear buried under twelve feet of snow in the dead of winter.

I suddenly felt a little restless and glanced down at the floor. Grenith was still sleeping under folds of quilts. The cushions were scattered around her in lumps under the covers. Her light blonde hair was scattered about her on a lump of blanket that her head was resting on.

I smiled a little, looking at her peaceful face and listening to her steady breaths. Glancing down even further, I was surprised to see that old Glimmer was gone. Then again, depending on what time it was, it wasn't that surprising at all.

Casting off the covers quietly, I untangled myself from the chemise, practically swimming in it. I swung my legs over the side of the bed and climbed down. This time I was careful to not hit my head. My feet barely hit the floor before I heard Grenith stirring behind me. I turned around cautiously, but she was already awake and smiling at me. Her face was the very picture of serenity.

"Good morning, Grenith," I greeted her.

"It is indeed," she replied in a soft voice.

"I hope I didn't wake you."

"No, I don't think so. It's time that I got up anyway."

Just then, Glimmer burst through the door, letting in a cold gust of morning air. I immediately wrapped my arms around me, not only thinking of the cold but my decency as well. I relaxed when I realized that it was Glimmer.

The old lady shut the door and turned around. "Oh," she said surprised, "you're awake! Splendid. I just got back from getting some new clothing for you, and I scared up a large tub for a bath." She saw our faces—they were a mix of surprise and shock—and said quickly, "Well, you're old clothes simply will not do. They are ratty and dirty. No amount of mending or scrubbing could fix them. And you must get clean, you're both simply filthy."

Now that I thought of it, my "new" dark green dress wasn't so new or fine as I thought it was. The skirt was splattered with mud and dirt, and there were many rips in it. The white blouse that went under it was hardly white anymore, and it too had its fair amount of rips and stains.

I could tell Grenith was simply astounded at the thought of a bath. I wouldn't be surprised if she had never had a true bath before, but still. When Glimmer heard, I thought she might keel over with some heart problem. She inquired with a shocked expression and tone, what then, did they do for getting themselves clean? Grenith explained that they would go out into the rain, when it did rain, and rub themselves. They did have a well just for the use of the slaves, but they never used the water to wash themselves, nor did they have the time to do so.

Miss Glimmer soon had a kettle on the stove heating water. By then, Grenith had gotten out of the blankets. We had folded and stacked the cushions, blankets and quilts in a corner. Glimmer insisted that we sit down on the stools, and that was when she noticed that we were shivering.

She felt so bad that she went into a tizzy about how she should have thought of it before. Soon enough, she had two soft, silky bathrobes pulled out of the trunk. We put them on over the white chemises and huddled closer to the stove.

It was quite some time before we got enough hot water for both baths. Grenith took the first bath, and I the second. The old lady was quite upset and concerned when she saw the scars from lashings all over Grenith's back. And she reacted similarly when she saw the remnants of the beating Master Abburn gave me. I still had dark marks over my back and sides, but they didn't hurt unless I pressed hard against them. She kept muttering angrily under her breath, her brow furrowed and lips pursed.

Ingeniously, Glimmer had gotten some of the men to carry water and leave it on her front porch, by the door. Whenever she opened the door to get more water, she would make sure that we were well out of view.

The clothes that Glimmer had gotten from some of the gypsy women were a little big, but we made them work. She had gotten two skirts that were of a coarse woolen fabric, dark in color. Grenith got a navy blue, and I got a brown one. Each had an equal amount of neat patches sewn on. There were cream, full blouses that buttoned down the front. Over these, we had long shawls made of thick cloth and lined with soft flannel. These were so large and we so small, that we could wrap them around our shoulders, cross them in the front, bring them around our backs and tie them in the front again.

After our hair dried, Glimmer gathered it back with cloth ties. She gave us plain bandanas that we covered our hair with to keep it cleaner.

Once we were done, we looked just as much gypsies as Glimmer did. By that time, it was well after noon, and Glimmer prepared us a fine breakfast. She had successfully chattered through all of this, asking questions, prattling on about this and that. She was rather entertaining and enjoyable just to listen to.

Miss Glimmer threw back the curtains and let the early afternoon sun in. She suggested that we go out for a little air. And that there was, of course, some people who very much wanted to meet us.

When we finished our breakfast, we went according to her wishes. She insisted that she could clean up just fine without our help, and that we should go out and get ourselves acquainted with the area and people.

With little reassuring smiles and glances, Grenith and I ventured out of the wagon. We closed the painted door behind us and stopped to take things in a little. We were near the edge of the gypsy camp, and there were a few other wagons around us, but the majority were out of sight and to our backs.

The wagons themselves are worth noting. They were very much like little houses on wheels. They were somewhat square, with flat or slanted roofs, had windows, and sometimes two doors, one on either end. They were all painted in dark colors with bright trimmings and decorative stenciling along the edges. All had a stove pipe popping out the roof. On either end there were steps to lead up to the doors, or the bench where one would sit if they were to drive a team. Some of the larger families had two wagons pulled side by side to each other.

Near the wagons there was always a smaller fire pit with pots, pans and kettles by it or on it. In the very center of the gathering of gypsy wagons, there was a place for a huge bonfire. They apparently did these often, telling stories around them, singing songs or just talking with their fellow campers.

Wide open fields and rolling hills surrounded the gypsy camp.

Grenith and I looked back to each other, then I stepped down the stairs first. Touching the ground, I took a few steps, then paused. I looked back to see if Grenith was following or not. She was.

We looked around some more. There were women stooped over campfires who looked like they were cleaning up from the last meal, and children playing around the wagons.

We had already attracted some attention, and curious looks came our way. Word had gotten around about the two strangers who were once slaves. It seemed nothing was kept a secret for long among these people.

Not liking to be the center of attention and really only wanting some peace and quiet, we chose to head out to our right and take a walk out into the fields a little. We wandered in silence for a while until Grenith said, "They seem really close here."

"Yeah. I feel like an intruder among them."

Grenith laughed a little, "Really? All I saw were curious looks. We're just different than them, and that's what makes them stare the way they do. Especially the children. They've probably never seen, much less met a slave before."

"I suppose," I answered a little sullenly.

"What is the matter with you, Limira? You're not yourself. What's wrong?"

That caught me off guard, because I was only just realizing that myself. "I'm not sure. I can feel something's not right. But I can't yet put my finger on it. I just, I just don't *feel* right. It's hard to explain."

"Well, if it's the gypsies, don't let them bother you. As I said before, they're probably just curious."

"No, I don't think it's them. It's something deeper than that. But it is only the first day being free. It more than likely has something to do with that."

Grenith left it at that and changed the subject. But that feeling didn't leave, not all that day.

When we returned to the gypsy camp, Glimmer had been looking all over for us. She scolded us lightly for not saying where were we going. But a few moments later, I'm sure she completely forgot about it because she was excitedly introducing us to pretty much every woman in the camp. She explained that the men and some of the younger girls—meaning girls our age and up without children—were out working in the fields and gardens. She quickly added that we might employ ourselves out working tomorrow if we wished. But the way she said it, it was more like we had to if we were to stay there for any amount of time.

❦

The gypsies were very kind to us. And just as Glimmer suggested, we were sent out to work in the fields and gardens the next few days. But we were glad to do it. Working for our own direct benefit was much more enjoyable than before. Everyone was, of course, curious about us. We spent many a night around the bonfire telling stories about our lives and adventures.

It wasn't surprising that Grenith readily made many friends among them. I had a more awkward time with it. The girls our age were very nice, and they and Grenith got along splendidly. But I found that I couldn't enjoy the same things they did. I was still uneasy. And I couldn't explain it beyond I didn't feel any different on the inside than when I was under Master Abburn. I had noticed something weighty deep down inside, but thought that it would pass once I got out of hardship. Well, it didn't. And now it almost seemed worse, because everyone else was happy, but I was miserable. And things on the inside soon spill out to the outside as well.

I told Grenith about it once on one of our long walks. We took them regularly, not being used to the friendly, always-with-someone lifestyle of the gypsies. Like usual, Grenith listened quietly, then said what she had to say in her soft tone. She gently explained what she thought it was, and how to change it. Which brought her into explaining all about the beginning of the world, how mankind made a mistake and were punished by being separated from Elohim to live how we wanted. But then Elohim sent Shalom to die to take the punishment for our mistakes, and how He rose from the dead three days later, conquering death and leaving it powerless. Then she explained that when we believe in Him, He would give us a new life in Him, free from the the power of death because of Him. His Spirit would then enter into us, and over time make us more like Him.

She went into more detail than that, but that was the general gist of what she said. It sounded a lot like what Nollem had tried telling us about. Only this time I listened. But I still wasn't sure. My childhood beliefs clung on for survival. I could still save myself, I wasn't in too deep that I couldn't pull myself out again.

Because of the conflict of what I had always known, and what I had just learned—but was leaning towards—I didn't make a decision one way or the other. I wanted to give it more thought. I also noticed that my Crown emblem was beginning to fade, and I wasn't sure how I felt about it.

Grenith was very respectful of it, adding that she'd been praying for me.

That ended that conversation, and we returned to camp.

Other than my inward problems, life there was very pleasant. There was nothing to complain about. Glimmer took the best of care of us, she said it was like having the daughters she never had. The work was pleasant and rewarding. The company was more than enjoyable.

One thing that awed me each night were the sunsets. Through the dark clouds shrouding the sky, the rays of the sun would filter through in the most beautiful colors. Dark oranges, pinks and reds streaked the sky each night. It reminded me of when you see the sun set through a haze of smoke. Except it was better, because all around us it was bleak greys and browns, all very bland colors. Then, as the sun sank lower, a burst of color painted the skies.

I began to sound like Grenith when we were in the slave shack at night, oh how we could go on about it.

There was also a boy there, his name was Haiblur, who had taken a fancy to me, I think. He was about my age and growing into a fine, strong fellow, but still a little awkward on his feet. Grenith was full of teasing me about him and his attentions. And I couldn't help but think that he really did like me. He sat by me, got all tongue tied and clumsy, and every time I looked in his direction he was staring at me. It was strange to have someone like me in that way. I didn't think anyone else had before. Grenith was all bubbles over it and I was content to think that he was just trying to be friendly. But inwardly, I wanted to believe that he liked me.

Some of the other gypsy girls noticed his attentions towards me, and joined Grenith in teasing and giving suggestive glances. I dare say it was rather laughable, and I can truthfully say that I am glad we left before things got more serious. But still, being a girl, I enjoyed it, and it still makes me smile whenever I think of it.

But our happy days were numbered.

Chapter 15
The Eighth Day

It was the morning of our eighth day. The gleam of the sun swathed everything in a luminous glow. It poured through the windows as Glimmer threw back the curtains.

The night before, Grenith and I had stayed up late around the bonfire, listening to stories and telling jokes. There was even some dancing about the large flames. Haiblur caught me up and turned a few circles around it, skipping and laughing. We flopped back into our spots, irrupting with laughter and smiles.

I was laying in bed, covered in the pine smelling quilts, replaying last nights events in my head when Glimmer insisted that we get up, or else the morning would quite forget us. Or we might forget the morning, and I think that's what she was more afraid of. She was throwing together breakfast while Grenith and I dressed for the day. By the time we arranged our hair under our scarves, fried eggs, ham and onions were served onto the tin plates. We would have to eat quickly if we were to make it out the door in time to head out into the fields with the others.

We finished and headed outside in a rush. We hadn't even touched the ground before I knew something was up. A gathering of twenty or so gypsies had congregated a little distance from Glimmer's wagon. They were all staring off into the distance and muttering among themselves.

I gazed out along the flat plains, searching for what they thought was so interesting. I didn't have to look long. A cloud of dust rose from a dark mass on the horizon. I could tell that it was a large group of horsemen riding furiously. I instinctively knew that it was Abburn—by then we had stopped calling him master—coming back for his slaves. He had threatened and now he was coming to carry it out.

Grenith and I exchanged a knowing glance, and we rushed back into the wagon. We blurted out everything at once to Glimmer who slowed us down, "Now, now, there's no need to jump to conclusions. But if you think that you could be in danger then I suppose we could get together a few things for your journey." She began to bustle about the small space gathering things up and putting them into two large cloths.

Staring at her, Grenith and I both asked at the same time, perhaps a little too sharply, "Journey?"

"Now don't go biting my head off, I'm only looking out for you two. Yes, journey. You obviously can't stay here, now can you? If it is this Abburn character, we had best be prepared to get you out of here. Can't have no slave trader bullying my guests—no, daughters—about and dragging them half over the world back to a place no person ought to be. Here take these," she handed two bundles with food and other such things into our arms. Waving her hands at us, she shooed us back out the door, saying, "Go on now, no time to lose."

We immediately looked back to check the progress of the daunting cloud. It was nearer than ever and would soon reach us.

By now almost all the gypsies had gathered, and some were running to arm themselves with tools and even a few weapons. They were going to put up a fight.

Old Glimmer, with tears in her eyes, turned us about to face her. She scolded us motherly like, as she gave us parting hugs, "You both stay safe, and be sure to stay warm at nights, they're getting colder. I'll miss you both dreadfully." She sniffed, wiping her eyes with the back of her hand. "Now go," she urged, "and don't linger longer than you have to."

I can't remember what exactly we said in response to her, but I knew that we would never forget her and that we would ever be in her debt.

We clamored down the steps and hopped to the ground. With a final look over our shoulders, we passed Glimmer's painted wagon and moved through the camp. I knew that we were headed towards the border, but had no idea how far off it was. I squared my jaw, trying not to think of those I was leaving behind.

Just as we were passing some of the last wagons, a shout rang out, calling my name. I turned around and saw Haiblur running to us.

"Wait, Limira!" he shouted running up to us. "I have to tell you something before you go." He stopped just short of me and said, "Stay safe out there, and," he leaned over and pecked my cheek affectionately. He whispered, rushed, "I love you."

I gave him a smile in return and embraced him. "I wish you the best of luck, mate," I replied earnestly. It was lame, I know, but what else could I say?

Then on the other side of the encampment, a great noise irrupted. The sounds of horses neighing and men shouting filled the air. It was time to go. We had waited long enough.

I gave his hand one last squeeze before I turned to go.

Grenith and I broke into a sprint. Haiblur stood there, looking mournfully after us. He yelled desperately after me, "If I can, I'll find you!"

I gave one final glance over my shoulder. He had turned and was sprinting over to the battle that I knew was commencing for our sakes.

Only then did it sink in what the gypsies were really doing for us. They were prolonging our pursuit. They and I knew that they couldn't very well resist the men Abburn would bring. If they did prevail, it would only be at the cost of many in their close community. But if they were overtaken, their wives and their children would be taken back as slaves.

They were laying down their lives to save ours.

Feelings of guilt and sadness swept over me. Part of me just wanted to turn around, run back, and give ourselves up. We weren't worth dying for. They were sacrificing too much for just us. But I forced myself to run on, knowing that they wouldn't have it any other way.

If we gave up now, their deaths would mean nothing.

So we ran. We ran from our past. We ran from our friends. We ran from our home. We ran from our deaths.

We ran for our lives.

It was dark before we stopped for any long amount of time. We had taken short breaks to catch our breath and get a little food and water from the bundles Glimmer had packed for us. Then we would set out again. Never certain of pursuit, but always leery of it.

Once complete darkness had set in and we couldn't see more than three feet ahead of us, we flopped to the ground exhausted, out of breath, and in desperate need of sleep. Not caring where we slept, we found a small ditch, more like a divot, in the ground. Curling up, we tucked our feet under our skirts, used the bundles as pillows and huddled close together to keep warm.

We passed the night uninterrupted and woke up in a frosty morning light thoroughly chilled. My hands and arms were stiff with cold, and my nose and cheeks were numb. We stamped our feet on the ground, trying to get the warmth back in them.

After we had a mouthful or two of brown bread, we set out, at a brisk trot this time, intentionally trying to get our blood flowing again.

There was still no sign of Abburn, or anyone else for that matter, but it was too early to tell whether or not he would be coming after us. And there was no way to know how our friends fared.

I was beginning to despair in anxiety for them. I was getting the feeling that I couldn't do anything to help, or gain knowledge of what had passed. In plainer words, I was beginning to feel small and helpless. Like I couldn't even begin to guess what the next day, much less the next few hours, held for me.

Onward we went. It was around noon that we slowed our pace to a walk. By the middle of the afternoon I noticed that the cloud cover was getting thicker and darker. Ahead the wall of black greyish clouds touched to the earth. At first I thought it was just the horizon, but soon I realized that it wasn't at all. It was the border. The eternal thick clouds sank and formed a wall of dark shroud. It ran on either side as far as the eye could see.

Suddenly, Grenith broke into a sprint, surging towards the dark barrier. I wasn't sure why, but I followed her anyway. We approached the wall much quicker than I was expecting. I grew more uneasy about it as we came closer. I couldn't see anything beyond the dark wall of oppression. I had no clue where we would emerge on the other side. And most daunting of all, I had no way of knowing what was *in* the darkness.

I consciously slowed down as we drew nearer. Quite the opposite, Grenith kept going steadily, unperturbed by the shrouded wall. She plunged into it and was instantly swallowed up by the swirling, dry mist.

I stopped immediately. Just feet from the moving mass, I stared into it, trying to perceive something beyond it. There was nothing.

I continued to peer in. Seconds drug by and felt like hours. I took a step forward. Then another. It wasn't quite so bad as I first thought. There was just something about it that captivated me. I was curious and fascinated by it, yet still, I had this unquenchable dread of it. I drew closer, taking the first step into the shroud. No, it wasn't so bad. I took a few more steps in.

I glanced over my shoulder, searching for the barren land behind me, trying to discern how far in I was. I could see nothing but swirling grey. I took a few more steps, wondering what would be at the heart of the blackness.

Then it closed in on me. I suddenly got a chilling feeling that tingled up and down my arms. Another step. In half a heartbeat, I was swallowed by the dark mass. Something, some force, had grabbed hold of my throat and was sucking the life from me. I gasped for every breath of air. The force pressed against me, squeezing me between its invisible mass. I struggled against it, but there was no use. It only clutched at me all the more.

It had me locked in a death grip. My limbs felt numb, my face clammy with cold sweat. I reached up, groping for the hands that held my throat. There was nothing there. All I could feel was the powerful force cutting off all airflow.

I began to choke, feeling unconsciousness gnaw at me. I felt like I could be strangled to death. I was completely powerless against this unseen beast. This unseen death.

Panic welling up within me, my mind raced through a whirlwind of thoughts. But one would always appear, pronounced and terrifying; I was going to die. I would never see Nollem again. I was going to die. Grenith would be on her own. Was she alive? I wasn't going to be. There was no way that I could save myself. This was beyond me. I couldn't do it alone. I couldn't do it at all.

I couldn't save myself.

Was there any way to survive? But did I really want to live just so that I would go on surviving again? Surviving was miserable. Look where it got me. Could this even be called surviving? It felt more like dying, but so slowly that it was hard to tell. Now it was obvious, I was dying.

I was going to die. I couldn't save myself. I had lived a horrible life, no good was done by it. I hadn't accomplished anything for any cause whatsoever. It was empty, meaningless, like a bunch of letters jumbled together into confused words. No purpose, no goal, no end result. No nothing.

I couldn't save myself. I needed to be saved. Because I was going to die.

I finally thought to plead with Shalom to save me now. I screamed with every inch of my mind for Him to hear. Grenith had said that the life Shalom offered was a gift, only in need of asking. I was counting on that. I knew that I needed Him.

There was no way that I could keep living in this world without Him. Death was closing in on me, I was lost, I couldn't save myself.

But He could.

I cried out, asking for His forgiveness and for Him to enter me. The only way I could live was if He was in me. There was no other way. It wasn't like I was forced. Right then I wanted, I desired with all my heart, to be saved, to have life, to have Him.

Save me, I know that I can't. I'll never be enough to save myself from myself. Only You will be enough, only You can save me from death. I give my life, for all that it's worth, to You. Please save me, I can't live without You.

It was there that I truly, whole heartedly accepted the gift of Shalom, the one He paid for with His life. The gift of a new life lived in Him and Him alone.

The suffocating force released its hold. I fell to the ground, gasping for breath. My mind was filled with thoughts of relief and gratitude and joy. He had saved *me*, the wretched undeserving person that I am. But He loved me enough to die for me anyway.

The dark mist, faded around me. I think I stumbled forward into the sunshine, but I really don't remember how I got there. I made it to the other side of the border, and the afternoon sun shone down on me. I fell to the ground, overcome with wonder.

Part 2

Chapter 16
From the Jaws of Death...

It was the most wonderful, indescribable feeling that I had ever known. I was filled to the brim with peace, love and joy. All because of Him.

I was no longer dead, I was *living in Him*. I was alive because He had died. I was made new in Him. He took my death away to give me Life.

Everything from that point on was different, my perspective changed. I couldn't look at things without seeing Shalom in them. The sun was brighter, the birds' songs were sweeter, the air was fresher, colors were prettier, flowers and grass more intricate. All because I now saw Shalom's finger prints all over them. I appreciated them more because He made them.

My perspective change wasn't limited to nature only. Beggars were kings and queens, the lowest of the low had value and were precious because they were precious in His eyes. Evil was more despicable, death less threatening, the Between more pitiable. All had hope of being saved. There was no point at which they could no longer be reached by His all-sin-covering love.

My eyes were closed, and I was smiling like I had never before. It was out of pure joy and peace. I was in the presence of my King, and I never wanted to leave.

After a few moments, I suddenly thought of my mark. I glanced down at it, having to lift my blouse collar a little. There, right where my Crown used to be, was a bush encircled by a curly ring. The bush itself still looked dead, no leaves, only branches lacing out from the twisting trunk.

I laughed. Never before had I thought that I would ever want to see that mark on me. But now, I was glad and proud to bear it as my emblem because it meant that I was in Him and He in me.

It was only then that I noticed Grenith. She was sitting on the ground, a few feet from me and a little to my left. I looked at her, a smile on my face. I didn't say anything. I didn't need to.

She knew and was grinning like I had never seen before.

There were a few moments of silence before I broke it. I whispered, still in awe, "I'm so... alive. I'm living now."

Grenith nodded, her face still glowing. "I know. It's such a blissful, incomparable, indescribable feeling."

I nodded in agreement, my mouth still parted in awe and joy. I was so happy that I might grow wings and fly off. No, not so much happy as... content. It was like no matter what happened, good or bad, it wouldn't matter. I wouldn't care. He was all that mattered.

"Now what?" I asked aloud, not really think about *where* we would go, but rather *what* we were going to do next. Grenith had never been out of Deceiver's land before, so she had no idea where we were. And, as I have said before, I never cared much for studying maps. And now I was paying for it. Note to the wise: study your maps. You never know when it might be handy to know where you're at and how to get somewhere.

It wasn't two seconds after I asked when Grenith practically blurted out in a most resolute, confident voice, "Let's go back in."

"You what?" I asked not because I hadn't heard her, but because I didn't believe that she was saying it. I was dumbfounded at the idea.

"Let's go back in," she reiterated. "There's an old Lightbearer's headquarters on the other side of Delth Marsh. There might be other Lightbearers still there. From there, we can talk to them and see how we can help with the war. What do you say?"

I stared at her with my mouth gaping open, "I say that we just got out! Why would any person in their right mind want to go back?"

"Limira," Grenith said seriously, looking me straight in the eye, "people are dying. I want to do everything I can to help them come into Life. That's what we're called to do. Love and serve Elohim with all our hearts, and bring others to the Life I've come to depend on. What's the point of knowing something, if you don't share it? Especially something that means life or death for thousands of people. And that's where a lot of lost people are. So why would I *not* want to go back in?"

It was a powerful message, and sincerely given, but I didn't see the beauty and truth in it then. All I could think of was that we shouldn't go back in, "Because we just escaped from there! In case you don't remember, we were just running for our lives!" It was a poor choice of words on my part.

"That's right. But now you've accepted Life. You've found Him. You know what it's like to be constantly afraid of death. Now think of the other people out there who have the same fear with no hope of ever escaping. They need Shalom just and much as you and I do, and you can help point them to Him. Shalom will do great things through us, if we let Him. There's nothing to fear. Shalom is with us, what can be against us?"

I was still skeptical. I had just gotten out from under Deceiver's reach, and now she expected me to go back in. And willingly too! It was rather silly of me, if you think about it. I was far from convinced, but I chose to trust in Shalom, and in Grenith's judgment.

I nodded slightly to show my reluctant consent.

Grenith beamed winningly at me and took eager steps towards the grey wall of clouds. As she passed me, she grabbed my hand, towing me along behind her.

Just as we passed into the mist, I closed my eyes. When I opened them, all I could see was grey. I couldn't even see Grenith. I saw her hand on mine, but a little past her wrist vanished in the shroud.

I didn't have the same apprehensive feeling as I had before, and I wasn't curious of it. It was despicable in my eyes, because of who it was wrought by and the destruction the darkness brought to the lands. It didn't feel oppressive either. It almost felt like it was glaring at us. Like it didn't want to let us pass, but was powerless to stop us.

I said to Grenith through the gloom, looking about me trying to pick out something, "If something goes terribly wrong, I'm blaming all this on you."

I heard a jingling laugh, just ahead but muffled. It was still unmistakably Grenith's. "Alright," she replied merrily, "it's a deal."

❦

We walked for a few hours, until it got dark. Well, darker than usual. It was an uneventful night, and boy, have I gotten to appreciate those.

It was the middle of the morning when things picked up a little.

Deceiver's land was just as bleak and desolate as I remembered it to be. Change in geography didn't mean much in this land. It all looked the same out here: rolling hills covered in sparse, dry, grey grass that I'm sure used to look green and pretty. But those days were long gone. There were even a few clumps of equally dead and grey bushes of old shrubs and briars. These were dotted all over the dusty tan hills in random dark mounds.

Wind was nonexistent. The heavy air was muggy and thick and stifling. The ever present clouds above us were moving though, so I knew that there was wind up there somewhere. I kept glancing up hopefully, wishing the breeze would come down and blow over us.

That's when I first saw it.

At first, I thought it was just the shadows shifting among the clouds. Then I thought for sure my eyes were playing tricks on me.

Suspended in the clouds, there was the dark shape of a flying creature. It looked like a shadow itself. From a distance, I thought it might be a dragon. It would have to be a small dragon, but a dragon none the less. Then I realized, as it circled about us, it looked more like a large bat than a dragon. It was too small for a dragon, but way too big for a bat. It was in the middle somewhere, about twice the size of an eagle, with black leathery wings. Occasionally, I could hear the snapping of the wings if the wind caught the sound just right. Even then it was very faint.

I had no clue what they were. I say "they" because the longer I watched them, more joined the first one, multiplying their number rapidly.

Finally, I brought them to Grenith's attention. And that was only because I was starting to get worried about their numbers. More and more congregated above us. "Grenith," I began slowly, hesitating, "what do you suppose those are?" I pointed up, staring at the circling shadows.

She looked up, catching the uncertainty in my voice. I saw her eyes get wide, then she quickly grabbed my hand and ran over to the nearest bush of dead shrubs, towing me along. It was a prickly thorn bush that had long since given up hope of ever being green again.

"Quick!" Grenith urged, "get under here with me!" She dove under the low hanging branches, digging her way into the middle.

I raised an eyebrow, viewing the large thorns skeptically. But I slowly got to my knees and wriggled in after her. The thorns snagged my clothing and left cuts and scratches over my hands, arms and face. It was a painful and slow process, but I got under. I lay beside Grenith on my stomach. I was far from pleased and wanted an explanation. Rubbing at some of the worst cuts, I grilled Grenith impatiently, "What is all this about?"

"Excuse me for attempting to save your life," she testily snapped.

"My life is saved!" I spat back. "Now what is this all about?"

"It's a good thing too," she said, dodging my second question, "we may be too late."

"Too late for what?" I asked still completely lost as to what she was talking about.

"They may have caught our scents."

"*What* may have?!"

"Orodumes!" She said like it was a no brainer. "Don't you know anything?"

I had never seen Grenith like this before. But I suppose everyone has that one part of them. Not that I was thinking this at that moment. Instead I was coming up with some good retort. "It's not my fault that I haven't spent my entire life in Deceiver's land!" I spat out. "In case you don't remember, I had a life before I met you! And it was just dandy in comparison to traipsing all over the world, facing perpetual danger. Speaking of which, shouldn't we be quiet if you're so worried about them?"

"No. They can't hear worth a penny. Nor do they see that great either. So from their altitude, we're quite safe in those regards. But they have the keenest sense of smell I ever saw. And they probably got a whiff of us since they're gathering. Start burying yourself with dirt and stuff. Hopefully, just maybe, that will cover our smells and we won't get attacked," she said this last part as she began scratching at the dirt around her.

I did the same. The top layer of dirt was crusty and firm, but below was sandy. So once I got past the first few inches, digging was fairly easy going. We were both silent, too busy digging to speak, which meant too busy to argue as well.

My fingers were cut, bruised and aching by the time I was done. They got shredded on the brittle roots of the bush and small sharp stones that I always discovered after the damage was done. I was glad that the Orodumes didn't have too good of sight, otherwise they would have seen the entire bush rustling.

Once we were sufficiently buried, we lay as still as possible, only chancing a furtive glance up every few minutes.

An hour or so passed. It felt *so* much longer than that. The Orodumes finally started to leave, slowly drifting in and out of sight.

It was a close call.

After the last one disappeared into the dark clouds, we unburied ourselves. Struggling out was harder than getting in because now we had to go backwards. After quite the ruckus, in which I think I might have kicked Grenith a couple of times by accident—well, maybe by accident—we got out and stood up. We stretched our muscles and flexed our aching backs. Then we sat down for a small break to cool our rattled nerves.

After a few minutes, we set out again.

It was early afternoon, and we were still dragging ourselves along over the barren, wasted land. And I was still brushing dirt out of my skirt and blouse and scraping it out of my ears. I was digging around in one ear, and I cleaned out another finger's worth of grit.

Then suddenly, the hair stood up on the back of my neck. Not even a second later, a bone chilling, hair raising, hissing voice rose from behind us. It was an unearthly voice that moaned in a long haunting breath, "*Deeaaattttthhhhhhh.*"

The very blood in my veins froze. I stood stalk still. I whispered slowly to Grenith, not really knowing if I really wanted the answer, "What was that?"

Grenith barely breathed, "Orodumes."

I exhaled a pent up breath. I didn't want to turn around and face them, but I voluntarily did. My eyes went to the sky, searching for them.

A dozen or more winged creatures were flying above us. I could easily pick out the razor sharp claws and red, glazed over, unseeing eyes. The scream of death rang out again.

My eyes went wide with fear. I turned on my heels and ran. I ran as hard and as fast as I could make my legs carry me. Grenith wasn't far behind me.

Glancing over my shoulder, I saw them swooping down, dropping lower as a group, and heading straight at us.

I willed myself to run faster.

They hissed their "*Deeaaatttttthhhhhhh*" again, this time much closer. In an instant, they were right behind us. They swooped in waves, claws extended and snatching at us.

I ducked and swerved, frantic to avoid their knife-like talons. I felt the air rush off my back, and heard the leathery wings snapping. Another hiss of "*Deeaaatttttthhhhhhh*" sounded above. Another plunge at me. Another miss.

They got closer and closer with every dive. I couldn't evade them forever.

I heard air rushing around wings and knew another was trying for me again. I ducked low to the ground, almost tripping on my skirt. A claw caught the back of my shawl, and tore a gaping hole in it. I cried out, not in pain, but in fear.

Strangely, all I could think of was Nollem. Well, something he said. He was sitting in the morning sunlight with that silly grin and peaceful look on his face. He was saying, "*You know, life with Shalom isn't promised to be all roses. In fact, there's bound to be more thorns than pretty roses.*" Those words suddenly rang true for me. Then my mind jumped to the night when I was attacked by the small creature, and the feeling of impending death crashing over me.

Death.

In Birset it felt like it was just around the corner simply waiting for an opportunity to snatch you up. It was like death was right around the corner, waiting to strike with a killing blow.

Now death was right there behind me, reaching with its dagger claws.

I didn't know how to fight it, I wasn't trained. So I had to run. Someday, I promised myself, I would stop running, stand up, and fight it. "*Just you wait until that day,*" I thought.

That resolve kept me going, even though I stumbled and tripped.

After a while, they only chased us, stopping all attacks. I think they were hoping to wear us out.

But we ran on. To this day, I'm not sure how we kept it up so long, but we did.

I was gasping for breath, sucking in every bit of air I could get. Suddenly I noticed that it had an odor. It smelled of rotting things.

As we ran on, the smell grew stronger and more pungent. It smelled like an old bog.

The bog! I vaguely remembered passing around one on our journey to Birset. Maybe the smell would deter the Orodumes!

Hope brought on a surge of energy, and I shot forward, eager to get to it. The closer we drew, the farther I wanted to be from it. The reek was overpowering and choking. Soon the ground got soggier. A new mist rose up before us, spreading over the wetlands. The smell was stronger yet.

Suddenly the Orodumes let out their chilling scream and paused mid-flight. Apparently their sensitive noses couldn't handle the stench. They turned reluctantly around. The flapping and snapping of their wings grew distant as they went off in search of other prey. They let out one final cry of death as they disappeared in the fading light.

Grenith and I stared after them in disbelief. I could hardly grasp the concept that they had gone. They were leaving. We did it!

Both Grenith and I were completely out of breath. We flopped to the wet ground, gulping down as much air as possible. Right there, we slept on the edge of the marshes, not at all caring about the exact spot.

Chapter 17
...Into the Clutches of Evil

When I woke up, the mist around us was already bright with light. Not that the sun got through to the ground, but it illuminated the mist and this was now making it glow. There was a definite night and day, but the day isn't comparable to the day outside of Deceiver's land.

I was shivering, so I inched closer to Grenith in hopes of stealing some heat from her. My muscles screamed back at me for disturbing them. They throbbed from the exercise they got the day before, eventually settling into a constant aching.

I bumped into Grenith, and she moaned. Her eyelids fluttered open, blinking in the brightness. "Oh, I'm sore."

"Same."

We both sat up, rubbed our arms then going to our legs, feet and back. After flexing our shoulders and necks, we dug into our increasingly smaller bundles that Miss Glimmer had given us. We sipped some frigid water and munched on some dried fruit.

"Well," Grenith began between mouthfuls, "I guess we get to go through today."

"Through?" I wasn't trying to object to every idea she had, but I was thinking that we might go around the bog. I didn't want to go through the slippery, stinking marshes.

"Yes, through." Apparently our tempers were short that morning. "Where else would we go?"

I blinked a couple of times at her, thinking what a stupid question to ask. "Around. We could go around it. I don't want to be swallowed alive by the bog."

"But if we go around, then the Orodumes will get us!" she objected soundly.

"Not if we stay close to the edge." I said matter of factly.

"They'll pick up our game just like that," she snapped her fingers in my face. "Then they'll attack us!"

"It's better than mucking through a bog for days on end! Besides we can run further into the bog if they do chase us."

"Then we might as well just go through! We have a better chance at survival if we go through!"

"Oh, and now we're back to surviving! What happened to no fear when Elohim is for us, huh?"

That stopped her and I both in our tracks. We fell silent for a few minutes thinking our own thoughts on the matter. Suddenly looking up at each other, we said at the same time, "Through."

So it was settled and we stood up. Vanishing into the mist, we trekked on, losing our footing on the slick stones and banks. Frogs and other crawling creatures jumped and slithered into the murky waters as we passed. The waters were dark and mud filled, not at all suitable for drinking. Otherwise we would have refilled our water skins. The mist swirled about us. I couldn't see more than twelve feet ahead in most parts. Picking out our path carefully, I hopped from one tuff of marsh grass to another. I think I was going fairly straight, but it was hard to tell.

Grenith kept saying how she was sure that she could get us to the old Lightbearer base. It was just on the other side of this bog. But it was, of course a little ways from it, because who would want to live near this old place?

I was trying to keep us in a straight line, but I don't think that I was succeeding very well.

Overall, it was very tiring, though I think we made good progress. The light was beginning to fade from the mist. And once it started, it got dark in a matter of minutes.

Knowing that we should stop for the night, I was searching for a good place to rest. We were caught right in a really wet part, with no decent patches of ground big enough for the both of us to curl up on for the night.

Grenith had fanned out to my left, also in search of a dry bit of ground. It was so dark by now that I could barely discern her silhouette. I went on, looking all about and jumping from one slippery stone to a tuff.

Suddenly I heard Grenith cry out in pain. I looked over to my left. I couldn't see her. I shouted uneasily, "Grenith? Are you alright?"

No response.

"Grenith?" I took a step in that direction, peering into the darkness, attempting to pick out something, anything. I called out again, "Gren—"

Before I could finish, a blurry form crashed into me, throwing us both into a sizable puddle. I threw the person off me and into the water, balling my fists, ready to strike out.

Then I realized that it was Grenith. She stumbled up, getting her feet under her. Her eyes were wide with fear, darting all around us. She was searching for something that wasn't visible. Her breaths came in rapid short gasps, and I noticed that she was cradling her left hand with the other.

Immediately, I got defensive and started to look about for something in the mists. I asked quickly, "What is it?" Which could have been translated as, "What am I looking for?"

"I don't know," she said shortly. "It appeared to blend right in with the mist, though it was only a little darker. But look what it did." She extended her hand for my inspection.

I grabbed it gently in my own hand and pulled it closer, trying to see if it really was what it looked like in the dark light. Yes, it was a burn mark. The skin was bubbled and a dark brown color. The bubbled skin was white and the entire wound was red around the edges. The mark was all over the back of her hand and extended a few inches above her wrist.

She smarted with pain as I flexed her wrist. I let her hand go, my mind whirling with thoughts as to what this creature might be. I had never heard of any animal giving that kind of wound. Well, except dragons, but that was too small. It must be something native to the marshes.

I searched our surroundings again. My imagination turned the shadows into leaping, prowling beasts. I looked closer in the direction where Grenith had been. There, the mists were darker, almost pitch black. The rest of the mist was a dingy grey. I searched for a sign of any creature. There were no eyes, no sounds, no other form but the mist. I puzzled over this, trying to make it out.

It was creeping closer to us. I noticed Grenith instinctively shrinking away from it. I took a step nearer to it. Closing the gap between me and the mist, I reached out my hand to touch it. Brushing my fingertips against the blackness, I gasped and withdrew them quickly. I looked down at them. The same burn mark appeared, white bubbling skin that throbbed with pain.

"It's the mist!" I cried, fleeing away from it.

I joined Grenith a few feet away. It was then that I saw the black coming towards us from the direction that we should have gone to get out of the bog. Instead of going northeast like we were, we pealed off to the right, running due east.

We slipped over rocks and banks, tearing through the wet pools and algae. We didn't care about staying dry now. It seemed the faster we ran, the faster the mist caught up with us.

Trying to keep up with our original course, we kept swerving to the left, attempting to beat the mists. But the black mist cut us off every time, driving us continually east. After a little while, and several burns, we kept to the straight course of east.

The black mist drove us from behind and from our left.

By now, my skirt was soaked up to my knees, and my arms were covered in burns and mud from tripping and catching myself in the watery muck. The cool mud dulled the searing, shooting pain all up and down my forearms.

We ran and ran. Whenever we slowed down at all, the black mist would catch us from behind, burning the backs of our legs and necks.

An eternity of wet and pain plagued us, until, finally, we burst out from the marshes. We felt our feet on dry, firm ground again. Dashing out of the mists that engulfed the bog, we flopped to the cold earth, catching our breaths and watching for the black mists.

The dark shadowy mist came up to the edge of the bog, and for a second or two, I thought that it might continue on to get us. But it didn't. It stopped along an invisible wall, and built up, forming a black mass of mist rising into the night sky. But it didn't go past that barrier.

Leaning back on my elbows, I breathed a sigh of relief. My legs were thoroughly chilled from the wet skirt clinging to them. Trying to get my feet under some dry patch of my skirt, I realized that there was no way we were going to make the night in wet clothing. We would die of hypothermia before the morning came. We had to keep moving.

As tired as I was, I stood up, wrapping my torn shawl closer about my arms and torso. I was already shivering. I looked about me, completely disorientated. My mind was foggy from cold and pain. I think I muttered something like, "Come on, we can't stay here," to Grenith while wandering in a random direction. Grenith followed me, also not knowing where we were headed.

I stumbled about in the night, tripping over unseen obstacles. My feet and legs were numb, along with my hands and arms. The only thing that I could feel was the searing burning over my arms and a little on my face. My eyelids were drooping with exhaustion. Things that I was seeing weren't what my mind thought them to be.

I began to hallucinate. I saw faces. I saw the dead face of Chimel, pale and cocked unnaturally to one side. I saw the snarling face of the female creature that attacked me that one night so long ago. I saw Master Abburn's face contorted with rage and a bright gleam of satisfaction in his eyes as he beat me. I saw the gypsy boy, Haiblur, laying on the ground. His body still with a dark red stain growing over his shirt. He was dead, slain by a sword through the middle. I saw Nollem, tried against a tree, death creeping over him. Dancing joyously around him was Alletta, with the same smile that I saw her with last.

Haiblur's dead body appeared on the ground right before me. I cried out, and jumped to one side to avoid it. In the mists I saw Dwin. He was staring at me, shaking his head and looking disappointed, angry and sad. In his arms he held the limp form of Kattim. He looked at me like it was my fault. I stopped and stared. I wanted to burst out crying, sobbing, asking for his forgiveness. But no sounds came from my gaping mouth. All I could do was walk towards them. As I drew nearer, I reached out my hand to touch Kattim's still, white hand. Just as I did, they both faded into the night.

I heard a cry of pain to my right. I whirled about and saw Nollem, crouching in the mist. He was pale and haggard, and long red lash marks striped his back. He cried out in agony. He was on his knees, pleading with me to make it stop. My eyes filled with tears, blurring my sight. His image slowly faded, his cries still echoing in my mind.

I turned around and around trying to avoid and hide from the images that appeared before me. There in the distance was a faint glow. I staggered over to it unsteadily. As I drew nearer, I saw that it was a fire, and I could see six forms huddled about it —the same number of my companions from the beginning of this journey.

I stumbled into the ring of light. All six of them, jumped up in surprise. I was expecting to see the faces of my friends. But these weren't them at all. Their faces had evil looks on them. They rushed me. I screamed and fought to get out of their grabbing arms. This time, when they touched me, they didn't disappear. Two big brutes, similar to the one who put me up on the auction block when I was sold, filled my blurring vision. They lay their massive hands on me, glowering down at me.

As they pulled me closer to the light, I felt dizzier. Then my limbs gave out from under me, and I fell senseless in their arms.

❦

I woke to feel a rough hand near my throat, passing over my collar bone. I opened my eyes with a jump. There was a big fellow, one of the big brutes sitting right by me, his face dangerously close to mine.

I moved my hands to push him away, but they jerked against tight ropes. My burns rubbed against the rope, and they repaid me for such a sudden movement with shooting, searing pain. My stomach wrenched and I tried to hold back a cry. A stifled whimper escaped my throat. I squirmed under the pain, wishing it to lessen.

Laughter irrupted from all six men around the fire. Their deep, harsh laughs bellowed out in cruel humor. I got a better look at them and suddenly how they acted made sense. They were Between men, and since it was night, their beastly appearances testified to their hearts.

I then turned to my own predicament. So apparently that last hallucination wasn't just that. I really had stumbled into the hands of a group of Between men. I looked around for Grenith. She was beside me, on my left. She was tied to the same tree, or post—I really couldn't tell then—as I was. She was still unconscious.

The brute sitting closest to me, reached down and gave the rope that bound me a sharp yank. Apparently, he thought it was funny the first time.

He jerked so hard that I cried out, pain crashing over me. I caught my breath and let it out a little at a time. I grimaced and turned my face skyward, bearing it as best I could.

Thinking this was greater fun than before, the Between roared and howled with laughter, doubling over to the ground. I thought I might have caught a whiff of strong drink on the man's breath. He leaned closer to me, then I could distinctly smell it over his clothes and breath.

I shied away, but he came closer. He still had his hand resting by my throat. He moved it across to the other side, trailing it downward. He was heading straight for my emblem. I tried not to squirm under his touch, thinking it might only encourage him to explore further. He brushed my blouse aside, holding it down to reveal my mark.

As soon as he saw my emblem, the bush, etched there, he withdrew his hand quickly with a small howl of surprise, and maybe a hint of pain. He clenched his hand in a tight fist, holding it in his other as if I had bit him or something.

All the other Between halted their laughing, and looked astounded and confused. I was just as confused as they were. I wasn't sure what had happened.

The Between looked at the big brute who had retreated a good five paces, then they looked at me, searching for what might have done him injury. All at once they saw the emblem. At first they just stared dumbfounded at it. Then they suddenly jumped up, scratching at their eyes, and ran out into the darkness. I heard them screaming, terrified and scared.

I, just as shocked as they, watched them tear off into the night, leaving both Grenith and I tied to the post. I blinked a couple of times, not sure if they had really gone. That could have ended a lot worse, and I was glad that it didn't.

Then I looked around thinking to myself, *"Great, now what?"*

I looked at the fire, thinking of its inviting warmth, and determined that I must get there to dry off and stay warm for the remainder of the night. My skirt was still soaked, and I found that I was trembling and shivering at the same time.

I slowly twisted my hands against the ropes. I bit my lip as pain radiated up from my burns. Using my fingers seemed to be the best option and the least painful. I felt around, getting an idea of how I was tied. I soon discovered that it was very poorly done, likely due to their being drunk. I could probably just slip out, but those burns would make it a slow, painful process.

I looked at the fire again. Its bright flames were dancing enticingly. In their haste, the Between had left their cloaks and blankets there. There was even some food and drink too:

roasted fowl on a stick, a loaf or two of brown bread, a broth from some soup or stew, and of course many jugs of drink, the majority empty.

It was too perfect of an opportunity to pass up.

Beginning small and hoping to work up to the harder parts, I started with my right hand. I shrunk my hand, tightly pressing my fingers together, causing the skin on the back of my hand to stretch. I smarted against the painful protest, and I slowly began pulling my hands through the first coarse loop. I clamped my lips shut tight, drawing in a sharp breath and holding it. I got my hand out of the first loop, and exhaled slowly, letting out a whimper. I braced myself for the second loop, and painfully repeated the last step, except this loop was a little tighter than the other so I scraped my raw burns. I moaned, closing my eyes. I was sweating by now, and my breath was coming quickly.

One last loop and my right hand was free. My stomach was churning and tied into knots. I groaned at the thought of having to do the same thing all over again with the left hand. No, this time, I decided, I would do it in one big go instead of three small efforts. I waited a few moments, bracing myself, and getting up the courage to actually do it.

I took a large breath, held it and pressed my lips together. I scrunched up my hand, and quickly pulled my forearm, wrist and hand out of the rough ropes. A scream tore from my mouth. Agonizing, shooting pain seared up my arms. I doubled over, gasping for calming breaths. I brought my hands forward and looked at the damage done. Some of the bubbled white skin had burst open and was streaming white fluid. It was all raw and red. I closed my eyes, not wanting to see anymore.

I moved lethargically over to the warmth emitted by the flame. I stretched out my shaking hands to catch the warmth. Then I spread out my wet skirt before the lovely flames. After a moment or two of basking in the warmth, I remembered Grenith. She was still tied to the post.

With arms throbbing, I crawled back to the edge of the firelight. Settling down beside her, I looked around to see how she was tied. Same as me, loosely, but just tight enough to rub against the wounds. Not wanting to put her through the same agony as I had endured, I looked for some other option. I glanced around, looking for something to cut the ropes with. On the far side of the fire, I saw a knife glinting in the dancing light. Swinging my head from her to the knife, I silently questioned, why did it have to be all the way over there?

Crawling back to the fire, I curved around it, grabbed the mean knife, and worked my way back over to Grenith. She was still unconscious, and for the first time, I noticed a bloodied gash above her forehead, half hidden by her hairline. They must had struck her, I concluded.

Slowly, half-mindedly, I cut through the thick ropes. Once I got her free, I puzzled over how to get her to the fire. It took me a while, in my groggy state of mind, to determine that the only way would be to carry her. Well, there would be no carrying on my part, so I dragged her instead. Hooking my arms under hers and joining my hands together against her chest, I heaved backwards nearly squashing myself under Grenith's limp form.

Half dragging, half heaving, I somehow managed to get her near the fire, at the cost of my arms screaming back. Thinking ahead, sort of, I grabbed a blanket and covered Grenith as well as I could. Then I pulled a big, thick cloak over my own shoulders and lay down. I was asleep in seconds.

❦

When I woke, it was far into the morning. The warm fire of the night before was reduced to ashes pealing up into the sky on a slight breeze. I blinked away the sleep from my eyes. Moving my hand up, I brushed away a stray lock of hair. I inhaled sharply, suddenly remembering the burns as they reminded me of their existence.

With that, all the night's events tumbled back into my mind. The black mist, awful hallucinations, the Between, the escape from bonds. I thought of Grenith and half sat up to look at her. She seemed to be sleeping peacefully, taking regular, steady breaths.

As I lay back down, a thought came to me. We had to run whenever opposed by Deceiver's men. We had no skills in fighting them. They were afraid of us, their running away last night after seeing my emblem was testament to that. No, they weren't afraid of us, they were afraid of Shalom, Who is in us. It wasn't *us* that sent them packing off, it was Shalom. That reminded me who was more powerful and who was in control. Shalom.

Already, I had reverted to thinking that I could make it on my own. And look where it got me!

It took me a long time to learn to be fully dependent on Him. Independence is a hard thing to give away, but it is necessary and fulfilling. I certainly had a lot more to learn.

Chapter 18
The Square, Stone Hut & Where
it Led To

By the time I drug myself out of my thoughts, Grenith had awakened. She rubbed at her gash, complained of a headache, and asked, "What happened?"

I explained as best I could, and she was just as surprised at the Between high tailing it out of here as I was. After a good stretch, we rummaged around the camp, looking for things that might be useful. I kept the knife. We gathered some of the food, eating some and stashing some in our thoroughly rifled through bundles. The Between had helped themselves to the remainder of our dried fruit.

Our water bottles had been dry for some time, so we indulged in a little of their drink. We found it extremely foul tasting, and the only reason we drank it was to quench our thirst. I filled my bottle with it, just in case we couldn't find anything better.

I think it was about noon before we set out again, guesstimating the right direction by the brightest spot—we hoped it was the sun—in the cloud cover. This time, we made sure to avoid the marsh, being on the far right side of it. Neither of us wanted to get into another scrape with the black mist.

It wasn't long at all until we found ourselves approaching an old forest. It was burnt, all of it. It extended for miles and miles on end. Having never seen a burned down forest, I looked in awe at the destruction. All the trees were reduced to either grey old logs rotting along the ground, or desolate grey skeletons cutting a jagged line across the sky. Their maimed, charred limbs stuck out in odd directions. All the underbrush had been burned as well. There was nothing but grey ashes and black charred trunks. The trees were like thousands of pencils standing on end, lining the country with their bleak, still skeletons. Occasionally there was a stone foundation, the last bit of a home that used to stand there.

Grenith told me what had caused all this destruction. "It was Deceiver and his army. When they attacked the land surrounding Dol Guliab, they burned it, leaving nothing of its former past. They scarred the land and claimed it as their own. That's what Deceiver does. He takes over the hearts of the people, destroying their lives, then he destroys all that is around them. He kills all who oppose him. Everyone else become his slaves. Such are the ways of Deceiver."

I couldn't help but think of those who used live here and what it would have looked like when everything was green and alive.

We had to travel through the burnt forest for several hours. It was all rather drab, and nothing too exciting happened. Well, nothing except Grenith getting her foot stuck between two fallen trees. It took us about twenty minutes before we could twist it just right and get it out again. It's funny how things go in much easier than they come out.

We had to stop every mile or so and give her ankle a break. She might have gotten a small sprain, but it was hard to tell. The stops were okay though, because it gave me a chance to get some drink and a little food.

I noticed that my appetite was almost nonexistent. I hadn't been hungry in days. And not because I had plenty to eat either. I found I had to remind myself to eat something.

Maybe it was because of the burns. They were constantly aching and throbbing, never ceasing in their painful complaints. Nothing seemed to appease them for any long amount of time. We had tried mud, but it only made it worse when the mud dried and we had to scrape it off. Wet leaves helped a tiny bit for a short time. We finally just gave up putting anything on, just letting them heal on their own.

Just before dark, we stumbled out of the desolated forest. The land reverted to the same hilly, smooth ground. Grenith said quietly, "It isn't far now."

So we continued on, not bothering to look for a place to stay the night. The light began to fade quickly. I tried to pick up the pace a little, but Grenith couldn't keep up.

She had worse burns than I did, and now her ankle was hurt too. I knew that she was in constant, piercing pain, but she never said a word. I don't think the drink agreed with her either, because she hardly had a sip of it.

Needless to say, I was getting worried about her. Wondering how far exactly we had to go, I tried to keep an eye on her for exhaustion and a look out for this Lightbearer base. She kept referring to it as old, and that there might not be others in it. I was seriously considering what our situation would be if it didn't exist anymore. We would be out in the middle of nowhere, with Grenith on the verge of passing out. No shelter, no suitable food, no place to even go for relief. Our future was beginning to look even grimmer.

Glancing over my shoulder, I caught sight of Grenith's stooped form, staggering behind in the fading light. It looked all too much like Dwin after the Weavel attack.

I turned back and came up to her, suggesting that we take a break. She wordlessly slumped to the ground. I sank to my knees beside her. I tried to study her face, perhaps see what she was thinking, but she sat with her head lowered.

I gently broached the subject, "So, how far away do you think we are?"

Grenith didn't say anything for a few moments. I was beginning to wonder if I would get a response at all, when she spoke in a hushed tone, "Not far." She paused taking a few labored breaths. "Look for a stone hut, square." Pause. "Down the staircase. Light the torch."

Nothing else. I blinked a couple of times, trying to decipher what she could mean. I studied our surroundings, looking for a stone hut. There was nothing in the way of buildings as far as the eye could see.

"Okay," I said slowly. "Then I guess we should keep going." I rose, then looking down at Grenith I muttered to myself, "Now this won't do." I knelt down again, saying softly to Grenith, "Here, give me your arm." She didn't move so I just put my hand gently around her waist. Draping her arm around my shoulders, I stood up again, this time fully supporting Grenith.

She responded slightly by trying to walk a little, but her steps were feeble. So I ended up half carrying, half dragging her. She was heavier than I had thought, and she wasn't getting any lighter as we continued either!

We stumbled slowly up a ridge, cresting the hill. There at the top, I stopped for a breather. Glancing up, I caught my breath at the sight down below. In the dusky light, I saw a small community of rambled, half torn down shacks and old houses.

On most all of them, their roofs were collapsed and nothing but their stone structures remained.

It was a little town that had long been abandoned and empty of any residence. I could only assume that I now needed to find the square shack, with a staircase leading down. Which meant that the base was... underground?

It seemed odd, but plausible. I started down the hill. Slowly but surely, we reached the bottom and were back on flat ground again.

As I drew nearer, it looked like the houses had been burned as well. Signs of Deceiver's work was everywhere. Charred roofs, stones with black smoke marks, burnt ground, remnants of pottery and other things of general survival lay about, black and eaten by fire.

We hobbled between the first of the houses, entering the decimated settlement. I looked about curiously and searchingly for that square, stone hut. I expected it not to have a roof on it. Square hut...

I pealed off to the right, hoping that it was off this way. Shifting Grenith's weight, I nearly dropped her. By now she was barely hanging on to consciousness. Just then, I had the idea of putting her down while I searched for the hut. I veered to my right again, approaching a shady stone house. I supposed that the walls were sturdy enough, since they hadn't blown over in all these years. I set Grenith down, leaning her against the stone wall below a pane-less window. Once I was sure that she would stay put, I stood up. I stretched my back, and flexed my shoulders trying to get all the kinks out of them.

Then I turned around, looking for anything that might pass as a square, stone hut. I ventured slowly out towards the middle of the small community of houses. I tried to be as alert and quiet as my senses would allow. You could never be sure what might lie in wait around the corner.

Through the structures I peered and wandered. Finally, I saw a sort of woodshed behind a larger house. It was made of stone and squarish. Well, just square enough to be considered square. In other words, it was basically a rectangle.

But it was the only small shack-like thing that I had seen so far, so I thought it was worth try. Approaching it cautiously, still paranoid that there might be men right around to corner waiting to jump me, I slowly inspected it from a slight distance. Then I took a few steps closer and looked inside. The roof had long fallen in, covering the floor in a rotting pile of thatch. But immediately—it was kind of hard to miss—I saw that in the center of the floor, the thatching had been scraped away to reveal a wooden trapdoor. It reminded me of the one we came out of in the streets of Divel, that first night we met Dwin and Kattim.

But the strange thing that stuck in my mind was that it looked like it had been frequently and recently passed through. In this old ghost town, who would still be living here?

I was instantly suspicious. I glanced over the hut again. Stone and square enough, I reached down and, as quietly as I could, wrestled the hatch open. There, leading down into the darkness was a—staircase.

It fit the brief description I was given, but still... It seemed shady and dangerous. I stared into the black hole, wondering what I should do next. Should I go in solo and make sure that it was safe? Or should I get Grenith and enter then? Safety in numbers, right?

I liked the second option better, even though I knew that Grenith wouldn't do me much good if we ran into trouble. Leaving the hut, I practically ran back to where I left Grenith, suddenly thinking that if someone was here, they might get to her first.

Dashing around the last corner, I halted in my tracks. There, bending over Grenith's still form, was the silhouette of a person. It looked like a boy, younger than myself, but I couldn't guess an age since he was in the shadows. He heard me come around the corner and swirled about. A shocked, surprised look was printed on his face.

I raised my fists, ready to put up a show that I might fight him. I did this only because I wasn't sure what he would do, and I wanted to assume he was there to harm us. So many others had, and I wasn't about to throw my trust on another stranger. I took a few determined steps forward, even though I'm pretty sure that my hands were shaking. I called out in as threatening voice I could muster, "Who are you and what do you want?"

He held his hands away from his sides, signifying that he didn't want to fight. He took a few steps towards me, getting out of the shadow of the building. Now I could see him a little better. He was a boy of maybe thirteen, with an innocent, boyish complexion. He looked at me and blurted out, uncertainty saturating his voice, "I could ask the same of you."

I didn't lower my defense, only staring at him harder. I wasn't going to be the one to say who I was. I asked him first.

He saw that I wasn't going to speak, so he fumbled, "I, uh, maybe you'll answer this. Are you a friend of Grenith's? A-And what happened to her?"

My turn to be shocked. My hands dropped to my side and my mouth gaped open. "You know Grenith?"

"Well..." he looked awkward, "yeah. Are you or aren't you?"

"Yes, I'm a friend of hers. But how do you know her?" I was still very confused, he had thrown a complete curve ball.

"I, I can't explain until I know I can trust you."

"I could say the same," I said quickly.

He nodded, still obviously uncomfortable with our situation. "Okay," he started, then an idea struck him, "show me your emblem."

My eyebrows shot up. There was a definite "no" stamped over my expression. There was no way that I was going to show him that. But I shot back, "Let me see your's first, that way I know I can trust you. I'm not about to show something like that to any stranger."

"Fine," he replied, by now trying hard not to lose his patience. He pulled his tunic and shirt aside, revealing a bush with a circlet around it.

My doubts were dispelled, and I slowly reached to my blouse. Undoing the first button, I slid it to the side just enough to reveal my mark.

He didn't look surprised, only satisfied with it. He said, much more relaxed than before, "Grenith's a part of the underground Lightbearer project. Everyone here knows her. She never told you?"

"No," I replied flatly. "Most people don't tell me much of anything."

"Oh." He paused, as if thinking, "You look worn out. Why don't we get underground, and we can get you both settled for the night, sound good?"

I was still a little skeptical. I didn't want to be taken advantage of again, and I was sure that this boy could tell. I didn't have a response for him, still trying to size him up.

"Um, I," he stumbled, "you don't... want to?"

"What's your name? And what do you have to do with that tunnel over there?" I was thinking of the one in the square hut, and jerked my head in that direction.

He knew exactly what I meant and proceeded, "My name is Findal. And I see you don't know much about Lightbearers. Time to fill you in. Underground—the tunnel you found is one of the entrances—is a network of extensive rooms and corridors. Deceiver and his men didn't find it when they came through. But everyone left, or was killed, so the network remains intact but thoroughly abandoned. To this day, people have forgotten about it, but we still use it as a sort of headquarters for projects behind Deceiver's lines.

"Grenith is a part of this. The projects involve sending out Lightbearers to live among the peoples, going among the slaves, and trying to live normal lives. But they're usually found out in two to three months, sometimes less. The Between and Vaudians are quite keen when it comes to spotting us. To put it frankly, Grenith has been one of the longest able to stay out in the field without coming back.

"Anyway, I need to get you both somewhere warm and dry. Surely you can see that? Grenith needs attention, and from the looks of you, you could use some as well. When we get under, you'll be able to meet some of the Lightbearers we have now. Will you come down with me?"

He looked so earnest, that I could hardly refuse him. Besides, he was right, we couldn't stay out here all night. So what choice did I have? Besides he was a Lightbearer himself, so maybe I could trust him. I nodded my consent, reluctantly, but I did.

His face lit up into a grin and he turned around, saying, "Great! Now come help me with Grenith."

I closed the distance between us for the first time and crossed over to Grenith's side. I couldn't tell if she was sleeping, or unconscious, but either way we needed to get her warm and dry. I took one arm and gently lifted her with Findal on the other side. We each wrapped an arm over our shoulders and started off through the buildings again.

Grimacing, Findal asked while looking at her arms, "What happened here?"

"Black mist." I answered shortly. "It was in the marshes a little way from here. I got it too. Stings like nothing else."

"Well, we can get some ointment that will help you both out some. Here, I'll go down first."

We were standing before the black pit. It gaped open like jaws just waiting for you to walk in. I shivered, thinking that we would have to go down there. I couldn't imagine that underground would be very comfortable.

Going down the steps with Grenith between us was a little challenging, but we managed with only a few bumps and scrapes along the way. After about two and a half flights of stairs, we were dumped out into a wide hall.

It had smooth walls with torches and lanterns to light it. They gave off a warm inviting glow and cast gentle shadows in the corners. The floor was smooth earth as well. I noticed that the air was warm and dry, not at all the damp, drafty, dark hole I was envisioning. The hall ran a straight course back with many other halls branching out from it. It was all rather impressive to have such an extensive underground organization.

Findal grinned at my awed facial expression. "Welcome home," he said.

"Thanks," I said briefly. We repositioned Grenith between us and started down the hall again.

Proudly acquainting me with the halls and such, Findal ran on about them as we passed by, "And down there is a few more storerooms, some bunks, and two other exits. And over there is a hall that runs around a square that holds offices and meeting rooms. It was all very official back in the day. ..."

I nodded slightly at every description, but I quickly lost interest, being too tired to care about it all at the moment.

He suddenly paused in his narrative to ask, "Oh, I don't think I asked you your name. How rude of me. I introduced myself and didn't bother to ask you yours. What is it?"

"Oh," I hadn't been expecting that question, and to be honest, the thought of names had escaped me. "I'm—"

"Limira!"

The voice echoed down the halls with an excited ring in it. The sound of hurried footsteps came with it. I immediately recognized it to be Dwin's. And sure enough, rushing down the wide hall with lantern in hand, came Dwin with Kattim just behind him. Their faces were warm and jovial in the light, their eyes have a certain gleam that I have grown to love.

I was so surprised and overjoyed at seeing them alive and well, I nearly dropped Grenith. I couldn't believe that they were here, right in front of me!

In an instant, they were directly before us, expressing their happiness. Both were nearly bubbling over with joy.

I was so shocked that I could only stand there, receiving their hugs with limp arms. After a few moments I said under my breath, "You're alive!"

"Yes!" Dwin replied, his voice booming off the walls. He stood before me, grinning, and studying my face. "Here," he said reaching out, "let me take Grenith. You look exhausted."

I gratefully surrendered her up to him. He handed off the lantern to Kattim, and then he picked Grenith up in his arms. We all continued down the wide hall side by side.

Findal was almost as surprised as myself. He blurted out questioningly, "You know each other?"

"Yeah," I responded quite honestly, "we've been through life and death together. Kattim, how are you alive? And how did you get here? Dwin, what happened with the slave market? How did all that work?"

"I'll explain it all later, Limira," Dwin offered, more like told me firmly.

Kattim added, "First, you definitely need to be sat down and looked at. We're almost there."

"Where's there?" I asked, not sure what they were talking about.

Findal piped up in his all important, all knowing voice, "Since this place is so big, we only use part of it for living in. We have a cozy large room with a couple of smaller rooms off it. We call it the Den."

"Oh, I see." And in a minute, I did see it. The Den was everything they said it was and more. It was warm, and well furnished with a large table, chairs, rugs on the dirt floors, benches, and a large inviting fireplace. Rows of pillar candles lined shelves dug out of the earth, the white wax spilling down the walls and forming intricate cascades of accumulated drips. Findal guided me over to a large padded armchair before the fire. I melted into it, gratefully soaking up the warmth and rest.

Kattim rushed over to a cupboard and pulled out a couple of thick wool blankets. She spread them over the large wooden table. Placing Grenith carefully on it, Dwin motioned for Findal to come over and give Kattim a hand. Basins of warm water were produced along with towels, bandages and bottles of ointment.

Just as Kattim was moving more light over to the table, Dwin crossed the room with his arms full of supplies. He knelt before me and set his things down in an orderly fashion around him. He dropped one of the towels into the basin of warm water, and turned his attention to my arms. As he rolled up the sleeves of my blouse, he shook his head clicking his tongue teasingly, "Limira, Limira, what have you gotten yourself into?"

"Black mist, in the bog," I answered shortly.

"Yep, that'll do it. I'll try to do this gently, but I have to get it clean," was his warning as he squeezed out the towel.

I bit my lip, bracing for the expected pain. My stomach was already in knots in anticipation of it.

He carefully pressed the cloth against the back of my bubbled hand. I drew in a quick breath, stiffening.

"Sorry," he whispered. "It's really raw. Can I ask why?"

He was probably trying to distract my mind as he slowly worked up my arm. He paused frequently to re-soak and wring out the cloth. It worked slightly, but I was trying hard not to cry out. So speaking was difficult and with many breaks. "Ropes," I said quickly, with a pain tainted voice.

"You just going to leave it at that? or do I get to hear more about your daring adventures?"

He was prompting me to speak more, so I did, slowly. I backed up a little ways to start, "We were in the bog, just Grenith and I. Ah!" I cried out, stifling it as it came. He had hit a tender spot. He paused then went on cleaning around it.

I continued tensely, "The black mist got us, and we ran out of the bog. I was—" I drew in a breath and held it. Letting it out as slowly as possible, I cringed as pain came radiating up my arm. For the first time, I realized that I was furiously gripping the arm of the chair with my other hand. I tried to relax a little —not very successfully—and continued, "I was seeing things and wandered into a camp of rowdy Between men." I paused again, biting my lip. "There were six of them. I think I passed out and woke up tied to a post." I stopped, the last few words rushed before I clamped my lips shut.

Dwin glanced up to study my face again, taking the damp cloth off and dunking it back into the water. He then asked, reapplying it slowly, "And you took all of them on at the same time, beating them to a pulp and escaping into the night, right?"

I half smiled at his attempt to be humorous. "No, not exactly," I said in a tight voice. "They saw my mark and then took off packing into the night. Oh, my emblem change—!" A searing pain cut me short and I whimpered.

"I know," he said quickly after I had stopped. "I can tell," he added with a smile that I had never seen before. "But tell me more about after the men left."

I nodded slightly. "Okay. They all left us tied to the post so I had to work my arms and hands out of their knots. They were drunk, so the knots were loose, but just tight enough to hurt." I paused again, grimacing. "Are you almost done yet?"

"Nearly," he said quietly. What he didn't mention was that he still had my left arm to do. "Well, since I think you've given me a short tale, I think it's only fair to give you some of what happened to me. Let's see here, I'm sure your tale is much more exciting, but I'll tell you anyway.

"Hmm, after you were led off by that nasty fellow, it was soon my turn to be sold. If you'll recall what I said to you in those final moments, I said not to be concerned, and that everything was going to be okay. I only half believed those words. I knew in the long term, they would come true. But I also knew that there was no way that I could save you from being taken halfway around the globe. I knew that I would be okay because I had friends among the crowd: other Lightbearers whose sole mission is to buy slaves who seem in particular need. To this day, I'm not sure how they choose out of everyone. They also get us fellow Lightbearers out of the system if we're caught. Unless they were put there intentionally, like Grenith. There," he paused, triumphantly dropping the cloth back into the by now filthy water, "halfway through. I'll go get some fresh water, then we'll continue." He rose with basin in hand and disappeared behind me.

I tenderly looked down at my arms, slowly raising them and bring them together. My right was so much cleaner and better looking than my left. It throbbed from being cleaned, but at least it looked better. Then I turned my gaze to the fire, watching the flame dancing up and casting strange streamers of shadows along the walls. Leaning my head back contentedly, I closed my eyes, just soaking in the heat.

I might have dozed off a bit, because the next thing I knew, Dwin had his large hand on my left wrist. He was gently applying the towel to the burns, sending pain up and down my entire arm. I looked down quickly, surprised at the sudden pain.

He must have seen it in my expression because he said gently, "Sorry, I didn't mean to startle you. Now, where was I? Oh yes," he said resuming his story, "I was telling you about the Lightbearers among the cities. You see, we have a few Lightbearers living in the major cities and in the outskirts, trying to make as much impact as they can. They usually don't last above two or three months before they're found out. Somehow Grenith managed to stay out there. She's definitely got the record for the longest field time without being caught."

I interrupted, asking quickly, "How long was she out there?"

"Well," Dwin took a moment to think, "at least seven or eight years. Once she got in the slave business, I think she changed masters three or four times. Each time she would give us the signal not to get her out, so it was her choice.

"Anyway, I knew there would be at least a couple of Lightbearers in the crowd and that they would recognize me immediately. I had no worries about myself and Kattim. I knew that they would get her when she was sold. But it was you I was concerned about. They wouldn't know to get you too, and there was no way I could get their attention and tell them without blowing everything. So I was in a real pickle, trying to think of what to do. No options presented themselves, so I let it ride. But I was sorely disappointed when I saw the man who bought you. He looked like a real mean one. I hope he was better than he appeared.

"I was bought by some friends, and we waited in the city for Kattim to appear on the markets. About a week later she did, and she was still not in good shape. She was thin, pale and droopy. It was obvious that she was in no shape for labor, so she went for a low price. We waited about two and a half weeks nursing her back into health before the journey here. It took us a good spell of time. We were intentionally taking it slow for her. We've been here ever since, trying to think of ways to see if we could find you and Nollem. So far, no luck. But now you've come to us! Only Nollem is yet to be found. Don't worry, Limira, we've got the underground searching for him."

He paused and dropped the cloth back into the water. He had just finished cleaning out my burns. They looked better, but they were a little redder with agitation. And every bit of that agitation, I felt doubled over again. I think my expression was one stuck in agony. At least that's what it felt like. I leaned my head back, closing my eyes again. I was really tired, and now all this added on, had completely exhausted me. All I wanted was a good night's sleep. I think Dwin understood and he silently moved on to the next thing. He pulled out the bottle and uncorked it. A sweet smell wafted from it, leaving a remnant of pleasant scent in the air.

He whispered, seeing that I was tired, "This is only going to sting a little."

I opened my eyes and watched him as he poured some cloudy liquid into the palm of his hand. I could guess what he was going to do next. I instinctively pulled my arms closer to me, not wanting added pain.

Noticing my reluctance, Dwin slowly reached out and lay hold of my fingertips while saying quietly, "Now come on, you and I both know that this is only going to help it heal faster. Come on, give me your hands. I'll do it as gently as I can."

No more convinced than before, I unwillingly surrendered. He slowly, tenderly rubbed the ointment in, trying go lighter when I whimpered.

My stomach tensed into a knotted ball that wound tighter and tighter. Sometimes I wished that I would just pass out like Grenith, at least then I wouldn't have to feel it. His rough hand slid just over my bubbled, aching skin. Even though he was going gently, it took all I could to not scream.

When it was finally over he pulled out the bandages. My heart sank with the addition of one more thing to torment my already smarting arms.

"Last one," Dwin said, trying to sound encouraging.

I barely nodded, still feeling the effects of his last tampering. This went much faster and smoother than I would have thought. Before I knew it, I had a pair of white wrapped arms. And he did it loose enough that I could move them without them getting too tight.

"Oh, one more thing," Dwin said. He stood up and went to the other side of the room. A few moments later he returned with a mirror and a clean damp cloth. He handed the cloth to me and held up the mirror.

At first I wasn't sure what to do with it—that was the extent of my tiredness. Then I got the idea that he wanted me to wash my face. To adjust the mirror so I could actually see myself, I reached out and brought it down some. I sighed with despair to see that the face staring back belonged to me. It was thoroughly covered in grime and dirt. It was tear stained and smudged. And there, on the left side of my face, were little bubbles surrounded by pale and red skin.

I washed my face, wiping away the dirty one. The warm cloth felt wonderful. Before I knew it, Dwin was handing me the bottle of ointment, motioning to the burns. I made a face at him, but poured some out into my palm anyway. I dipped my fingers in it and rubbed it gently over the irritated areas.

Dwin took the bottle and gathered up his supplies from the floor. With a word of, "Don't run off on me," he vanished behind me again.

I really didn't care. I leaned my head back again and presently fell asleep.

Chapter 19
Recovery

I woke sometime during the next day. The first thing I noticed was a scratchy thing brushing against my cheek. I wasn't sure what it was, and I wasn't sure that I wanted to find out. After much inward, groggy debate, I finally opened my eyes just a tiny bit. It was a wool blanket. I suddenly felt very silly, and was certain that I would have blushed had I not been struck with the next thought.

Where was I?

I opened my eyes completely and swept my surroundings. I was on a cot, before a fireplace with a wool blanket around me.

Oh yes! The underground Lightbearer base. But how did I get here? The last thing I remembered I was in a chair. Someone must have moved me.

Just then I became aware of hushed voices behind me. I slowly turned around on the narrow cot, nearly falling over the edge in the process. Did I ever mention that I don't have good balance when I'm sleepy? Well, I don't.

On the far side of the room, Dwin, Kattim and Findal were sitting at the table where they had laid Grenith the night before. They were talking quietly and didn't seem to notice my moving around a bit.

Grenith. Where was she at? I glanced about me again, searching for her. At the foot of my cot, she lay on another cot near the fire. She was still sleeping, but looked very peaceful.

I lay back thinking and waking up slowly. This was a nice place, cozy, secluded and, best of all, hidden. I wondered what we would do next. Oh yeah, I wanted to learn how to fight so I wouldn't have to run the next time trouble came my way. I would have to ask Dwin about that. Nollem was yet to be found. Who knew if he was even still alive. I wouldn't be surprised if they never found him. Alletta could have done her job well by stowing him in some dark hole. Though that was never really her style. She liked leaving them out as warnings and trophies.

Oh well. I supposed that I should get up, but part of me just wanted to lay there forever. After quite some time, I finally sat up and crawled out between the layers of wool blankets. It suddenly reminded me of Glimmer, and I wondered how my gypsy friend was getting on. I wondered if they had won, or if they were now slaves. Haiblur came to mind, and I couldn't help but smile. He was a funny one. I wondered if he survived, and if he did, was he now wandering the plains in search of me like he said he would do?

Shoving my thoughts aside, I approached the table, and greeted everyone with a good morning. They all grinned and said in return, good afternoon. I smiled, realizing how late I had slept. I took one end of a bench with Kattim across from me and Findal beside me on my left.

After the usual greetings were exchanged, I asked quickly, "How's Grenith?"

Kattim responded, "As well as can be expected. She'll make it, but with a lot of rest. Slavery's a hard thing to overcome, physically and emotionally. Especially when you've been under it for so long. It will take a while for her to get back into good health. Though, I could say the same for you too. But you'll be better sooner than she will," she added as a bit of hope.

While she was speaking, I studied Kattim's face and saw something new in it. I liked it, and wondered what had brought around this change. "You know," I remarked as a sort of teaser to get her to say something about it, "I think that's the most I've ever heard you talk."

She smiled, hearing both the humorous and serious side. "Yes, I think that is the most I've ever spoken in front of you. While I was being held before I was sold, I got to think about going back into slavery. I dreaded it. But the more I thought the more I began to realize that I had never really gotten out of slavery the first time. I was still bound by the chains of mistrust. Because of that, I held back giving my entire life, every aspect of it, to Shalom. I wasn't sure that I could trust Him. But when I realized that, I gave it all away, and He freed me from my chains. I've come alive like I was when I first believed. Now, because of my love and trust in Shalom, I can freely extend the same to others. I know that I'll get trampled on a few times. But with those whom I do trust, my relationships will flourish because of it. I'm not holding back, I'm being totally honest with myself and others."

I wasn't sure how to respond to something like this. I was glad that she came to that decision, but I wasn't sure what to say. Thankfully, Dwin covered for me by asking eagerly, "So, do we get to hear your side of the story? All of it?"

"Uh, okay. I'll start when I first met Abburn, since you already know the things before." So I launched into my tale, describing the manor, its inhabitants, Abburn and Meddella in particular. I told of Abburn's wild temper, but I intentionally left out the parts that came so readily during his fits. Somehow, I didn't feel like I could talk about that. Then I told about our escape, plan and execution, our meeting with the gypsies, and our brief stay there, and why it ended. Then I went into the most detail when I told about passing through the border. I continued on how I thought Grenith was crazy for wanting to go back in, our journey and attack from the Orodumes. Then how the marsh saved us and our run-ins with the black mist and Between men. I skipped over the hallucinations on purpose, in fact, you're the first person I've told about that. I went over seeing the burnt forest and ended with our arrival at the base.

Findal inquired laughingly if I would tell about our first meeting. I laughed and said that I would let him tell, since I had been fair and not told of the arguments that had passed between myself and others of this party. I glanced at Dwin, and we exchanged a mischievous wink.

Findal was then begged to tell the tale, and he obliged with only a few interruptions from me correcting or adding in my side it. Sometime within that time span, Kattim got me a plate of food. I munched slowly on it through his story, still not being truly hungry.

Once he was done, I asked of Dwin, "Do you think that you could train me to fight?"

He was thoughtful for a moment, then asked, "Why do you want to fight?"

"Because I'm tired of having to run away from my enemies: the Orodumes, the Between men. I wish I could defend myself, but I'm not trained. That's why."

He nodded his head, liking what he heard. "That's a good reason. Defend the faith, defend the innocent and those unable to do so for themselves. I'll train you, but only after those arms have healed. I won't have you overdoing yourself too soon."

I grinned at the prospect. Soon I would be able to hold my own in a good fight. "Thanks, I can't wait until we start."

"But you'll have to wait," Kattim broke in. "Speaking of your arms, how are they feeling?"

"A little better. They don't sting as much as they used too. I think that ointment helped, thanks again Dwin."

After a while of more catching up—it was fun just to sit and talk—Grenith woke up. That was when we started getting things accomplished. Findal and Dwin moved our cots into an empty room they had cleaned out earlier that morning. Meanwhile, Kattim scrounged through old trunks and closets searching for something suitable for us to wear. It was obvious that we couldn't keep wearing our gypsy clothes. I was rather sad to see them go, I had grown fond of them but more importantly the memories that went with them.

Women's clothes were in short order in the base. We found some under clothing that would work well enough, and we could use them for night clothes. After a thorough search we found some old ragged skirts that were used by the Lightbearers going out into the field. They would certainly blend in well enough out there, but they were hardly better than our own. Kattim found one that was in slightly nicer shape, and it fit Grenith very well. In contrast, I got stuck with boy's pants and a jerkin-like shirt. The pants were baggy and it took some doing to ensure they would stay up. The jerkin was made of thick warm material, and had sleeves that came just above my elbow, and the hem came down mid thigh. It was also completely oversized, so I found a belt and managed to retain my waistline.

Kattim also found some leather strips and, after combing out my hair thoroughly, tied it back into a ponytail. Grenith's had the top parts pulled and tied back, leaving some hair streaming down her back.

Overall, Grenith looked the female and I sported a different look. I had never worn pants before, much less a jerkin, so I was feeling awkward in them, almost exposed. After wearing them among the girls, I grew a little more comfortable and partially forgot that I was wearing them. But pants always feel weird after you've worn skirts your entire life. It must have been an hour or so before we reappeared from out of Kattim's room.

You should have seen Dwin's face when he saw me in boys' clothes. He burst out laughing. Though I could tell once he saw my embarrassment, he tried to hide it. He wasn't at all successful. Findal smirked with a comical expression written over his face. Kattim scolded, Grenith explained, and I blushed.

It took quite some time before Dwin could stop smiling whenever he looked at me. I didn't find it funny at all. Especially since I was the one being laughed at, and all I wanted to do was feel normal in them. It was hard enough without their remarks and laughter.

Right from the beginning, Grenith and I were put on extreme rest. Neither of us were supposed to lift a finger. Which I think Grenith was grateful for. She slept most of the day away. But I, on the other hand, never really liked inactivity before I came on this journey, adventure, thing. I was anxious and constantly begging them to let me go up and explore a little.

They did consent to us going up for some fresh air. In fact they made us do it once a day, but at first for only a few minutes. Then it lengthened into fifteen, and eventually a half hour. But we always had to have someone with us to keep us punctual.

❦

After a month, my burns were reduced to small scabs and fresh white skin. It was amazing that there were no scars left behind, for which I was grateful. I was back to health and regaining my former muscle.

Grenith, on the other hand, still tired easily and was just beginning to loose some of her scrawny, underfed look. She began to fill out again, her cheeks getting less gaunt and her ribs growing less pronounced.

It was then that Dwin consented to begin training me. On the first day, I could hardly contain my excitement as he led me to a room solely for the use of storing weapons. The room was a little smaller than the Den and was lined with racks holding swords, bows, knives, shields, maces, and anything else one could want for defense and attack. The blades gleamed in the torch light, reflecting coldly the warm glow.

I had never seen so many weapons in one place before. My mouth parted slightly, and I fell to examining them. There were plain and ornate, fancy and practical. The swords particularly caught my eye. There were so many of them, and each with a different inscription down the middle and decorative design.

Dwin went off in a different direction, searching for something in particular. He waved the torch over the shimmering blades. As each one reflected the light, it seemed to say, "Pick me! I'm the one you want." But he chose none.

He worked his way down from the broad swords to the dirks and knives. Occasionally he would pull one off the wall and feel it, testing its balance and weight. He would mutter to himself as he did so, and ended up putting it back into its place.

After seeing him take a few off, I started doing so myself, trying to look like I knew what I was doing when I held it up before me. They felt heavy and awkward in my hands, but I wasn't about to admit it.

By now Dwin had worked his way somewhere in between the regular swords and the daggers. He pulled out a short sword and felt it. He smiled slightly with grim satisfaction as he came over to me.

At that moment I was handling a nice broad sword, running my fingers over the etching down the middle near the handle. He came up to me and held the short sword out to me. "Here," he said, "try this."

I made a face at the small sword. It was about half the size of the one in my hands, not even close to having the same grandeur. I replied with a tone of disgust, "It's so small."

"It's your size," he insisted. "Try to swing that, see how far you get with it."

I took his suggestion more as a challenge. I held the sword awkwardly in both hands, and extended it away from me. It got even heavier.

Dwin backed up.

Determined to follow through, I made the attempt to arc it from right to left. I failed horribly. I barely cut it through the air, only to lose control and have it crash into the floor. Thankfully, it was only dirt and not stone so it didn't ding the blade.

Suppressing a smile, Dwin came closer and handed the short sword to me without a word.

I grudgingly took it, giving up the broad sword. He replaced it in its spot and motioned for me try again. I repositioned my feet so they were planted firmly. I held the sword further away from me, already feeling the lightness of it. I arched it smoothly through the air, cutting a half circle in an imaginary foe. Even though the sword was easier to handle, it still felt strange in my hands. It wasn't natural.

Dwin smiled, trying to cover it with a thoughtful hand raising to his chin. He asked, without a trace of laughter coming through, "And how was that?"

I sighed, even then not wanting to admit it, "Better. I guess it will have to do. But," I thought of a good excuse as to why it wasn't the best idea, "won't I be at a disadvantage? They'll all have longer and bigger swords, and I'll be stuck with this little thing."

He handed me the sheath for it and said, "Not the way that I'll teach you. You'll have the advantage if you learn it well."

This piqued my interest, but I didn't get to ask about it because he quickly added, "Come on, let's get started."

Part 3

Chapter 20
Training

Dwin walked out of the armory, and I trailed behind him.

The shadows closed in behind us, taking the only light with us. I hadn't really remembered which way we came, but it seemed that we weren't going back to the Den. He was taking me down dark and foreign passages. I wasn't so much worried about where he was taking me, but curious as to where we would end up. He silently led me down turns and straight tunnels, all with the same smooth dirt floors, walls and ceilings.

Eventually we came to a dead end. Here the tunnel widened considerably into a pleasant cove. At first I thought it was just that, but I soon saw a sturdy wooden ladder leading straight up. Dwin reached over to the side and hooked the torch in a sconce. It sat there, contentedly dispelling the darkness.

He scurried up the ladder and stopped briefly at the top. I heard the familiar sound of a thump and knew that there was some sort of trapdoor up there. I was immediately curious where it would lead us to.

I followed him up the rungs quickly, poking my head above ground. I blinked in the bright light and looked around. I vaguely picked out the shapes of stone walls about us. We had surfaced somewhere in the colony of stone skeletons which I assumed was a part of the desolate town that lay over top the old base. Dwin offered his hand and I accepted it.

He practically pulled me out of the hole by the hand, and set me on my feet on the cold ground. The first thing I noticed was the dramatic temperature change. I knew it was getting on to the middle of winter, but every time I came up the cold took my breath away. It was so much warmer underground. Especially in the Den.

Which reminds me of something I thought was curious when I learned of it. At first, I was wondering where the smoke went from the fireplace. As it turns out, every fireplace has a chimney that lets it out above ground. These chimneys were aligned with the chimneys of the houses that were built over it. In that way, they avoided immediate detection. It was only conspicuous now because the town was abandoned.

Anyway, we were dumped out in the middle of what used to be someone's house. The hatch looked like it might have led to a cellar. The tumbled walls of the house were fallen in around us, leaving large gaps and a jagged roofline. Grass and weeds had replaced the floor that had once been there, and stray stones had imbedded themselves nearly level with the rest of the dirt. On these and the walls, greenish-grey moss had taken over, and a few black smoke smudges still lingered. A cold wind whistled and moaned over the protruding stones. I shivered slightly, thinking of the family that once lived here. And to think that they were now as forgotten as their town.

Dwin broke through my thoughts by saying, "This used to be a cellar." he motioned to the opening. "We opened it up into the tunnels after the burning. Now it serves as another entrance or exit. Come with me."

He walked out of the rubble and struck out straight ahead with long strides. I hurried to keep up, trying to watch my feet and take in my surroundings at the same time. It didn't work out so well, and I got tripped up quite a few times. But that is the nice thing about pants, they don't get tangled around your legs if you loose your footing. By now, I was completely used to the feel of boys' clothes and actually enjoyed them, seeing the bright sides of wearing them.

It seemed that we were going down a commonly passed street. The ground was harder and only tougher weeds had grown up around the half hidden cobblestone. We rounded the ruins of a sizable house and the street opened wide before us. It turned into a large courtyard, still cobblestoned and mostly intact. I was surprised to see such a large area so clear of the wreckage. Four other streets spilled out into it, all leading out between the grey houses. Overall, it seemed the perfect training courtyard.

"This," began Dwin, "used to be the marketplace. Here, every Saturday, men and women would cram in to sell, buy and trade goods. It was quite the center of the town. It was where they'd hold their celebrations and announce important things. Many a wedding happened here." His voice grew sober, and his eyes took on a sad look. He sighed and continued, mustering up a somewhat normal tone, "And here is where your training begins."

He strode out into the center. He stood facing me, drew his sword, and tossed the sheath off to one side. He smiled, beckoning me closer and saying, "I've genuinely been looking forward to this."

I wasn't sure if I should be glad to hear that, or be afraid. I awkwardly pulled my short sword out of the leather sheath, catching the tip on the inside as I tried to wrestle it out. I think Dwin was grinning at my efforts, but I didn't really notice because as soon as I got it out, he came charging straight at me with his sword held over his shoulder, yelling like a madman.

Completely caught off guard and terrified out of my wits, I threw my arms over my head and shrank to the ground. The same crouching fear that I got whenever Master Abburn would strike out, crashed over me. I cowered tensely there on the cold stones, expecting to receive a hard blow along with harsh curses.

But nothing happened.

Cringing with fear, I glanced hesitantly to the side. I saw Dwin's pant legs just inches from my curled self. My eyes trailed slowly up to his face.

To my surprise, he wasn't grinning like I thought he would be. He was staring down at me, studying me silently with his sword hanging limply by his side.

Relaxing a little, I sat back on the hard stones, hugging my knees. My sword lay totally forgotten an arms length away. My heart was racing, palms sweaty. I calmed my breathing, trying to collect myself.

Dwin extended his hand, quietly offering to help me up. I reached my own up and realized that my hands were shaking violently. Dwin noticed too. He was the last person I wanted to see that.

Once I was on my feet, I meekly apologized, "Sorry."

"No, don't be," Dwin replied solemnly while retrieving my sword from the ground. "I do that to everyone to test their instinctual response. I have a hard time believing that would have been your response six months ago. The Limira I know was slinging pebbles at Weavels and Vaudians."

I knew he was asking, without saying it out right, what had happened between then and now. I bit my lip, not really wanting to say it. He kept looking steadily at me, and I knew that he wanted his answer. I sighed and quietly responded, "Master Abburn..." I wasn't sure if I could finish, no one had ever asked me about things like this before. When I told Grenith about it, she knew exactly what it was like because she had been through it. And she always made jokes of it, making me feel better. No one had ever wanted to seriously know. I felt shame and uncertainty nagging in the back of my mind. I pulled up enough courage and said, "Master Abburn used to... well, yeah." I still couldn't say it directly. "When he would..."

Dwin gently finished for me, "When he beat you, there was no other defense. If you stood up, more punishment. Right?"

"Yeah," I affirmed meekly, staring at Dwin's boots, "that's it."

"Limira, first thing, I'm never going to hurt you. Understand that now and we'll be off to a good start. But you have to get over that, can't be curling up at every blow. Now's the time to fight back, muster up your courage. Now, let's start with some basic moves, okay?"

I nodded, still studying the stones. He gave the sword back to me, and I took it in hand. Brushing my fingertips over the flat of the blade, I held it up, staring into the cold steel. It grimly stared back at me.

After a moment, Dwin cut in by saying and illustrating, "Now, hold your blade like this. A little higher, and over your shoulder a bit... There. Perfect. Now swing it forward. Harder. Feel that?"

And so our first lesson began, and already he was prying into my secret places. But somehow, I knew that it was safe to tell him those kinds of things, as uncomfortable as it was. Once we got started, we got into a roll. I seemed to be picking things up quickly enough. The sword began to feel less like just a piece of steel and more balanced and fluid.

By the end of that hour I was mastering thrusting. He would do it with me, to make sure that I kept up with him. Then he would stand beside me and watch me do it a few times. That part usually entailed him instructing me to do it better and tapping my heels with the tip of his sword, saying, "No, move that one forward. Now back again. One movement. Try it again... See! That wasn't so hard! Do it again."

I would lunge forward, conscious of my footwork, and retreat back again.

After this was properly mastered, he concluded the session, much to my disappointment. He justified his reasons by saying, "We should call that good for today. I don't want you to be too tired that you won't be able to do it again tomorrow."

Seeing the logic in that view, I reluctantly followed him back to the trapdoor and underground again. I felt fairly confident with the two moves that he had taught me. The first was how to hold my sword properly, while fighting and running. And then to maintain a good form. Then he taught me a downward arch (which I thought was rather easy, but he was stingy on the good form part of things). Then it was the thrust.

I left feeling rather productive and well learned. Little did I know that there was so much more to learn.

Chapter 21
The Regrettable Journey to Moneth

The more we trained together, the more we got to know each other. We started to race each other to the arena, well, market square. Sometimes instead of fighting, we'd go for a run, or work with daggers. I was pretty horrible at knife throwing, but Dwin was patient with me. I couldn't have asked for a better trainer than him. After two months, we were into intense fights, and I was soon—after about a month or two more—able to beat him too! Though personally, I think he was going easy on me.

Findal was told by Dwin that he had to instruct me in maps and coordinates. He did so eagerly because that was his passion, and he finally had someone who would sit and listen to him for hours on end. I only agreed because I was told I had to. If it had been up to me, I wouldn't have been the least interested in even starting. But once we did, I found that I enjoyed it... to an extent. I couldn't ever be as excited about it as Findal, though.

Kattim also took it upon herself to give me some lessons on cooking. I had never needed to do so before, having servants and the like back at home, so it was a totally new experience for me. It wasn't too terrible, but I must say that I enjoyed gathering and cooking things in the open plains more. It was more of an adventure that way. And I had come to realize that I rather liked adventure. I loved the excitement and uncertainty. I thought that then, but I was sure that I'd want to eat my words as soon as I got into a pinch. It was bound to happen eventually.

❦

Adventure came sooner than I expected.

Every once in a while, more like when she felt the need to go, Grenith would make the journey Moneth, which would usually take about two and a half to three days on horseback at a steady pace. But seeing how we didn't have horses and as it was Grenith who was walking, it would take about seven or so days to get there. She still held many marks of her years in slavery, one of them being she tired more easily than the rest of us. She also had to carry all the provisions she might need over an eight day span—we always pack for one day extra than planned—and fend for herself out in the rolling open plains. Despite all these factors, she still insisted on going. She was determined to go and visit some contacts in the underground Lightbearer world that she had known from forever ago and just had to see how they were fairing, it being years since she was in the area.

Personally, I wondered how she knew that a) the people she knew from long ago were still in Moneth, and b) she wouldn't merely be in the way. But that wasn't for me to determine, nor was it my place to tell her that she couldn't go.

The main thing we were concerned about was that she would be alone with no one to protect or look after her. But after a week of persistence and persuasion, she finally managed to convince us that she would be just fine under the supervision of Findal.

So they were off, we missed them both terribly, and they returned after three weeks time. End of story.

Not quite.

That all played out about a month and a half ago. Grenith wanted to go to Moneth again. Findal agreed to accompany her once more. We were preparing to send them off again. And this is where I cme in. She wanted me to go with them to Moneth, to the scum hole of detestables, to the rotten, drunken pigpen of all Deceiver's land, to the last place I wanted to be. I was already stuck in Deceiver's ashen, fruitless land, why would I want to go deeper into disgusting muck and slime?

Regardless, in less than a week, I was trudging along side Grenith, a pack on my back, a cloak draped over my shoulders, and my short sword strapped at my side. Somehow—I'm still not sure if there was any one reason that made my decision definite—Grenith and Findal, plotting together in a scheme against me, had convinced me to go with them. They gave a number of good reasons, among the list that was it would be a good learning and growing experience. It would get my head out from underground (that was one from Findal), and it would give me a better view of things going on in other places that I haven't seen, giving me a better Kingdom mindset and aspect. I already *knew*, in my mind, that people were fighting to spread Elohim's Kingdom all over the world, but I hadn't actually *seen* it, and, as Dwin pointed out, that if ever I began to doubt or wonder if anything I did made any difference, or if there was anyone else out there fighting for the same cause, I could remember when I saw it in action and be encouraged that Elohim was still working.

All in all, there I was, the chilly morning air just beginning to warm, my shoes wet from dew, and the low, grey, ever present cloud cover hanging its gloomy self between me and every bit of sky above.

Both Grenith and Findal had just been filling me in on everyone whom I would meet, whom we would be staying with, when meal times were, our sleeping arrangements and practically everything *but* what I wanted to know. That is, I wanted to know *what* we would be doing this entire week long stay in Moneth. Every time I asked, either Grenith or Findal, they would give this curiously funny look, smile, and say that they didn't know or it wasn't for them to decide.

I thought it was all rather poor planning and very bad hospitality on the part of the hosts. It was rude to not have anything planned in advance, and it was equally rude, if not more so, rude not to include the guests in the plans for activities.

Before the outskirts of Moneth were clearly visible, I knew we were close. I could smell it. Literally. At first I only caught a whiff of it on the breeze, then it infected my nose like a swarm of angry hornets, then it leaked into my mouth and I could *taste* it. If you could imagine all the worst smells you have ever experienced, combine them all together, times it by ten, then you might have something vaguely similar to what I was being raided with. The stench was something like a combination of rotting flesh, burnt feathers, decaying feces, and strong rum.

Before I knew it, and long before I wanted, we had entered Moneth and were seemingly deep into the gutters of the city. Already, desperation and poverty surrounded us on all sides. I felt overwhelmed by the oppressive sights and smells the city displayed with unashamed flagrancy. Clusters of poorly dressed residents stood about on the streets and in doorways, staring. Some staring blankly, others very intentionally staring with evil glares of contempt, scorn and mockery. Even most of the children held similar expressions as the adults. As we passed down the street, everyone, on both sides of us, would pause in whatever they were doing just to give us our icy, hateful reception with those darks stares. Complete silence. Staring grim faces. Eyes boring into our backs. Then the slow returning to their previous tasks. A low murmur rose up behind us.

I made eye contact with only the first few who did it. But as we continued down the street, I let my eyes skip frantically on the mud road, avoiding any contact. Chills shivered up and down my spine. I hugged my arms tighter to my sides and shrunk my shoulders in just a tad. I had no intention of looking threatening in any capacity. This was one town I would definitely keep my head down in.

And it wasn't even nightfall yet.

My heart sank even further into the darkest, smallest recess of my chest. If this is what the people were like during the day, I dreaded seeing them at night when their hearts' true colors ran irrepressible and unchecked. I not only had to witness that mob of vileness, I had to *live* among that mob of vileness. I seriously began regretting coming on this trip. I don't care what Grenith and Findal had said about it being a good time, this was going to be one miserable week.

My shoes were already thoroughly caked with the muck of the streets, my lungs burning with the odor wafting up from the scum of the city, and my soul oppressed by the presence of darkness that permeated my entire being.

Even Birset was more endurable than this! Birset, the slave city full of Vaudians, traitors, and overall villainous characters, the very same place I was sold to Abburn.

Thinking all the more of turning back, I glanced over my shoulder, partly to measure how much distance I would have to return back through, and partly to ensure myself that I was committed because I had already come a sizable way into the city. I sighed with dismay. There was a mere fifty feet stretched between me and solid ground.

Inwardly, I knew that I couldn't go back, returning the way we'd come wasn't an option.

Findal, who was striding beside me, looked at me just as I was facing the city again. He caught my gaze and gave me a reassuring smile, saying in a quiet tone, "Don't worry about them, they're just staring because they know we're different. People don't like those who are different than themselves."

I attempted to return his smile, but only managed a very weak, pathetic one. That wasn't what I was thinking of just then, but it was heartening to know that I wasn't just paranoid about the stares.

"It's perfectly alright," Findal was speaking again, "I found it unnerving at first too. But you'll get used to it."

Unnerving? Yes. Used to it? No. There's no way I could ever be used to this much blatant, unabashed hatred. Avoiding their stares, my eyes flitted back to the bystanders, glancing cautiously at them. On many of them, there was no clear evidence of their being Between, no gruesome scars, no bubbled, blackened skin, no fungus or growth visible. Only those who stood in the shadows of doorways or eves had the indications of death. But they were too veiled to see anything in detail, for which I was grateful. The moving shadows of those concealed by darkness stared defiantly back at us, some with violent snarls, most gave us mocking, proud sneers.

Night was falling, and the already dark land was getting noticeably darker. Soon, all would be revealed as they truly were, disguised and protected by the ink of night. The visual signs of death were repulsive, truly ugly and stomach churning. It was strange and disgusting to me that I once thought the signs of decay fascinating.

I shoved aside my thoughts and returned my attention to where we were headed. After a few turns onto side streets, yet always nearer to the heart of the city, we landed ourselves on the muck covered cobblestone sidewalk before a slumping house with a crooked door and sagging roofline. Moss and dark slime dripped from the eves. Shutterless, cracked and mud spattered windows were so dilapidated that they revealed only a hint of light beyond their blackened panes. Stone walls were hidden beneath layers of mud, moss and slime. To top it all off, painted symbols, blood red and black of hue, marked the door with strange and dark images.

Chapter 22
"Didn't expect to find you here..."

MY eyebrows went up and my eyes grew wider. Taking in all the details in an instant, I immediately glanced at Grenith and Findal, hoping that they had the wrong address. But no, both stood confidently before the door, Findal raising his hand to knock.

A pace or two behind them, I took a hasty step forward, stuttering out my concerns, "Uh—"

Findal's knuckles rapped lightly upon the wood planks of the door, cutting off my complaints before I even got the chance to say anything about it. My mouth hung open, my tongue still forming the words.

Grenith turned her head to look over her shoulder, a slight frown clouding her brow.

She had heard me, and doubtless she knew it was I who uttered the sound. And I knew it. Snapping my mouth shut and forcing my eyebrows to return to a normal position, I closed the remaining gap between us with a forced smile plastered over the expression I knew was full of distaste.

Grenith's further inspection of my reaction was cut short, thankfully, by a loud creaking then a sheet of light glaring from the doorway. In the center was the dark silhouette of a woman, momentarily wreathed in warm light.

I hadn't realized how dark it really was out on the sidewalk until the glow of the house burst into the street. In a moment, the brightness faded as our eyes grew accustomed to it, though it seemed more like the darkness on the streets swallowed every stray ray of it, consuming it in its black jaws.

The woman's form became clearly visible, revealing a shorter, middle aged woman in dark mud spattered garb. She wore a home spun navy blue dress with a woolen shawl wrapped around her torso. Her silver speckled dark hair spilled over her broad shoulders and down her back. Her face crinkled into little creases from smiling, a radiant and warm welcome in large contrast to the former reception we received. Both her arms opened wide to welcome us, a soft yet firm voice beckoning us to enter.

It was obvious from the way that Grenith and Findal acted that they had met her before. They instantly entered, exchanging hugs and greetings with others in the room. I came in behind them, feeling like an outsider already. As soon as I got past the radius of the door, it swung with another creak back into its former resting place, shutting out the night and fully enveloping us within the warm, glowing light of the room.

I half turned when the door moved, expecting to have something attack me with weapon raised high. It was nothing of the kind. A young man, about my age and slightly taller than myself, appeared from behind it. He had the softest expression of quiet reserve in his demeanor that I had ever seen in anyone. He gave me a smile though, as sheepish and meek as it was.

Sticking out a boney hand, he said in a voice that matched his manner, "Creedal."

I took it, receiving a squeeze and shake from him, replying, "Limira," while meeting his steady gaze. He was so earnest and sincere, that I didn't know what to think of him at first. There was so much depth in his brown eyes, yet innocence. He immediately struck me as a servant and leader of men. There was so much gentle authority in those quiet eyes.

Grenith's hand on my shoulder tore my attention away from the fellow behind the door named Creedal. I turned back to the room and was met by the beaming face of the woman who admitted us. She immediately enfolded me in her round, loving arms, even before Grenith introduced us.

"This is Limira," she said smiling wide at my hesitancy of receiving such a generous hug from a stranger.

The woman held me all the tighter and gushed, "I've heard so much about you that I feel like I've known you for years."

My eyes widened, my eyebrows shot up again, and I gave Grenith a look that clearly asked, "What have you told her about me?"

Grenith laughed at my expression and concerns, brushing it off lightly.

The clingy woman finally released me from her smothering embrace, saying, "My name is Fraisa. I'm so glad to finally meet you in person." Her twinkling eyes were nearly lost in the creases of her beaming face.

Just as Fraisa stepped back, a towering figure appeared behind her. Looming nearly three heads taller than his wife, the massive man bestowed the most homey, gentle smile of them all. Creedal, the young man behind the door, was very similar in appearances as this man now advancing his calloused hand. His hand folded over the entirety of mine, giving it a firm squeeze between his leathery palm and fingers. His soft eyes too glowed with warmth, yet contained a gentle and resolute depth to them. His name was Tolgariden, but it was usually shortened to Tolgar.

Findal and Grenith took over the conversation once more with Tolgar and Fraisa. Between the four of them, they managed to say quite a bit without my needing to contribute. That gave me an ample chance to take in my surroundings.

In contrast to the outer parts of the house, the inner section was cozy, warm and wreathed in cheery firelight. The walls were clear of any growing green things, the compacted earth floor swept smooth and clean, the mantle and hearth invitingly warm. Half of the exposed rafters were laid over with boards, creating a floor. Across the opening between the roof and where the boards stopped, a thick blanket was hung, sealing off a private room. Various things hung from the other half of the rafters, from herbs to bundles to buckets and every other manner of things that could be easily stowed away up there. Two oil lamps hung from the rafters as well, casting a spray of golden light on things below.

Before the large hearth several rocking chairs, stools, benches and every other assortment of seating were arranged tightly about the warmth of the flames. Most of these chairs were occupied. Everyone had stood up, but it was clear that they had previously been seated in a semicircle.

To my left, there was a kitchen dimly lit by an oil lamp in the rafters. It was a well used, small yet tidy kitchen, nothing of modern conveniences to speak of, but I'm sure it suited their needs. A large table was in the center of the kitchen area. All the chairs and benches had been removed from around it and to the fireside.

On the other side of the room, to my right, were different essential household pieces of furniture and work things such as basins, tubs, shelves with foodstuffs, etc. The second oil lamp dimly lit this section of the room.

Movement in the far corner caught my eye. In the shadows, two people were gathered around a third, a girl about my age, curled in the corner. It look like she was crying. Sobbing would better describe it. The two friends were down on the floor with her, arms around her and it looked as if they were praying. It looked like a very tender moment, and I wondered what had happened to bring it about. Before I realized it, I was staring at them, completely engrossed in the scene of three friends supporting each other in their brokenness.

In my peripheral vision, a tall person appeared beside me just to my right. Catching my attention, I turned to see who it was, slightly startled that someone was there. Creedal. He snuck up on me again!

He was looking at me in such a manner that I knew he had seen me staring a the trio in the corner. I couldn't help but ask, "Is she alright?"

Creedal smiled slightly, nodding in the affirmative, "Yeah, she'll be fine. Just learning and growing that's all."

Just then, Tolgar and Fraisa beckoned us further into the firelight and introduced us to all who were present. They all went around in a circle saying their names and how long they'd been in Moneth. There were so many, and I was so tired, that I hardly remember anyone's name. But of course, Grenith and Findal already knew everyone present.

Then after a few long minutes, during most of which some of the newly met people came forward and struck up conversation with me, they slowly began to take their leave in large groups. I was yet again surprised to see how dark it was outside.

Quite frankly, I don't remember much of what happened between then and me suddenly finding myself on a cozy cot in the room in the rafters, which was created by blankets hung from the eves. I was soon fast asleep with three other girls around me in their own cots.

🌱

Bang!

Startled out of sleep, I glanced around me in the tiny loft leaning on an elbow, the cot creaking with my movement. Whatever that was, it was close. Too close for my liking.

Sounds of voices, some high with shrieking laughter and some deep with bellowing anger, permeated the walls of the house and came blaring into my sleep sensitive ears. Tramping and scampering feet padded and squished in the mud out on the streets, a loud, constant hubbub of movement and crowds were in the background.

But that was what had awakened me. Directly in front of the house, on the raised walk as far as I could tell, were either a group or only a couple of the rowdiest people I had ever heard. Their animal-like voices brayed, growled, screeched and barked at one another in undistinguishable phrases. From the amount of ruckus, it must have been a group of people, definitely Between from their sounds.

So this was what it was like, to be surrounded on all sides with the purest form of evil, the hatred carried by the servants of Deceiver unleashed at night in their true forms. I was glad that I hadn't grown up with this kind of riffraff in Monare Pelm. Only in the poorest, most centered districts had the occasional wild ruffian, but they never came into the refined, outer areas where I lived.

My thoughts were drawn back to the present Between just below on the other side of the wall. Another bang! I perceived just the slightest tremor in the floor boards and one of the lamps hanging from the rafters rattled. There was a sort of honk of pain and fear mixed together. A laughing growl came directly after that, obviously from a different member of the party down there. There were other snickering grunts and squeals on the street a little further away. More pleading honks from the victim. The next thing I heard was a crunch and a thump as the same unfortunate slammed against the wall. A wheezing moan reached my ears, and I wanted to grab my pillow to block it out, but I couldn't move. I was wondering too intently what would happen next.

There were more chuckling growls and shrieks of women's cackles. More shuffling and I think the group moved on down the street, hooting and rumbling in garbled voices. I was relieved that they had left, but unsure what had become of the unfortunate victim. He was probably left behind in a sniveling heap against the house wall. I wondered if he was going to be there in the morning.

The riotous din from the streets still roared on. There were obvious fights going on, girls' high, flirtatious giggles, drunken voices all around, smashing of wood and clay, slimy splats as people stumbled and fell into the mud. Occasionally there were unearthly screams echoing into the night air. Everything of disorder, confusion and immorality you could imagine was sure to be going on.

I wasn't certain I could go back to sleep for all the noise. Glancing around the dark loft, I saw that no one else had woken up. They must have been used to it. Flopping back onto my cot, causing a considerable creak, I readjusted my blanket and prepared for a long night.

❦

Very few citizens of Moneth were out and about the next day. The frolicking atmosphere of the night before had sunk into the usual threatening and suspecting air, and the stares were revived with vigor. Many slunk from doorway to back alley to taverns. At least, that was how it was around Tolgar and Fraisa's home. With Creedal as our guide, Findal and I emerged from the house early that morning.

Apparently I had fallen asleep the night before, because the next thing I knew Grenith was shaking my shoulder to wake me into a grey morning. Every morning in Deceiver's land was grey, but this one seemed even more so. It was probably because it was much earlier in the morning than I would usually be out above the Den. We four girls dressed and went downstairs to help with a breakfast that finished faster than I could have thought possible. Then we set out in groups to do various things that I didn't fully understand.

Everything seemed to go quickly that morning. Grenith and a few other girls set out with Tolgar before I could catch what they were off to do. Fraisa shooed Creedal, Findal and I out the door to get aquatinted with the city some while she took care of things there.

So, before I knew, I was going down the muddied walks with Creedal in front, explaining things and sights and smells to me. Findal was beside me when there was no need to go single file, which was quite often. We had been fully immersed in the heart of the city, where all the markets, well known taverns, and people could be found. All the buildings were in the same sagging disrepair, and the market stands and carts weren't much better. I was surprised that anyone would buy a single food item from this place. I wondered how any of it could be sanitary. If the muddy streets and sagging, mossy structures weren't bad enough, there were rats and large rodents sitting about in plain day, snagging food from the stands or cleaning themselves on the edges of the containers.

All the people were no better, with their grimy hands, clothes and faces, their coughs and snivels. The worst of it all was that the people here weren't the least bit shy about their Between deformities, nor the latest wounds from night brawling. And it wasn't like there were only a couple people here and there with these awful marks, every one of them had something, and there were so many. Throngs of them, crowding the markets and especially the taverns.

We returned to Tolgar and Fraisa's home for dinner around noon. Grenith and Tolgar and the other girls had returned as well. We all sat around the huge kitchen table, and the conversation buzzed with excitement around me. But for some reason I found myself lost in thought. All I could think of was the people in the streets, lost in desperation and hopelessness, hungry and cold. My own food looked unappetizing, but I shoveled down as much of it as I could.

After dinner was over, Fraisa produced several baskets full of food. The others began to pair off and take two baskets each. Dares and playful teasing jumped from group to group as they bet who would make the most connections. As soon as I realized what we were going to do, I offered to stay and help clean up after the meal. Fraisa smiled, and Grenith caught me by the arm, insisting I go with her.

Before I could get two words of protest in, Grenith handed me the last basket and directed me to the door.

"Now the purpose of these," Grenith explained as we trekked through the muddy streets, "is not merely to give them food and leave, even though we are helping them and making ourselves feel good too. The thought is more that these baskets are vessels, a way to start a relationship. I know it's kinda hard for us because we aren't planning on staying in Birset very long.

And it's hard to not let that fact inhibit our hospitality towards others."

And then Grenith was knocking on the door of a small battered hut. I stayed behind her and to the right. Remaining silent, I watched as everything went down with curiosity and a foreboding feeling rising up in my soul. Grenith made it look so easy, so simple to initiate conversation and make the other person so at ease. I watched it twice, as she handed out her two baskets.

Then it was my turn, and I honestly don't remember anything I said. Though I do remember feeling very uncomfortable and awkward, and Grenith stepped in a few times to help guide the conversation.

It was over before I knew it and we walked back to Tolgar and Fraisa's, me feeling quite numb from it all. I hadn't seen this kind of brokenness before, and it left me shook to the core. I felt helpless as the weight of need was too large for me to carry. But I didn't know I wasn't meant to carry all that, and it crushed me. The desperation, the hopelessness, the enormity of it was all I could dwell on for the rest of the day.

I was grateful when it was time to turn in, and looked forward to sleep mercifully taking my thoughts away. But it didn't, I lay awake for hours, tossing and turning. When sleep finally came it was riddled with dreams that left me unrested by morning.

My relief was great when Creedal and I were directed to go on an errand for Fraisa. We were given instruction to buy bread and a jug of milk from the market. Findal decided to come with us, and we set off to the crowded markets.

I was again confronted by the sights and smells of the Moneth market. The people with their marks and scars made me very uncomfortable. At least they weren't staring at me though. Everyone was very busy bartering for their goods.

And that was when it happened. The last thing I was expecting to happen on this trip, happened without warning.

I was just thinking over the disgusting appearances of the Between in the market when a face caught my eye. Delicate, blanched skin. Pale flashing eyes. A bright red mouth in contrast to her skin. The tattered remnant of a dress. Small of stature. Slinking in form. The innocence that I once saw there, had now vanished, replaced by cunning and cruelty.

I knew that face.

It was like one from a nightmare. A long ago nightmare yet still very present in my mind. An unnamable fear was connected with that face. It was the creature who had attacked me on that third night in Slaggar Forest, knife in hand. It was most definitely the creature, the same beastly complexion mixed with sly trickery. And that smile, I knew it as well, though it wasn't from the beast. It was the same cunning smirk that Alletta wore when she was standing by Nollem, herself unguarded, in Post Neth, the last time I saw either of them.

Then it suddenly all made sense. She was the one who had killed both Chimel and Bilham. She was the one who had attacked me. She was the one who summoned the Weavels that first night. She was one of Deceiver's servants. Which meant she didn't have the emblem of the Crown at all.

And most importantly, she knew where Nollem was.

All these thoughts whirled through my head in a matter of seconds. Without saying a word to Findal and Creedal, I plunged off the side of the raised walk and into the muddy streets swarming with Between. I went straight for Alletta, never taking my eyes off her face. I picked through the rough citizens, whom were all walking as if I wasn't even there. Findal and Creedal shouted after me, but I barely heard them, and I certainly didn't stop.

Alletta looked over in my direction, apparently attracted by the shouting. Twenty feet from her. She saw me, her eyes getting a hair wider. Ten feet from her. A large, burly man passed between us, blocking her from my view. I quickly dodged around him, catching sight of Alletta's fleeing figure darting through the crowd. In an instant, I too was zigzagging between people, determined to catch her. I couldn't let her get away! She was my only hope for finding Nollem.

Distantly, as if through a fog, I heard Findal and Creedal behind me, shouting for me to wait up. Alletta burst through the crowded market and down a side street, running much faster than I would have thought possible for her stature. But I was gaining on her. She skidded around a corner. I dashed after her, getting closer. She quickly ducked between two houses into a narrow little alley, just big enough for her to squeeze through. Turning to one side, I brushed against both walls, keeping my eyes on her silhouetted form to see which way she went. Right.

Emerging from the little alley, I burst forward, getting closer yet. Alletta took a nervous glance over her shoulder, then darted to the left, down another street. But this time she didn't calculate so well.

I rounded the corner shortly after she did and saw her staring at the three walls of houses, her back turned to me. It was a dead end. And I was between her and the only way out. She whirled around, her look of surprise and terror at being stuck melted into a loathing, piercing glare. That wicked, cunning smirk returned. She held her hands slightly away from her sides and crouched slightly, starting to move to her left. I moved over to block her, just feet away.

Her smirk got wider, her gaze more gloating and malicious than before. Something inside me snapped in that moment. I lunged at her, my hands grasping the neck line of her tattered dress. She didn't resist like I expected her to. The force from my lunge carried us both backwards. She spun slightly to her left, swinging both of us into the wall on the right. I had her pinned against the stones, her slight form strangely relaxed. I wondered what sort of tricks she had in her dirty mind. Our faces were inches from each other.

I pounded her into the wall, demanding, "What did you do with Nollem?!"

She hissed through pointed teeth, "Didn't expect to find you in this city. Thought you'd be in Birset, or better yet, rotting in one of Master's cells."

I rammed her again. "Tell me!"

Chapter 23
The Shock

She grinned all the wider at me, licking the back of her rotting teeth with her blackened tongue. "You don't know? I thought you were smarter than that, Limira."

I heard footsteps behind us, presumably Findal and Creedal. They stopped suddenly, a small distance from us. I tightened my grip on her bunched up collar, shouting, "I'm not going to ask again! Tell me!"

"Since you insisted, alright." She smirked with a strange glint of satisfaction in her eye. "He was great sport, you know. Valiant to the end, he was. We roughed him up a bit and tossed him in a hole. Great fun we had. I wish you could have been there yourself, to see him grovel in a pathetic heap at our feet, offering to do anything to spare himself more pain. He was weak, Limira, your brother was a coward. He even offered to compromise all of Monare Pelm to save himself. He would have shown—"

"No!" I couldn't hear anymore. My sight was blurred by hot tears. Every inch of my mind screamed back at me. Nollem couldn't, wouldn't, have done that. It couldn't be! "Just stop!" I yelled.

Alletta's face was still twisted in a smirk. She cackled, "Oh, but he did! We didn't take him up on his offer, we just let him have it then threw him in a dark hole. Somewhere in a remote, desolate forest, with nothing but the beasts to gnaw on his thin flesh."

I snapped my eyes closed, trying to block out the images she was painting in my mind. Under something like an impulse, I suddenly pulled down her collar. I had to be sure.

I stared blankly at her emblem. I couldn't comprehend it, I blinked a couple of times to be sure that I was seeing it correctly.

Black against her transparent skin, the figure of a crown with a curly circle surrounding it blazed out with glaring clarity. She didn't have Deceiver's mark at all. But she was Between and had called him master. What? My entire childhood shattered before my eyes right in that moment. My shock and disbelief must have been written over my face like bold lettering.

Alletta laughed, thin cracking laughter that gloated and mocked me. She sneered, laughter still threaded in her voice, "Oh, my dearest Limira! You didn't think that people who have the mark of the Kingdom are actually *good*, did you?" She laughed again, "Aww, you poor, silly girl! Deceived from birth that the people of Monare Pelm are somehow better than the rest of us. Well, you were wrong. Everyone is just as black and cruel as Betwe—"

Just then I heard something whiz over my right shoulder. Alletta's voice gurgled as she gasped. Her body slumped against the wall. I scanned her to see what went wrong. A dark shaft protruded from her chest, a blackened stream of red soaking down her dress. I released her collar immediately, springing back with a scream. I brought my hands up to my mouth, then

I looked over my shoulder, half expecting to see another arrow flying towards me. But instead, a dark figure against the grey sky darted out of view over the roof top, disappearing behind the crest.

Involuntarily, my gaze returned to Alletta. Her pale skin was even more ashen than before. I couldn't think. I stared in blank silence. I felt Findal's strong arm clasp me around my shoulders. The warmth from his body felt strange, mine seeming to have gone numb. I saw Creedal approach Alletta, him crouching before her.

I swallowed a hard lump down the back of my throat, silent tears sliding down my cheeks. Tears for Nollem. Tears for what he went through. Tears for my innocent childhood belief. Tears for me.

Nollem was dead. For certain, he was dead. The Crown emblem meant nothing. All this time I had carried a fancy that Nollem might still be alive. How foolish could I have been? Everyone in Monare Pelm were Between. Including my parents. Including me! Nollem, dumped in a hole, a mangled wreak. Did I go night prowling like the Between here? Why did I never see my parents like that? Why was there never any evidence of decay? Alletta was on Deceiver's side. She was against us the entire time. Nollem was gone. As in never to be seen again. As in dead.

Creedal stood up again. He shook his head in dismay. Findal, his arm still wrapped around me, turned me away and slowly took me to the mouth of the street. I was staring straight in front of me at nothing but empty space. I didn't notice anything till Findal spoke, "Limira, who was that?"

I swallowed, my mouth suddenly felt very dry. I looked up distractedly, my jaw slack. "She was against us from the beginning... I trusted her."

"You knew her? How?"

"She killed Nollem," I blurted in a mechanical manner, then with more force as if I didn't hear myself the first time, a hint of hysteria cracking my voice, "She said she killed Nollem!"

"Slow down. Take a deep breath and start from the beginning. Who killed Nollem?"

I had continued to mutter while Findal was speaking, "Crown emblem doesn't mean anything. We're all like them." But my thoughts jerked back when Findal mentioned Nollem. "It's true, isn't it?"

"What is?"

I didn't hear him. "... Dead," was all I said before a fresh flood of tears came. Big, hot drops rolled down my cheeks. This time they weren't silent. I sobbed. My shoulders caved forward, shaking with deep gasps of breath.

I felt Findal embrace me, his other arm linked about my shoulder, his hand resting on the back of my head. Leaning further on him, I fully and unashamedly accepted his embrace. He stroked my hair and said gently, "Hey there, it's going to be alright. Just cry." Pause. "Just cry."

Somehow, I was suddenly sitting on a stool before the huge hearth. The boys had gotten me back to Tolgar and Fraisa's home. It must have been a long walk for them. I'm sure they were very kind and understanding through all of it, but I don't remember a thing.

When we got back, I was ushered to a spot before the fire, and given something warm to drink. My tears had subsided, mostly because I forced them back in the presence of company. I didn't want to talk, not now. I stared into the flames. Thinking. More thinking. Nollem was... I stopped myself there. I didn't want to cry again, not yet.

Shoving those thoughts to one side, I started a new line of thought, one that puzzled and baffled me. How could Alletta be Between, yet have the emblem of the Kingdom? That meant that my parents were Between, yet I never saw them act like it. I started tracing back through my memories of them during the night hours. There were parties, but those were always well lit, so it didn't count. Was there any time when it was dark or mostly dark when I saw them? I thought about that for a while, and nothing came to mind. In fact, you never saw anyone at night without them having some sort of bright light source. I always thought it was to keep the vagabonds away, but now I saw that that wasn't it at all. But the strange part was, everyone thought they carried a light to keep the vagabonds away. No one knew any different, that was the only reason we carried light at night.

That made sense, but what about the deformities, the skin growth? Why didn't I see any of that? Were none of us to that stage yet? But that didn't make sense. I could only recall strange, dirty looking people in the slums, the center of the city where all the poor lived. They could definitely pass for Between, they were ugly and no one ever wanted to touch or even be around them. But the main questions still remained, who determined that the regular citizen was suddenly too deformed to live among normal society? And how were they so quietly disposed of?

Well, that wasn't a hard one. Every once and a while a family or a single person would disappear, just vanish. It was always widely spread that they had done or said something against King Hobbel IV and his official staff. It seemed as if no one was safe from being arrested at any moment for whatever crime they had supposedly committed. Though, if you kept your head down, lived life like a good citizen of Monare Pelm, did plenty good in the name of King Hobbel IV, you had a great chance at being left alone. That's what my family always did, and it had worked so far. But now it became evident that it didn't matter how good of a citizen you were. Eventually you would be sent down to live with the untouchables merely because you couldn't hide who you were anymore.

Bursting through my thoughts, Grenith and the group she had been out with came in the door. There was the usual joyous greeting then a few hushed words between Findal and Grenith. I didn't need to hear what they said to know that they were talking about me. I didn't move. In my mind I could picture them, close together, Grenith's expression growing more concerned.

A quiet murmur of voices hummed in the background, the whispering of Findal and Grenith distinctly different than it. I couldn't hear exact words. The hum continued, along with general movement.

A hand slid on my shoulder. I jumped under the touch. Glancing up, I saw it was Grenith. A faint smile crossed her face, her gentle gaze meeting mine.

"You want to go upstairs?" she asked quietly.

I nodded, wanting badly to talk with her alone. Standing, we picked our way through the circle of furniture around the hearth and up the into the loft. We sat on my cot. I heaved a deep sigh. Grenith wrapped an arm around my bowed shoulders.

Tears began to silently trickle down my cheeks just thinking of it. How could I put words to the depth of my thoughts? How could I even say that Nollem was...? Praying for strength was the last thing I thought of, and the last thing I wanted to do. I much rather would have liked to sob for an eternity of time. Sob till there was nothing left.

Grenith gently broke into my thoughts by asking, "What's on your mind?"

More tears even at the thought of it. My chin began to quiver. I choked on the lump of sobs rising in my throat. Then like a dam suddenly topples under the sheer weight of built up water, tears and words came gushing out, sometimes one overpowering the other. But out it all came, finally. I explained about Alletta and Nollem, feeling the need to back up to the first few nights that started all this. Then I told about the Crown emblem, and how my entire childhood beliefs were crumbling before my eyes.

The more I told, the more the crushing ache relieved, and the more the tears dried up. I was getting all cried out. When I ran out of things to say about the most recent shocks, I continued on about the things that had been pressing on me within the last few days, with our journey and our brief stay here. The desperation, yet total ignorance, or stubborn denial of it, in this city had really gotten me down. To see the young children, all dirty and underfed, playing in the mud holes. Their big eyes and wondering looks. How anyone could live in such squalor was beyond me. I didn't understand it. I didn't understand any of what I was crying over. Why Nollem? Why did Alletta hate him? How could I have grown up so ignorant of a growing problem, a disease, in my own city? It was right before me, and I didn't even suspect anything was wrong, much less did I desire to fix it. Why was I such a mess?

Grenith stayed quietly by my side the entire time, listening to every word and only interrupting on occasion. At the end of it Grenith said, "I wish I could give you advice or a word of wisdom that would answer everything. What I really wish is that I could at least hand you a small bit of a Book that would answer your questions, but I don't have access to even one. But one thing I can say is this. You're going to have to work this out between you and Elohim. Start a conversation with Him. He will tell you what you need to know, over time. Only He can heal hurts like this, just give Him a chance and you'll see. Pour out your heart to Him and know that He always hears. I can't tell you how much He loves to hold us closer.

"I'm going to head downstairs. Think, talk, get some rest. I'll come back up to check on you when supper is ready."

With that, she gave my arm a last squeeze, stood up, and disappeared down the ladder.

Left alone, I laid down and curled in a ball, hugging my knees to my chest. She made it sound so easy. Prayer felt pretty one sided lately. In my head, I knew that it never was, and I also knew that He is always here for us and that He works everything out for His glory. But right then, I didn't *feel* it. Nor did I feel like praying. I knew I should, even though I didn't feel like it. Maybe I should just try to talk with Him anyway. Maybe I would put a little more effort into our relationship, be more intentional about getting out of the whirls of life to spend time with Him.

I didn't understand why He took Nollem from me, maybe I never would. But at least I would have Him. And maybe that would be enough. But at the time, it didn't ease much of the pain.

❧

I felt trapped, suffocated almost, the rest of the week long stay at Fraisa and Tolgar's home. Everyone was very understanding and kind, but I just wanted to be alone for even a mere hour. The loft wasn't enough, I could hear everything below, and they could hear everything I did, from the cot creaking to my muffled sobs. I longed to get out into the open country again, even if it was the grey barren country of Deceiver. I wanted to feel a fresh breeze against my face, I wanted to smell the earth, see just a tiny flower. But I wasn't allowed to go outside without a traveling buddy, preferably a guy.

Just about every day, I grabbed either Findal or Creedal and escaped from the city for a half an hour or so. It wasn't even close to being alone, but at least it was out of the muddy, smothering city. It was still winter beneath the perpetual cloud cover, so there wasn't a green thing in sight, much to my dismay.

Neither Findal nor Creedal and I ever spoke much on these outings. Once we got out in the open, they would hang back some. But I always felt their gaze trailing after me, watching me like an eagle would its young. The short half hour would pass too quickly and I would find myself back in the warm, most of the time crowded, living space.

In the last couple days, I tried to be more social, but usually failed in any attempt. My mind constantly drifted away from the conversation I had started.

On the final day, goodbyes felt slow and half hearted on my part. Then Grenith, Findal and I were finally headed back home.

❦

Dwin and Kattim took the news harder than Findal or Grenith had. Which made sense, they actually knew Nollem, much more than just a name and an association as my brother.

My efforts in prayer had begun to be a little rewarding. At least, it was much easier to talk with Him than it had been before. The more I reminded myself that I am loved by Him, so much so that He died for me, the more other things mattered less. I didn't care quite so much what others thought of me. I didn't care quite so much about my failures either. This was the beginning of living differently than I ever had before.

Training with Dwin was a much needed outlet of physical and some emotional energy. It also distracted me from thinking about Nollem, which was a relief. I found that keeping busy was a good distraction, but it by no means became my sole way to deal with grief. I had to let it out, not stuff it in.

But overall, I got back into a regular routine rather quickly. And it was nice. Nothing unexpected was planned, and nothing unexpected was going to happen.

Chapter 24
The Things I Get Myself Into...

At the end of six months total of training, Dwin and I went up to the old market place that we used as an arena like usual. It was mid April by now, and green things were just starting to appear. I was surprised that anything green actually grew in Deceiver's lands. But they did. Nothing very big, due to lack of sunlight, only small flowers and trailing, creeping vines. These vines slowly overtook the ruinous stone houses, turning dull grey and brown into fresh greens.

We didn't run this time, but walked along, laughing and smiling at the tiny bits of life sprouting up.

I think its fair to say that by now I was strong and fit again. Even stronger than before. Training had toned my muscles. And it felt amazing. For once I could run and keep up without being totally exhausted afterwards. Grenith, on the other hand, didn't do any training. She was busy getting caught up with everything that she had missed. She also never really got back to what I pictured as normal. She still had obvious traces of slavery. She couldn't keep up with us, and she would get tired easily. Dark circles under her eyes refused to leave, and she was still too thin.

I still feel for her, not being sure if she'll ever get completely well. But regardless, the physical shortcomings never affected her emotional energies. She was happier than I had ever seen her before. A new love of life blossomed in her and it spilled out in such joys that I wouldn't have believed if I hadn't seen it. She was way beyond the point of human happiness. She drew her strength from Shalom, and in that way she was much stronger than the rest of us.

She and Kattim got on very well, enjoying the time they spent together. I assumed that Grenith knew how to fight, but saw no evidence of it. I asked Dwin about it once, and he had said that yes, every Lightbearer was trained to fight in some capacity. Though some were more trained in certain skills, like Findal in maps. So I at least had the comfort of mind that she knew how to defend herself.

As the days progressed, Dwin and I did our usual training in the market square. One day at the end, Dwin proposed an idea that he and the others had formed for me. "Limira," he started slowly and thoughtfully. And I knew immediately that he was going to suggest something that wasn't really a suggestion.

He continued, "We've been thinking about your training." He saw my anxious expression and quickly said, "Oh! Don't worry, you're doing marvelously. But we had an idea. You see, when we were all taught, there was no place to practice all this, like for real. So we came up with a sort of 'final test.' In this, you'll go out alone, with provisions of course, and you'll have to find a location using a map. Then after you take notes of the surroundings and anything that looks interesting, you'll come back and report to me. It'll be a three to four day trip, depending on how disciplined you are. So, what do you think of the idea?"

I thought about it a second, at first being intimidated by the idea. It sounded rather scary, to be honest. But I said the exact opposite. "Oh! That sounds fun! When do I start? And what kind of weaponry do I get? And how much provisions can I have?"

"Woah, slow down. We'll go over the details in a second. Are you sure that you want to go through with this? There's bound to be some challenges, and there won't be anyone to help."

He must have seen through my guise of glad anticipation. I really was nervous about it. I couldn't be sure that my skills would hold up to the test. But I slowly nodded my consent, saying, "Yes, I'm sure. I think it will be a good test, and I'm willing to go through with it. So, that's that."

"If my opinion is of any help," Dwin offered, "I'm not worried about you at all. I think you've been well prepared and will have great success with this. Besides, we wouldn't have suggested it if we thought it was going to be dangerous. So it's a go then?"

"Yes," I said with much more confidence than I felt.

Dwin beamed with pleasure and clapped one of his big hands on my back. He exclaimed excitedly, "Great then! We'll get some things together for you, and you can start tomorrow."

He started walking back to the tunnel. I just stood there, thinking with surprise about what I had just agreed to. I started screaming at myself, my inward voices protesting my decision. What did you just do? Are you nuts, Limira? Did you really just agree to go out for three days and live off the land? Well, they did promise to give me some provisions, I argued in my defense. The opposing side lashed back: but knowing Dwin, he's probably only going to give you a knife and send you off on your way. You're an idiot to agree to such a thing!

But Dwin wouldn't be that mean, right?

"Limira!" Dwin's voice interrupted. He was standing at the edge of the market, staring back at me. "Are you coming?"

It was just then that I realized that he had left and that I hadn't gone with him. I quickly sprinted over to him calling, "Yes! Yes, I'm coming."

He gave me a strange inquiring look as I approached. I briefly replied, "I was lost in thought, that's all."

"Are you sure that you—"

"Yes!" I cut him short, "I'm sure that this is what I want to do. It'll be a good experience."

And that's what I told myself when we got back to the Den and told everybody. And that's what I told myself when I learned that they were only giving me a small loaf of bread and a water skin to live off of. Though they were going to give me a pot and some utensils for cooking—I would take anything I could get. And that's what I told myself when I was told that I had to pick my own weapons without Dwin's suggestions. And that's what I told myself all through the sleepless night that I passed prior to the big day. And that's what I told myself when I set out the next morning, saying goodbye. A chorus of farewells and good lucks sang out as I went.

It'll be a good experience. Sure...

Regardless, I had started, so there was no backing out now. I was equipped with a map, a compass, five matches, a sack with my "provisions"—if they could be called that—my short sword, and a small dagger. I had even been given a special set of clothes for this mission. They made sure that everything was dark greys and blacks. I kept my pants but got a new jerkin with half sleeves. It was a dark grey, of the same coarse wool material. I got new boots—well, new to me—and a wrapping cloak of sorts. It was more like a big warm scarf that wrapped around my shoulders and covered my back. It's hard to describe, but it was warm and that was the important part. And by now I was thoroughly used to boys pants and found them to be very comfortable.

Now I was really regretting this. I had never traveled alone before, much less expected to live well out in the wild. I was starting to wish that I had company. But I didn't, so I might as well not dwell on it. At least, that's what I told myself.

I passed out of the stony ghost of a town. I reached the ridge that Grenith and I had first stumbled over that night six months ago. Looking back, it seemed like a big nightmare, like it didn't really happen. I paused at the top, and glanced back over the grey ruins. It looked so desolate from here, but it held special meaning now that I knew what lay beneath it. It was such a contrast between its appearance and what it actually was.

But returning to the journey that I had to do, I remembered my instructions. I replayed them in my mind once more. First, get to the hill south of the base. Dwin described it and Grenith confirmed that it was this very one that we had first come over. Second, I was to look at the map that was given to me and read the directions it gave on the back. I was to follow the directions which, if I did it right, would lead me to my destination. Where I was supposed to end up was a small cottage or hut. Kattim suggested that I look for things such as what kind of crops or livestock they were raising. Also the number of occupants and their general living conditions. These were mere suggestions and it was made clear they wanted more information than that. Then I was supposed to bring back a detailed report of what I observed there.

It seems simple enough on paper—as you would say—but it was quite the challenge seeing how it was a three day trip. Besides, he made it clear that I wasn't to be seen, so even harder. It had been a long time since I last had to remain nothing but a shadow slipping by.

Overall, it was daunting.

I pulled out my map, in compliance with the first instruction. It was a piece of thick brown paper done in ink. It was an obvious copy of a section of a map, but I could tell that Findal had fun with it. I unfolded it and took a peek at what it mapped out. It was a simple copy, showing the old Lightbearer base, a few hills to indicate the terrain, the edge of the torched forest, and not much else. I was disappointed, hoping that he would have given me a few hints as to where I was supposed to go. I flipped it over and read the directions on the back:

First, go southeast till you come across a strange, large boulder formation.

Second, from there, go southwest till you find a pit. It's a great big pit, you can't miss it.

Third, from the edge of that, go east, southeast. When you cross over a stream, you'll know that you're close. Go just beyond the stream and you're there. Again, you can't miss it.

And that was all that consisted of the directions. I read them once, then read them over again. Just to make sure that I had got it right. I was having a hard time grasping that I, me, had to follow this and end up in the right place. I immediately decided to mark out my progress as I came to each land mark.

After a moment of thinking, I looked back at the first instruction. Southeast. I pulled out my compass, glad that they had allowed that at least. I struck out in the right, or so I hoped, the right direction.

The once dismal plains were bursting with green. Up close, it was obvious that not much green had grown, but if you looked over the stretching plains, it looked like a luscious green meadow. In the early morning, a light dew had spread over all the land, leaving everything sparkling and twinkling. The air was crisp and felt fresh. It was quite lovely, and I enjoyed the view as I went alone over them. It appeared that the rolling hills and flatlands would never end.

I suddenly felt very small and lonely. And figuring that I had nothing to lose, I broke out into a sprint, keeping a steady pace, like Dwin had taught me. The early morning air burned slightly in my lungs, but I was used to it and didn't mind too much. Eventually the cold air warmed up some. Around the middle of the day, I paused and took a drink. I wasn't sure what I should do next. I knew that I had to start thinking about what I was going to eat. So I kept my eyes pealed for edibles as I continued on. I paused to gather them whenever I found them, and I hastily stuffed them in my sack.

Every once in a while, I would pause to check my bearings and correct my course if necessary. The afternoon slipped by slowly and uneventfully. As the light faded from the dark clouds, I looked for a place to stay the night. I soon found a little niche, more like a small cove, in between some large rocks. Seeing how it would protect me from the wind and give me something to cover my back if I got attacked, I chose it and prepared to hunker down for the night. I started with setting down my sack and foraging for some tinder and burnable things. After traipsing over the smooth hills and collecting dried grass and such, I finally returned to my cove with both arms full of fuel.

Somehow, I managed to coax a flame out of them and started toasting some roots and a chunk of precious bread. I had found some berries on a few of the scraggly bushes that dotted themselves over the plains. Putting some of them over the piece of toasted bread, I enjoyed a little treat that I wouldn't have thought to do back at the Den. Mainly, I suppose, because I had more resources there and didn't have to make do with what slim provisions I had.

Overall, I think supper was a success. I mean, I didn't starve or die the next day so I must have done something right. After supper, feeling quite content, I piled on the rest of the dead grass and such to let them burn through the night. Curling up under my cloak, wrapping thing—which turned out to be much bigger than I thought—I scooted closer to the warm flames. Exhausted from the productive day, I fell asleep quickly. My final thought was that even though I felt alone in the cold dark night, I reminded myself that I never was.

Chapter 25
Of the Difficulties of Landmark Hunting

When I woke up early the next morning, a cold dew covered the ground and left a damp layer on my boots and cloak. The fire had long since faded into a pile of smothered grey. Stretching, I quickly got up, ate some roots from yesterday and took the last swallow of water from my bottle. I immediately wondered where the next stream would be. Just then I thought of looking at the map, to see if any were marked. I didn't remember seeing any, but that didn't mean much.

I pulled out the map, unfolded it and scoured it. It didn't take long to find that no streams were marked. At least, I hoped they weren't marked. I was rather disappointed, but was determined to keep a stiff upper lip through all this. After all, I was the one who got myself stuck in this.

I took one last look at the map, suddenly remembering that I was going to mark out my course. But so far, I had nothing to report because I had no clue where I was. I looked up, and glanced around. It was then that I noticed the enormity of the rocks that I had been sleeping by. They were like a dark shadow, jagged against the light grey sky. Rising high above me, they loomed overhead, frowning and standing solemnly guard.

Rock formation! This must have been what Findal was thinking of!

I flipped the map over and read the instruction:

First, go southeast till you come across a strange, large boulder formation.

Well, this was a strange and large looking pile of rocks out in the middle of nowhere. But was it *the* rock formation? I figured the only way to find out was to see if there was any other rocks around. Gathering my things up, I set them safely under a small ledge. I stowed my sack and sword, taking my dagger just in case. Hoping they would be safe, I then looked up at my next task: climbing to the top.

I had never done any rock climbing before, like never. It was kind of a scary thought, but that's what I decided must happen, so guess what I did? I went rock tumbling. Which is only different from climbing in the fact that I did more stumbling and tripping and falling than climbing.

Hoping to find a place where I could start, I hastily sought out a ledge low enough for me to reach. I felt up along some ledges, testing the depth. It took a while before I found someplace low and deep enough for me to feel confident enough to try. By then I was about a fourth of the way around the rock formation. It was all smooth and weathered rock, not to mention that my fingers were freezing.

Anyway, I found my hold, jumped and latched my fingertips over the edge. My feet left the ground and my fingers got a sudden strain. For a few seconds I just hung there, trying to get my head around the fact that I was actually doing this. Shaking myself out of my stupor, I pulled up, my fingers turning white. My muscles strained and my arms started to shake. I wasn't sure if I would make it. I dropped back to hanging, my arms straight. Mustering up for a big push, I gave one giant pull straining and grunting with the effort. I got far enough up there to put my elbow up and I pushed all my weight onto it, heaving myself up onto the foot wide ledge. I rolled over the edge, flopping on my back. Steadying my quick breathing, I lay there for a while. I shook my hands, trying to make them stop tingling.

I had made it! I could hardly think about anything except that for a few moments. I was feeling so proud of myself, I had defeated it! I was patting my back and praising my own effort.

Until I remembered that I still had the rest of the rock formation to climb. Glancing up, the sight doused my joy, and I immediately felt foolish for thinking how great I was.

Taking a last breath, I prepared myself for the next stage. Picking myself off the smooth stone, I looked around, seeking another handhold. There were none directly near me, so I moved down the narrowing ledge. I was soon at the very end where the once foot deep ledge was nothing but five inches before it dissolved into the rest of the vertical cliff. Right above this point, there were some jagged, narrow, nothing more than an oddball stone poking out here and there, handholds.

Cocking an eyebrow at the prospect, I looked up and down my route. I looked up and down again. Then I hopefully glanced to the side, praying for some new route to open up.

None did.

Ugh. Of course. It had to be this.

Sighing heavily, I sized up my situation again. My conclusion was that there was no way around it. I had to find out if there were any other rock formations around, and there was no other way to the top than this. I sighed again at my logical thinking, trying to find any excuse that I could get away with, except possible death.

None came that I wasn't already facing—I had forfeited my life when I started this entire journey. Steeling myself, I reached up and clutched at the nearest handhold. My other hand followed. I heaved myself up, scrambling for another handhold. I scraped my boots over the smooth surface, searching for anything to catch them on. I finally found a divot and stuck my toes in it. I bent my left foot at the toe using pure tension to keep it there. Feeling secure enough, I looked up in search of another handhold.

There, about a foot above me and to the left. Half swinging, half jumping, I stretched out and hooked my fingers around it. My left foot found some hold. Steady, I reached up again grabbing a tiny ledge. Once my hands were tightly gripping a hold, I would move my feet.

I slowly inched up the face of the stone. Eventually, I rolled over to the top of that rock, only to be surrounded on three sides by stone walls running straight up and down. The space I had now was only a foot wide and a foot deep.

I nearly melted right there. Thinking there was no way that I could ever do that, I sank against one of the sides to catch my breath. Mustering up courage and a slight sigh, I stood up and looked closer at my next obstacle. Upon rising, I could see that it wasn't totally vertical, but the slant wasn't very significant either.

Screwing my face into a frown, I reached up, feeling and looking for somewhere to hold onto. My search was unsuccessful, and I quite literally turned up empty handed.

Great, now I knew that the only way to get up this was going to be quite strenuous. It would require me stretching out and pressing against the sides. Spider climbing. Boy, oh boy.

Mentally preparing myself, I thought of all the worst case scenarios possible. Every one of them ended with either multiple broken bones, or death. But you know, I told myself, death wasn't all that bad. I would get to meet Shalom and live with Him. I smiled at the thought. Until I realized that the others would not know what had happened to me. They would come searching and they would find my body, if I had followed the directions correctly.

No, let's just go back to being with Shalom, that was much better.

But, the other option was that I could actually make it up, and live to see the next day. Regardless, I prompted myself to get moving so that I could get to the top and back down again in a timely manner.

Oh no... Back down.

My heart sank. I allowed a dozen overwhelming thoughts bury my hope before I shoved them aside and resolved to cross that bridge when I came to it. I wasn't going to worry about it before hand, there was no point. That's what I told myself anyway.

I took the one step fully into the corner, pressed my hands firmly on either side, jumped up and spread my feet a small distance below my hands. I awkwardly sat there, suspended and crunched together in mid air. I cautiously inched my hands up, then shuffled my feet up after them. Every muscle in my body was tight, straining to keep my balance.

My eyes were wide with horror that I might fall, and wonder that I hadn't yet. My heart was pounding in my chest, and I was certain that everyone within a mile's radius could hear it thumping away. A couple more shuffles up and I made it to the top, only to be faced with the difficultly of how to get over the edge. The walls stopped short at the beginning of the the next ledge. Gulping, I scooted my feet up closer under me, crumpling myself together. I was nearly doing the splits, which I had also never done before.

Suddenly, I was feeling very unprepared. Why couldn't Dwin have given a class on rock climbing? But then again, I would have thought that it was useless and probably wouldn't have paid attention anyway.

But back to the real problem. I was stuck. My feet and hands were only inches apart from each other. Okay, I told myself, brace with your feet, and reach up quickly to the top then pull yourself up. Simple.

Biting my lip, I pressed harder with my toes and released pressure on my hands. For the breathtaking, heart stopping moment that my hands were in the air, I thought that I would fall backwards. I could feel my body weight slowly sinking back. I panicked and scrambled wildly for the ledge I knew was there. The tips of my fingers brushed against it. Hard cold stone never felt so inviting. My fingers latched on with a vise like grip. My feet fell out under me, leaving me dangling by my fingertips. A small cry of dismay came out of shaky lips. All I could think of was the drop.

Holding on for dear life, I practically screamed when I felt my left hand slipping. Only the tips of my fingers remained on the ledge. I grimaced, fighting to keep my grip. In my repositioning, my stiff fingers slid over the edge in one smooth movement. My arm fell back and I hung awkwardly by one hand. Immediate strain applied to my remaining hold. I glanced down frantically judging the distance of my fall.

My stomach churned into a melted knot. It was a good twelve foot drop to the bottom of the tiny ledge I started the spider climb from, then the fall down the rock face below. The ground was far below me, and it wouldn't be a pretty landing.

I fixed my gaze on the ledge above me. I had to reach it. Swinging my hand up, I curved my fingers, stretching to get a hold of it. Success! My fingers latched around the lip. I crept them further around on the ledge, hoping for a firmer grip. My arms and fingers were quickly tiring.

It was now or never.

Taking a deep breath I pulled up as hard as I could, striving to get over the edge. Grunting with the effort I barely got a peek over the edge, when my strength gave out. I flopped back straight armed against the hard rock. Breathing heavily, I could feel both my sweaty fingers start to slide back. I whimpered and strained to lift myself up. My toes scraped against the smooth stone, trying to gain elevation. There! I could see over the edge! I slowly reached an elbow over the lip, planting it firmly on the hard stone. Forcing it to hold my weight, I heaved over the edge, landing on the smooth stone ledge.

Rolling over on my back, I just lay there. I let out a yell of triumph among my quick breaths. I lay there for some time until I regained my breath.

After a few minutes, I stood up and inspected my next route. From here, I saw the way was going to be a bit easier. The large smooth rocks were replaced by a bunch of smaller more pointed and jagged ones. I started out, clambering up them. They were still large rocks about as tall as myself, but all piled on top of each other.

As I climbed, I noticed that they were sharper too. I banged my knees, tearing holes in my pants, and acquiring a few cuts over my hands. But these injures weren't serious enough to stop me. As I got closer to the top of the giant mound of strange rocks, I grew more daring and even jumped from a few rocks to others.

Before long, I was at the very top. The first thing that I noticed was that it had a completely flat top. Its surface was smooth and neatly chiseled. In the very middle there was some sort of stone table that rose up conspicuously.

Climbing over the last edge, I stood up and peered about me. A cold wind blew over the flat top, tousling my dirty blonde hair. The dark grey cloud cover seemed much closer than it had ever been before. The grey covering moved lazily despite the wind. I took a few steps nearer to the center, intrigued by the small, round table. Wondering what it was for, I circled it slowly inspecting it closer. Around the perfectly curved base, there were strange marks and symbols. It almost looked like they might be lettering of some ancient script, but it could have been anything. The entire table and surrounding rock was a darker shade of grey than the rest of the stone.

It was then that I remembered my original task. I looked up immediately and scanned the sight that spread out before me like a real life map.

With the green returning, the plains and small rolls of hills were one blank sheet of green. It was only interrupted by occasional dots of brown where the scraggly bushes of thorns and such grew. The light green canvas was shaded in darker hues where there were either hills or more clouds to block the sun. No direct sunlight penetrated the dark cover that blanketed the entire scene. But I was used to it, so it didn't look unnatural.

Down below, I could pick out the faint course of a meandering stream. My heart skipped a beat in my excitement. That meant I could get more water! I took a few more steps nearer to the edge so I could trace it. I saw that it ran right by the base of the rock formation. It must have been on the opposite side of the formation because I didn't see it when I first came.

I could see for miles on end in each direction. It was breathtaking. I'd never before seen such a view in my life.

And, just as I suspected, there was no other rock formations in sight. But now I knew for sure and didn't have to keep second guessing myself.

Next was to get back down. I couldn't even guess what direction I needed next. I had left my compass down below so that wasn't an option.

I stared longingly out over the plains again, searching for the next landmark that I was given. Findal had said that it was a big pit, and I couldn't miss it. But unfortunately I couldn't remember which way it was, not that I could tell direction anyway. I went round and round in my mind for a few minutes. I finally gave it up concluding that I would just have to get back down and check.

Down.

That was going to be difficult. I certainly couldn't go back the way I came, I barely got up using that way. I looked all around the edges of the circular top. My eyes strayed back over that strange table that was as round as the floor it was sitting on. Then a thought struck me. If there was a table, and this was chiseled out by man, then there must have been an easier route to get up. Like maybe a path or something carved out of the sides.

Quickly walking to the edge, I peered over, looking for any signs of passage. Very soon and rather suddenly, I found what looked like a narrow pathway of deep steps. The first step was a foot below the rim of the large stage, making it invisible from standing on top. I thought it was rather clever, only I was so stupid not to find them before. It would have saved a lot of unnecessary trouble. But no, I had to do it the hardest possible way.

While mentally lecturing myself, I carefully proceeded down them. The stairs curved around a bend as they descended around the rock formation.

Slowing my pace, I cautiously rounded the blind corner. Uncertainty built up as I turned it, then deflated when I saw that there was nothing except more steps. But it was better safe than sorry. Just then the stairs grew shallower and closer together until they faded altogether into a smooth path. It just then struck me that it was strange that everything was so smooth, it was like a crew of men went over everything with chisels, rounding corners and sanding out bumps and rough parts.

That thought took my breath away and stoked my curiosity as to what this place was. I would have to ask Findal later.

I quickly made it down. About halfway, the path turned into switch backs so that was easy. I nearly ran down them in my eagerness to get on my way again. I had wasted enough time with all this.

When my feet touched grass again, I paused, relishing the feeling of stable, squishy ground. Then I had to wonder where I was in relation to my camp from the night before. I paused in my thinking, trying to remember and calculate my trek combined with where I had gone back down and where I was now. I got lost in the tangles of thoughts and came up with nothing. But then, I remembered the stream. It was on the opposite side where I came up, so if I could find that I could just pick a side. I remembered where it was in relation to where I had come down the path. I needed to go to the right.

I turned dramatically on my heel, setting a steady pace in that direction. In a few minutes I found the stream. It was about four feet wide, rather shallow, had the clearest water I had ever seen and the most refreshing flavor I had tasted in a long while. I was surprised to find such a fine stream in the middle of Deceiver's land.

Once I drank my fill, I set out again to my right, so that I would pass nearly all around the entire formation. I followed alongside the stream for a bit, then peeled off to the right of it. Before long, I found the little niche that I had slept in the night before. My sack was in its proper place, as well as my sword.

Strapping my sword on my back, where I had it before, I flexed my shoulders and picked up my sack.

Now to go back to the stream. I felt like I was traversing half over the world with all this back and forth. I was feeling the time crunch, it being at least noon by now. But what could I do?

I reached the stream, filled my bottle, took another long drink, crossed it, and set out on my way again.

It was just then that I remembered that I had to change directions. All that effort to identify a landmark had apparently distracted me from my real mission. I stopped right there, knelt on the grass and pulled out my map. Luckily, earlier that morning, I had remembered to place in my sack a bit of charcoal in a small square of cloth.

Unfolding my map, I spread it out on my knee, guessed how far I had gone, and marked it out. I put a small dot for the rock formation. Then I looked on the back for the next instruction.

Second, from there, go southwest till you find a pit. It's a great big pit, you can't miss it.

Southwest. I pulled out my compass and laid it on my other knee near the map. I traced with my finger the direction. I had no clue where the "pit" was, but I paused my finger on the map a little ways down. I glanced at the back again, reading the next instruction.

Third, from the edge of that, go east, southeast. When you cross over a stream, you'll know that you're close. Go just beyond the stream and you're there. Again, you can't miss it.

I traced my finger over the map and frowned.

Chapter 26
Of What I Saw at the Destination

Wait a minute... first I go down, then to the left, then cut over to the right again. I could cut out that entire little jig jog by just going southeast. But, then again, I had no idea if there was anything of importance in going southwest. Findal had put it there for a reason, so it must have been important.

I determined to follow the directions to the letter, and maybe on the way back cut some corners. I checked for southwest on my compass, and looked in that direction. I couldn't see anything, but that didn't mean much.

Stuffing my things back away, I set out.

It was a rather droll trip, and it took me about four hours of loping until I found the "pit" Findal was talking about. I took one look at it and said to myself, "Yep, can't miss it."

I was standing on the brink of a deep pit with steep sides about forty to fifty feet down. The ugly earth was dug out in an oval shape. An old, odious stench rose from it. And I soon saw why.

It didn't take much hunting to discern piles of unearthed skeletons and remnants of bodies half covered with earth. It was one huge mass grave. White bones protruded conspicuously against the dark soil. There were also more fresh bodies dumped over the earth that no one had bothered to cover.

My face contorted with disgust. I didn't stay long, not long at all. As soon as I could rip my eyes away from the sight, I backed up and shook my head, trying to clear away the sights. It reminded me all too much of Chimel and Bilham. Their still forms, deathly white and in unnatural positions.

I suddenly couldn't help but wonder if Nollem was among them, just dumped down there to rot. He was certainly dumped *somewhere* like all those below, if not here.

Unbidden tears filled my eyes. I couldn't imagine finding him in a pit like this. I wondered if we were missed by our parents, if they worried about us, if they even cared that we had disappeared. They didn't even know Nollem was gone. They probably thought I was as well. It had been long enough. Had they sent out search parties for us? Were notices put out to watch for us? Would they find Nollem's body shoved rudely in some hole and assume that I had come to the same end? Did they care? Did anyone back home care?

The tears slid down my cheeks, one after another. Soon all I could think about was Nollem. In all these six months that I had been in the old base, no word had come. Findal and an old man, Brene, were in communication on a weekly basis. Brene gave Findal reports of the doings of the Lightbearers, and Findal would tell us. Each week, no news of Nollem. Parties were still searching.

If I had had it my way, there would be no parties, no word, and no raised hopes just to be dashed each week. No, it wasn't even dashed hope anymore, it was the throbbing pain of reminder, like the reopening of an old wound. A reminder that he wasn't here. The news would never be any different, only the same fresh reminder.

Within the first week of my return from Moneth, Dwin and I had a blow up about it. I dreaded the day when Findal would come back with the latest news. It came at supper, and the news of no news was shared. My face burned with anger, and I slammed my clenched fist onto the table top. Findal had barely got the words out of his mouth before I yelled at him, "Why?! Why are people still looking for him?! All they'll ever find is a heap of bones! They're wasting their time!"

Dwin sighed, looking up at me, "Limira—"

I bitterly cut him off, spitting spiteful words at him, "Don't! I know what you're going to say. But there is no hope! Regardless of what you all think, I'm holding onto reality. I can't afford to entertain the thought that someday he's going to come walking through that door over there!" I pointed a furious finger at the entrance to the Den. Hot tears were burning my eyes, threatening to spill out the corners.

"Limira," Dwin tried again, his voice firm, his eyes flashing, "You don't know if what Alletta said is true—"

"I saw, not only heard, I *saw* her say it. There's no way that it couldn't be true. She meant every word of it, grinning and cackling like the fiend she is! You all can think he's still out there, but I know the truth." Rising in a fury from the table, I stormed into my room and sobbed on the edge of my cot for the rest of the evening.

None of them had given up hope yet, but I had. I wiped my face with the back of my sleeve, leaving wet marks on it. I sniffed a couple of times telling myself that I had to get back to the mission. I couldn't let my personal feelings get in the way.

I pulled out my map and compass again, checked my bearings and started off in the right direction. I tried to dispel those nagging thoughts about Nollem, but I couldn't stop thinking about him. Where was his body now? What kind of animals had witnessed his death with pleasure? What did Alletta have against him anyway? What kind of blind hate could prompt someone to do that? How long had Nollem spent in agony? Why him? Out of all of us, why him?

All of these questions remained unanswered. I soon tired of asking them, finding all the doubts and sorrow to be overwhelming. Then a phrase that Dwin had muttered so many times entered into my mind: *"It's out of my hands."*

Suddenly it made sense. Dwin wasn't the raving lunatic that I thought he was. Nollem's death was out of my hands and in Shalom's. Shalom knew what had happened to him, and He had never left him alone, wherever he was. Now Nollem was with Him, far beyond my reach, far beyond every sorrow and hurt, far beyond anything separating him from his King.

That was what I continued to remind myself of and sometimes it helped. But today it didn't. I missed him too much.

❦

Evening was falling, the light fading from the clouds. The land grew darker than what it already was. I began looking for a place to sleep. While I was searching, I began to worry about the amount of time I had already spent. I was just completing day two and it was supposed to take three days round trip. So I might be a little late. But I had spent a morning climbing the rock formation, wasting a bunch of time.

I thought about it further as I gathered together fuel for the fire. I continued on a little more and stumbled across a stream. And I mean, literally, nearly stumbled over a stream. If I had taken one step more I would have fallen straight into the cold water.

That goes to show how distracted I was.

I decided to bunker down for the night by the stream. I coaxed a fire, ate some food and wrapped up for the night. I fell asleep with the thought of, "I wonder if this is the stream that Findal was talking about...?"

When I woke up enough to think about actually getting started with my day, my first thought was to check my map. I scoured it, looking over the lines that I had added. I could only guess and trust that this stream was the one that Findal meant.

I ate a quick bite and set off again, eagerly anticipating finding the place that was my destination. Dwin had described it as a hut or a small shack. That should be easy enough to find out here. I kept my eyes alert looking over the plains and found myself hardly watching where I was going. I *might have* tripped over some obvious obstacles like a large rock, a deep hole, and a couple of scrub bushes. All the training that Dwin had poured into me could never quite cure my clumsy ways.

After a few slips and close calls, I finally started paying more attention to my path. It was then that I noticed the grass and other dead and live things were diminishing and giving way to dusty, dry earth. It took on a reddish hue.

I glanced up and saw a ridge line, it had a few bumpy spots that stuck out like a sore thumb against the grey sky. The ridge spread far on either side. I figured it was nothing more than a large, notable hill. But boy was I wrong.

As I drew nearer, the ground sloped up. My curiosity fully roused, I craned my neck up to see over the crest. At first all I could see was the dull grey clouds, then I saw the horizon far in the distance, dim with haze. I was nearly at the top.

It was a good thing that I was watching where I was going, otherwise I might have walked right over the edge. The hill turned out to be a full scale, top notch, tallest and sheerest I'd ever seen, cliff.

Halting in my tracks, I stared wide eyed at the drop for a moment. My only thoughts were if I had fallen over... Fill in the blank yourself; that's what my mind did.

When I forced my thoughts out of what could have happened, I noticed for the first time what looked to be a small establishment at the very bottom. There were a few buildings nestled against the cliff face. Well, as I took a second glance, I could hardly call them buildings. They were more like shacks and huts, which fit Dwin's description perfectly.

I smiled at my success, inwardly throwing a victory party for following the directions correctly. I figuratively patted myself on the back, got my hand shook and a metal given to me. I, naturally, felt proud.

The glorious moment ended when the next part of my mission struck me. I was supposed to go down there and spy, then get back up and back to the base. My mission was only half done, if that.

The problem of getting down was the first thing that stared right back at me. I would have to find a place to climb. At least this time I could say that I had a little practice at it.

Deciding to go to the right first (because right is always right), I picked my way along the edge, hoping to spy out a path before I wasted another whole morning. After some long searching, and me nearly giving up the idea that right is always right, a path presented itself. It was nothing fancy, far from it.

At best, it was a mere goat trail that snaked all the way down the cliff in switchbacks. It offered no cover whatsoever, but I wasn't about to be picky. It was better and quicker than having to climb down the face of the cliff, fully exposed and in constant danger of falling.

I started the steep trek down, carefully bracing myself and trying not to tumble forward. Suddenly, I wished that I was wearing pale red or at least tan clothing, but no, it had to be black and greys. Maybe I should wait for the cover of darkness? No, I would waste an entire day and be gone that much longer.

But really, I crouched to contemplate, was this *really* a good idea to do in broad daylight? I would have more chances of discovery now, and it was rather risky. But imagine me coming down this at night, in the total dark, to spy on some uninhabited remnants of a farm. That sealed the deal. During the day it was.

Besides, it wasn't like there were very many people around either. In fact, I had seen no sign of life anywhere.

Eventually, I made it down the cliff path in one piece and that was when the real fun started. Going into stealth and sneaking mode, I crouched as low to the ground as I could and stole from one bush—which wasn't much more than a bunch of twigs congregated together—to another. I dodged from one rock to another, then to a corner of the farthest outbuilding, more like out-shack. I had a big grin on my face. I hadn't done anything like this in forever, and to be honest, I enjoyed it more than I thought I would.

I soon lost my smile. Things started getting a little more serious when I heard a sound from the largest shack closest to the face of the cliff. I paused, uncertain if I had actually heard it or not. Could someone actually live here?

I crept closer, watching my footing, skirting brush and loose pebbles. I was still twenty feet from the hut that the sound had come from. I had checked all the other buildings as I went, all were empty of anything other than rubble and dusty, discarded things. I stole behind a small tri-cornered tent, half of its cloth covering pulled to one side. My eyes darted around, landing on a rag fluttering in the wind and a weed waving. Everything else was still.

I swept the horizon. There! In the center a column of dust rose against the dull sky. I strained to pick out who, or what, was at the front. In a large pack, slightly spread out to make them look bigger, was a group of tall, burly men. They were coming this way!

Catching my breath, I dashed behind the large shack, hoping that they wouldn't find me. There was just enough room for me to squeeze in, crouching between the wooden slats of the shack and the firm red earth. There were large gaps between the slats, and I peered in.

Through my limited gaze, I was surprised to see that people were indeed living there. Not just people, but a family. The parents looked young, maybe in their mid thirties. They had three young children between the ages of maybe five and two. It was hard to tell, all were frightfully undersized, likely the result of lack of food. The children's faces were hollow and thin. They glanced cautiously about with a vacant look in their eyes. Piled into a corner, they all huddled together. The woman was of the shrinking type, and she glanced nervously about her. The man, who was busying himself with something in the far corner, occasionally looked about him with an authoritative air. A rasping sound came from his lap. It seemed that he was the only confident one, yet there was something about him that I didn't like. He had a cold manner and snapped at the children when they whimpered. The woman would then send a reproving word and he would apologize in an angry tone.

I soon realized that he was stressed and worried about them, not angry. They had seen the pack of men coming their way.

The woman shuffled to the corner and wrapped her arms protectively over the children. It was then that I saw her face. I recoiled, half so she wouldn't see me and half out of shock. She had the definite mark of a Between on her. She had an ugly, mean look that was only softened by motherly affection. She had a fungus-like pocket of skin growing over one side of her face and she had discolored marks over her arms and legs. She was most certainly a Between.

I slowly peered back through the crack, and caught a glimpse of her husband. He too was a Between. This was something that I wasn't expecting..

I continued to watch as the group of men drew closer, and the only way I could tell was the reactions of the man in the corner. He grew tenser with every moment.

I soon found the source of the rasping sound. The man in the corner was sharpening a knife. Occasionally, I caught the cold glint of it. It appeared to be their only defense.

I grew more engrossed with their story. It was like I wasn't even there, but watching from behind a window. I soon forgot I was in danger too.

Searching for anything else they might be using as defenses, I saw the door had a bench leaned up against it. All the windows had some sort of covering over them, whether it was an old shirt or just a torn bit of cloth spread over them.

And that was about it. I and they knew that they didn't stand a chance.

Before I knew it there was a considerable amount of stomping outside. The children began whining which was quickly hushed by the mother.

Suddenly there was a bang and the entire hut shook with the force. The door bowed in, and two panels splintered around a fist that protruded through the door. The children screamed. The husband jumped up brandishing his dagger fiercely.

The hand disappeared, and burst through the hole again. Iron-like fingers latched around the boards. With one yank, he ripped the entire door out of the frame. The mother gave a cry of dismay, and the children began to weep openly. The first hulking figure stooped through the doorway, a towering silhouette ringed with dim light.

The first thing I saw was his eyes, glittering with a cold light and wickedly finding pleasure in the whimpers he heard within. As soon as the first big form came through another took its place and entered. Then another and another.

Once the first came in, I recognized that it was a Vaudian. I shuddered, remembering my experiences with them.

At that moment, the man who had been waiting by the door jumped at him, knife blade shining as it flew through the air.

With a grunt the Vaudian caught the man's wrist midair and gave it a savage twist. The man cried out in pain as he was wrenched around, his arm pinned cruelly behind him.

Six other men had filled the small hut, some Vaudians, some Between. They made straight for the woman and children in the corner. Their grasping hands tore the woman away. Her screams and sobs rent the air in horrible spasms.

The man being held by the Vaudian struggled and screamed for them not to hurt his family. The Vaudian grew impatient, he drew a dark bladed dagger and in one fluid motion swiped it across the man's throat. He fell limp to the floor, a pool of scarlet staining the dust redder.

The woman screamed an anguished cry as she rushed over and pawed at her husband's limp form. The children just sat there, squished together, staring wide eyed at the scene unfolding before them.

As the woman was sobbing over the fallen form of her husband, a Between slunk up behind and plunged a dirk into her back. She crumpled over.

I clapped a hand over my mouth to stifle the cry that threatened to come out. I watched breathlessly, my eyes glued to the horrible scene of destruction.

The children wailed to see their mother so. The oldest of them tried to put on a brave face for the rest of them, tears still streaming down his face. He defiantly slid the back of his hand over his face and stood up, puffing out his chest. The Between and Vaudians laughed at the sight. They stood there mocking and jeering at him. More tears slid down his streaked cheeks.

With one final laugh, they scooped up the young ones. Holding them in their strong arms, they rushed back out of the hut. I watched as they fanned out, overturning everything in their path. As they ravished the farm, they set the slouching structures ablaze with the touch of a torch.

I watched in revulsion as they moved through the small farm. One of them came back to the shack I was hidden behind. I was so shocked that I didn't realize the danger until the whole front of the dwelling was consumed in flames. I stood up abruptly, shrinking as far against the cliff wall as I could get.

To my relief, it was the last hut they set on fire, and they left without watching the spectacle. They ran off in the direction they came, leaving with the youngsters and anything else of value that they found while pillaging.

As soon as I dared, I slipped out from behind the burning shack. The roof collapsed as I slipped to a boulder. I crouched behind it, catching my breath, feeling like I might vomit. Choking smoke burned my eyes and lungs.

My vision blurred and the world rocked before me. I tried to get a hold of myself, knowing that this wasn't the place for it. I couldn't stay here. I had to go.

Stumbling to my feet, I leaned on the boulder for support. Forcing myself to move, I staggered unsteadily back in the general direction that I came. I hugged the cliff side. Out of pure fear and delirium, I risked furtive glances over my shoulder, afraid of pursuit.

I had to get away.

Somehow I managed to get back up the mountainous trail and back onto the familiar rolling slopes of the plain. I tumbled into a heap in the dip of a small knoll. My frame shook with sobs. I was gasping for air with tears streaming down my face. Never before had I witnessed such a horrific scene. Such cruelty and unfeeling that I couldn't comprehend. I hadn't realized that I cared so much for life, that I would cry over the loss of it. They were strangers too, people I had never met. They were even Between!

But that didn't matter any more, all life mattered to me. The destruction of it was grieving. They were so innocent, those children. What had they done to anger the Vaudians? What had any of them done?

The answer was nothing. They had done nothing but been there. Those men didn't need any other reason than their hate for life.

I cried for a long time.

After an immeasurable amount of time passed, I finally got a hold over myself. I was all cried out, feeling exhausted and worn down. I fell asleep just as a headache began to come on.

When I woke up, light was just beginning to fade from the sky. I picked myself up off the ground, took a brief check of my bearings, and set my course. This time I was just heading northwest, it being the direct route.

The scene replayed before my eyes on repeat. Each play only instilled my former feelings all the more.

Then the thought struck me—I had never before valued life so much. When did this love start? I couldn't pinpoint the time, place or exact situation, but I knew that it must have been during training. The more I learned about Shalom and His ways, the more I marveled and loved Him. I suppose that love was spilling over on His creation too. I saw the beauty in ashes and bones, seeing new life possible.

Part 4

Chapter 27
The Unbearable News

The journey back to the old Lightbearer base was uneventful and spanned a day and a half. I could hardly wait to see everyone again. It seemed like an eternity since I had been among them and I missed their loving company.

Once I got underground, I ran to the Den anticipating a warm welcome. I burst into the cozy, inviting room that had grown to be my home. Before I turned the corner, I could smell some lovely stew brewing over the fire and soft bread baked to perfection. My eyes darted around the room and found everyone to be seated or lounged about, each doing something of their own invention. Kattim was bent over some mending near the fire. Findal was draped dramatically over a bench, staring at the ceiling and tracing shapes and pictures in the air with an extended finger. Dwin was whittling on a chunk of wood; it was small in his hand, and I couldn't tell what it was. In another corner, Grenith was pouring over a book, looking anxious and tense as her eyes darted over the pages.

All their quiet occupations were soon abandoned and forgotten as they tore from their places in joyous triumph over my return. A thousand words of gleeful greeting were exchanged between us, and even more knowing and expressing looks given and returned.

It was nearly supper time, and Kattim and Grenith flew about serving it up. In a jiffy we were all seated around the familiar table with steaming bowls of wonderful smelling stew. I suddenly had a new appreciation for real food.

I was soon bombarded with requests for my tale of the last few days in explanation of my being late. They told me that they had been dying with worry ever since the three days had been spent. All, except Dwin of course. He loudly clarified that he had "no concern for me," that I could "handle anything" on my own with his training under my belt.

I laughed heartily at his confidence and proceeded to tell about my trip. I retold everything as best I could, only purposefully holding back my reaction after witnessing the ordeal. I couldn't just then tell them in depth what I felt, but I did retell the sadness and horror of the entire thing.

When I finished, there was a silence that fell over the table of solemn reflection. Overall, the mood had been the same throughout the tale, only interrupted by great hoots of laughter over my rock climbing skills, or lack thereof. Many jokes at my expense were made off that predicament for a long time after. It seems that I will forever be stuck as the worst rock climber ever.

Everyone was momentarily lost in their own thoughts, each either staring at the grain of the wooden table or picking at their hands distractedly. I was glad when Grenith interrupted the growing awkward silence by exclaiming, "Oh!" and looking so excited and eager that I thought she might burst.

Suddenly, as if this outburst reminded them of something important, everyone around the table exchanged winks, excited nods, and all knowing looks filled with joy and expectation.

Cocking an eyebrow, I looked quizzically at each of them attempting in vain to find out what they knew that I obviously didn't. My searching gaze returned and settled on Grenith's face brimming with uncontainable joy.

"You won't believe it!" she exclaimed vaguely, but so unfeigned that she leaned over the table towards me on her elbows. "You just won't believe it!"

I gave her a blank expression with only one question etched over it. "What?" I asked with caught breath. I hardly knew what they were talking about, but their excitement overflowed to me. Everyone else had leaned in closer and were staring at me to catch my expression when I heard the news.

Grenith blinked in elation and blurted out in short staccato sentences, "We've got news! Word was brought by Findal. He got it from his contact, you know the old man who occasionally comes by, Brene. Two days ago. Nollem's been found, Limira! He's been found!"

My jaw dropped with incredulity. A crushing weight of shock and sadness overwhelmed me as I thought of the remains they had found. Tears welled up, blurring my vision. My shoulders drooped. I hardly dared to ask where and what was left of him. I didn't even want to know what his condition was. I knew that Alletta had spoken truthfully about this. I *knew*. Why was this so hard to hear? I hadn't entertained even the slightest hope, so why was my heart crushed like never before? Staring at the grains on the table, I barely uttered, "Do my parents know?"

There was a slight pause before Findal replied hesitantly, "Well... no."

I nodded my head numbly. It was too soon before anyone could have gotten to Monare Plem. "Where is he laid?"

"Laid?" Findal asked, complete confusion is his voice. "He's alive, you goose!" exclaimed Findal with a laugh.

Those first two words rang in my ears, yet seemed not to go any further. Alive? No. That couldn't be right. Could he really be alive? I looked Findal straight in the eye. The words formed slowly on my lips, "Are you... are you sure he's alive?"

Findal laughed merrily, "Why would you ask such a question? Would we look so excited if he wasn't?"

"No, I suppose not," I replied slowly and soberly. "It's just, Alletta... she said he was dead."

Dwin smiled reassuringly, "But he's alive, Limira. She lied to you. He's alive."

As the thought sank in, thoughts of anger and shame filled my mind. How could I have let her dupe me? Why was I so stupid to believe her? All this time, I've insisted he was gone. I would have halted all search for him if I had had my way. All this time I've been wasting away in self pity and sorrow when I could have been putting more effort into finding him. He could be half dead because of me. No matter where he was, I had to get to him. I would waste no more time, so much had already been spent.

Kattim solemnly continued with more details, "He's been found in the dungeons of Dol Guliab. Alive, but in poor condition, as expected."

"We have to go get him," I blurted with blind urgency. I half stood from the bench, saying, "I'll get some things together. We'll need—"

"Hold up," Dwin interrupted, grabbing my arm and pulling me back into my seat. "That's the last thing we need to do, be all hasty and enter without a plan and proper provisions."

"Yeah," chimed in Findal, "this *is* Dol Guliab we're talking about here. It's not just a simple little outpost of Deceiver's, this is Deceiver's palace."

"Findal's right," joined Kattim, "we'll need some serious planning if we're going to get in and out with our lives."

Grenith smiled slightly at me, "Four to one. Looks like you're overruled."

I slumped on the bench, defeated.

"Besides," Dwin added, "You're hardly in the condition to be out and about. In case you haven't noticed, you're a bit thinner than usual. And while you're getting some meat on those bones, we'll be making a plan. First, we have to get into the dungeon without being seen. Then we have to get Nollem, he'll probably need to be carried, get him out and escape back down the mountain without being slaughtered by hoards of Vaudians and Orodumes. And then we'll need to get back here carrying Nolem and without leading Deceiver's men directly to the base."

Everyone fell into a dreary silence at the prospect. Findal sighed, bemoaning, "How come everything is much simpler on paper than actually played out?"

There was a chorus of agreements, then Dwin slowly said, "Well, it's a four day ride there, and... Findal, do we have any maps of Dol Guliab? I know it's two mountains sidled together, but where are the dungeons located?"

Findal screwed his face up in obvious thought. All eyes were fixed on him. "Uhh," he finally sighed out, "We'd have to look in the map room... which, would be a mess. Yeah, big mess. But," he added with a hint of hope, "we can try it."

With a general consent reached, we—more like they—decided to tackle it in the morning, seeing how it was getting late already. They all ganged up on me and force me off to bed under the pretext that I "must have had an exhausting day," and that I "must be completely worn out." I protested with all the wits and words I could conjure up. Though I epically lost the battle, I went down with a fight. As I was whisked into my room by Kattim and Grenith, I managed to catch myself in the doorway and scream out my final threat to my much amused friends, "You may have won the battle, but I will win the war! Let it be known that I surrender under protest!"

While Grenith and Kattim settled me in for the night, my threats melted into pleas, and my pleas melted into grumblings. My motto, which I kept up even as they went out the door, was a pitiful groan of, "If only you guys would stop raining on my sunshine..."

But in all truth, I really was tired and worn down from my journey. Even with the excitement of Nollem being alive, I drifted into a deep sleep and slept the entire night soundly.

"Why didn't you wake me?!" I exclaimed indignantly, a spoon full of runny porridge frozen in mid air halfway between the bowl and my mouth. I had just been told the time.

I was sitting at the table with Dwin and Findal across from me, their places void of any breakfast food stuff. Kattim and Grenith were busily cleaning up from the morning meal.

With a comical expression written over his face, Findal spread his hands wide and appealed in their defense, "It's best that you got as much sleep as possible. You were obviously tired enough. We thought it best if you woke up on your own."

Deflating slightly, I admitted, "Well, yeah, I'll give you that." Then after a moment of reflection, I fired up again, "But you could have awakened me *before* noon! We have things to do, plans to make, Nollem to rescue!"

Dwin, a silly grin over his face, reasoned, "It's important that you're back in shape, otherwise we'd have to leave you behind, or we would have two people to carry back. And we all know that it would slow us down and endanger all of us."

I sighed and avoided having to say anything further by filling my mouth with porridge. But I did manage a rueful glare at Dwin which plainly told of my sentiments. I inwardly fumed that he made too much sense! He couldn't be argued with because he was right, and he knew it and I knew it.

Dwin smiled at my antics. Teasingly, he leaned over to Findal and said in fake private conference to him, "Now if only Limira over there would hurry up, we might be able to get to the map room in a timely manner."

While Dwin was speaking, Findal over exaggerated and emphasized large, business-like nods of his head, throwing disapproving, authoritative scowls at me.

Hearing Dwin's remark doubled my excitement and efforts to finished breakfast. I hastily spooned the runny porridge from bowl to mouth, slopping more over my chin and the table than actually getting it into my mouth.

Less than two minutes later, I wiped my chin and pushed the white streaked bowl away from me.

Dwin and Findal had retained their comical critic airs. As I pushed my bowl away, Dwin snapped down his index finger as if it was a stop watch. He exclaimed in a thick voice, "By jolly, she's got it! Downed that entire bowl in one minute and fifty-eight seconds flat."

Findal skeptically leaned over and peered into the bowl, inspecting it with his authoritative eye. After a moment, he declared his final conclusion in an equally solemn yet comical voice, "You're right there, by George. She's actually done it! Broke the world record that one. Better write it down, mate."

Kattim and Grenith were doubled over laughing; they had been concealing snickers during the entire interview. I frowned, not at all enjoying the joke at my expense.

My frown only made things worse. Dwin and Findal fell over each other in laughter at their little charade and my response. Their laughter was contagious and my frown slowly melted into a slight smile. Then before I knew it, I was laughing as heartily as the others.

Once we settled down enough to breathe, we left the cozy confines of the Den, and set out for the mysterious and long forgotten map room. Evidently, Findal knew where it was, maps being his most avid interest. Findal also had an extensive knowledge of locations and their main points of history, as I soon learned.

After traversing through a head spinning amount of tunnels, twists, and turns, we landed ourselves before an old, dusty, wooden with iron pins and bolts, door. It's safe to say that it was a traditional medieval door, cobwebs and squeaky hinges included.

While Findal wrestled it open, he admitted that he got lost the first couple of times that he tried to find this particular room, and that he had to do a full body slam to open the door. With the added help of Dwin, the door gave way to admitting us, but only with many protesting groans.

Dust swirled up from the floor by the violent draft we created. Our light caught the particles and made them gleam. Cold air, the type that seeps into your bones, wafted out to greet us with an icy reception. The room seemed like a black hole, like open jaws waiting to devour us. I could see nothing beyond the reaches of our torch.

Findal, torch in hand with Dwin following, entered into the abyss.

Hesitating and being left behind by the light, I quickly stepped after them, trailing in the shadows.

Chapter 28
Digging amongst the Dust

I glanced cautiously and uncertainly to either side of me. I half expected to have some unnameable creature come hurtling out of the darkness to attack me. I tried to suppress the feeling, but I couldn't shake it.

Keeping an eye on Findal, Dwin, and the bobbing light ahead of me, I tried to keep up and watch my back at the same time. I wasn't succeeding by a long shot. I walked straight into Dwin, colliding with his warm woolen jerkin. Startled out of my wits, I recoiled, closing my eyes tight and throwing up an arm to shield my head. My mind jumped to the conclusion that I had run into a Vaudian.

Dwin turned around to find me cowering and cringing at his elbow. I think I startled him with my reaction because he stared at me for a moment, clearly surprised. He gently reached out and laid a hand on my raised elbow.

Flinching under his touch, I slowly opened my eyes, half expecting to see the towering form of Master Abburn and half amazed that it wasn't.

Our gaze met when Dwin had lowered my elbow away from my face. His look was steady and clam with a hint of questioning. My frightened, wild eyes calmed when I saw that it was him. I suddenly felt ashamed and embarrassed. My crazy mind had run away with me.

Dwin looked more concerned than anything else and asked in a low whisper, "You okay, Limira?"

"Yeah, I'm fine," I nodded briefly, standing straight and attempting to look normal.

Just then, a bright light ignited ahead of us and a little to our left. Findal was clearly visible in the light. He had touched his torch up in a groove in the wall, slightly below the ceiling. Quickly the fire spread along the track, running like a tidal wave all around the upper edge of the walls until it reached to other side of the doorway. The flames illuminated the edges of the room brilliantly, but left the center slightly dimmer.

My gaze was directed to what lay below the strip of light. All I could see was bookshelves; the walls were lined from the floor to a few inches below the fire groove. The shelves were packed with scrolls and folded sheets of paper crammed together. The papers were yellowing and torn with a great deal of dusty webs clinging to them.

While I was absorbed in the enormity of maps, Findal had crossed to the center of the room with the torch. The bounding light revealed an equally dusty and webbed, iron chandelier. Directly below the large chandelier, an even larger, square table sat, completely buried under stacks and piles of assorted maps. It had a few unlit candles in dishes sitting under inches of brown dust. Lighting the chandelier, Findal returned to near the door and placed the torch in a sconce.

The chandelier finished wreathing the room in light, illuminating everything from floor to ceiling. It was perfect for a map room.

Lost in the thoughts of so many maps, I completely forgot about the incident with Dwin just a minute ago. I wandered over to the wall and gently, reverently fingered the pages as I went down the shelves.

Dwin's inquiring voice drew my attention away, and I looked to see Findal and Dwin standing near the table. Both were looking despairingly at the amount of maps we would have to pick through.

"So," Dwin asked slowly, "what are we looking for and how do we find it?"

I wasn't sure that I wanted to hear the answer, it all seemed so overwhelming to actually find anything in this mess.

Findal took a moment to think before he answered, "Well, considering the age and extensiveness of this collection," it was obvious that he was extremely proud to be the sole caretaker of such a treasure horde, "I would say that we should try to find a more recent map of Dol Guliab. Which means that it would either be on the table, or on the shelves on this side of the door." He pointed and waved his hand over the far right wall which was interrupted by the dark door.

I suggested, "Wouldn't we need a map of the dungeons as well? Is there one?"

Findal struck a pointed finger in the air as he turned to me with a triumphant manner. "Yes, and there is." He got that certain look about him that I knew he was soon to go off on a long spiel of knowledge. He often got into that mood when he showed me maps and such in the Den that he had retrieved from this very room. He had never actually brought me here before, always giving his lectures in the comforts of the Den. He smiled knowingly, cleared his throat (another such sign that he was about to begin a capital lecture on his most loved passion. As I said earlier, maps are his thing), and started with an expressive voice, "Back in the day, long ago, Dol Guliab was not inhabited by Deceiver. It was actually built by men and they called it Dol Wenaith, meaning 'twin wealth.' They carved extensive mansions and palaces out of the mountain side and mined the earth for precious jewels and metals. They were very prosperous in their industries. But an inward feud broke out, dividing the two mountains. one side wanted to continue mining, and the other wanted start creating the largest library ever complied. That's when Deceiver got his chance and took them over. He entered in and joined the two sides of men with one purpose. Give them a common enemy, and they work together again. He twisted their love for explosions, used gold and diamonds to bribe, and won their hearts to him. But, of course, they never got, nor ever will they get, their promised payment. Now here's the key for our problem. When Deceiver took over the mountain, he turned their mines into an expansive prison. Though, he only used ground level, level zero as they call it, which is the main entrance for the right mountain." Here Findal scrambled on the table, leafing through the spread out maps. He selected one, pulled it to the top and smoothed it out for our inspection. Placing a finger over two depicted mountains, he said, "Here is where we need to go. And here," he moved his finger slightly, "is where the mines are. Now, no one has been able to explore the tunnels and shafts from the inside, so we have some guess work to do. But that is where a map of the mine tunnels will come in handy. We need to find an air shaft, get into it from the outside, and find our way to the prison. Sound good?"

There was a general nod between Dwin and I, but Dwin clarified with a frown, "So we need a map of the mines?"

"Precisely," Findal replied in a crisp tone while he turned in serious contemplation towards the area he thought the map might be located. He mused to himself as he glided past the ancient scrolls, "Now they made the maps when they were first digging out the mines, and that puts it way before Deceiver ever took it over..." He perused till he was on the far side of the room, his brow knit in thought, "...unless the maps weren't made when they began the project... no, who would make tunnels then map them all out later...?"

Dwin and I stood at the table, staring silently at him. We exchanged a few looks of wonderment, Dwin making a few faces and gestures indicating that Findal was a little loopy. A giggle escaped me by mistake. It was coldly responded to by a shooting glare from Findal. Both Dwin and I cleared our throats, stood straight and tried to act as if nothing had happened. When Findal returned to scouring the shelves, we relaxed and grinned at each other, enjoying the joke silently.

"Ah-ha!" came the exclamation from a dimmer corner of the room. "Here," Findal triumphantly announced, "is where it should be. Somewhere in this general area." He extended his hands in indication to a rather large section of the floor to ceiling bookshelves.

It was five feet in diameter, and crammed to the point of overflowing. My eyebrows shot up and my jaw slackened.

Dwin cocked an eyebrow and commented, "This general area, huh?"

Findal was already at work, inspecting the dusty papers. He gave a nod without a word or even a glance.

"You couldn't have narrowed it down a bit?" I asked, not at all looking forward to having to find one map out of hundreds which all looked the same to me.

With his back still turned, Findal responded in a dry, icy tone, "This *is* narrowed down, Limira."

I sighed in bewilderment, making an exasperated face. Dwin shrugged, grabbed the two candles from the table, lit them, and advanced to the search area. I followed more slowly, still reluctant. I moved between Findal's crouched form, and

Dwin stretched up to look among the higher shelves. Falling to the task with a candle in hand, I scanned, flipped and shoved maps and old folded papers as I peeked into them. After about half of the first shelf I had started on, I took a step back and frowned. "Wait, Findal, what are we looking for again?"

Findal audibly groaned, swung his head back to look up at me, and gave me the most disgusted look I had ever seen on him. "Ugh, weren't you listening?"

"I was, and it was very interesting, but I want to make sure that I'm looking for the right one. All these maps are starting to mush together in my mind."

"Fine," Findal consented, then warned, "you had better listen this time. Let me spell it out for you so you don't miss anything. You are looking for a map. It should be in a packet about this big," he gave me rough dimensions with his hands, "and it should be together with a bunch of others about the same size. I'm not sure how thick the packet will be, or how it's kept together, if at all. The specific map we're looking for will be labeled Level Zero. You'll know it by a shaft being labeled near the main entrance."

"What was the shaft for?" I asked, truly curious, and yes, sad to say, just that ignorant of mines and such things like that.

Another groan from Findal. "Must I explain everything? It's for getting to other levels of the mines. From there, you could either travel up to the peak of the mountain and every mine tunnel in between, or you could go down further into the earth. The mines are very extensive, and set up as levels, like house stories. All were accessible by a complicated system of elevators. Can I get back to looking now?"

"Sure. And thanks," I added lamely. Returning to the search, I began to ignore any smaller maps and oddball ones. It probably wasn't the smartest thing to do, since the information I was going off of was guesstimated, but I did it anyway.

Minutes dragged by ever so slowly. My hands were thoroughly covered in dust from touching and fingering up the old maps. Some of the pages broke into little crumbles in my fingers. Then I got the dust that Dwin was shaking down from his search efforts. My hair took on an even more light blonde look than before due to the amount of dust that landed on it. Somehow, I only coughed and choked a few times, nearly gagging on the dry particles that found themselves in my throat.

"One would think," Dwin broke the silence with a somewhat regretful tone, "that with all these maps and books and such we would have a copy of Elohim's Words."

Findal leaned back and looked up at Dwin, agreeing, "Right? You know we used to. Personally, I don't understand why they didn't make more copies, or partial copies, to leave here."

I glanced from one to the other, "What are you guys talking about?"

Both looked surprised at me. Dwin finally asked, "You've never heard of Elohim's Words?"

"No."

Findal inquired, still more amazed, "As in never ever?"

I glanced innocently at them, replying meekly, "Well, no."

"Woah," was all Findal managed to say.

Dwin shook his head slowly and turned back to thumbing through maps. Findal did the same after a moment, leaving me to look from one to the other rather annoyed. Frustrated, I demanded more than asked, "Aren't you going to explain?"

Both boys snickered at my overreaction. Then I realized I had been duped intentionally by the pair of jokesters. I didn't think it was very funny.

After a few moments to collect himself, Dwin finally explained, "Alright then," he grew more sober, "Elohim told us about Himself, what is pleasing to Him, how we are to live, treat others, and well, it's basically a manual to life, or everything that is important in life. He has revealed Himself to us, and men of His choosing through the ages have written down what He told them. Those writings have been compiled into a book, or in some cases just pages bunched together. There are only a few complete copies. One used to be here before they moved headquarters. I think there's at least a few books in Monare Pelm. I'm surprised that you haven't heard of them before. There are men and women who dedicate their lives to copying His Words."

I couldn't believe what Dwin was telling me. Imagine! Elohim giving us His Words to read and live by. It was amazing to think that He did that. He had things He wanted to tell us! It wasn't like any other book, fiction or historical, because this was written by the King over all, the One who knows present and past. I would give anything to read just one part out of all the manuscripts complied together. Wonder illuminating my expression, all I said in a soft voice was, "That's amazing. I wish I could read it."

Dwin shrugged, turning back the shelves, "Maybe someday you will."

It's hard to say how long we were in there, it must have been close to an hour and fifteen minutes. Our backs, shoulders and heads were aching. A sizable cloud of dust had formed in our part of the room. The candles had burned down significantly, their smoke adding to the cloud of swirling dust. Dwin had made his way down, and Findal up, squishing me in the middle of their "search zones." As we moved down the shelf, we would collide with each other until we figured out a system of weaving and swapping places that seemed to work well enough. No one spoke except a few apologizes for bumping into each other.

Just when I was about to suggest a break, Dwin exclaimed in an elated voice, "I've found it!"

I glanced up at him, a map scroll in my hands. "You what?"

"I've found it!" he repeated, his eyes scanning over the document in wonder and excitement.

Findal rose from his knees, his face looking skeptical, "Let me see that."

Dwin held it out, and Findal snatched it out of his grasp. Brow furrowed and eyes squinting, he scanned the map, picking out the details of it. "Huh, you're right. This *is* it." He handed it back to Dwin, and I craned my neck to see. Findal added, "I never doubted you for a moment."

I ignored Findal's laughable comment, totally absorbed in the detailed map. Its faded ink was a maze of lines and tunnels. On the bottom of the map was the obvious label of "Level Zero." It was in the middle of a large stack of likewise faded and dusty papers.

Findal elbowed his way between me and Dwin, blocking my view from further inspection. We moved over to the table and spread the map out, next to the one of Fairlend. Findal dug about on the table a bit more and pulled out a map while muttering to himself. When he laid it out, I saw that it was a close up of Dol Guliab, the twin mountains of Deceiver. It was a newer map, as Findal explained, it was made by Lightbearers who had actually seen and witnessed the things. It showed where the prison was, aka, where the main mine entrance was, some buildings carved out of the mountain side, a large tower, and it had a curious line around the bottom encircling both mountains. I also couldn't help but notice that the mountains seemed to have some sort of shading over them. Around the front of the mountains, facing southwest and the rest of the valley of Slaggar, were a bunch of little dots that spread over the majority of the front sides of both mountains.

I pointed to the small dots and asked, "What's that?"

"That," Findal returned to his normal teaching voice, and I knew it was safer to ask more questions, "those are Vaudian camps. We reckon there's thousands in those camps. They're very well established from what we can tell. And they guard the gateway." He pointed to a place where the curious line that was drawn around the base of the mountains was interrupted by an arch. The arch was right in front of a tower, which was located on the lower front side of the right mountain. Findal continued, "The gateway is the only break in the barrier that surrounds both mountains." He traced with his finger the curious line.

"So," I mused, "we have to go through that to get to the mines?"

"No," Dwin corrected before Findal could, "it's not that kind of barrier. When Deceiver first took over, he conjured up some spell, or something of the like, to make the cities and villages over the mountains be invisible. You can still see the mountains, and they look beautiful, you'd never suspect the evil that is truly on them."

"Right," Findal cut in, "The gateway is the only part where you can actually see what is on the mountain without being inside the barrier."

I inquired, really only thinking about how to get to Nollem, "So, we can go through the barrier, but we won't see what's on the other side till we've crossed?"

"Right again," Findal replied. "Now I was thinking that we could go on the back side of the mountain, and that works out perfect because there's an air shaft." He pointed to the map of the tunnel system.

"Okay," Dwin said slowly, trying to think things through a bit. "So we have to go all through these tunnels to get to the other side, right? And once we're there, how do we get Nollem out without being seen, especially since we'll have to carry him?"

I suggested, "Why don't we just go back through the tunnels, then our horses—" I paused with a thought, "we are getting horses for this right?"

Findal looked to Dwin with an expression of "it's out of my department." Dwin puzzled over that a few minutes, then said, "Yes, we'll need horses for this one. I guess we could pester Brene to get us some, he could probably scrounge up some."

Brene was the older man who was in contact with Findal once every week. Usually Findal would go and meet him, but occasionally Brene would make the trek and bless us with his cheery spirit. Brene got us all the information we had, since he was directly in the underground link of informers. It was quite handy to have a guy like him around.

"As I was saying," I continued with the thought I had going, "We could go back through the tunnels and our horses would be right there, then we could get off the mountain and get home, very possibly unnoticed."

"Well," Dwin burst my bubble with reality, "probably not completely unnoticed. Orodumes are on the constant guard from the skies. Nothing moves without their knowing. But if we get in and out of the mines quick enough, we shouldn't come to much harm. But we have to be quick, or else we'll have a company of Vaudians to deal with."

I cringed at the thought of having to fight off skilled, seasoned, and well organized Vaudians with Nollem being a sort of drag weight. It wasn't going to be easy, but with horses we might be able to outrun them, escaping to safety.

It all depended on speed.

Chapter 29
Under the Shadow of Dol Guliab

Over supper, Dwin, Findal and I discussed our plan, leaving it open for suggested improvements. Dwin had been done most of the explaining, and he gave credit where credit was due. He finished up by saying, "And Limira thought of just heading back out the way we came, mounting our horses, and riding off the mountain. We would have to take a couple extra horses, of course. So I think our request for horses should number seven, one for each of us, one for Nollem, and one for supplies. Of which, Kat, how are our stores looking?"

Kattim, who seemed strangely unattached from the conversation, said shortly, "Fine. I'll have to get some things together. How many days?"

Dwin bit his lip, calculating in his head, "Uh, eight days round trip. So pack for nine, just in case."

She silently nodded, spooning more supper to her mouth.

Grenith piped up in her gleeful, enthusiastic voice, "I think it sounds like a marvelous plan. Well done team, especially Limira for thinking of a crucial part, and for her perseverance through all these daunting oppositions."

I smiled slightly, but more embarrassed at the compliment than anything.

Findal chimed in, raising his mug of water, "Hear, hear!"

Dwin said, with a proud hint in his voice and a fond look on his face, "I'll raise my glass to that. Limira's done quite remarkably, with her little test, and now this. Well done."

My smile grew a little wider and I replied, looking around at their beaming faces, "I could have hardly done it without the help of all of you. Dwin, I wouldn't have survived the test without your training and guidance. Findal, I would have gotten lost without my newfound knowledge and appreciation of maps. Grenith, Kattim, I couldn't have gotten on without your constant, unwavering encouragement and joy. So really, thank you."

Everyone smiled, paid their meek welcomes, and the conversation moved on. Only Kattim hadn't said anything. She had just stared all the harder into her bowl. I hadn't noticed then, nor had anyone else I don't think.

Supper was soon over, and we all stood up to clear the table. Dwin and Findal retired to the fireside, maps in hand, to work out some details of the route. I started picking up the dishes from the table and carrying them over to the washing basins. Grenith did the same, and she bubbled off about how exciting all this was. Kattim began to help clear the dishes, but she glanced at Dwin and Findal leaning over the maps and earnestly conversing over some undiscussed problem. She stared at them a minute then set the dish down, saying in a curious tone, "Limira, you wouldn't mind helping Grenith tonight, *would you?*" The way she said it, it was more like a statement than a question.

I shook my head, "No, not at all."

"Great," was the distracted response, "I'll go help out with the plans."

With that she moseyed over and joined Findal and Dwin. She was warmly received, and she sat in between them, occasionally adding in her suggestions.

Grenith and I exchanged a confused look. I commented, "That was strange."

"Yeah, she's been acting kind of funny lately," Grenith agreed, then added as if to make up for smearing her name, "but it could just be the stress and prospect of rescuing Nollem. I know it's been a while since she was last on a mission."

I shrugged, returning to the dishes. I occasionally chanced a glance over my shoulder to see them huddled together and laughing quietly, their forms silhouetted by the dancing flames.

❧

It was a chilly morning, but it was slowly warming to a pleasant temperature. Evident signs of spring were everywhere in the blossoming flowers, new leaves on the shrub bushes, and new sparse blades of grass poking up. The sunrises were very pretty, full of color and brightness. They reminded me of the sunrise that Nollem pointed out to me that one morning so long ago, the morning after we had just gotten off the mountain range before we entered Slaggar Forest. We were all exhausted, but Nollem took the time to point out the beautiful colors, remember the Maker of it all, and even make an unappreciated joke.

It seemed so long ago. But I could remember him so well it was like he was sitting right next to me, on the cold hard boulder, staring at the sky with that silly expression of contentedness on his face.

I smiled at the picture, so vivid before me. It only made me miss him all the more.

It had been eight days since Dwin, Findal, and I had scoured the map room, swimming in old papers which were buried under layers of dust. It had been ten days since I witnessed the atrocities of the Vaudian raid upon the Between family.

Those days seemed a lot farther in the past because of the busy days between then and now. We had finalized our plans, gotten our supplies together, and were completely ready on the third day since my return from the test. The only thing was Brene couldn't get the horses to us till the next day, so we were delayed four days in total before we could leave.

Now we had traveled four days already, and we were nearing Dol Guliab. The journey had so far been smooth, and much more enjoyable than any other I had taken. This time we didn't have to walk the entire way, we had sufficient provisions, and plenty of bedding and warmth during the night. Not to mention there were no unexpected attacks, no injuries—despite the incident of Findal getting a thorn from a thistle stuck in his thumb—and almost everyone was enjoyable for company. Everyone except Kattim, that is.

It was only as we drew closer to the twin mountains that everyone grew progressively quieter and the stress of the situation caught up to us. When I caught my first glimpse of the mountains, I suddenly got knots in my stomach and my palms got sweaty. The dark form of the smaller mountain loomed up, towering over us shrouded in a dark mist and cloud cover. It was in the early afternoon of the fourth day that we sighted it.

As we got closer, the mountain only got bigger and more imposing than ever. Then the second mountain, the farther one and the one we needed, appeared. First only as a vague, dark outline behind the other, then it grew in size and distinction.

Dwin was right, I couldn't see anything in the way of habitation on the steep slopes. Some of the mountain sides, but only near the very base, were a slight shade of green with grass and shrubs, others were the bold, white face of rock cliffs and formations, but the prevailing color was various shades of grey.

Which reminds me to mention that I did ask Findal—when we passed the memorable rock formation on the first day—about the strange table thing on the top. He said that the rock tower used to be a post for Vaudians. Their trademark for their posts was a table of sorts around which they would lay bundles of wood and other burnable things then set the whole thing ablaze. It created a signal fire to proclaim that they had taken over the land, and gave them the enjoyment of destruction by fire. If there's anything that gives Vaudians the most pleasure, it's to create fire and watch it destroy.

Quicker than I wished, we were engulfed in the shadow of the dark clouds and shroud that covered the mountains. An ominous, dark feeling settled over me, suffocating my courage and hope as if it were a wet blanket. I couldn't help but want to get away. Escape from the dark feeling of oppression. But I had to do it for Nollem. I had to be brave. This was something that I couldn't back out of.

No one said a word. We passed beyond the first mountain, and came directly under the second. It loomed high, frowning down at us with dark shadows. I quailed under its stoney gaze. I could see nothing that was situated on the mountain, and that made me more nervous than anything. I had no idea what lay just yards from me, but anything on that side of the barrier would know exactly where I was. My nerves were high on edge.

At every strange, unfamiliar sound I would jump and frantically look in the direction I thought I heard come it from. But there was nothing there.

I only hoped that no one had noticed. I think we were all too busy hiding our own feelings to notice anyone else's.

Dwin and Findal guided their horses together in silence. They met up at the front of our group, and quietly, just above a whisper, decided where we would start up the mountainous slope.

My attention was drawn momentarily to their plan making. I tried to pick out what they were saying, but everything was one inaudible droll. Then suddenly they broke apart into silence again. We continued on, even Grenith was strangely quiet for her usual self. She still had a slight bright look about her though. Normally she didn't have to say any words, her joy blossomed out in just her very expression. But today was different. She looked anxious.

Kattim was solemn, her expression vacant of any other emotion than grim disinterest. Occasionally she would sneak darting glares at Grenith who rode next to her. It seemed as though she was angry with Grenith, but for what reason I don't know. But I do think, though I hate to say it, Kattim wanted to make everyone else unhappy because she was. At least, that's what it seemed to be.

Suddenly, like a waving wraith shrouded in mist, Dwin brought his arm up and fluently brought it down to his side again, pointing to the right. Likewise he turned his horse to the right. We all got the signal and followed suit.

My eyes grew wide, and my heart leapt to the back of my throat when I stood face to face with the second twin of the shadowy mountains. Dark mist rolled off the steep slopes. Its peak was hidden, suppressed by a thick layer of non-penetrable cloud. I thought I could pick out the barrier. The bland grey rocks on this side of a definite line were slightly brighter, and the grey rocks on the other side were slightly dimmer. That was the only way I could tell where the barrier was.

I got the same feeling as when I was standing in the midst of the border, all those days ago. Grenith had passed through, but I had been caught behind by a pressing force. A new fear, rising out of distinct memory, entered me. I started to imagine that I could feel the same force clutching at my throat, suffocating the life out of me. I felt panic rise in me. My breathing quickened. The more I tried to fight the feeling, the worse it got. Dark, blurry pictures of the night in the marshes appeared before me. The same feeling of terror engulfed me. A flash back of Chimel's ashen face with that horrendous red smear over his throat. His blank, unstaring eyes. I fought the sickening feeling that swelled in me, but I sank into a lethargic state. My eyes rolling, I slumped forward in my saddle, losing all sense of balance.

I vaguely heard someone approach on my left. The next thing I knew there was a hand on my arm and Grenith leaning nearer to me, her face full of concern, saying, "—okay?"

I blinked a few times, trying to focus on Grenith's face among the blur of images fighting for my attention. After a moment, I seemed to shake myself out of it, meeting Grenith's eye, she being the only thing before me. I hadn't heard her question except for the last word. I blinked a few more times, then stuttered, "Uh, yeah, sure. I'm fine."

She didn't look convinced but slid back to her place next to Kattim. I looked up and saw Dwin just turning forward in his saddle again. He had seen it all.

I studied the coarse hair of the horse's mane that I was riding. But I didn't really see it. I was thinking. Terrified partly because of what I had replayed, and partly that I had slipped back so easily. Just when I thought I was safe, they came crashing down with more force, making themselves more obvious than ever. I was really more at risk when I thought I was the safest.

The barrier was only feet away, and I forced myself to focus on that. I was here to save Nollem. I had to keep my head in the game. Everything depended on speed and clearheadedness. I couldn't afford to mess up now.

Dwin and Findal were just inches from the barrier. I thought that they were going to disappear, but their horses started acting up. They shied and whinnied nervously, avoiding the dark barrier. Dwin and Findal tried settling them down and urging them forward, but they refused, dodging and rearing.

We girls had stopped a safe distance away, just enough to not be in the way. Our horses seemed to catch onto the feeling and shifted nervously, stepping in small edgy movements.

It was soon evident that we couldn't make the horses carry us beyond the barrier. Dwin and Findal eventually backed away from the barrier and joined us. Dwin spoke what was on all our minds, "We'll have to leave them behind, out here. Have to walk to the air shaft."

Grenith asked, "Where should we tie them?"

Looking around, Findal pointed out a tangled mass of trees and briars. It was the best we could do, so we moved over there, and tied them up as securely as possible. Gathering our weapons from their places on the saddles and the torches we had made for the tunnel trek, we set out to climb the slope.

There was no further discussion. Findal seemed to know where we were going, though he had no map in his hands. It was securely tucked away in his mind.

With Findal in the lead, and Dwin taking up the rear, we walked with an even pace in single file. I was right behind Findal, and I saw him disappear once he crossed the barrier. It unnerved me, but my sense of duty to him, if something was on the other side and were to attack him, hurried my steps to go after him.

As I passed through, there was only a slight tingle to denote that anything had changed. I actually closed my eyes as I went through, so I can't truthfully tell you anything about what it looked like. The next thing I knew was a chill racing through me and then seeing Findal just ahead. Grenith nearly bumped into me as she came through, so I moved quickly to join Findal. That dark feeling of horror renewed itself with more vigor than before. Now we were really swallowed by the dim mists and clouds.

Glancing over my shoulder, I watched Dwin as he slipped from the outside to this side. The barrier became visible, only around his outline, for just a second or two. It was a ripply blur that strongly resembled water just as if the surface had been disturbed by a dropped pebble. It was strange indeed, and I would have missed it if I had blinked.

We had all made it through safely enough, now only the climb remained. I lifted my eyes up to survey the route we would have to take. It was steep, with many broken bushes and stones. Hardly a blade of grass poked its fresh head above the rocky surface beyond just a few feet from the barrier. It was even more desolate than the burned forest with all its white trunks and skeleton limbs jutting out against the dull sky.

The prolonged silence continued as we climbed, only broken by the sounds of our heavy breath and shifting stones underfoot. After a long spell of time, Findal looked over his shoulder and barely breathed, as if even to speak above a whisper would bring sudden disaster upon us, "About halfway, so I reckon."

I passed it on, then heard the message quietly echo till it reached the end of the group. It was just then when someone, I believe it was Kattim, but I don't really remember from the excitement about to come, hissed the one word that sent chills up and down my spine: *"Orodumes!"*

All heads turned to the sky, and sure enough, like black blots against a dark grey canvas, the winged creatures wheeled slowly through the mists. All I could think of was their razor-like claws that had very nearly become the end of me. There was no damp marsh to save us now.

Even as we watched, the black creatures multiplied and dropped closer to us. One of their most effective weapons was their slow, drawn out approach, then their initial attack was speedy and sudden. During all the time that it took them to come, our nerves kept us on edge. The sense of urgency pressed down on each of us like a heavy weight.

A battle was sure to come.

As the Orodumes dropped closer, I started to pick out their low moaning hiss of *"Deeaaatttttthhhhhhh."* I fought the panicking urgency to break into a run and book it for the nearest cover.

I heard the familiar sound of Dwin's sword rasping out of its sheath. That was the general signal, and similar sounds echoed through my ears.

Holding my short sword—of which I had grown much more fond of since the first day Dwin picked it out for me—with both hands, I spread my feet apart, braced and steady. I looked up, scanning for the Orodumes, assessing their numbers, their flight patterns, and their possible first attack point.

Dwin didn't even have to call for a circle, we formed one naturally, everyone covering each other's backs. An anxious, uneasy feeling spread over us, all flexing our muscles, repositioning our grips, and just waiting for the onslaught to begin.

I stared them down, putting on my best fierce face. They were drawing closer. The grimness of battle was settling over me. My fears were beginning to fade into the background. I knew what I had to do, and I knew how to do it. No running this time.

Time oozed by slowly like the last few drops of syrup in a bottle. My eyes started playing tricks on me, the colors fading and bleaching because I had been staring up for so long.

Then, suddenly like a long anticipated storm, the Orodumes hit us with a heavy force of sheer numbers. They darted down from all angles, swiping at us in a synchronized pattern so that they didn't run into each other. Though it was a pattern, it was hard to get ahead of because there were just so many of them.

It seemed like two came at each of us at the same time. Two black beasts with claws extended and wings snapping, swooped full force at me. My first instinct was to crouch. I ducked slightly, holding my short sword up to block them. I closed my eyes, fully expecting to be sliced by their long knives of claws. A stinging blow knocked against the blade as a claw collided with it. My hands shook from the sheer force, but I kept my grip.

Both Orodumes flew overhead, their claws just missing the top of my head. I stood up straight, equally pleased and surprised that I had survived.

Another pair of Orodumes, heading straight for me, jerked me out of my shocked moment. This time, I stood my ground firmly.

Their unearthly war cry of "*Deeaaattttthhhhhhh,*" hissed out, their eyes full of black hatred. I returned their cry with the most challenging shout I could muster. It didn't seem to work for they came at me with undaunted boldness. But I wasn't about to be intimidated.

I raised my sword, giving it a forceful swing. A satisfying screech spilt the air. I had caught a wing tip with my blade. The second Orodume was met with the same reception, and it obtained a slash on the bottom of its foot. I didn't have time to gloat over the injuries I had inflicted, as another Orodume whizzed by. Just as I saw it, I was able to duck as it swooped over me in a flash. A startling sting suddenly seared through my shoulder. With a quick glance, I saw a clean cut through my jerkin and undershirt, and a red mark growing over the exposed skin.

The urgency of battle kept me from tending to it directly. I had to ignore it for the moment. But it reminded me of its painful presence every time I moved my right arm.

Another Orodume charged, one after the other. Another swing, now missed, now hit. The black creatures kept up a continuous stream of attacks on our small group. We fought them valiantly, taking down only a few among many. It was soon clear that their tactic was working. Wear us down, give us no break, and when we were spent, finish us off.

We all had the same thoughts going through our minds. We couldn't last forever. Somehow we had to get to cover.

I called out above the din, while taking a slash at the nearest Orodume, "So what happens if they just keep coming?"

Findal hollered back, "We just keep— " he paused, ducking and raising his sword, a shriek of pain ringing through the air in response, "—fighting!"

"I've got a plan!" Dwin shouted, "Findal, how far to the shaft?"

"Uh, not too far."

"Not too far to run?"

"No, not for us."

"Great. Findal, take the lead. Grenith, Kat, follow him. Limira, help me to hold them back. We'll make our retreat shortly after. Findal, now! Go!"

Without a word, Findal, his sword poised at a high guard, dashed further up the slope, his footing slipping on the loose stones. Grenith and Kattim followed shortly after. Before I knew it, Dwin was back to back with me. His breathing was heavy and quick.

We took a few slashes at the descending creatures before Dwin shouted to me, "Come on! Watch your back and fight them as we go!"

He made a mad dash up the slope, the others not far ahead.

Chapter 30
Dash From Death

It took me a second to realize that he wanted me to fight and run at the same time. I had never done that before.

I scrambled up the loose ground after Dwin and fell behind within seconds. His fast pace and long strides speedily out doing mine.

Oh, come on! Give me a break! I mentally screamed at the creatures. Another three came in for a strike all at the same time. Two from either side and one from behind. I whirled around, readying my sword. The Orodume coming directly at me was slightly faster than the others. It reached me first and was about at my level because of the slope. Thinking fast, I bent on one knee, and slashed my sword over my head in one fluid movement. I felt the rush of air pick up stray strands of hair and race down my back. The soft underbelly of the beast collided with my upturned sword.

There was a sickening tearing sound, my sword was dark with blood, and my back got sprinkled with red drops.

I might have screamed.

Rising, I turned to my right, preformed a downright blow, nicked the neck of the creature, and curled to one knee again. In that moment, my left foot slid out from under me, and I crashed awkwardly to the stoney ground.

I panicked, fully aware of the third one coming at me. My back was turned to it, fully exposed to its deadly razor claws. The snapping leathery wings were so close I was certain that I would be dead in moments. In a futile attempt, I flopped over, hoping to at least face it. I only made it about halfway before I thumped to the ground, landing on my left side. My sword was resting limply in my right hand.

I saw a black blur coming straight for me. Instinct kicking in, I hugged the ground, throwing my arms over my head and curling into a ball. I squeezed my eyes shut tight. A small cry of fear and anticipated pain escaped my lips.

A rushing whirl whooshed over me. I felt the distinct draft on my face then heard the snap of wings as it ascended again into the sky.

I barely had time to exhale in relief before Dwin's strong hand pulled me to my feet. Standing up I uttered a quick thanks, and we charged up the hill. Dwin's breathing was ragged by now; he stumbled and tripped as often as I did.

But still the Orodumes came. Another dropped low coming at me from the side, and slightly in front of me. My hands shaking with adrenalin, I held my sword in high guard, ready for a downward blow.

It came at me, and I ducked just before it went over me. I held up my sword and caught this one with the tip, barely penetrating the underbelly. It screamed in pain and wheeled to the right. The only thing that I didn't realized was that Dwin was a little behind me and to the right.

The Orodume, writhing and driven to anger all the more with pain, collided directly with Dwin, knocking him flat to the

308

ground. Lashing out with claws and wings, the Orodume tore at Dwin's exposed form with wrathful vengeance. Dwin's screams of pain gripped my full attention. I spun around, only then realizing what had happened. I ran to them, slipping and nearly landing on top of the mess. I attacked the back and the wings of creature, slashing down as hard as I could. Somewhere in the pile of wings, scales and man, Dwin's sword arced and blurred, doing damaged of its own.

I didn't dare plunge through the back, even though I had the opportunity. I might hit Dwin. I chanced only glancing slashes.

So suddenly that it startled me, the glistening tip of a sword protruded out of the back, near the shoulder blade of the Orodume. Giving a few struggling kicks before its death, it fell limp pinning Dwin underneath.

The creature was about as big as Dwin, but I tugged and shoved at it anyway, trying to get it off. From below, Dwin pushed it half off him, and I struggled with the other part. When I first saw Dwin, my heart sank and my mouth parted. His front was bloodied, but not all of it was his. He had numerous cuts and gashes over his arms, face and chest. I offered him my hand. He accepted it with his own bloody one. He unsteadily got to his feet, then pulled his sword out of the Orodume.

With a sigh and a grimace, he continued up the mountain. I followed behind him, in shock and screaming at myself in anger and regret. It was my fault. I could have killed that thing before it even hit him. I could have just ducked and it wouldn't have landed on Dwin in the first place. If only I had done *anything* differently, it would have been better. I deserved for that beast to have fallen on me. It was my fault. Now I'd endangered the entire mission. If Dwin couldn't carry Nollem, there was no way to get him off the mountain. We definitely couldn't carry both of them, and our horses were all the way down at the base.

Another lone Orodume swooped at me, I ducked, dodging its claws. I knew that eventually they would go low enough that I couldn't duck them anymore. It was only a matter of time. I had get to the shaft. I had to get Dwin to the shaft without further harm.

Dwin was already a few paces ahead of me, but his head was bowed and his steps dragging. I sprinted to catch up with him, and practically danced circles around him, trying to fend off as many of the flying creatures as I could. We slowly made our way up, and before I knew it, we were only about ten yards from the shaft where the others were waiting.

Seeing the opportunity, I emerged under Dwin's arm, lending support. I shouted at him, "Only a little to go! We can run it!" With that, I set the pace at a jog and he picked up on it, then forced me to go faster.

Findal's head poked out from a square box that looked like it had just grown out of the mountain slope. He saw us and urged us on with shouts of encouragement. Five more yards. I heard the rushing of leathery wings behind me. We had to get underground before it caught up with us. There was no fighting this one. Two more yards. The rushing and snapping of wings grew louder, drowning any other sound into silence. Findal ducked under. Dwin and I jumped for the wood lined opening. Landing hard on the stoney ground, we were sprawled out, our fingertips just touching the hole. I felt a razor-like claw catch and tear through the back of my jerkin. Not a second after, the tip of a claw scraped over the back of my scalp. I inhaled sharply.

Dwin paused in his wriggling towards the hole and looked back at me.

I urged him on, mentally shoving him into the hole myself as I heard the sounds of another Orodume coming up behind me. When his boots disappeared, I followed, getting one last glance over my shoulder before I was dumped to the damp floor of a dark tunnel. Another Orodume's black shape momentarily blocked out the light as its form passed over. It was closer than I realized.

I think I might have landed on Dwin, because I heard him groan and felt his legs move under me. I scrambled to one side, blurting out a million apologizes. He groaned again, and said something like, "It's fine," but he muttered it, and it didn't help me feel any better. I barely made out his form in the half light. He had sat up and put a hand to his head.

Then Findal's voice echoed from further into the tunnel, "Is everyone here? Grenith?"

"Yup."

"Kat?"

"Yes, I came in with you, remember?"

"Only checking. Dwin?"

"Yeah," came the strained and pain filled voice of Dwin.

"Limira?"

"Yeah, I'm here," I responded while sinking heavily against a damp earthen wall, adding, "we barely made it."

Findal again. "Kat? Do you still have the torches?"

"Yeah, I gave Grenith a couple too."

"Anyone got a match?"

Dwin responded, breathing laboriously, "In my pocket."

I heard him shifting around then he said, "In my hand."

Findal's form appeared in the half light, his hand reached out. Just as their hands met and the match was exchanged, a loud thud interrupted our repose. The light from the shaft was blocked out again, leaving us in pitch blackness. The head of an

Orodume appeared through the opening, its blood red eyes glowing with hatred, its white teeth snapping at thin air.

Dwin and Findal jumped back, scrambling to get out of reach. I clambered further into the darkness. The head disappeared, then the claws started tearing at the hole, ripping back the loose dirt and rocks, only to have more fall in its place.

We retreated further into the tunnel, only to watch in horror as our escape route was torn to pieces. It seemed that several Orodumes were working to clear a hole in the side of mountain. But the earth slid in their way, only frustrating their plans and efforts. But at the same time it was burying us further from our planned escape. We couldn't get back the way we came now. I suppose it was a blessing in disguise, because in blocking us from our plan, the rubble was protecting us from another, more savage attack. But I wasn't thinking of it like that in the moment. All I saw was our escape being foiled. We would have to find another way out, and that wasn't going to be easy.

It was soon apparent that they had stopped their digging on the other side. All of us had stood transfixed, staring in disbelief, at the wreckage. The growing cloud of dust rising up forced us to fall back into the darkness, stumbling along the passage. Once we thought we were at a safe distance, we all flopped to the ground, leaning against the cold, damp walls of the tunnel.

Then suddenly, I heard the sound of a match scraping, and a bright light flickered up. The small light illuminated Findal's dirt smudged face. Wordlessly, Kattim handed him the first of four torches. Bright flame caught and filled the tunnel with a blazing glow. Immediately, everyone was visible, all crouched and limply resting against the walls. It looked as though everyone was fine, except Dwin. If there were any injuries on anyone else they were minor, like the cut on my shoulder. But Dwin, oh, Dwin...

He leaned back with his eyes closed, his face drawn with pain. One leg was extended out, and the other bent at the knee. It looked like his breathing had steadied somewhat.

Sitting opposite to him, all I could do was stare and think of how it was all my fault. I replayed the scene over and over again, adding in what I should have done differently. I was a failure.

All my ideas were failing. We couldn't take the horses beyond the barrier, the shaft got closed behind us, Dwin got seriously injured. The very things that this mission depended on, I was messing up. Now speed and stealth were no more attainable than growing wings and flying out.

With a torch in hand, Grenith moved over to Dwin, her brow knit as she began to inspect his injuries. Her footsteps echoed, making it sound like she was shuffling her feet, even though she wasn't at all. At the sound, Dwin opened his eyes. Mustering a faint smile, he shifted his weight, sitting up straighter.

Grenith returned the smile, and knelt by him. "Looks like you got into quite the scrape."

"I don't think even half the blood is mine," He said, looking down his front. Those were brave and optimistic words from him.

"How bad does it hurt?"

By now, everyone's attention was fixed on Dwin.

"Uh, not as bad as it looks... I think."

"That doesn't really help," Grenith frowned softly at him.

Findal asked, his voice loud and echoey, "Can you continue on?"

"Yeah," came his slow answer, "but a break might be nice."

Grenith smiled, still looking him over, and replied, "That's one thing we can arrange for you. Stay still, and don't worry about rushing, we could all use a rest."

She stood up and let him be, rejoining the small huddle of Findal and Kattim. I stayed put, closing my eyes, leaning my head back, and feeling miserable.

I heard Grenith whisper quietly to Findal, "I wish I could clean out his wounds. As he says, most of the blood isn't his." Then adding the optimistic note, "I don't think it's too dreadfully serious. After a rest, he should be able to go on."

Findal nodded his response, all the while staring at Dwin with anxiety.

The positive note didn't help me feel any better. Even if he was going to be fine, he was still in pain, and it was still my fault.

Busying himself with the next stage of our rescue mission, Findal pulled out the map of Level Zero from under his jerkin. It had safely made the dash up the mountain slope. He studied the map once and moved his torch to look further down the tunnel that we were in. I could tell he was mentally writing down the directions.

I also knew, from looking at it earlier, that there were several ways to get to the main entrance where the prisoners were. We had mapped out one way, but I knew that he was weighing the other, possibly faster routes. But I didn't really care, nor did I care to offer my opinion. My suggestions were failing.

It felt like much longer than what it actually was before Dwin thought he was ready to continue. I wasn't sure whether or not he had fallen asleep during that time. It was hard to say.

Wallowing in my guilt and frustration didn't help the time pass any faster. The more I thought about it, the more blame and anger I threw on myself. I was such a worthless person. Nothing I could say or do would amend for the damage I had done. I deserved that Orodume to fall and attack me. It should have been me. It should have been me...

But no, Dwin had to suffer for my mistakes. And I felt wretched about it.

When Dwin lifted himself up, slowly, painfully from his position, I didn't even offer to help. I was afraid that I would somehow manage to hurt him all the more. Kattim offered her assistance, and it was accepted gratefully. Once he was up, he said he was fine and it was by Elohim's grace that the Orodume hadn't gotten to his legs.

Findal organized everyone, and we soon set off down the passage. It got muggier and damper as we went. The tunnel also became wider.

The torches were evenly distributed and cast a yellow light. It reminded me much of the candle light that we had back at the Den. It was comforting, somehow, to see the darkness dispelled as we moved forward. But it was equally chilling to see the shadows accumulate and stack up behind us. It was like they were hunting, prowling after us. They made me nervous, as if they actually would attack if we had our backs turned for too long.

More silence. It seemed as if everyone was oppressed under the complete darkness that emanated from the mountain. More time passed. Soon we came to a true 'Y' in in the tunnels. Findal took the right side without a second thought. He was relying on that mental map. No one said anything.

Eventually, the sound of a drip and a splash echoed. I thought nothing of it till Grenith exclaimed, breaking the prevailing quiet, "Water!"

We all knew what that meant, and we picked up our pace a little. Sure enough, the torch light reflected off the little jewels of liquid just ahead. There was a trickle of water, dripping and sliding down a path smoothed out of a rough bank of broken up rock, ending in a lovely little pool. That bank of rock had overtaken our tunnel. It sloped in a large mound, like the tunnel was a throat and it had vomited all this out. It blocked our passage. We needed this tunnel.

The water was a great sign, but the cave-in made the excitement die quickly. Forgetting the water, Findal stood before the mass of rubble, his hands on his hips, contemplating what to do. Grenith and Dwin sat by the little clear pool. Kattim, just behind Findal, surveyed the damage as well. I slumped on the other wall, opposite of Dwin and Grenith. Everything was falling apart. I suddenly had no thirst for water, though my mouth had run dry.

Grenith had started by wetting a strip of cloth she tore from her undershirt. She too had changed to boy's clothes for the mission, though she found them much less comfortable than I did. Dwin leaned back patiently. Grenith started cleaning out the dried blood and dirt from his wounds.

She looked up, glanced around, and her eye fell on me. She motioned with her hand for me to come over. Standing up, I reluctantly went over and knelt in front of Dwin, waiting to see what she wanted, though I could guess.

"Help me out with this, would you?" She wrung out the cloth again. "It'll take me too long by myself."

I nodded in agreement, but I didn't really want to. I tore a strip of cloth from my undershirt, wet it, and set to work. Dwin only had a few claw marks, but they were deep, like dark red furrows against his pale skin. To this day, neither of us are sure how he got so few injures from that, all things considered. Most of the blood over his front was from the Orodume.

Chapter 31
Pit of Death

When Dwin winced if I pressed too hard, I cringed. The third time this happened, I breathed, with a tense voice, "Sorry."

He turned his eyes from the studying the tunnel ceiling to look directly into mine. I couldn't meet his steady gaze and dropped mine, dodging looking into his face.

"Hey now," he said, carefully putting his hand over mine to stop me from the vigorous cleaning that I had so suddenly and studiously started, "it's alright. It's not your fault."

Biting my lip, I wanted to scream out while bursting into tears, "Yes it is!" But I said nothing.

He continued, "It was an accident, I was standing there and you had no idea what that creature was going to do. If you want to point fingers, point it at the Orodume, it was his fault for crashing into me."

That didn't help. An unwanted tear slid from my eye and down my smudged cheek, "If I had just killed it, if I had just raised my sword a little more, this wouldn't have happened to you!"

"No, Limira, don't do that to yourself. I hold nothing against you, I don't blame you for this. Neither should you."

I only nodded my head, brushing away the tears that slid down. Dwin let go of my hand and reached up, catching a stray tear with his thumb. Sniffing once in an effort to show that I was back in one piece—which was far from the truth— I returned to dabbing away the blood and dirt.

I couldn't look at his face again, nor did I look at Grenith. I knew she had seen and heard it all, and frankly, I was embarrassed that she witnessed it. I was never fond of showing my emotions to others. The person I was most comfortable sharing my feelings with was Nollem. But I had felt that I couldn't trust him just after he became a Lightbearer, so I shut him out. Now I couldn't be more sorry and more willing to regain that trust.

Dwin was soon as cleaned up as he was going to get, and I collapsed against the wall next to him. I closed my eyes, resting my head back again, a new problem weighing on me. How were we going to get to Nollem?

Findal had gotten out the map, and he was bent over it, studying it with uncanny fervor. After a while, he looked up, and glanced at each one of us, making sure that he had our attention. He cleared his throat and began rather reluctantly, "Well, this tunnel being blocked, we now have to find a new way."

That was obvious enough, I thought to myself, what do you really mean to say?

He cleared his throat again, and continued, "Well, I'm sorry to say that there is no other way."

My eyes grew so wide that they might have fallen right out of the sockets. He wasn't going to say what it meant. But I was thinking it. If there was no way to get to Nollem, then there was no way to get out of the mines. We were stuck between cave ins. Bad just turned to worse.

"But," I was amazed that Findal had something to add to this news, "There is another passage. We can go down the left side of the 'Y' intersection we passed. According to the map, the end of that tunnel lands us pretty near another tunnel that would lead us right into the prison area. So I think it's worth a shot to try to break through the small separation. It means some work, but it's better than giving up."

Everyone agreed to that, and we backtracked to the 'Y'. Dwin seemed to be doing better with every step we took. Either the water, the rest, or both helped him in some tremendous way.

Everyone kept to their own thoughts, which I was pretty sure were all about our doom. Our focus suddenly shifted from Nollem to our own survival. In a futile attempt to distract myself, I tried to keep my mind on Nollem. We were here for him, to rescue him. I had to get to Nollem. I had to rescue him. He was depending on me.

We reached another intersection, one tunnel going straight, another to the right, and another to the left. Here, Findal stopped dead in his tracks. I watched as his head swung in each of the directions. His forehead was wrinkled with confusion. As his confusion deepened, his hands followed his head as he tried to figure out the problem.

The rest of us had no clue what that problem was. But none of us wanted to interrupt him while he was in "the mood," since that would not usually end in a pretty scene.

He finally pulled out his map and scoured it. Then he tapped his finger knowingly to the side of his head and he uttered an, "Ah ha!" He got a funny smile on his face and muttered more to himself than anyone else, "I knew something was up."

I felt like my mind would explode if he didn't start explaining himself. Thankfully for the safety of my brain, Findal turned on his heel and faced us all, a bright, knowing, I'm-feeling-smart expression over his face. "This," he pointed dramatically at the tunnel to the right, "ladies and gentlemen, is our ticket out."

Still just as lost as before, I blurted, "What are you talking about?"

"This here tunnel, is not on the map." He made a pause for added effect before he continued, "Therefore, my fine friends, it is likely that it leads out to the main tunnels. since it was added *after* this map was made, it more than likely will lead us to a main corridor."

Kattim spoke up, clarifying for the rest of us as well, "So you're saying we should follow it and see where it leads?"

"Precisely, Kat, precisely my point."

"Okay then, let's do it."

"Alrighty, follow me to victory, and the way out!" He dramatically turned on his heel and marched down the tunnel to the right with his torch brightly illuminating the way.

We all followed him, and he led us after some time to a place where the tunnel ceiling rose high, and the walls widened to create a big, black hole, eagerly waiting to swallow us. I stepped cautiously out of the smaller tunnel. The sounds of our footsteps echoed in such a different manner that I could tell we had entered into a large, spacious room. The light of the torches was lost and drowned out before it revealed the sight of a roof. This chamber was very large indeed.

Findal halted once more and pulled out his map. He looked about him, then back at the map. Somehow, I think from guesstimating our diverged course to where we were now, he put things together and located us on the map. Though he said that he couldn't be sure that this room was on the map, because the new tunnel showed that this map was outdated.

That bit of information nearly threw me into a panic, because now we really had no way of knowing what lay ahead. But Findal did add that the tunnels laid out by this map had to still be there, because miners never reburied a tunnel once it was dug, they only added on to what they dug out.

That was a slight comfort, but not really. Then he looked around once again and pointed, saying, "If my guess as to our location is right, then there should be a tunnel to our left, and that should split into two tunnels that meet up and form one again."

In accordance, he ventured in the direction he indicated, his torch held out at arms length. And likewise, there was a tunnel that tapered down to the usual size. Findal had been right so far, and only a bit more before he could definitely prove our location.

I strained to see beyond the others and into the darkness beyond. But nothing new would appear, no matter how hard I tried.

There! the tunnel was split into two tunnels that branched away from each other! We were found! Findal whisked out the map and traced the route to the prison area with his finger. He exclaimed, "By jolly, all we have to do is go straight, hang a right, follow that one tunnel to its end, and bingo, we're there!"

New hope blossomed out, and our steps were revived to a quicker, lighter pace.

There's a saying that I have found to be true: "When in doubt, follow you nose."

Not that we were in doubt of where we were going—the tunnel was rather straight forward—but there was doubt of when we would come upon the prison. Well, our noses cleared that up for us. We knew immediately when we were getting closer by the stench that wafted up the tunnel to torture our noses.

I wrinkled my nose and lifted a hand to cover it. I even tried to filter my breathing with my wrap, but nothing helped. It only grew stronger as we went on. I eventually gave up my attempt to protect my nose against the offending odor.

Up ahead there was a slight bend in the tunnel. It was curved just enough to block from view what rested beyond it. I had a funny feeling about that corner. It did not vary in appearance to any other we had passed, but I just knew that something was going to be different. I anticipated the thing that lay on the other side. I moved to my left, trying to catch just a glimpse. Nothing... Nothing... There!

Oh, no...

As I rounded the bend, the sights, smells, and feel of the odious cave battered my senses, leaving nothing but a cold sinking feeling in the pit of my stomach. Nollem had been here how long? And I had not come for him sooner?

A faint light dimly outlined everything in shades of dark grey and black. The tunnel broadened into a vast room carved out of the earth and stone. It was long and narrow, and divided into "cells" by earthen pillars and rows of metal bars. None of the cells had doors on them, leaving the inhabitants to wander as they pleased. Old, musty, rotting straw had been spread over the floor, from the looks of it, years ago. Waste, piles of rags, and who knows what else, lay strewn in corners and against pillars. There was no movement except rats lazily lumbering over the piles. Even as we approached, the rats showed no fear.

I saw no people at first, then I realized that the heaps of rags had people under them. No, the heap of dirty rags was the person. The only reason I figured this out was because a foot, thin and sallow, was protruding from a pile in a corner. To my shock, I saw that the rest of the person was just as ghostly and faint as the foot. He appeared to be sleeping, yet his eyes were wide open. He was staring at nothing, eyes vague and large in his gaunt face. His skin sagged at the joints and clung to his bones everywhere else. He was barely alive, his ragged breaths wheezing in and out like a pebble rattling in a tin can.

His skin, so pale and grey, blended in with the stone walls he was curled up by. He was half covered with shreds of rags, his upper back completely exposed. Long old scars ran up and down his back.

I shudder at the thought of what could have made those. A realization sprung upon me with startling urgency; if Nollem looked like this man, he didn't have much time left. I had to find him. I frantically started searching in the corners for his face. No other thoughts entered my mind.

The others caught the idea and we fanned out, searching through the expansive prison.

Every person I passed resembled the first one I saw. It seemed that his condition was the story of everyone here. All looked near death, and all looked like they would welcome death. In the back of one cell, in the darkest corner, a group of rats had congregated, crawling over a heap much like the ones I passed. I did not pause to consider more thoroughly what the rats were doing. Skeletons, picked clean, were everywhere. The live people and the bones nearly looked the same.

Very few of the heaps moved when I passed. If they did, they shied back in fear, a crazy wild look in their pale, large eyes.

I practically ran from one person to another, my eyes only looking for one face. I grew more frantic when I saw the far end of the prison getting nearer. There was no sound except the footsteps of my companions and I, my quickened breath, and the rats. Another heap of rags, not Nollem. Too old. Another ashen skeleton.

From a far corner to my left, in the very back of the prison, Findal's voice rang out, "Over here! We've found him."

I spun on my heel and dashed back the way I'd came, searching for a way to get to the third and final row of shallow cells. I ran back to where we first came out of the tunnel, hung a quick left, and dashed down the third row. I caught sight of Findal and Kattim, crouching on the cold floor, looking closely at a heap against that wall. A pillar blocked my view from seeing the heap, all I could see was a foot and part of a leg.

Running over to them, I passed the pillar and saw Nollem, what was left of him, at least. Under a few soiled rags was the huddled form of my brother. He too was strangely thin and pale. His eyes were closed and it looked like he wasn't moving. I immediately feared that we might have come too late. He looked so much like the skeletons I passed by.

I fell against the wall he was propped up against and threw my arms around him, not caring about the dirt and grime. A sick feeling swept over me when I felt no response from him.

Findal grabbed me by the arm and hauled me off him, saying, "Limira, careful, you'll crush him."

I was crying by now, and I pawed after his hand, enfolding his cold, thin one in my own. I stared into his face, his deathly pale and hollow face. He looked like nothing but a shadow leaning against the wall.

The others came up behind me, all stopping one by one to look on sadly. But I didn't notice. My heart broke inside me for the loss of him, my mind racing to things I wish I hadn't said and done, and to the things I wish I could say, but never would be able to. I sobbed out, crying his name over and over, "Nollem! Don't leave me! Don't you die on me! Nollem, Nollem, please be alive."

Nothing.

Findal bowed his head. Kattim looked away. Dwin moved up behind me and put a hand on my shoulder.

I could do nothing but stare deploringly at his still face. It was seared with pain and agony. He didn't even go peacefully. How could he be...? I couldn't even bring the word to mind.

Then his eyelids fluttered just a bit. I caught my breath, seizing for any shred of hope. He opened his eyes about halfway and jerked his hand in mine. Pulling away in fear, he coiled further into a ball huddled against the wall, only chancing a glance at me.

I stared at him, only the more concerned by his behavior, though I understood it at the same time.

His pale grey eyes stared back at mine in fear for few moments. Then something changed in them; they grew softer with recognition. He relaxed a little, and whispered, breath slipping laboriously between his lips, "Limira, is that really you?"

New tears of joy flooded my cheeks, I nodded my head, drawing him into my arms, "Yes, it's me." No words could thoroughly describe my feelings, nor what passed between us in that moment. Only joy and relief could begin to.

He had no strength to return my embrace, he only rested his head on my shoulder. He whispered faintly, "I knew you would come."

I nodded again, just holding him. When my tears finally subsided, I began to notice the more practical things. He was dressed in dark tattered clothing, barely covering him. He shivered with cold, the rags he had covered himself with had now fallen off.

Pulling off the wrap I had about my shoulders, I wrapped it snuggly around his gaunt frame. That's when I saw his back and sides through the tears and holes in his shirt. He was laced with scars. Some older, some newer. His arms, neck and chest were dark with bruising, and he had deep cuts that were crusted with dry blood.

My anger flared, and I wanted to demand what they had done to him, but I knew that this wasn't the place nor the time. I also knew that, just like I couldn't begin to tell all of what Master Abburn had done to me, I might never know what had really happened to him these last nine months. There would be some questions that he wouldn't be able to answer. I guess I had to start preparing myself for that now, rather than later.

Dwin moved in closer. I knew that he was thinking of the next stage in our flight.

The worst of it was yet to come. We had to get to the other side of the mountain without being caught or killed, with Nollem as he was. It was obvious that he would have to be carried, but I had never imagined his injures to be as bad as this.

An arm still wrapped around Nollem and one hand safely in mine, I said softly to him, trying to explain things a little, "We're going to get you out and back home, a cozy place called the Den. Dwin here—you remember Dwin—is going to carry you. I'll be right here for you. There's no need to worry."

Nollem merely nodded his acknowledgement, his eyes drooping closed again.

Dwin stooped down and gently picked him up, suppressing a painful grimace. Nollem's frail form looked so small in Dwin's secure arms. I continued to hold his hand.

Nollem, in Dwin's arms, turned to face me. In his faint voice, he urged, unfeigned concern in his eyes, "Limira, wait, we can't go yet." There was a pause for him to take a breath. "We've got to get Arkona too."

I frowned, not fully understanding what he was saying, "What's that?"

He took another breath, "Arkona, we've got to rescue Arkona too."

"No," I said quickly, "we've got to get you out of here."

He actually frowned at me, his voice gaining more force, "No, I can't leave without her. I promised—!"

"Nollem, *I* have to get you out of here, we don't have time." And that ended that, Nollem's strength failing him.

Findal took the lead, and we picked our way between heaps and pillars to the entrance of the prison. It was wide and lofty, allowing for a chilling draft to rush in. The air was frigid and the sky full of sooty smog. I couldn't imagine what it must have been like during the winter months. I didn't want to know.

The entrance had no gate, as I was expecting to find. We filed out of the cave to find ourselves on the inside of a fenced in area. I would call it a yard, but there was not a blade of grass to be seen, it was one big mud bowl. The fence consisted of a bunch of wires stretched loosely between posts. It didn't look like it would keep anybody in, but I afterwards realized that it wasn't the fence that kept them in, it was the fear of being caught.

There was a large, imposing iron gate at the far corner. It was wide open. Not that we cared much about it. I figured that we wouldn't be using it.

As soon as we emerged from the old mine opening, a shout irrupted from near the gate. Immediately, I looked to find the source. My worst fear were coming true. There were at least fifteen Vaudians who had been sitting by the open gate, but were now on their feet. In the harsh language, they shouted at us with anger, surprise and rage. After a moments hesitation, half the group started to trudge towards us through the muck. The other half of the group jogged along the outside of the fence, moving to cut us off as we slipped through the fence.

Findal turned straight for the wire fence. Our steps were hurried with the urgency of getting out before they reached us.

Getting through the fence was easy enough. Findal spread the loose wires apart and we slipped through. Nollem was a bit of a challenge, but we soon had him through. The Vaudians within the yard quickly realized they wouldn't be able to do anything, and they ran back to the gate to join the rest of their party. We formed a circle, our backs to the fence, our swords ready. Dwin, helpless with Nollem in his arms, stayed behind us all.

The Vaudians were soon right in front of us, their ugly black swords raised, their faces contorted with malice and an evil pleasure at cruelty.

We all knew what would happen if we didn't kill them. We would either be thrown into the prison after a sound beating, or tortured slowly till we were dead. Or both.

Nollem would be killed in agonizingly brutal pain. That much was for certain, but there was no way of knowing what other cruelties they would invent for particular use on us. The thoughts were grim and steeled our minds to not allow that outcome, no matter how desperate the fight became.

The first one charged at me. Waiting till the last second, I raised my sword quickly to block his large descending one. A metallic ring filled the air as they collided. The sounds of other battles commencing rang off the mountain side and echoed all around me. It became nothing but background noise for me.

The Vaudian grunted in anger: he thought for sure he was going to capture me. He pulled back his sword and swung down at me with twice the strength as before. I raised my sword again, blocking it at the cost of my hands tingling from the impact. Determined to stand my ground, I curved my sword, throwing his blade from mine. I quickly completed the maneuver in one fluid motion, nicking just under the armor that protected his knee. He let out a scream of rage and pain, though more rage than pain. The Vaudian responded by letting lose a torrent of blows, raining down on me.

Using every technique I knew, I blocked them as best I could, being forced to retreat a step, then another. I knew that I was losing ground. The thought threw me into severe defense. I waited for the right time, feeling his pattern. Just as he was in a break, there! I thrust my sword up and under his breast plate. The heavy, black sword lowered, mid strike. He doubled over, driving my sword home. His sword dropped to the ground. The Vaudian's eyes rolled back, as he fell over on his side. His face was still and vacant.

I stared at him, my hands dropping to my side, having let go of my sword when he fell over. It protruded out of his middle, a dark wet mark appearing around it. In shock, I reached for my sword and tugged it out.

I had actually killed him.

Chapter 32
The Cost of Life

I had never killed anyone before.

My sword was dark with blood, leaving drips on the stoney ground. I had never killed anyone before. Strange to say, I was sorry that I had killed him, even though he was a Vaudian. I had actually killed him. As in... dead.

I stared at his motionless body. A sick feeling swept over me. Somehow, the thought of all the things he had done to deserve it didn't make the feeling go away. I had still killed him.

I was given little time to further contemplate what I had done. Another Vaudian took the place of the last one, charging at me, sword raised in a high guard. He was upon me in an instant. Our swords clashed, a metallic ring joining the others. With every blow I deflected, the bolder I grew. I switched the tide, rushing a torrent of blows on him from various sides. This caught him completely off guard, and I dispatched him with a blow to the neck.

A third Vaudian rose up in his place, giving me no pause to think or even recover. My sword blurred and whirled, racing to block and deliver blows. This one was angry, purely angry, and his emotion played out in his execution of blows. He was quick and forceful, yet reckless. That was his eventual downfall.

But he kept me quite on my toes till then. He drew me away from the tight knit circle, leaving a gap and my back exposed. The worst part of it was I had no idea that he was doing it until it was too late. I was busy blocking his powerful strokes. Our swords were locked in a dual of strength. My arms were shaking, straining to keep my ground, he was grinning like nothing else, and he looked over my shoulder once or twice. I should have caught the hint.

Dwin's voice rose over the din, filled with urgency and alarm, "Limira! Watch your back!"

As soon as I heard it, I realized what had happened. I didn't know what to do. I couldn't just disengage with this fellow: he would slice me in an instant. But on the other hand, my back was completely exposed.

In my hesitation, the Vaudian, who had come up behind me, let his sword descend with a blow that would cleave me in half.

With a quick glance over my shoulder, I saw the sword dropping rapidly out of the corner of my eye. Immediately ducking, I disengaged the lock I had with the first Vaudian, and slipped to one side. The move caught both of them by surprise, and neither had time to recover. The Vaudian from behind couldn't stop his cut, and the Vaudian from in front was pressing so hard on me that he pitched forward, right into the blade of the other Vaudian.

I regained my position and readied myself for the next one.

The Vaudian who had killed the other stared blankly for a second at the dead creature at his feet. His sword was sticking out of the fallen Vaudian, and that seemed to be the only proof that he had actually killed him. The Vaudian quickly came out of his momentary shock, seized his sword, roughly pulled it out, and charged recklessly at me.

I blocked his first blow. It was heavy and forceful, nearly knocking my sword from my sweaty grip. We exchanged a few blows, both blocking them well enough. I was getting tired, and it was starting to show. Sweat beaded down my forehead and ran down my back. I wasn't able to withhold the full impact from a heavy blow either.

He delivered two strokes, one from each side. I caught and deflected the first, but didn't get my sword over fast enough to fully block the second. I caught his sword with mine but didn't have enough force to stop it completely. His black sword cut into my right shoulder, nearly over top of the scratch the Orodume gave me. I cried out in pain. My sword dropped slightly, my arm radiating with pain, but he drew his sword back. My left hand flew to my shoulder. My right hand, with sword in it, dropped to my side. I cringed, gasping in air. I raised my sword in a valiant effort to show that it wasn't that bad. I held back a small cry threatening to come out.

Catching on to the indicator, the Vaudian, with a wicked grin on his scarred face, got me locked into a hold, our steel blades collided and froze. The ultimate test of whose strength and willpower would outlast the others. I brought my left hand down, now slippery with red blood, to help out. He pressed harder. I screamed as darting pain shot up and down my arm.

It was pretty obvious whose strength would fail first. I didn't stand a chance and I knew it. With a new air of disparity, I searched for anyway to get out of the lock.

The Vaudian pushed harder. I was forced to take a step back, then another. I didn't want to go too far back, seeing how it would push me further away from the group. I had to stay by them, or else all hope was gone.

Painfully, I held my sword, tightening my grip as I felt the pommel slipping. I thought of turning my blade to the side, but I couldn't move my arms without the threat of his sword going right through me. My grip was slipping again, this time I couldn't hold it still. His sword slowly advanced towards my face. My arms bent at my elbows, my blade coming nearer to my shoulder.

The Vaudian's grin widened.

Just as I thought I couldn't hold him back any longer, the tip of a sword protruded out of his chest. Then it suddenly disappeared. His force against me stopped, his sword dropped and he fell to one side, dead. From behind the body, Dwin, his red stained sword in hand, stood staring me in the eye.

My mouth gaped open in surprise and shock. I actually dropped my sword, grimacing in pain as the wound reminded me of its existence. My left hand clapped over the bleeding cut. Then I looked up at Dwin. It was then that I realized that it was Dwin who was standing there. My first thought was, "Where's Nollem—"

Dwin held up a hand to stop me, and replied, "He's fine. He's over there leaning against the fence. No one else could help you, so I put him down and came." He looked at my shoulder, "You okay?"

While he was speaking, my gaze wandered over the four dead Vaudians at my feet. I stared in horror at their contorted faces and the growing dark red stains. I vaguely heard Dwin's last question in the distance, and it took me a moment to recall it, then give an answer. I dumbly nodded my head and said in a distant voice, "Yeah, sure..."

I'm pretty certain that Dwin said something else but I didn't hear him. My eyes had fallen on the expression of the Vaudian who had gotten me so close to defeat. His scarred, brown face still held an eerie grin on it. His eyes stared at nothing, his grin growing wider in my mind. It was almost like he was coming to life. In my mind, his eyes were moving, and they were looking straight into mine. I trembled, and took a step back, having no other response but to stare back wide eyed.

A shout from Kattim roused me from my stupor. It sounded like she was in pain. Jerking my head up, I saw Grenith dispatch a Vaudian that was attacking Kattim. Kattim was leaning over, her face drawn into a grimace, her hand clasp over her upper left arm. Red was seeping through her fingers and over her jerkin sleeve.

Grenith recovered her sword and stood ready. She and Findal were staring down the final Vaudian, both with faces of grim determination. Dwin moved over to Kattim, and I joined Findal and Grenith in putting up a brave face. I raised my sword, but without the same imposing look.

The remaining Vaudian, who stood a few feet from us, looked from one of us to the other. His eyes darted nervously from us to the rest of his former companions at our feet. He took a step back. Then another. His eyes getting more frantic and desperate. Another step.

Findal took an impressive step forward, deepening his scowl.

That quailed the heart of the Vaudian in an instant. He took one hasty step back then turned on his heel and ran for his life back down the mountain. He was dashing towards the dark city that lay below us. For the first time since we had emerged from the prison, I noticed it. It was rather a grand set up, all the buildings carved out of stone, a great stone tower rising up among them. I didn't get much chance to view it further before we were running away from it.

Kattim had rolled up her sleeve and was holding the material against her wound to help stop the bleeding. I didn't have time to do anything with my cut. I held my arm, cradling it in attempt to ease the throbbing. My first cut from the Orodume had split open during the sword fighting. The second was much deeper and two inches off my shoulder.

I got one last glimpse at the Vaudian who nearly killed me, his still form laying there, the dark spot on his back growing.

I was practically dragged away by Grenith, her arm hooked through mine. Dwin had picked up Nollem again, and we were off, trying to get as far as we could before we had a new company of Vaudians pursuing us.

It was rather slow going at first, Dwin finding it awkward to hold Nollem and watch his footing at the same time.

I kept looking to the sky and looking back, expecting to see a dozen or more Orodumes circling, waiting to attack in their slow way, and a hundred angry faced Vaudians racing after us. It kept my nerves on end. At any sound that even resembled the signature low moan of an Orodume or the harsh, throaty sound of a Vaudian, I would jump and reach for my sword.

I kept telling myself that I was overreacting, that I should stay calm, that everything was going to be fine, like I had told Nollem. But I failed to convince myself.

Slowly, we made our way around the mountain. My edginess caught on, soon everyone was looking to the sky and over their shoulders, anticipating the worst. But either they weren't there, or they refused to show themselves. The latter was more likely.

And it proved true, just not at all when we were expecting. The barrier was in sight, about where we had first crossed through too. We were fifty feet from it when a score of Orodumes swooped down as one unit. They came suddenly which was very uncharacteristic for them.

Likeminded, we didn't even bother to stand and fight. Though I did draw my sword in all readiness for a fight, only with great protest from my shoulder. Instead we dashed for the barrier, running with all the strength we could muster. Dwin had the hardest of it. I had mentally determined that I would hang back with him if he fell behind, but I found myself running as hard as I could just to keep up with him.

Almost to the barrier, it blurred and rippled as everyone passed through it. I was last. Just before I passed through, I took one glance at the Orodumes. They were flying low, and had nearly caught up to us. Then they disappeared as I crossed.

We kept running, hanging to the right, hoping to reach our horses before the Orodumes reached us. At any moment the whole pack of Orodumes could come bursting through the barrier. I continuously glanced over my shoulder, every time expecting them to dart out right behind us. None did.

We got to our horses, untied them, mounted, and rode northwest. Dwin kept Nollem in front of him. Nollem had fallen unconscious sometime during the trek. We didn't bother then to tend to any wounds, it was more important to put as much distance between us and the mountains as possible.

Still no Orodumes or Vaudians.

Chapter 33
The Beginnings of Healing

The return journey to the old Lightbearer base was long and nerve wracking. It took us six days to get back because Nollem couldn't travel very well. We were all concerned about him, me most of all. Sleep was haunted by nightmares of Nollem, and I would wake up scared half out of my wits. Every time I had to make sure, beyond a doubt, that he was still alive. He always was, but I would do it all over again several times that same night and the next few nights to come. When morning dawned, I would wake up and make sure, just as the sun was rising, that he had made it through the night.

There was no reason for so much of my concern, he was already improving with proper food, water and clothing. But my mind tortured me with the thought that he would die, that he was dead, or that he would suddenly take a turn for the worse and die during the night. But every morning, I would wake up and find him alive, if not more alive than the night before.

Even if he was not actually struggling between life and imminent death, in my mind he was. Death was so prominent, those Vaudians, those heaps of rags huddled in corners, those people on the streets of the city where I was sold as a slave, the citizens of Moneth, Chimel, Bilham, that family of Between murdered before my very eyes. It seemed like every death came forward in my dreams, taunting and tormenting me with all those whom I saw.

But Nollem was alive. I couldn't give up on him. He was alive, even if my mind thought he was dead. He was alive and I needed to think of him as so.

I was alive, and I needed to think of myself as so. Death had no hold over me, even if it was on my doorstep, or waiting around the corner to get me. Death had no authority over me. I was under the authority of Shalom, the love of Shalom. Nothing could take me away from that. But still, the reign of the nightmares lived on.

It was these things that were constantly brought up and debated in my mind. I knew that they were true, but it was very hard to put that knowledge into practice. I was struggling, with very little hope in sight. No one seemed to notice. No one asked about it. All energies were focused on Nollem and getting home.

Kattim got a proper bandage for her cut, and I got mine looked after too. It continued to hurt and bother me, adding to the sleepless nights. I did my best to ignore it, but amid silent tears, there was an occasional cry of pain stifled in my wrap late at night.

During the day, I was devoted to Nollem, glued to his side. I was constantly fretting over him. And Dwin was constantly fretting trying to stop me from fretting.

Grenith was still subdued, she hadn't quite recovered to her usual bubbly self. She seemed thoughtful and remorseful, but when asked, she said it was nothing and put on that fake happy face. But it was just a mask.

Kattim was just plain sullen and hateful. She always had very curt, angry responses for anything that I said to her. If I asked for her to get something for Nollem, she would roll her eyes and grudgingly get it, giving me all the grief she could manage. I had never seen this side of Kattim before, and it wasn't a very pleasant one. Her mood was not at all helpful, and only made my day more miserable. I soon, sad to say, caught myself wondering what was worse, night time terrors and pains, or day time nagging and unpleasantness.

Findal tried playing the general peacekeeper, but he gave up after a while, since it only succeeded in riling himself up.

Dwin also attempted to be a peacemaker, but his own set of troubles seemed to occupy his attentions.

Overall it was a stressful six days. And it didn't help when we found ourselves a little short on food rations.

But we all lived and made it back to the Den without ripping each others' hair out, so I guess that counts for something.

When we got into the Den, it was in the late evening of the sixth day. Kattim went directly to bed, complaining of a headache. Findal took care of the horses, making sure they had a place to rest for the night. Grenith was kind in offering to help bring the necessities from the horses into the Den. Dwin picked up Nollem who was either unconscious or sleeping, and carried him down, while I flew around them, giving my advice and making quite the scene. Once we got into the Den, I set up a cot before the fire with plenty of warm blankets, by order of Dwin. Laying Nollem down, Dwin settled to making a fire. I put myself to the task of tucking Nollem in with much fuss.

I then insisted on staying the night with him. Dwin, tired of my nagging, consented, not seeing the point of opposing me. I quickly got my cot and settled it by Nollem's. It was hard to tell if Nollem would be fine for the night, if he was comfortable or not. I couldn't tell if he was unconscious or just sleeping. His breathing was steady and he had a peaceful look on his face, so I contented myself with that.

Not really feeling sleepy, I pulled off a wool blanket from my cot and curled up under it in one of the big armchairs by the hearth. Dwin let us be and returned above ground to help with the final settling of things.

I stared at Nollem's calm face, studying every line, hollow and mark. I was impressing his image in my mind. I didn't ever want to forget what his face looked like, even in the current condition. My mind strayed from thinking about him to everything else that had happened. I remembered the Orodume attack, Dwin's injuries, his face creased in pain. How late we were, how we couldn't go back out. Kattim and I got injures from it. Nollem had to endure the trek around the mountain; it was all my fault. It was my fault that Nollem was the way he was now. I had failed to find him sooner, I hadn't even thought of what he could have been going through while I was living safely and joyfully at the Den. He was going through the worst of times, I the best of times. Even worse, I had given up, thinking he was dead.

I was such an awful person. I had made fun of him, I had resented him for believing in Shalom, it should have been me in there. But it was Nollem. He had such a good heart. He had even wanted to bring...

My heart despaired even more. He had even wanted to rescue a friend he had made there. Even while being rescued from the worst of places, he was thinking not of himself, but of others. And what had I done? Pushed him off. I didn't care about anyone there but him. I had passed by all those heaps, all people waiting, needing to be saved. And I just went right by them.

Even when Nollem insisted on saving someone, I pushed it aside. What was her name? And didn't Nollem say that he had promised? And what had I done? Nothing. Absolutely nothing.

❦

I woke up to the see Dwin stoking the fire. I brushed the sleep from my eyes, stirring in my seat. I was surprised to find that I was in the chair. I must have fallen asleep while I was thinking.

Dwin glanced up when he heard me moving and he whispered, "Sorry, I didn't mean to wake you."

I shook my head and whispered back, "No, it's fine." My gaze fell to Nollem, still stretched out on the cot. It looked as if he hadn't moved all night. My mind jumped to the worst conclusion, and I watched for breathing, holding my own breath in anticipation. His chest rose and fell gently. I let out a pent up breath, and glanced back at Dwin. It was then that I realized he was staring at me.

I managed a half smile, as if to say that I was okay, even though I was far from it.

I knew he took note of it, but he didn't mention it. "You want to help me clean up his wounds?" he asked as he stood up.

I nodded my reply and stretched in the large chair. I heard Dwin gathering things together in the kitchen. My mind jumped back to the time when I had first arrived at the Den. It was late, Findal and I had gotten off on the wrong foot by accusing each other of the worst we could think of, and when we finally made peace—ish—we came down, and Dwin and Kattim gave the warmest of receptions. I thought more particularly of when Dwin so studiously cleaned the burns on my arms. Pain had fogged the details of the event, but I remember the basic parts. He had tried distracting me by getting me to tell of my adventures. It only half worked. I smiled at the picture of what we must have looked like. Me grimacing and trying not to scream because of the pain, and he trying to be as gentle yet thorough as possible and distract me at the same time.

I startled out of my thoughts. Dwin had reappeared with a basin of steaming water, some cloths and a few glass bottles. It was all too familiar.

I threw off my blanket and joined him on the smooth earthen floor. He put the cloths in the basin, then turned his attention to Nollem. He carefully removed the blanket, pulling it down to his waist. I moved to help unbutton his shirt, but my shoulder complained loudly against it. I had forgotten about it and was both surprised and pained by it. I drew in a quick breath, pressing my lips together tightly.

Dwin glanced up, his quick eye catching everything. He said quietly, "We can take a look at that after this if you'd like."

I quickly responded, "No, it's alright. It doesn't bother me much." It was a lie and we both knew it.

Dwin gave me the look that said, "Really?" and he added with just as quiet a tone as last time, "Not buying it."

I sighed in frustration. "Fine, but make sure it's well after Nollem's been taken care of."

"I'll settle for that."

He had unbuttoned and laid open Nollem's tattered shirt. I bit my lip, holding back the urge to cry. His chest was black and purple with bruises and had nasty deep cuts along it. Scars from other wounds lined his sides. Some of them rounded in continuation from his back. Dwin wrung out a cloth and handed it to me, while he got the other.

With my left hand, I started with one of the cuts, soaking away the dried blood and dirt.

The job was a tough one, and it took a long time. But once we were done, he was clean, and his wounds bandaged with ointment put over them. Then we changed him into a set of clean clothes. They hung sadly about his shrunken frame, making him look even smaller than before.

Nollem slept peacefully through it all, only muttering a few inaudible words once or twice.

It was then that I asked where everyone else was, only just realizing that I hadn't seen any of them yet.

Dwin, picking up the things and readying to go back to the kitchen, replied, "They're still asleep."

I frowned. We had been up for a while. "What time is it?"

He shrugged and said, "Probably around six thirty."

I stared at him incredulously, "What time did you get up?"

"Oh, around five, I suppose," was his guesstimated answer.

I continued to stare at him.

"What?" he asked with an air of innocence, "I couldn't sleep."

Oh, sure, I thought to myself, *likely story.*

He busied himself over in the kitchen again. I moved back to the big chair and wrapped myself in the woolen blanket. I stared at the dancing flames, occasionally glancing at Nollem. Then Dwin appeared from around the chair and settled next to me, a basin of fresh water and a roll of bandage in his hand.

I sighed testily, but held to my word in allowing him to clean my cut better. Grenith had only cleaned it a little then put a bandage over it. That was five days ago. I wasn't sure how I felt about Dwin doing it, but he was insisting. But still...

He looked expectantly at me.

I returned his gaze, and said, "I'm not taking my jerkin off! I'll roll up the sleeve."

"I wasn't expecting you to," He replied softly.

Ignoring his comment, I set to rolling up my sleeve, but didn't get very far. Dwin stepped in and rolled it up all the way.

Thankfully the jerkin was big for me, otherwise the armhole wouldn't have allowed itself to be pulled over my shoulder.

The white bandage Grenith had placed over it was now soaked through, a dark red stain over the cut. I sighed when I saw it. I knew what that meant; we'd have to soak the bandage off. And that hurt.

Dwin bit his lip and set a wet cloth over it gently. I winced, it was still really painful to the touch. Dwin's eyebrows shot up and he commented, "Doesn't bother you much, huh?"

I shot an angry glance at him, but chose not to say anything back. I wasn't in the mood for an all out battle with him.

Silence reigned and after a little while he removed the wet rag. Then he cut the bandage and pulled up the first layer. I lifted my arm with a grimace, and he rolled the top layer of the soiled bandage under my arm. Then he paused when he reached the top of my shoulder. The next layer was dried on. He placed the wet rag on it again. And the whole process started over again.

It went on for a while, feeling even longer because of the awkward silence that we both kept so perfectly. Small talk only failed and threw us back into silence. Small talk had never really worked between us in the first place. Finally, after a long silence, Dwin spoke, "You know, I used to be just like those Vaudians."

That caught my attention. I quickly looked at him, confusion clouding my countenance. "What do you mean?" I asked with uncertainty.

It was a little while before Dwin spoke again. When he did, his voice was low and thoughtful, "It was a long time ago now. I lived in Birset when Deceiver took over the city. I was just a boy then and went by my given name. Lord Gernton saw me, I don't remember what he saw in me, or why I agreed. I don't recall much from the nights, who's to say what I did as a Between?

"Lord Gernton was a powerful general in Deceiver's army. He trained me and under his supervision, I became a commander of Between myself. At some point during this, I too became a Vaudian, my night appearance becoming permanent. I keep thinking that I was just like those who attacked us. Mindless, filled with violence, brutish."

I had never thought that Vaudians could change, but somehow Dwin did. During his pause, I asked softly, "What happened between then and now?"

"I was commissioned with my men to raid Post Balder. The men of Monare Pelm won, killing most of my men, taking the rest of us captive. I was severely wounded during the battle. All I remember is that I was in the house of the Kelvin's, in the village of Divel. The Monare Pelm soldiers had moved on, considering me basically dead. As I recovered, Mr. Kelvin taught me about Shalom, and he completed my training in weaponry. I went by my father's name when I was with the Kelvin's. Then he commissioned me to return to Deceiver's land and live for Shalom. That's how I became a part of the Lightbearer resistance. I worked against Deceiver for many years."

"And that's how you met Kattim?"

"Yes, a while after that."

"What was this base like? When it was full and active with Lightbearers?"

He smiled at distant memories, explaining, "I wish you could have seen it. It was quite the hopping place. People coming and going, Lightbearers commissioned and being received. The communication department coordinated movement and made attack plans when we would raid Deceiver's camp. The kitchens were busy nonstop."

"Where are they now?"

"I'm not sure," Dwin paused, thinking. "When Deceiver overtook the town above us, they moved to a different location, but I could never find it again. And I searched too."

He stopped again, reminiscing. When he continued, he had a certain smile, one I had never seen before. "There was a girl who worked in the communication department. She had fiery blue eyes and yet such a gentle spirit. We had known each other for quite some time, growing closer. I finally asked her father if we could marry. He gave his blessing, she said yes, and we set a day for four weeks in advance. I was sent on a mission, and when I returned two weeks later, the town was desolated and all the Lightbearers had vanished."

I was surprised. I had never known that Dwin even liked a girl, much less almost married her. I knew she must have been very special to have caught his attention. "Have you ever seen her again?"

"Nope." He said briefly. "I searched for months, during which I met Kattim. After several years, some of them spent searching with Kattim, I thought maybe the Kelvin's would know where the new Lightbearer base was. That's one of the reasons we went to see them, and they hadn't heard anything. Then we met you, and here we are."

"What about Brene? He's in contact with the new base right?"

"Yes, but since they moved, its location has been keep hidden from almost everyone. They really tightened security around it, hoping the less people knew where it was, the less it would be in danger of discovery by the enemy."

"I'm sorry." I was at a loss of what else to say, and we fell back into our own thoughts. After a few moments, a question came to mind that I just had to ask, "Dwin, what was your emblem when you were a Vaudian?"

"It was the Crown. Why do you ask?"

Just then, Kattim came out from her room, and she sighted us immediately. Like an angry mother who has spotted the two culprits who broke her best Sunday dishes, she came storming over, a classic scowl plastered over her face.

Both Dwin and I exchanged questioning glances, wondering what we had done to upset her so much. Upset is a light word for what she was, a more fitting adjective would be furious, outraged, or boiling over with vexation. She stomped right up to us and practically shouted, "I've had enough—!"

"Shh!" Dwin and I hissed at her, motioning to Nollem.

She fell silent, but glared at us twisting her lips with new rage.

Dwin whispered, knowing how best to handle Kattim when she was like this, "Let me finish with this then we can talk in another room. Okay, Kat?"

She stiffly nodded her head once in agreement, still staring icicles at us.

Dwin turned back to dressing my wound. He gave me a knowing look that was a warning and a reassurance at the same time. I read it as, "Let me handle this," and, "She'll be fine after a good talk."

He finished rather quickly, wrapping my shoulder back up and suggesting, "I wouldn't use it very much for the next few days. It needs time to heal without being opened up again." Then he stood up and said to Kattim, "Alright, I'm ready."

She nodded, turned on her heel, and lead us towards my room. I stood and followed.

"So we don't disturb the others," Kattim said curtly. She marched in first, a frosty air in her wake. Dwin followed, wondering what could be eating at her. Last of all was me, waiting for a blow up with myself as the cause of it all.

We formed a loose circle in the middle of the room. Dwin and I looked at Kattim, she looked at us, still with a fire kindled in the back of her eyes.

Dwin said, "Well? What do you have to get out?"

Kattim took a short breath in agitation before blurting out, "What do I have to get out?! I'll tell you! I've had enough of seeing you two dote on each other!" My eyebrows shot up. "Especially you, *Dwin!* Ever since *she* went on that stupid training mission, all you talk about is *her!* Limira did this, Limira did that, I'm so proud of Limira. I'm tired of it! How you heroically killed that Orodume, which was *her* fault for it attacking you, then say it's fine, it's not her fault that it collided with you! Rubbish! How you look after her, she's your first concern, how you clean her wounds. You even came to her rescue when she was struggling against the Vaudian. Yes, I saw you! But I also noticed how you didn't think of me when I was struggling against a Vaudian! And now I have this," she indicated to her cut mark on her upper left arm, "to remind me how you ignored me! I can't even begin to tell you how frustrating this has been for me! *I* used to be your best companion, *I* was your confidant, *I* was your trainee, your prize. What happened? We used to be so close, then *she* stepped into the picture, and stole my best friend away from me! What do you have to say to that, huh?"

Dwin stared speechless at Kattim.

I started, seeing that he wasn't going to say anything, "Look, I—"

"No," Dwin cut me off. "Let me answer," he turned to Kattim, "since your main complaint is against me, it's only fair. I'm sorry that I have neglected you. My regard and value for our friendship has not lessened any more than before. It's true, I do watch Limira more carefully than you. But only because I have a trust in your skills. You have proved to me by experience that you can handle yourself in a pinch. Limira, on the other hand, is still rather new to all this. So of course, I'll be watching her, to make sure that no harm comes to her. I did the same to you when I first taught you. Sorry that it's irked you so much. But why didn't you tell me? Why didn't you just say that this was bothering you?"

At this point, I felt like I shouldn't have been there. It seemed like a personal thing between Kattim and Dwin.

Kattim took a minute to compose herself before she replied, "I didn't think that it was bothering me so much, not until it felt like I couldn't say anything about it. There were no open communications, no one asked as if they were truly concerned about what was going on."

"So you've carried this little grudge against me in your heart all this time, and as it grew, you started taking it out on Limira?"

"Yeah, I guess so," the fight was all out of her and she looked repentant.

"I think you know what you need to do," Dwin said softly.

Kattim sighed slightly, turned to me, and said, "I'm sorry, Limira. I wasn't directly angry at you, I didn't mean any unkind things I said and did. Will you forgive me?"

I nodded my head, readily wanting this sourness to pass, "Yes, I forgive you."

There was a pause before Dwin said, "Though, you know, you're right on one point, Kat. We've all been stuck in our own little worlds, we haven't been very open or real with each other."

Just then the door opened and Grenith's head poked through, "Hey there everyone. Party in Limira's room and I wasn't invited? What's up?"

Chapter 34
Deceiver On the Move

There was an awkward pause. None of us knew exactly what to say. We looked from one to the other, waiting for anyone but ourselves to answer.

Dwin finally cleared his throat and answered vaguely, "Uh, we were just, um, making up."

"Oh, I see Kat looks better already. Mind if I join in?"

No one had any objections and she stepped in, joining the circle.

I summed up the last few minutes to catch her up, "So we were just saying how it feels like we haven't been talking about things with each other."

"Well," Dwin added with more clarity, "It's more like we haven't been open or honest with each other. And I think we've all suffered the consequences from it."

"Yeah," was all Grenith could say, her face falling.

It hit home in all of us.

Dwin started slowly, "Well, I guess the only way not to fall into this again is to start being honest." It was rather obvious to all of us, but someone had to say it. "I guess I'll go first. Uh, I admit that I've been neglecting our friendship, Kat, and I'm sorry."

Grenith piped up next, "I, I have this foreboding feeling whenever I think of the prison. Don't get me wrong, I'm glad we rescued Nollem, but there's something unsatisfying about it, something still irking about it. Almost like we didn't do the right thing. And I can't put my finger on it. Besides I feel so sad for everyone we left behind."

I nodded, saying, "It's the crime of just passing by. We didn't care, it was only about Nollem."

Dwin agreed, summarizing after a moment, "Think if Shalom had only cared about one person, we'd all be without life. We shouldn't be choosy, He certainly wasn't."

"Now hold up," Kattim spoke up, "We've got to do this right. We're not going to fix anything by ourselves."

"Right," Dwin caught on quickly, "We have to start with Elohim first, then us."

"Meaning?" I asked.

"Meaning that we need to get right with Elohim before we can help others get right with Him. Our focus needs to be on Him, then everything will sort of follow along. Genuine love for others spills out of genuine love for Him, not anything we can muster up..."

So began the long days of watching, waiting and wondering. I never left Nollem's side for more than ten minutes. Days dragged into a week. The usual things went on all around Nollem and I, passing us by as if all we did was watch it go on without us.

Nollem would wake for a few minutes, then fall back asleep. Every moment that he lay awake was like a diamond, and I hated letting it go. He didn't even have to say anything, talk about his experiences, or even ask about mine, I was content just sitting by him, exchanging a whirlwind of messages through our expressions. To my joy, these moments lengthened with every day.

Before I knew it, he was sitting up and asking to be allowed to do something other than lay in one spot. We consented only to allowing him to sit by the fire. He did so. The first time was rather shaky in getting him from his cot to the chair, but it worked out in the end.

We would sit together, and that's when we started to actually talk about what we had done in the last nine months of separation. He asked what I had been up to, and I told him, relaying everything that I could remember since the journey to Moneth in the arms of Vaudians, through my imprisonment with Dwin, slavery, the gypsies, my first encounter with Orodumes, the marshes, finding the base, my training, my trip to Moneth with Grenith and Findal, my test mission—he also thought my rock climbing skills, or lack there of, were hilarious —then the recuse mission. I didn't go into great details on the last event, in fact, I offered nearly no details about it, being unsure of how he would react. And he didn't ask, so I was safe for a while at least.

When I had finished, I desperately wanted to ask what he had done, but I didn't have the courage nor the heart to do so. He kept asking about things that I had done, and I was getting the impression that he didn't want to talk about his side of things.

❦

Life continued to go on around us. Findal returned the horses to Brene, the old fellow from whom we got nearly all our supplies and all of our information. The next week, when Findal returned from meeting with Brene, he brought an interesting bit of information.

The very moment that Findal entered the Den, we all knew that he had some piece of news that none of us knew. We could easily tell by the way that he moseyed in with that particular look on his face. But when we asked him, he shook his head and held out his hands in innocence. We pestered him till he promised that he would only tell us at supper if we let him alone, otherwise, he wouldn't tell till breakfast.

We reluctantly agreed and we all nearly died of curiosity. The entire afternoon was spent discussing and guessing what this prized info might be.

By the time supper came around, we had determined from Findal's reaction when we mentioned it in front of him that the news wasn't someone getting married, a new recruit coming to stay with us, we had been given new assignments, the Lightbearers wanted to return their headquarters to here, nor had Brene finally got the donkey he had wanted for years. The last suggestion was offered in desperation.

When we all sat down with supper plates steaming on the table before us, Findal then cleared his throat dramatically. He looked at each one of us, directly in the eye.

We all hung on his every movement, supper momentarily forgotten.

He folded his arms before him, resting them on the table. Raising his chin just slightly, he proceeded to say, "Brene has promised me a new set of maps for next week! Isn't that awesome?!"

There was a loud groan as we all deflated in our disappointment. It was at that moment when I solidified the common supposition as a fact; Findal loved gaining every bit of attention he could.

Dwin's hands flew up in the air, his questioning, outraged expression the same as the rest of ours. He complained loudly, "What kind of news is that?!"

Similar complaints rose against him.

"You kept us in anticipation *all* day for that?"

Findal returned in his defense, "But they're new and updated."

"Oaky, that's it. From now on, *I'm* going to meet with Brene and actually get some real, *important* news."

"But that was important, come on guys!" Findal's reply was quickly drowned out.

"Oh, sure."

"We thought it was life and death!"

"And that had to wait till now?"

The hubbub lasted a good five minutes before Findal's voice rose above everyone else's. He was grinning from ear to ear, obviously rather pleased with himself. "Guys, that wasn't the information!"

We all stared at him again, silence reigning as we tried to determine truth from fiction.

"Wait," I asked, mentally questioning his motives and validity, "you mean to say that that wasn't the piece of news we've been waiting for?"

Findal burst out laughing, doubled over and pounding the table. The rest of us were dead serious about this, and we waited solemnly for his response.

Once he calmed down enough to speak between laughs, he asked of us, "Did you really think *that*?" He looked at each of us, and settled down even more. "Wow, okay. Make one joke and any previous trust is out the window. Do you really think that I would make you wait for that? I'd be way too excited to hold that back till now." He paused for any response.

I raised an eyebrow. None of us were impressed.

"It was a joke," Findal said, "would it kill you to lighten up a bit?" No response. "So maybe it would. But anyway, the information that I found out today... and yes, this is the real thing. So as you all know, I went to see Brene today, and I got to see our horses one last time before he had to send them back to wherever he got them from. Daisy is looking great, by the way —"

Kattim blurted out, "Just get to the point!"

"Fine," Findal returned, "he told me that Deceiver was on the move. But here's the important bit. Apparently word reached him that a group of *twenty* Lightbearers forced their way into the prison, got a prisoner, who was very important in the eyes of Deceiver, and left, overpowering numerous guards and killing several Orodume. We, my friends, are the strength of many. But that's not all, in revenge for the loses Deceiver has felt, he vows to march upon Monare Pelm, since he thinks that's where the attack originated. Though, I'm at a loss as to why he would think that, but whatever. So he's gathering his forces together, planning for an attack centralized on Monare Pelm, but we all know that he will destroy everything in his path, and maybe even a little out of his path. That, my friends, is the news I have."

Dwin spoke first, "That certainly is news. Do you have numbers?"

"No, none besides the fact that he's emptying Dol Guliab, and he's sending out word through Birset and Moneth to rally to Dol Guliab. We're looking at tens of thousands of well trained Vaudians and angry Between. It's going to be a mess."

"It's going to be bigger than a mess," I said. "Monare Pelm doesn't have the resources nor soldiers to combat those numbers. They're going to need help, and if it's anything like I know it, they won't admit to needing it."

Grenith asked, "So what are we going to do?"

Nollem's voice called from over by the fire. We didn't think he was up to sitting at the table with the rest of us yet. "Limira's right. I've seen the forces Deceiver has. Monare Pelm doesn't stand a chance. They'll need some serious reinforcements."

I looked over my shoulder. I frowned when I saw his thin face, pale with fear and memory. I said to him, "Nollem, I don't think you should—"

He cut me off, "It's fine, Limira. I can talk about it."

I nodded, more wanting to silence him before he looked even worse than actually agreeing with him, "Later, then." I turned back to the table. Everyone had witnessed it without saying a word. The discussion started once more, and Nollem didn't interrupt us again.

Findal spoke up, "I say the best thing that we can do is go over to Monare Pelm and try to warn people."

I quickly said, "They won't listen, I would know."

Dwin agreed with Findal, "Not that it matters, they still need the help, regardless if they acknowledge it or not. I say it's the best we can do."

Grenith added with a winning smile, "I say it's a smashing idea!"

I had one objection, "But, Nollem will be coming with us, right?"

Dwin replied, "Well of course, we can't just leave him behind, now can we?"

I just wanted to clarify, "So we'll wait till he's ready?"

Findal said with a smile, "I don't see how we can't. Besides, you wouldn't have it any other way."

The rest of the evening was spent eagerly making plans and seeing to the details of it. We would have to pester Brene for some horses, but that would be later when Nollem was feeling up to it. We mapped out our route, got a general list of things that we would need, went to bed with our heads filled with thoughts of adventure and saving lives. During the discussion, I held back from offering any ideas, seeing how well they went over last time.

Nollem stayed silent through it all. He sat in his chair before the hearth, with his lips pursed and eyes glued on the flames. When it was time for him to retire to the cot, he insisted on doing it without any assistance. Those were a very tense few moments for me.

But, despite my concerns, he made it in safely.

For the last couple of nights, I had slept in my own room, seeing that the worst of his recovery had passed. But tonight, I had a funny feeling and couldn't sleep. So I grabbed a blanket and crept out of my room into the Den. By the light of the dying fire, I moved over to one of the large armchairs and curled up in it.

I stared at Nollem's sleeping face, watching his chest rise and fall gently with every breath. The light from the fire cast funny shadows over his face, making his hollow cheeks look like deep bowls. Though I must add that he was looking better.

I was just about to drift off, when I heard Nollem moaning softly. I opened my eyes in an instant to see if he was alright.

He was still asleep. His expression was twisted and wrinkled in concern and pain. His head rocked back and forth, getting more violent each time. His lips were moving but no sound came from them.

I was just about to get up and wake him when he stopped moving. His breathing was quick and he fell to muttering something under his breath. I caught one word that he repeated several times: "Arkona."

Chapter 35
Scars

It was after breakfast the next day before I sat down with Nollem again. Grenith had joined me, in the other seat, a mug of steaming tea in hand.

Nollem started by asking in his unpleasant, yet civil voice, "Is later now?"

I knew immediately that he was referring to last night's exchange, and I nodded, saying, "Sure."

Grenith looked between the two of us, then said, rising, "I think I'll bow out here, um, yeah. Let you two have some privacy."

She quickly walked out of the Den, in search of the others, who had all gone out for some reason or another.

Once the heavy door closed behind Grenith, Nollem made a move to go over and take her seat. I jumped up, offering a hand of support. He held out a hand to stop me and he rose shakily. He hobbled over to the seat and sat back with a sigh of comfort. Then he turned to me, his grey eyes staring piercingly into mine, and asked bluntly, "Why didn't you let me speak last night?"

Fumbling for an answer and trying to delay giving it, I sank slowly back into my seat. I thought I formed one and replied as if I had had it in mind since the night before, "You looked so pale that I was concerned. And I didn't want you over exerting yourself, or causing any more pain from thinking of..." my sentence trailed off.

"Of my time in Dol Guliab," he finished for me.

"Right," I said quietly, then I added, "I was only worried about you."

"I've noticed," he commented. "I've also noticed that you all have been careful not to ask about what happened, in fact, you haven't even mentioned it within my hearing. Why?"

"We only wanted to spare you pain," was the truthful answer.

Something in his eyes flashed with anger and he spat out, "And you thought that by not saying anything I would forget about it?!"

I blinked in surprise at his sudden change. Uncomfortably, I shifted back in my chair, my mouth slightly parted.

Passing a hand over his eyes, Nollem sank back into his normal self, looking older and defeated by some invisible weight. He sighed, his hand still over his eyes, and said quietly, "I'm sorry."

I wasn't sure what to say in response. I finally stuttered out, "No, I'm sorry. I should have—"

He raised his other hand to stop me. I fell silent. He didn't move for some time.

I finally asked in a small voice, "Who was Arkona?"

He looked up immediately, his eyes sharp. He demanded, "How do you know her name?"

"Well, when we were rescuing you, you stopped us and insisted that you couldn't leave without her. Then last night, while you were asleep, you muttered her name over and over."

He sighed again. "Yes, I remember the dream. And it takes a weight from me to know that I at least thought to ask for her. I couldn't remember, it's all like a distant memory for me. But you asked who she is. Arkona was the only one who ever looked up when I was dragged in. She was the only one who bothered to tend to my wounds, though with such limited resources it's amazing that she was able to do what she did. She was the only one who even offered the slightest bit of hope when there was nothing but prolonged death surrounding us. She was the only one who was a friend to me, even though her attentions got her in trouble. She was my friend."

His voice trailed off, his eyes glassy and distant. He wasn't seeing me, he was reliving moments with her.

He picked up his narrative, "She taught me to hope that you would come for me. I told her so much about you, she might even recognize you if you passed in the street. I promised her that I wouldn't leave without her. I promised that when you came for me, we would take her with us. And now, I didn't... I didn't save her."

My heart broke within me. It was my fault that she wasn't here with us. I insisted that we go immediately. It was my fault. "Nollem, I... It's not your fault that she's not with us. You insisted on getting her, but I, the selfish, unloving person I am, hurried you off. I cut you off and was only concerned about getting you out. You, even in the joy of being rescued, didn't forget the needs of others. I'm so sorry, Nollem. I'm so sorry."

There were tears in both our eyes, mine threatening to spill out. He stared at me for a moment then said in a husky voice, "No, don't blame yourself. You didn't know. How could you? I just hope that she hasn't come to further harm because of me."

"Nollem," I started hesitantly, "if I may ask, what did Alletta want with you? What did she do to you? All these months, I have cried and thought you to be dead, dumped rudely in some hole. I thought you had been killed without reason. What did she do to you?"

His look changed, becoming distant again. "It's so long ago... I can hardly remember. She and the group of Vaudians took me to some city, after they killed all the Monare Pelm soldiers at Post Neth. I was blindfolded most of the journey. I think I was taken to some lord of one of the cities. He questioned me, asking things that I didn't really know about. Apparently he wasn't satisfied that I had told him the truth because they drugged me and the next thing I knew was pain. There was a new person asking questions. More questions, more pain." He stopped, resting his forehead on the palm of his hand. "They put me in the dark tunnels. That's when I met Arkona. It seemed like every few days some men would come in and... well, there's no need to say what they did. I have proof enough by the marks over me. Days and nights blurred together. Days, weeks, months, all passage of time was one continuous drawn out memory of pain."

He ended, still bowed by memories. I was touched that he confided all this to me, yet I knew that there was so much more that he wasn't going to tell, nor was he going to be able to ever tell. There's no way to describe some things.

"Those people in the prison, the misery they suffer, the prison itself, dark and dank with the reek of death everywhere, the pain without hope. Everything sticks out in my mind and replays, during the day as visions and sounds that I think I hear, at night in horrible images. There's no way to get rid of them. It's always before me, always there."

I stared awestruck at the similarities in feelings we had. He said it so perfectly; it was always there. "I have the same thing.

Only, its not images from one particular event. I see things collided together with other. Mostly of death. Death that happened, death that might have happened. Death is everywhere."

We had both sank into a deep thought, each in our own world of images. A voice from the far side of the room startled us out of our introspection.

"Though," Findal stood in the doorway, "death may be everywhere, there's life too. We have that Life, we know that Life, why still live as though we are in death? Death has been conquered, it has no power over us. Why leave others to wallow in death, when we have the key to Life? They may not accept that Life, but at least it was offered to them." He came over to us, continuing, "I know there's death everywhere, I see it too. But if we do nothing, is the love of Life really in us? That's why we have to go to Monare Pelm, that's why we have share Shalom with the world, we can't keep Him to ourselves.

"The past, yes, it has happened. I'm not denying it, and I'm not asking you to forget it. But the past is gone, the future is now. If we spend the future lingering in the past, what should have happened, what could have happened, then we waste it. Move beyond it, learn from it, you've been forgiven, you've been saved, there's no need to linger there. Now, don't get me wrong, it's very good for you to talk this out; I encourage it, but I beg you, don't stay in death. Live like you're loved, because you are."

He paused to let it sink in, then he added, "Sorry if I interrupted you both, but I needed to say it. Please think about it."

He walked off, over to the kitchen, and began rattling things around. Neither Nollem nor I noticed. We were too stunned by the speech that we so desperately needed to hear.

"He's right," Nollem started, "Death is conquered, it has no hold over us. Limira, I needed to hear that so much. I have only true Life, I have the ultimate Love, I have Shalom. He can take all the death away, all the images, the pictures, all of it, gone. I just need to ask and let it go. Would you mind leaving me alone for a while? I have some things to give away."

I understood what he meant, nodded, rose from my seat and said, "Sure," as I walked over to my room. I took one last glance at Nollem before I closed the door. He made it sound so easy! So pleasurable to give things up to the One Who holds it all. I had tried a few times, but it seemed like I couldn't truly give them up. I wanted to snatch them up for myself, hide and huddle them under me, guarding them from any attack. I had this doubt that if I gave up some of the hardest things, my memories of everything I had seen and heard, they wouldn't be secure, and maybe they wouldn't really be gone. I wanted to call them my own, I wanted to say I had lordship over them, even though they ruled me. I knew I had to give them up, but I didn't want to. It was almost like I didn't trust Shalom to really take care of them, like He wasn't safe to share them with.

It sounds ridiculous if you really think about it, but those were my fears and they were very real. I wanted to mask the fact that they ruled me by distrusting that He could handle them.

What could I say to Him? I had already given my life to Him once, at the border. It seemed like I had snatched it right out of His hands. What else could I do but repent?

Right there, I fell on my knees and poured out my heart to Him. I can't even begin to say the things that I uttered before Him. Besides that I begged for forgiveness, I asked Him to take everything, I didn't want it. He took much better care of things than I ever could. I even started a list, giving away my rights, one by one, just to remind myself that I had given them up. I can't tell you how long I was in my room, just me and Elohim, just getting to be with Him. Time seemed to slip by unnoticed and unheeded. I didn't care.

I determined to just be with Him every day, if I could. More days than I would care to admit slipped by without me fulfilling this, and it wasn't that I didn't have time to. But oh, the sweet moments when I did set aside the time. It was worth far more than I could have imagined for every second we spent together.

And I can truthfully say that the more I sought, the more I found, and the more I found, the more I loved Him. He changed me, through and through.

It was three weeks before we set out. We might have been ready a week earlier, but Brene couldn't promise horses at all until we passed the border, so we had to wait until Nollem thought he could make it.

After five weeks total of recovery, Nollem was looking fairly normal again. He still didn't have the same healthy flush to his cheeks and he wasn't as filled in as I would have liked, but he was significantly better than before.

It took us five days to cross the border, with Nollem we went a little slower than we had anticipated. We traveled around Moneth, going above it, north of the outskirts. We didn't want to get close to it, so we left quite the berth between us and them. It was for the best, that way we didn't run into any trouble.

There's nothing really to report from those days. It was rather average, standard traveling with a goofy group of friends. Unlike last time, the seriousness of our task had no effect over our funny sides. Many jokes were made and many laughs were had. There was no way that we could go an hour without someone making a crack to produce laughter. Sometimes we laughed because it was actually funny, and other times we laughed because the attempt had failed so badly. Even now, I couldn't tell you everything that passed between us, but I can tell you that the fun and the companionship has forever stuck in my mind.

Passing through the border was much different than last time. I had no feelings of dread, no invisible forces, and best of all no smothering, dying feeling. I walked right through it without flinching, and it almost seemed like the dark mist spread away from me, as if it was afraid to even touch me.

When I emerged to the other side, color and brightness seemed to jump at me, enveloping me like a warm blanket. Everything was so beautiful and full of color. I had gotten so used to the greyness of Deceiver's land, that the things people take for granted, like bright blue sky and lively green grass, were new and fresh to me.

The early summer midmorning was at its peak. Wild flowers blossomed in the height of their season, birds sang merry, little tunes in the trees. Bright sunshine filtered in lacy patterns, its warm fingers touching the even brighter green grass and tiny sprouts just poking their heads from the warm earth. I hadn't heard a bird sing in months, nor had I seen actual rays of sunshine. Every thing was so alive. And I felt like I fit right in.

There was an arranged meeting place to get the horses we needed, and we made our way there, our eyes staring with wonder at everything. The fingerprints of Elohim were all over.

We soon found the man whom Brene had sent, waiting for us. We thanked him, and he rode off after telling us about some particular peculiarities of the horses, and that he had given us an extra one just in case. One of them hated to be ridden by someone with a heavy frame, another couldn't stand the sight of any weapon—which was rather inconvenient for we all carried something in the way of protection—and another had this strange habit of eating a mouthful here and there while it walked along. I got this last one, to my disappointment. It was rather annoying because this horse, which I affectionately and aptly named Jerk, would yank against the reins and go out of his way to catch just a mouthful of new leaves, or anything else that was in any way desirable. Before I got used to it, he would catch me completely off guard and nearly make me fall. Sometimes, well more than sometimes, it seemed intentional and thought out before hand.

The one thing that was certain, though, was that he didn't like me and I didn't like him. So at least we could agree on that point. Though eventually I won him over to my side by peace offerings of apples and other young plants that I could find.

Anyway, once we got the horses, we made a slight change in direction, instead of going west like we had, we went more southwest, hoping to reach the pass over the Slaggar Mountains before Deceiver and his armies. On our new course, we traveled through the forest lands, engulfed by lovely trees and other woodland sounds. It was much more enjoyable than my last trek through Slaggar forest.

Sometime, I think on our second day of traveling in the forest, we came across an odd thing, that ended strangely. In a small clump of tight knit trees, there was some sort of encampment. There were old canvas tarps stretched between the trunks creating a makeshift tent. It looked lived in. There was a smoldering fire, wisps of smoke curling softly to the sky. There were some buckets with water in them, and tin dishes, frying pans, plates and such utensils were organized neatly on the inside of a small awning that branched from the tent.

We halted, looking on from our perches on the horses. We exchanged a few looks, and Grenith voiced what we were all thinking, "I wonder who lives here?"

"I do," came a gruff voice from behind us.

I reached for my sword at the sound, whirling Jerk around. We all moved for weapons as our first defensive instinct.

There, standing firmly between two massive trees, was a strong, tough, yet young man. He had an impressive scowl on his face and held a large branch in his hands. His hair was severely overgrown. What wasn't tied back into a ponytail fell into his face, shading his glinting eyes.

I was surprised at his appearance and could definitely tell that he was putting on a fake air to scare us off. None of us knew exactly what to do. He didn't seem that dangerous, but he wasn't going to put down his defensiveness till he trusted us. And that would be the hard part.

None of us drew any weapons upon seeing him, in fact, we let our hands drop to our sides. Dwin cleared his throat and said in the most gentle voice he could muster, "Um, I'm sorry if we intruded, but we're just passing by. So, I guess we'll go now."

"Wait!" came the sharp order. He took just a step closer, and asked, a hint of real curiosity in his voice, "Where, where are you going?"

Dwin answered, "We're going to Monare Pelm, hopefully we'll be able to reach the pass in a few days time."

At this, he dropped his defense completely, the boyish hopeful side coming out. He asked, his face full of eagerness, "Can I... can I go with you?"

I was even more surprised at his question than his angry first appearance. I looked at Dwin, wondering what he would say. I was alright with the idea, though it might be a little awkward at first.

For a moment, we passed knowing and questioning looks at each other. It was soon determined that everyone was fine with it and Dwin said, "Sure, if you'd really like."

He earnestly replied, "Yes! Let me get a few things together, then I'll be ready to leave."

With that he darted past us and into his makeshift tent. There was some rustling then he reappeared with a sack over his shoulder.

Dwin motioned to the extra horse that we had, while saying, "We even have a ride for you. Won't have to walk, that's a plus."

He smiled funnily as he walked up to the animal. His fingers carefully, almost reverently touched the mane and he slid it down the sleek neck. After a moment he swung up into the saddle and commented, "It seems like I picked the right travelers to stop."

There was a general smile, and we set out again. Nollem didn't have much to say. Grenith, not being comfortable, slid back into her imaginary shell and didn't speak unless spoken to. Kattim grew quieter too. Findal and Dwin kept him talking enough for the rest of us though. They were trying to find out more about him, and thankfully he replied loud enough that we all heard him. His answers were polite, but sometimes vague. I noticed that he especially dodged the questions that pertained to *why* he was camping out in the woods by himself, and that he enjoyed the subject of himself.

He said his name was Harred, that he came from beyond the border, and was hoping to make his way to Monare Pelm. He said he had heard that Monare Pelm was the place to be, that it was safe and prosperous. And that's what he wanted, safety and a good life. Apparently he hadn't heard about Deceiver's new plans, but we weren't about to tell him. Not yet at least.

I was curious to know what his mark was, which emblem he bore. Not that I was going to ask, but I somehow doubted that it was a bush, so it had to be a crown, which, as I was slowly beginning to understand, meant that he was just like Between and Vaudians.

But he was nice enough, a little rough around the edges, but overall not bad to hang out with. The time passed pleasantly, even more so as we got to know him a bit better.

When the shadows of evening began to lengthen and the birds settled down, that's when we came across the sight that has forever been engrained in my memory. It was one of complete destruction.

We were just thinking about finding a spot to camp for the night when we saw a clearing ahead. It looked strangely dark so we went forward to investigate. As we drew nearer, I noticed that Nollem seemed to recognize what it was before the rest of us. He started to shrink back in his seat and as his eyes gained a distant look.

I knew it immediately and dropped back to keep an eye on him. As we passed the distinct tree line, I understood.

Spreading out before us like a dark painting come to life, the forest had been turned into nothing but smoldering heaps of fallen and ashen trees. As far as the eye could see, a wasteland of grey and smoke spread in the stead of the green, lovely forest that bordered it.

I knew the scene; it was one so familiar to me. Deceiver had left his footprint by decimating everything to ashes and rubble, stamping out the beauty, and leaving nothing but death.

Everyone but Harred knew what it was from. We took it in with grief and shock. Were we too late? It seemed that he was far ahead of us.

Harred's demanding voice broke us out of our stupor, "Will someone tell me what this is? Why must it be me who is always out of the loop?"

Nollem said under his breath, in a strange haunting tone, "It's the destruction of Deceiver."

Harred looked rather alarmed at the mention of Deceiver. In a scared voice he asked, "What is he doing beyond the border?"

Dwin answered, "It's a long story. Why don't we head back in the trees and settle down for the night, then I'll tell you."

We all agreed and were soon thoughtfully contemplating in our own worlds around a warm fire. That's when Dwin started with the tale that would inform Harred of everything he needed to know about us. "It all began with a rescue mission in the heart of Dol Guliab. We, as a team, broke in and left with a prisoner of some importance. As you can imagine, Deceiver was really angry over that and he swore revenge on Monare Pelm, because that's where he thought the attack was from. So now he's parading over the country, destroying as he goes. We were hoping to reach the pass before he did, but it seems that we might be too late. We might have to go another route over the mountains."

"But wait," he interrupted, "why do you want go to the very place that he's about to wipe out? I'd want to go the opposite way, as far as I could."

"I was about to get to that. We're going because we care about the people. They need to be warned and, from what I hear, they need to know that there's hope for life."

"So, you're going to offer them some hope after telling them they're doomed to die? What kind of loonies are you guys?"

I couldn't help but smile and commented to myself, *"I've never been called a loony before. But there's a first time for everything, I guess."*

Dwin smiled too, and I could tell that he wasn't sure exactly how to answer that. He finally said after a moment to think, "Uh, I suppose you could say we're crazy. We're definitely crazy about Shalom. And it's definitely crazy the love Shalom has offered us."

"Woah," Harred held out his hands and leaned back from us, "no, I don't do religion. Let me get that clear now, I'm not interested in any weird religious stuff. Leave that out of the picture and we're fine."

"Well, I can't just not talk about it, it's a part of me and I'm unashamed to say so."

Harred looked at all of us in shock and disgust, "Are you all the same way? Or is he just the black sheep?"

Each one of us said something along the lines of, "Yeah, we all believe the same that he does."

"Yeah, okay, no," was the response gained, "I'm out of here, you all are just too strange for me." He started untangling himself from his blanket.

Dwin looked at him and said, "Alright, no one's forcing you to stay. But you'll have to leave the horse behind. It is ours, and we might need it."

That stopped him. He halted in his getting up, and slowly sat back down with a dejected look. He shot a glare at Dwin and said grudgingly, "Fine. I'll stay with you. But no talking religion. Deal?"

"I can't make that promise," Dwin returned, "but I won't preach at you, if that's what you're worried about. Just remember, no one's holding you back from leaving except you."

"Right," he said, still unhappy with how that all went down. "I'm feeling tired, so if you all wouldn't mind piping down, I would like to get some sleep. And don't wake me till the sun is well risen."

With that, he rolled over, his back to the fire. We exchanged a few smiles at his antics and nestled down for sleep ourselves.

I stared into the fire for a long time, watching the flames flicker and dance. I couldn't help but wonder what path we would take over the mountains now. Then I looked past the fire into the dark night and I shivered at the blackness that stared back at me. It reminded me of the nights so long ago that I spent in the very same forest. The images of horror flooded back. A sick feeling of nervousness came over me at the remembrance of the night I was attacked. I could only hope and pray that we would stay safe this time through.

I tried to calm myself down so I could actually sleep. But nothing seemed to work. I finally cried out to Shalom, asking Him to take away the thoughts, the feelings, the images.

I was soon asleep.

Chapter 36
Reviled & Rejected

In the morning, we decided to cut back into the forest going northwest, then cut over due south. In that way, we hoped to skirt around Deceiver and his armies and still make it over the pass.

We set out immediately, and as we went we got to hear more about Harred. I wish you could have heard it all first hand, since I can't equally relay it. He talked on for hours, and every other sentence he used the word "I" with either some impressive adjective to go along with it or some heroic deed to add to the quickly growing list.

I thought it was humorous, and I had never imagined that someone could have that high of an opinion of themselves. He wanted to make sure about once an hour that we were not going to run into the armies of Deceiver. Along in the same paragraph he would ask if it was really safe to try to cut them off to get over the passes. He would add affectionately that he wasn't at all concerned about our welfare, but he was only looking out for his own. Oh, and by the way, don't be offended; it's nothing personal.

Overall, he was very funny to listen to, but after a while I started to pity whoever was riding next to him, that usually being Dwin. Then I just got sick of hearing him rambling on about himself. Soon I started wondering if I was the same way. And I made the inward joke that he made up for the talking that he had missed out on while alone in the woods.

Still, nothing very memorable to say about the trip as a whole. When we got to the base of Slaggar Mountain range, we cut over heading south. Somehow, I'm still not exactly sure how, we made it to the pass before Deceiver and his armies.

As we climbed higher, I looked out and saw a dark blot with smoke rising high behind it. The dark spot was long and wide trailing over the flat-looking earth like a river of ink. I had known that Deceiver had large numbers of troops, but I had never imagined the amount I saw spread out. A wide ribbon of dark ashes, fire, smoke and scorched earth trailed in their wake.

The air grew thinner and colder. For early summer, the nights were bitter, and I wouldn't have been surprised if it started snowing on us.

I suddenly knew we were close to the peaks when the narrow trail widened and turned to mud. The thinning trees gave way to slumped old houses, half covered in mosses. It was the familiar little town of Divel, where we escaped the grasp of the soldiers thanks to the help of Mr. and Mrs. Kelvin. I looked at their dilapidated house as we passed. It was dark and cold, not at all the inviting homey one that I remembered. Though at the time, I didn't see it as half so nice as now. We didn't stop and I wasn't expecting too, I only hoped that the Kelvins were already safe in Monare Pelm.

❦

The narrow city streets, the bustle of city life, the hubbub of people, the pressing of crowds; it was all the signs that we had arrived in Monare Pelm. It hadn't changed much, hardly at all. Everything was just as I remembered it. The streets were hot and crowded, salesmen reaching out from their stalls to sell the latest item that you just had to have, the yelling, the bargaining, the happy looking masks the people wore, the official looking soldiers that paraded up and down the streets yet had no real authority, the pages and young people dashing to and fro on unknown errands of apparent importance, the latest news shouted from every street corner. It was all the same in the heart of the city.

Even the outer parts, the residential areas, the tall stone and brick mansions towering into the pale sky, the doorsteps swept clean by servants who had no value in the eyes of their masters. The hushed rows of houses filled with hushed lives and hushed comings and goings. It was all the same.

We were tossed between the shoulders of a sea of people trying to get past to wherever their destinations were. Both men and women pursued the passerby as they rushed past the zone of the stall. Most everyone was dressed nicely, there was no *real* peasantry in Monare Pelm. There were too many citizens out doing their good works by helping the poor.

As a whole, the city benefitted from it, and that's perhaps why the king and his officials encouraged it. But the people who did the service got no reward from it, not besides a warm fuzzy feeling inside that died to emptiness the next day.

Because of the generosity of the citizens, there was also a lack of social classes. Everyone was pretty much on the same level as far as finances went. The "poor" were just as poor as the people who gave them monetary help, sometimes it seemed like they had more money than the so called "rich." Those who did have any wealth to their name were labeled as "stingy" and "uncaring" and "nonreligious." The only exception to this was the king, Hobbel IV, and his staff of officials. If anyone dared to call them any demeaning names, they weren't ever seen again. No one knows exactly what happens to them, but it seemed that they would disappear the next day never to be found again. Stories and rumors would spread, but nothing could be confirmed.

This kept the city in a fearful silence from saying anything negative about the rulers. It seemed like they always found out who had said what with uncanny accuracy and precision. Spies and informers were everywhere. And that's why it was such a big deal to be a Radical in Monare Pelm. The unjust things done by rulers went undisputed for so long that it was a horror if you had anything to say against them. Fear kept everyone in line. It was also the reason why the happy mask was so commonly worn: if you looked unhappy, it was assumed that you had something against the rulers and were stirring up rebellion within the people.

I had always been able to see behind the masks that everyone wore. It was obvious that they were just that, masks. But now I saw clearly what was beyond the mask. Brokenness, lonesomeness, emptiness, hopelessness, fear, and sometimes, obvious evidences of Between. Most everyone had painted faces, and I knew what all the paste and powder hid. All these people, jostling and hurrying by me, were Between. They were all just as lost as the person next to them, yet they didn't know it.

And yes, this is the city where I grew up. This was the atmosphere that surrounded my every day. Maybe now you have more of an understanding about the way things work around here.

This was also the city where it all started. This entire adventure, the ups and the downs with everything in between, began here. And I can't tell you how funny it was to be back in the city where we were first run out because of our beliefs. And the even funnier part is that now I actually fall under the accusation of being a Radical, whereas then, my worst fear was to be even *thought* of as a Radical.

Funny how things change.

I wasn't exactly sure how we would even begin to tell people that their lives were in danger. The old side of me that grew up here implored me to keep silent and put on that happy mask, hide the fact that something was wrong. The worst part of it was that it felt like I was the only one who was getting this pressure. I guess Nollem had already fought against it once, so a second time wouldn't be that different. Besides, he now had those who supported him, whereas the first time everyone was against him.

With Dwin as our nominated leader, we picked out a bustling city square. As soon as we talked of finding a place, Harred took his hasty leave. He found it too awkward, and it was an equally awkward goodbye, for me at least.

We had left the horses at a small outer cluster of homes, outside of the city wall. That was where we were supposed to leave them. And I was glad that we did, though it might have been easier to get through the crowds if we had had them. We also had to leave our weapons with them, since strangers without papers aren't allowed to take them past the city gates. I felt like I was missing something, the place where my short sword usually hung was empty. And I felt very exposed.

Picking our way to the center of the square, we situated ourselves at an ornate public fountain, which was exactly in the middle of everything. It was there that we, well more like Dwin, Grenith, Kaṭṭim, and Findal, started to accomplish the very thing we set out to do. Their voices rang out over the swirling sea of the masses, competing with the newsboys selling papers on the corners and the street vendors lining the perimeter.

The reaction of the people was very characteristic to the city. They smiled at us and passed by at first, refusing to listen and acting as if they hadn't a care in the world. I could see right through the smiles and straight to their real emotions. They weren't at all happy that we were shouting the upcoming doom from the city square. After a while, their smiles became more strained and forced than ever.

There were two general responses we got as we continued to shout out: one was the laughing, brushing us off as if it were all just a joke; the other was genuine anger, all masks were thrown aside and real angry people thronged against us. It raised to its peak when we started proclaiming the good news of the coming of the true King.

I smile at the remembrance of it. It's amazing the different responses people have when they're confronted with Truth. It was a little scary at first, but it was reassuring at the same time, because I knew that we were saying the real thing. Anything other than the Truth wouldn't have riled them up and offended so many.

When the crowd got to its utmost point of anger, the officials stepped in. Guards, their armor shining in the afternoon sun, elbowed their way through the jostling people. We saw them coming long before they ever reached us. We complied with their requests as best we could.

The leader of the small unit called out over the racket, saying the things required, "You've been arrested for disturbing the peace. You'll have to come with us."

My eyebrows raised in alarm. That phrase could mean anything. We could be let off with nothing but a warning, we could go to court and be shot or hung the next day, or we could skip the trial and be hung from the nearest post. That phrase could mean anything.

As soon as the officials showed up, the crowd went crazier and started pawing at us, pulling us away from the fountain. Strong hands grabbed my arms and yanked me into the sea of angry faces. I didn't fight their holds. The forceful hands swept me further from the fountain.

A guard with a grim look on his face moved over to me. I could see him set his jaw and try to keep his official, stern demeanor as he pushed off the rough hands that were clawing at me. I intently looked him in the eye, trying to ensure that he wouldn't lose me. Shoving hands off himself and out of his way, he picked through and approached the group that held me. His scowl deepened and he demanded in a husky tone, "Hand her over!"

Very suddenly the hands released, and I was shoved from behind. I fell forward a couple of steps, crashing right into the armored guard. The crowd roared with laughter as I tried to right myself, the man pushing me off. Once I got my feet under me, the guard, his rage heightened by my clumsy fall, swung his metallic fist that descended to my cheekbone.

I let out a small cry, my hand reaching up to my stinging cheek. Warm, wet blood stuck to my fingers. I winced in pain.

The guard seized my arm just as roughly as the crowd had and dragged me over the rest of the company. I was the last to arrive. It seemed that everyone else had been gathered without injury. The bright red smear over the back of the guard's gauntlet denoted our brief scuffle.

The guards formed into a double file and marched out, one of us with each of them. I was towards the back. Cheering and jeering irrupted all around us. The sea of people closed back around us as we passed.

We were soon out of the main market square and into a side street. The people didn't follow us out, thankfully. Things quieted down as we moved farther from the square. If I knew the streets, we weren't heading towards the center of the city, so that meant we wouldn't be brought before the council and held on trial. That left two options: let go (which was highly improbable from the looks on their faces), or killed immediately. The last was more likely. We had, after all, been teaching about another King coming to rule, and that was definitely against the law. But usually they would just say that it was rebellion, not disturbing the peace.

I was undecided as to what they would do, but I was fairly sure it wouldn't end in our favor. By now we had passed all busy areas and were in a narrow street with no one in sight. They stopped and silently lined us up against a wall, our backs to it. Then they withdrew a few paces, staring at us grimly.

My hand still at my cheek, I looked at them, then glanced to Dwin, then Nollem. Nollem and I passed a message of solemn confirmation, basically saying, yep, we're dead.

The leader of the group stepped forward. Catching my attention, I stared at him. We all did, hanging on his every word. He drew a breath dramatically before saying in a slow calm voice, "You have been arrested by the authority of King Hobbel IV, and his council of worthy nobles, for violation of the thirteenth law, twenty second amendment. You have disturbed the peace, and must be labeled as disturbers of the peace. I now release you to go as you please with a warning. If you are caught disturbing the peace again, you shall be fined, jailed or worse. Do I make myself clear?"

We all nodded, fully understanding what he meant, but no less determined to do it all over again.

The leader nodded his head in an official manner, saying, "Then I release you to live your life as you please while you still can."

With that, he turned on his heel and marched back down the street, his double file of soldiers following his every step.

I breathed a sigh of relief and deflated against the wall. Everyone else relaxed as well, and Findal commented, "Well that was close."

Nollem added, "I thought we were goners for sure."

Everyone agreed. I couldn't help but smile at the scene Harred would have made if he was arrested with us. It would have been something similar to the scene I put up when Nollem and I were chased out of the city by the guards when being accused as Radicals.

Grenith's hand touching my elbow brought me back to the present. She peered at my cheek, her other hand resting on my upraised wrist. "What happened here, Limira?"

She gently pulled my hand away while I replied, wincing, "The guard caught me with the back of his gauntlet."

"Well, he left quite the mark. Though I think it looks worse than it is." She pulled a cloth from her back pocket, she now kept clean cloths on her at all times, and dabbed at the oozing blood. All I could see was the white cloth rise up, feeling it sting, then saw it come back down a new shade of red.

While Grenith was tending to me, the others had formed a rough circle and were talking about what to do next. The sun was sinking and the thought of shelter for the night was on everyone's minds.

It was Nollem who suggested, "Why don't we go and ask my parents if we can stay the night with them?"

Dwin, Kattim and Findal all exchanged glances. And Grenith looked to see my reaction. I was the first to speak, and I did it rather hastily, "Are you sure they'll receive us?"

"There's no harm in asking. Besides, they've offered homeless the couch for the night, and we're their own children, why wouldn't they?"

I replied, in a sour, doubtful tone, "We didn't exactly leave on good terms."

"There's no harm in asking," he repeated again.

I had nothing further to say. I wanted to believe him, I wanted to believe that they would take us back with open arms, but something inside kept me from truly believing it.

Everyone else waited for our sibling battle to end, then Dwin spoke up, "Like Nollem said, there's no harm in asking. We can at least try it. Lead the way."

Dwin's confidence seemed to boost mine, if only a little. Nollem took the lead and we threaded our way through the familiar streets. As we drew nearer, my doubts began to melt away with every recollection of the things they did for strangers. Surely they would accept their children back. By the time we were standing on the smooth stone steps before the massive double doors, I had confidence that they would be glad to see us again, and only a small sliver of me still doubted they wouldn't receive us. After all, wouldn't they be glad to know that we were alive and safe?

Nollem's attitude seemed unchanged. Everyone else seemed to hold it with open hands. They would be grateful if we were let in, but they also wouldn't be too disappointed if we were turned away.

With Nollem and I in the front, the rest of our group spread out behind us on the steps. Nollem took a breath to calm himself before he raised his hand. My heart was thumping loudly. He knocked, his knuckles rapping against the hard wood.

An anxious few moments of silence passed. I held my breath, straining to catch just the faintest sound of life from within the house. Nollem was just about to knock again when we heard the distinctive clack of heels against the smooth stone floor of the entry hall. It was the distinct walk of my mother. I could picture her striding quickly, yet composedly, down the echoey hall. The tall ceiling loomed above her and the decorative wood pillars and painted wall panels rose up around her. She was smoothing her hair back and brushing out her long skirt. It suddenly made me remember that I was wearing pants and a jerkin. I had never even thought of wearing boy's clothes before, it was completely unacceptable in Monare Pelm. Especially in upper class families such as ours.

I suddenly felt extremely awkward, but it was too late because the bolt slid over and the door opened just a crack. My mother's head poked out, it was just as I remembered it to be, young and caring, with just the first traces of silver speckling her blonde hair. She too had that familiar, social mask over her face. When she saw us, her expression fell, it was one of disbelief and coldness. She barely whispered under her breath, "You're dead." She opened to door wider, standing full in it. Her arm against the door grew stiff. She called over her shoulder for my father, "Jeklin, there's someone here for you."

I heard the faint, "Yes, dear." calling from the study. The voice was so familiar and filled with such richness that I longed to throw my arms around him again. My father appeared, a moment or two later, his tall, kind figure coming down the hall. His jovial smile faded as he drew nearer. He stood tall behind my mother, his jaw tense, his eyes darting from me to Nollem.

A great deal of my confidence in their hospitality sank low, leaving a sorrowful, longing in its stead.

He stared at us for a moment then demanded sharply, "What do you want?"

Nollem swallowed, then replied in a steady voice, "Father, we've come to ask to stay the night with you. We won't be in your way, and we'll be gone in the morning if you so desire."

His reply was crispy, "I desire for you to leave."

Nollem asked again, "It's only for a night, please. That's all we want."

"Out of the question."

I broke out, pleading with him, hating to see him so cold, "Father, please. We're your children! Daddy..."

For just a second, his eyes softened, and he looked me in the eyes. I could see his former self, his loving, caring side break through for just a moment. Tears filled my eyes. Then, just as fast as he changed, he returned to his cold, stiff expression. I could see tears forming in his own eyes, but his voice remained the same icy tone, "I have no children. I have no daughter. They're dead."

"But I'm her," I interrupted him.

"No!" came the sharp denial, "the daughter I knew would have never come begging for a place to stay the night. The daughter I knew, even if she did, would not come in search of a place for her friends as well. She would have only thought of herself. You clearly are not her. And my son," he turned to Nollem, the tears sliding down his cheeks even as he spoke, "he has been dead longer. He died when he rejected his parents' lifestyle and took one for himself. He has been dead to us for a very long time. Neither of you could be my children, they're dead."

Tears overflowed and dripped down my cheeks. I couldn't believe the words I heard.

Nollem tried again, crying out in a desperate voice, "But father—!"

He cut him off before he could go any farther, "Leave! Leave us be." He choked over the last words as he closed the door on us. I reached out my hands, wanting to seize the door and fling it open. The bolt slid over in the lock and the footsteps hastily receded back into the house.

Chapter 37
A New Ally

I crumpled against the heavy door, sobs shaking my frame. I couldn't believe that they would do that. Yes, I knew there was a good possibility of them not receiving us, but I had never imagined that they could turn us out so heartlessly. Tell us to our faces that we were nothing to them, that their son and daughter were dead. Every fond memory with them flashed before my eyes, my heart treasuring them up, wishing to relive them, but knowing that I never would. I suddenly regretted not being closer to them. I regretted that the daughter my father knew, was at one time me. I hadn't cared about anyone else but myself. And that was the Limira he knew.

It was a while before I composed myself enough to leave the doorstep. Nollem's shoulders drooped and his head bowed. His fingers pressed against the smooth wood of the door. He was fingering one of the small roses carved out of the wood.

The rest of the small group stood silently, waiting for us, feeling the distress that we were going through.

I was finally able to stand up, wipe away the tears, and square my shoulders. Nollem broke away from the door and turned to go. I moved with him, taking a glance over my shoulder at the friendly old door as if it was the last time I would see it. I reached out my hand and gave it one last caress before I followed Nollem down the steps.

We wandered down the street some, then just before turning the corner, I took one last look at the old house of my childhood. It stood there, looking as inviting as ever, squeezed between two equally large houses but not half so warm and welcoming as my home. The sleepy windows of my upstairs room blinked back at me, their thick curtains drawn. The lovely large windows of the parlor showed a homey view of the familiar room. It was arranged just as I remembered it. It was in that room where I got to stay for my first "grown up" party, and I spilled my punch over a rich woman's dress. Because of that, I wasn't allowed to attend the next party that my parents put on.

There was also a tea stain on the carpet near the upholstered chair, where I spilled my tea once when guests were over. I had to clean it up and the next time guests came over I had to spend my time reading a book on manners instead. In the hall was where I knocked over the heirloom vase, it shattering to the floor, while I was running out the door. I also got in trouble for that. In the dining room, a large room tucked on the far side of the house, was where I managed to fling a fork full of mashed potatoes through the air and landed it straight on the dark mustache of Uncle Berhern's portrait. Father had laughed so hard he accidentally spat out a pea he was chewing, Nollem choked on his drink spraying water over his plate, and mother tried hard cover her smile with a scowl.

Grenith's hand on mine startled me back to the present. She didn't say a word, but I knew that we needed to go. She gave my hand a gentle squeeze and a slight tug as she took a few steps back, guiding me into the narrow alley. I followed her, not looking back intentionally.

We went through the alley and wandered down some other streets, but I didn't really notice. My mind was still back in the house, reliving the big moments of my childhood.

I never heard the plan as far as what to do next, but the thing I remember doing was finding myself in the lower end streets, filled with dirt and muck. The sun had sunk below the horizon, and daylight was quickly fading from the sky. We found an empty corner between slumped houses, and settled down in it. It wasn't the cleanest nook I had ever seen, but it certainly wasn't the dirtiest either. I huddled up in the farthest corner and tried getting some sleep, but none came. I lay awake for some time, staring at nothing, thinking, reliving, and longing.

❦

Pale early morning light streaked across the sky. A cold breeze passed through the streets and a chill came over me. Hugging my arms closer together, I shivered, stretching my stiff limbs. I had never spent the night in the streets of my own home city before. With everyone closer to the main street than I was, I felt secure enough. Besides, it seemed that no harm had come during the night hours.

I sat up and leaned against the cold, damp stones of the wall I had slept by. A yawn escaped me, and I flexed my back. It was only a little sore from the cramped position. My cheek suddenly got a twinge, reminding me of my injury. I tenderly reached up and passed my fingers over the crusted marks. I winced. It might be a while before that healed completely.

I remembered well what had passed the evening before and there was still an aching in my heart, but I felt better after the night's sleep. I could process what had been said and what it really meant with a clear head. I felt like I could start to move on now. I would always miss them, but I wasn't really surprised by the reception we were given. They still loved us, their tears testified to that, but they would never allow themselves to show it. Their hurt turned into callousness. We were rejected because we had accepted Shalom. That was the way it worked sometimes, but it didn't make the pain lessen. A part of me would always have a scar.

It wasn't long after I sat up that the others started stirring. Findal was the first to wake up fully. He was refreshed and bouncing again, ready for whatever today would throw at him. The rest sort of woke up at the same time, each exchanging the usual good mornings.

Just as my stomach started to growl, we began to discuss what we would do that day. It was quickly decided that we would try in another part of he city to warn the citizens of the coming of Deceiver.

The imperative danger of Deceiver pulled me out of thinking about what had gone down yesterday and startled me into thinking of the present problem. People were going to die if we didn't do anything.

With empty stomachs, we set out for the nearest market square, knowing that it would be far enough away from the last spot, and we would more than likely have a different crowd. And we did. Though we were still smiled at from those masks. Then, just as last time, the masks melted away and revealed the angry person behind it. We soon had another mob on our hands. This time I was better prepared for it though. And it started smaller than the last one, but it was growing to be about the same size.

The noise of the crowd elevated to a whole new level and that's when Dwin called for a retreat. I was caught off guard by that. I was expecting to wait it out like last time. But no, I was standing confused, trying to figure out what he meant by shouting "Run!" over the cries of the mob. I watched Dwin, Grenith, and Findal, peel off and make their way to a lonely side street. Nollem was working his way over to join them.

That's when missiles of unpleasant things started sailing through the air. Kattim dashed over to me and grabbed my hand, dragging me after her. I ducked an apple core as I was pulled away in the direction the others disappeared, Kattim's hand still clasp mine. We dodged outreached hands, and ducked under arms in our flight to get to the side street. Kattim and I caught up with the others, joining them in the entrance of the little street. There was an obvious lack of people. It was just then when I heard the shouts of angry, authoritative soldiers.

I looked back but couldn't see them over the sea of heads. There was some laughter from the crowd. The missiles didn't stop flying through the air. I looked back to our group and I saw Dwin hastily counting us, his finger jumping from one to another. "... Five... Six. Great. Let's get out of here."

He dashed down the little side street, the rest of us following. We made it down a few streets before I heard the sounds of heavy footfall behind us. I glanced over my shoulder and saw a troop of soldiers, all in the king's armor, chasing after us. A shout of, "Halt in the name of the king!" rang through the air, bouncing and echoing off the stone street and walls.

We didn't listen. If anything we sped up some, taking more twisting corners. We were on one street with a couple of cross streets to either side. On the left, I saw a dark head pop out from around the corner. The head saw us, then looked back and saw the guards following. He looked at us again, then beckoned with his hand for us to come around the corner.

Dwin made the decision without any input from the rest of us. He made the corner, dashing around it and out of sight. I flew around the corner. I was half expecting to run into someone as I tried to stop, but we were still running with the tall boy in the lead. We took another sharp left, then the boy disappeared into an old shack. Dwin followed him without hesitation. I was the last to come through the narrow doorway. The darkness of the room hit me like a blanket, and it took a few moments for my eyes to adjust. Outlines and a faint glow from the far wall were what I first saw.

The glow was a dying fire, the outlines sticks of furniture, expensive mixed with old, cheap ones. Everything was dirty. Everything was worn and used. The boy who brought us here stood bravely before us, not shrinking at all. He was tall, had dark hair and eyes, and this certain look of breathless excitement about him, but it wasn't a childish look either. He looked about our ages, maybe a little older. He ducked low, and motioned with both hands for us to do the same.

I dropped to the floor, my breath paused, listening. The sounds of the soldiers racing by came then faded in the distance. Once I couldn't hear them at all, he stood back up and the room relaxed.

He looked at us again and asked briefly, his voice still quiet, "Lightbearers?"

Dwin nodded.

"Let's see your marks."

We girls exchanged looks. He noticed.

"I have to be sure," he added.

Each of us pulled back our jerkins and revealed the viney bush encircled by a curling ringlet. He didn't seem satisfied though, and he said, "Now take your finger and rub it."

That part puzzled me, but I did it. Then he seemed satisfied and replied to our inquiring looks, "We have to make sure that it's not painted over. Deceiver's men are getting trickier. Now, are you the six who made that big stir in the main market square yesterday?"

I almost wanted to ask why he wanted to know, afraid that we might be in for trouble if we answered yes.

Dwin obviously didn't have these doubts. He nodded again, saying, "That was us alright."

The tall boy smiled, "Good. We've been looking for you." He seemed to change into an action mode, like time was short and the entire city was looking for us. He spoke quickly, in the same low tone, as he moved over to the door and looked out the windows, "You may call me Greyskies for now. I'm going to be your guide, and I'm taking you to our headquarters of sorts." He suddenly trailed off in a muttering tone as if talking to himself, "We really have to find a name for it... The Haven? No, that's not quite fitting. Anyway, are you with me?"

We all nodded.

"Then stay close." With that he ducked out of the narrow door. Dwin shrugged and went out after him. One by one, we slipped out. Preferring to be in the back, I moved out accordingly. We slipped stealthily from one corner to another, avoiding the sight of any people on the streets. Occasionally we made a serious back track, dodging back around one corner then another. By the time we arrived before a rather large, upper scale house, I was thoroughly lost by the maze of corners and streets we went through. I had no idea where we were, and I had grown up here! I knew that we were somewhere in the edges of town... or we could have been near the center, close to the palace of King Hobbel IV. It was really hard to say.

The tall boy, introduced as Greyskies, darted up the steps leading to the front door, taking two at a time. He landed quickly on the mat and rapped out a certain pattern on the door. Not only was the sequence odd, but there was a door knocker just above where he knocked.

The bolt was drawn back and the right side of the double doors swung open. Greyskies bounded into the hall, the rest of us following him in. As soon as I passed the threshold, the heavy door closed and I skirted to one side to avoid being hit. A short girl with curls bouncing around her shoulders appeared from behind the door. She saw me and her young eyes got wide. She whispered delicately to me, "I'm sorry, I didn't see you."

I gave her a smile and waved a hand to show that it was no big deal. She accepted my forgiveness and skipped down the hall, dodging around those who stood in her way. My gaze trailed after her, and followed her out the short hall until she disappeared around a corner to the right.

Then I turned back to the hall. It wasn't lavish, but it wasn't drab either. It was nice, homey, I guess is the best adjective that comes to mind. Greyskies led us out of the hall and to the right. Immediately the room opened up and formed a sort of parlor with a kitchen and dining table—larger than the one in the Den —attached to it. Comfy sofas and upholstered chairs sat arranged around the room. There were some paintings up on the walls and a few small house plants scattered in corners on small side tables.

There were a few smaller children, the little girl with curls among them. The mother was in the kitchen, a young toddler hanging off her skirts. She stood upright from leaning over an oven when we came in. She smiled, it brightening her whole countenance. "Well hello there, Breylin. Nice to see you brought the guests safely in. You must be the six who caused that big stir the other day."

We all looked at the tall boy, whom we thought was Greyskies, when he was addressed as Breylin. He didn't seem to notice but introduced her to us, "Guys, I would like you to meet Mrs. Nettira Heldings. This is her and her husband's home. We kind of congregate here. And I'm sorry I don't know all your names, so you'll have to introduce yourselves."

"My name is Dwin. And thank you for admitting us into your home."

"Findal is my name."

"Kattim."

"Nollem. Nice to meet you."

"Grenith, and this is a lovely home you have here."

"My name is Limira. Also a pleasure to meet you."

Nettira replied equally to each of us then introduced her children, pointing to the girl with bouncing curls first, "That's Hetta, she's my oldest." Hetta bobbed a curtsy. Nettira pointed to the one boy lounged over the sofa, looking over the shoulder of another. "That's Dagget, and Sorth." She gestured to the young girl hanging onto her skirts, "And this is Tesha." Then she added, "Please, make yourself at home. Everyone should be getting back in a little while for dinner."

Breylin, the tall boy who brought us there, took her up on her offer and flopped down in an armchair. He gestured to the other seats and we sat down as well. Dwin was the first to speak, "So, Greyskies is it?"

"Oh, yeah. Sorry about that. It's more safety stuff. I'm not supposed to give out my real name before Nettira gives the okay. She can somehow tell who's safe and who's not. She was quicker than usual this time though. Dwin is it? what's got you on the run this time?"

"We were just about to get caught for disturbing the peace again. The lead official made it very clear that we wouldn't get a second chance if we were caught again. So I was making sure that we weren't caught. Thanks for helping."

"Sure, that's what we're here for."

Findal asked, "What exactly do you do?"

"Well, we're kind of like a refuge house for Lightbearers. It being illegal, and with King Hobbel cracking down with laws and patrols lately, we thought it was a real need. Though actually we've been around a while, there's just been less of a need." He called out to Nettira, "You know, I've been thinking. We really need to find a name for this place."

Nettira replied, "Why not call it the Haven?"

Breylin called back, "I thought of that too, but it doesn't seem to quite fit. Maybe... the Hall, or the Shield, or something neat and meaningful."

"Why not the Rock?"

Breylin wrinkled his nose, "This doesn't exactly look like a rock."

"Well yeah, that's the point, it's supposed to be a code word for this place. It's not like I'd want to call it by the address."

"Still," Breylin mused, "it's not quite fitting. We need something original, something with meaning, something like... "

"The Haven," Nettira finished for him, a big smile over her face.

Breylin sighed and said, "Well, I guess it's better than the Rock."

Kattim, I think a little agitated at the seemingly useless banter, interrupted it by asking, "Do you guys know about Deceiver coming at all? Or do you not care?"

"Yeah," joined in Nollem, less annoyed with the previous conversation than Kattim, "what are your plans as far as Deceiver coming?"

Breylin brought his attention back to us and explained, his excited air increasing as he went, "Oh, we definitely care. We've known for a while now, and just as you, we found out that very few other people cared or believed us. We kind of gave up on the warnings, it only ended badly. So since then, we've concentrated our efforts on preparing for an attack. You know, gathering weapons, strength in numbers, stock piling food in case of a siege, that sort of thing. It's been rather successful, though we're short on weapons, and the total number of us remaining Lightbearers has decreased. It was small to begin with, but now..." His voice trailed off for a second, then he returned to the present and continued, "We might have enough weapons to arm you lot, though you'd be the last."

I spoke, thinking of the empty space since my sword was gone, "We have weapons. They're outside of the wall though."

"Well that's easy enough. We can just smuggle them in. Done it plenty of times."

Kattim still anxious to do something thing, summarized, "So, you've done everything? There's nothing left to do?"

Breylin was about to reply when Nettira called over from the the kitchen, "We can pray, and that's plenty for us to do. Elohim's the ultimate doer here."

I suddenly felt very silly for not having thought of that before.

Chapter 38
Battle

And so the waiting began. It has to be the worst part about any war. The anxious calm before the storm. The tense build up of emotion and preparation, with no release. Not yet.

Eight days after our arrival, refugees from Divel came flooding into the city. They came with meager supplies, low spirits, and terrifying stories of destruction. Plumes of dark smoke rose into the grey sky along the mountain ridges, adding to the blanket of clouds coming our way. The city, which was previously in denial of any upcoming danger, was thrown into a panic when they realized that Deceiver actually was coming. That day was the most hectic I'd ever witnessed in Monare Pelm. People were flying through the streets, stocking up on food and other necessities, mobbing stores and markets. Blood was shed. Soldiers were rushing all through the streets trying to restore as much order as they could and mustering up every weapon and able bodied man they could get their hands on.

There was a general silence from the king and his council of worthy men. There were no proclamations, no new laws, no speeches urging the people to remain calm nor evacuation plans. There was nothing. It led to a discomfort among the people, and the whispered word on the street was that he didn't care or he thought that it was hopeless to even prepare. It was like we had no ruler.

The same day, other soldiers were busy barricading all the gates, closing us in. The growing group of citizens who wanted to leave the city were stopped. They were angry about not being allowed to leave. Blood was shed.

By evening of the same day, the wall tops were lined with soldiers and other citizens geared up with any pieces of armory that could be found. Darkness fell early that evening.

That was when the silence drifted over the city like an invisible mist.

The next day, the ninth since we'd arrived, the streets were empty, the markets deserted, all doors and windows were closed and barred. Everyone was huddled together, waiting out the storm that hadn't even begun yet. Dust and trash blew down the cobblestone street in the slight breeze that had picked up. There wasn't a sound of life. No birds, no people, no nothing. Even the patrols that had passed by on occasion were nonexistent.

We, everyone who called the Heldings' home their home, sat around quietly. The older ones of our group were silent, each lost in their own thoughts of wars gone by. Over the past few days there had been a great deal of sayings like, "When I was a solider..." or "Back in the day..." But not today.

Dwin, Findal, Nollem, Breylin and a handful of others had left the day before when the soldiers first came to round up men. I felt completely useless sitting around, fretting over the battle. Kattim and Grenith felt the same way, but Kattim by far was the most vocal about it. We all knew how to fight. So why weren't we up there with the men? Other women had been recruited. And they would definitely get desperate once Deceiver's army came into sight.

But we took no action because of the pleadings of Nettira. She kept saying that if they needed our help, they would come and ask for it. Till then, it was best to assume that we would simply be under foot.

Our reasoning was she had never seen the destruction wrought by Deceiver. She hadn't seen the burnt forests, the decimated plains and cities that he had picked over. The posts in the path between here and Deceiver's land, Post Baldar and Post Dagget, had been wiped out. No survivors had returned to the home city, Monare Pelm. Which meant if there were any, they were wandering around in the forest, trying to get back here, but were completely cut off by Deceiver's armies. There would be no reinforcements, no aid to send for.

In the afternoon during our hours of sitting around, somehow we got on the topic of Elohim's Words. When Nettira heard that I had never read even a sentence of it, she quickly rushed me into a long and narrow closet that was under the stairs. The walls were lined with shelves filled to the brim with books, scrolls and manuscripts. Unlike the map room in the old Lightbearer base, these shelves and books were well dusted and organized. Lighting a candle and handing it to me, she led the way to the very back and pulled three books from the bookcase along the back wall, one from the second shelf, one from the top shelf, and the last from lowest shelf. They looked just like regular books to me, leather bindings and covers. Nettira handed them to me and said, "We only have ten parts of the book, and some of them are short. Enjoy, and come back out once you're done. Oh, and do your best to keep the pages in order, sometimes it can be hard to juggle them."

The last comment confused me, but I gave her my thanks as she returned to the parlor. I sat down, leaned against the shelves, and opened the book on top. Just as I did, some of the front pages slipped out of the binding and fell deeper into my lap. My eyes went wide, and I scrambled to put them back in the cover. Then I saw what Nettira had meant. The pages were loose from the binding. They had never been stuck into the cover, just placed inside the cover probably to disguise them.

Once I got past the thought that I had broken it, I delved into the Words of Elohim, pouring into the messages and truths written. During that time, I realized these pages confirmed everything I had been taught by Nollem, Dwin, Grenith, Kattim and Findal. Not a thing was contradictory. And there was so much more that I didn't know before, some so deep that they're almost too hard to write down or even try to explain.

I don't know exactly how long I was in the little closet beneath the stairs, but I read them all over twice, and by that time, the candle had burned down significantly. That was my time of quiet peace in the midst of the chaos of the impending battle.

❦

Supper was over and the sun was just setting before we convinced Nettira that we could go to the ramparts. We girls made a pact with her; we take supper to the men there and if they didn't need us, we would come back with the dishes and latest news. But if we didn't come back, they would know that we were needed.

Kattim, Grenith, and I rushed out the door eagerly, our weapons at our sides. Before I slipped through the door, Hetta, the young girl with bouncing curls, grabbed the hem of my jerkin, stopping me in my tracks. She stared up at me solemnly, then gave me the biggest, warmest hug I'd ever received. I returned it as best I could with full hands. She stepped back, then gave me her childish smile of confidence and security.

I held that moment, cherishing her smile. That was what I was fighting for. To protect the innocence, to fight for the good, to bring glory to Shalom.

Slipping out the door, I ventured down the street with Kattim and Grenith. For a long while, we were the only ones in sight. I felt very conspicuous as I walked between the dark houses, laughing and talking of merry things. Our voices echoed off the walls and danced down the streets, sometimes laughing back at us.

As we drew near the walls, soldiers and other young men half in armor were walking around aimlessly. Most of the forces were condensed at the south side of the walls, at the main gates.

We quickly went up the nearest stone stairway that led up to the rampart. Men were lounged all along the walls, sitting and sprawled out over the steps. We dodged legs and other men coming down. The wind was cooler and blew just a little stronger up on the top. Most of the soldiers up there were looking out over the dusky plain, looking for the first sign of the enemy. Occasionally we passed a woman, or a young girl, but most had already come and gone with supper for loved ones.

Picking our way across the rampart, we eventually found our group. They were grateful for the food, which was still hot from Nettira's oven. We settled down by them and kept up small talk, mostly about any news. There was nothing that we hadn't already heard.

After a while, Kattim carefully breached the topic of us staying and fighting. Breylin looked skeptical at first, but Dwin, Nollem, and Findal vouched for our fighting abilities. He was convinced and said, in his defense, that it wasn't that he doubted our capabilities, it was just that not many women he had known had any interest in fighting. So to find three, trained and willing to do so was strange to him.

I understood where he was coming from, having grown up in Monare Pelm too. Mentalities here were much different than in other places. Here, survival didn't depend upon fighting abilities, it depended on how well you bartered and swindled the other person.

Only one problem arose. We would have to ask an officer for his permission to stay and fight. That would be the hard part.

After they had finished their supper, Dwin, Breylin, and Nollem went with us to find an officer. All we had to look for was a fully armored man standing aloof from the rest with a cold air of distain about him. It didn't take us long before we found one.

He was tall, with an unfeeling expression stamped over his features. He had dark hair and an over done mustache, curled to fine points at the ends. His chin was held high, and he moved his eyes to look at us as we approached. He hardly even looked at us girls.

Dwin fearlessly stepped up to him and began respectfully, "Excuse me, sir. May we have just a moment of your time to ask your permission for something?"

He shot Dwin a sideways glance, only looking at him out of the corner of his eye. He licked his lips loudly, and gave just the slightest shrug of one shoulder. Then his gaze went back to the darkening plain and mountain ranges and he studied them.

I could tell Dwin wasn't quite sure if this meant he was ready to listen or not. But he cleared his throat and pressed on, "We were wondering if you would allow my friends here, Kat, Grenith and Limira, to stay on the wall and fight with us?"

When Dwin mentioned us, his beady eyes turned to us and fell to studying us with cold disinterest. His chin never moved. He didn't say anything, he only stared.

Dwin added on, "They're good fighters. I've been in many battles with them."

The officer cut him off by quickly saying in a crisp voice, "Oh, I don't doubt you. It's just that we're not supposed to have women up here when the battle starts. Safety and all that. Besides, I think we have plenty of able bodied men that we don't need to stoop to bring on women as well. Don't you agree?"

His beady little eyes looked out of the corners again as he stared down Dwin. He elevated his chin just a tad bit more, and sniffed.

Dwin opened his mouth to say something, but he never got the chance.

A shout irrupted from somewhere on the wall. All eyes turned to the mountainous terrain, especially the wide outlet where the road that led to Divel was. As the last traces of light faded from the sky to the right of us, deep shadows fell over the pass. In the darkest recess, faint dots of light flickered into life. The dots of orange multiplied, starting closest to us, then rippling back up the steep road. The lights continued back and out of sight as they rounded a slight bend in the road. A wide ribbon of lights had appeared, their orange glow ominous.

We all knew what that meant. Deceiver's armies were here.

A low murmur of frightened voices ran through the ranks stationed on the ramparts. The stiff officer, with whom we had been talking, drew a breath, his eyes getting noticeably larger. His hands were trembling.

He turned towards us, facing us full on for the first time, and said hastily, "You may stay. And please, if you have any more friends, bring them up."

Then he turned and hurried to another part of the wall, giving out weak pats on the back and shaky encouragement as he went.

Desperation had gotten the better of him.

We went back to our places on the wall and crouched down. All eyes were watching the moving ribbon of blinking lights. As the closest lights advanced, more just kept coming around the bend. The flow was unceasing.

I watched them come and kept expecting to see the end of the blinking lights, but there was none. A cold, numb feeling came over me. I was frightened, very much so. Our outlook was grim, there was little chance of survival. I would probably die here on the wall, pierced through by many arrows. I started praying. My thoughts seemed jumbled, but the phrase that kept reoccurring was, "You get the glory."

I believed that Elohim had His hand over this, but I was still scared.

Complete darkness filled the sky. It shrouded everything except those blinking lights. Eventually stars appeared, faint and cold, winking in an inky canvas. Dark clouds stacked up in the east, slowly overcoming the whole sky. Everything was so still. The murmurs of uneasy men had quieted. No sounds from the approaching army drifted into our hearing. Only the occasional shifting of armor and weapons broke the silence.

Everyone was lost in their own thoughts of doom. The night slid by slowly, ever so slowly. Tension and anticipation kept everyone awake and staring at the slow advancement of the army.

After what seemed like much too long, the end of the glowing ribbon came around the corner in the road.

A few hours before dawn's first light, the small outer villages, a short distance from the wall, rose up in flames. The bright light illuminated a portion of the front of the army. The flames danced into the sky, engulfing everything in its path. An orange glow reflected off the cloud cover that had formed and thickened as the army drew closer. Black smoke rose in pillars to the ashen sky.

We never saw the morning light. The thick clouds had shaded us over in darkness. It was similar to what Deceiver's land had been like. It was all in darkness, no light had penetrated it. Not yet.

The fighting started suddenly. I'm not sure who ordered the first volley, the soldiers of Monare Pelm, or Deceiver's men. But as if on cue, we were both firing volleys of arrows at each other. I had never used a bow and arrow before, so Dwin gave me a quick lesson as we went. I'm pretty sure, though, that my arrows did nothing but glance off the heavy armor of the Vaudians and Between.

Rows of Vaudians, Between and other mutilated creatures spread out in neat columns over the fields. Being near the big main gate of the city, I got the best view of everything. It seemed as if most of the efforts were centralized at the gate. It also meant that I was in the most perilous place there was. Not that I thought of it then.

A group of strong armed, enemy archers were busy firing continuous volleys at us, forcing us to stay low. Meanwhile, another group came over to the gate and started pounding against it with a heavy battle ram.

We tried to fire at the Vaudians near the gate, as well as the others firing at us. Arrows whizzed over our heads like angry hornets. Sounds of battle irrupted from everywhere. Horrible guttural shouts and unearthly wails roared deafeningly from below. Loud shouts rang out from the commanders on the rampart. There was the bang!

A shudder shivered through the ramparts as the heavy main gates were assailed by the blackened iron head of the battle ram.

I fit another arrow to the string. Drawing it back, I stood quickly, aiming in the general direction of the gate. I released the dart and ducked below the wall again. I pulled another arrow from a bucket that was occasionally replenished. I ran my fingers over the fletching, then fitted it to the string. Taking a deep breath to help me calm down, I watched the dark arrows shoot over me. Then I did another quick pop up over the wall, fired, then dropped out of sight.

It seemed like that was all we could do.

I could hear the sharp cracking and agonized groaning of the gate, the shivering of the surrounding stones, as the timbers were rammed against. A party of uneasy soldiers had formed near the gate, ready to take the first wave of Deceiver's men that burst through.

I popped over the wall again and released another angry arrow. And that's when I saw it. While we were busy with staying down, several lines of Vaudians had approached the walls. They carried crudely crafted ladders with them. I could easily guess what would happen next.

I dropped below the wall again and shouted at Dwin, rather alarmed at the prospect, "Dwin, they have ladders!"

He was just fitting another arrow to the string. "I know," was his hasty answer before he stood up and released an arrow.

"But what are we going to do? If they breach the walls, the city is doomed!"

He reached for another arrow with fierce speed. "We're going to fight. And fight hard."

He shot another arrow and came back down in a kneeling position. I reached for an arrow and silently continued on. Arrow. Fit to the string. Pull back. Stand. Release. Drop.

Repeat. My arms ached and my back was stiff from bending over. My fingers stung.

Every time I looked over the wall, it seemed as if two more Vaudians had appeared in the place of the last one. The ladders swung smoothly in an arch, racing towards the tall stone walls. They collided with a sharp thud. The tops began to quiver as the first of the creatures began their ascent. Two ladders had appeared rather close to me, one on each side with me in between.

I rose to look over the parapet, I aimed at the highest Vaudian climbing up. I released. The arrow missed, soaring two feet over his head. I ducked down in frustration and picked up another. I tried for a second time. When I looked over, he wasn't there anymore, and the ones below him were rising steadily. I aimed for the thick of them, hoping to down at least one of them. I let the arrow go and watched in satisfaction as it struck home, protruding from the neck of a Vaudian. He fell off the ladder, dropping straight down and taking out a couple other ascending creatures with him.

I smiled grimly at my success, a new surge of energy rushing through my veins. I darted down and grabbed up another arrow. I put it to the string, urgency making my raw fingers fumble. Reaching over the wall, I aimed down, expecting to see the head of the line where it last was. Boy was I wrong. The first beast was almost to the top. I aimed and let it loose. It glanced off the back of his shoulder, leaving nothing but a shallow scrape along his heavy armor.

I grabbed another arrow from the bucket. The number of ammunition was rapidly decreasing. Suddenly I took a few steps back and looked at the other ladder that was near me. The mass of climbing creatures was nearly to the top as well. I glanced back and forth again, an arrow against the string in my hands. We would have to forget bows and arrows soon, it would be sword fighting. I liked the thought of that better. I was certainly more skilled with a sword than a bow.

I pulled the string taunt and aimed for any head that would show itself over the parapet, on the right ladder. My eyes narrowed, looking for the first sign of a dark head. There! Just the top came into view, but I needed more. Just a second and... Now! I released the arrow. It sprang eagerly from the string and whizzed towards target. And it hit! A straight shot hitting home. The Vaudian screamed in pain and fell sideways off the ladder.

I couldn't believe that it had actually hit him! There was no way that *I* had done that. My moment of glory was cut short by the first Vaudian jumping over the wall to my left. He drew his mean, dark sword. The soldiers around him drew their own. They suddenly engaged in an intense battle of life and death.

Just seconds after the first came over, another was jumping onto the cold stone, his sword ready.

I looked back over to the right just in time to see the first Vaudian jump from the parapet with a descending stroke that hit hard. The solider under his blow crumpled to the stones. Another burly creature was jumping to the wall.

I dropped my bow and drew my short sword from its scabbard. The dull rasp was familiar and welcomed. Firmly planting my feet apart, I readied myself for the first creature to come at me. I knew they would make their way to me, I would just have to wait. My sword stood straight out from me, ready for the first blow. Adrenaline surged through my veins.

I couldn't wait any longer. One step at a time, I advanced. I watched as the heavy swords flew and arched, cutting down soldiers like grass. Another fell to the ground. Another Vaudian jumped over the parapet, fresh and eager for a fight.

Taking a few hasty steps forward, I charged at the nearest, a big fellow about two heads taller than myself. I wasn't thinking about fair size ratios, at that moment I felt like I could take on anyone.

I yelled something fierce and tried out my best intimidating face. I swung my sword in a descending cut aimed at his torso. He raised his sword and blocked it swiftly. He quickly retaliated with a whirling blow, his sword nothing but a dark blur. I raised my sword and blocked it, going on complete defense. A volley of forceful blows rained down on me. I parried all of them as best I could, but was forced to retreat a couple vital steps. I was suddenly very conscious of the fact that this wasn't like fighting on a meadow, on a slope, or in the forest. There was a distinct drop off when the edge of the wall dropped a good distance to the ground. A fall like that could be deadly.

I was feeling for his rhythm, his pattern, waiting for a break in it. The sheer power in his blows was staggering, and I wasn't sure how long I could hold out without making a fatal mistake. If I struck too soon and it wasn't his actual break, I would be dramatically overstepping and leaving myself exposed. If I didn't do something, he would have me backed up to the edge and I would have no where to go but down.

These thoughts raced through my mind as I blocked and chanced a weak thrust or cut here and there. He went for another rain of heavy strokes, leaving my arms feeling like jelly. He executed a final stroke from the right aiming for my torso. I caught it and twisted his sword to the side, jumping the opposite way. It was a bold move, and I wasn't sure if he would fall for it, but I had no other option. I stood ready, facing him with my posture regained.

The maneuver caught him off guard, and I don't think he knew what exactly to do with it. He followed me, turning to the side to face me again. He did a quick thrust. I saw it and dodged it. While he was extended forward, I jabbed at his shoulder. My sword tip found its way between his plates of armor.

He roared in pain and surprise, recoiling a step. I jerked away from him, pulling back into my sword stance. He looked at me with a new rage kindled in his eye. Out of reckless anger he charged me, throwing himself sloppily to further engage. The first thing he did was a thrust at my torso. I knew he would do it, and waited until it was too late for him to recover to duck under his screaming blade. It worked perfectly. He surged forward and realized too late that I wasn't in front of him anymore. He lurched forward, trying to recover the force. He was nearly stumbling over me when I raised up my sword and drove it up under his breast plate.

The Vaudian doubled over, dropped his sword, and landed full on me. His dying breath was exhaled on the top of my head, my hair moving under the air. I cringed, his huge body crushing me. I still had one hand on my sword which was stuck up in him. I tried moving my other arm, but had no success. I squirmed under him, then stopped, trying to collect myself. I took a few shallow breaths, trying to think it through clearly.

I let go of the hilt and slowly moved my hands up to the chest of the Vaudian. I pushed up with all the strength I had. I threw my body weight to the left, somehow managing to roll him off me. I landed next to him on the cold stones. I took a few breaths then stood up and regained my bloodied sword. I looked down at my front. Right around my midsection was covered in dark wet blood. At first I thought it might have been mine, but then I realized that it wasn't mine at all.

Shoving aside the sick feeling that flooded my stomach, I forced myself to look for the oncoming enemy. My attention was quickly grabbed by a charging shorter beast. It was a little shorter than me and very round. He had a stubby sword that matched his stature. Even as he rushed at me, I couldn't help but see the resemblance.

After the huge Vaudian, the short little tub would be easy to deal with. I flicked the tip of his blade to the side and arched mine down at his exposed torso. He caught my blade, quickly recovering. He held it there, pressing against it. I circled my sword, pulled out of the hold, and aimed another stroke at his chest. He caught it again, and we exchanged a few blows that didn't really do anything.

Feeling bold from the success of my last encounter, I advanced on him, forcing his retreat as he scrambled to block each of my sword strikes. His eyes grew wider with surprise as I backed him further and further. His heel struck against a fallen warrior and he lost his balance. He stumbled backwards, trying to regain his footing. Only tripping further, he fell back and a let out a cry of pain. His eyes went wider with shock.

I stared at him, wondering why he didn't get up. Then I saw it. He had fallen on the sword of the warrior beneath him. I turned away, not wanting to watch what would happen next. I looked back at the ladders. Soldiers and men had regained ground and were pushing against the ladders. It took me a moment to realize what they were doing. They were pushing the ladders away, and as they careened backwards, screams and shouts irrupted below. The roar of battle was deafening.

All over the walls men were pushing the ladders back over the sides, sending them crashing to the ground. The shout went out from the officers all over the walls. The arrow supply had been replenished, and we picked up our bows, or any bow we could get our hands on that wasn't damaged from the fight.

I pulled a handful of arrows out of the bucket and went over to the parapet. I fitted an arrow to the string. This time, I knelt on one knee, my head between two stones at the top. I wasn't sure how I hadn't thought of it before, but I was glad that I did. It gave me ample protection, while I could still see where my arrows were going.

I pulled back the string and angled up, shooting my arrow high into the sky then dropping it into the masses of dark creatures whom had swarmed up to the walls. I shot out another arrow, this time not watching where it went but quickly firing another.

I focused on only that, speed counted more that accuracy. Down there it was sure to hit someone. Out of my peripheral vision I saw a ladder swing up and rest against the wall. I was just beginning to wonder if someone would push it down, when it shot back, hitting the ground with a sickening crunch.

After a few more arrows, I looked out and watched one fly from the string. It arched up, soaring against the grey clouds. Then it dropped down, and I lost it against the dark mountains. I looked over the black mass of moving bodies. The ground was littered with fallen dark creatures, some still, some writhing, dark creatures—from Vaudians to Between. I was shocked to see so many dead. It seemed like two fell for every one arrow we shot. There was no way that it was us either. Elohim was definitely here and working. You can't tell me that He's a silent, inactive King, because He's not. You might just not notice or see where His hand is working. But if you look hard, His fingerprints are all over everything.

I kept firing arrows, watching Elohim win the battle for us. My firing rate decreased with exhaustion, my arms getting tired and fingers aching. That was when I noticed Breylin was next to me. He had a beautiful long bow in his hands. He looked over at me and flashed a smile.

I returned it, then went back to shooting myself. I wondered where everyone else was and if they were okay from the raids that had come over the walls.

And that's when it happened. I still don't completely know how, why, or where it originated, but suddenly the tables turned for the worse. I had just released an arrow when my attention was attracted to a massive black figure in the middle of the dark sea of creatures. A chill passed over the wall, I could feel it sweep over us, emanating from the black figure. He was tall, shrouded in an ebony robe with the dark hood drawn over his face. His armor was blackened and jagged. In his gauntleted hand he held a large sword, the blade stained with dark blood made it look black as death. He was mounted upon a fearsome steed. It was inky black, darker and blacker than any other thing in the sea of dark creatures. The steed had massive leathery looking wings protruding from its shoulders. Even from the wall, I could distinctly see the blood red eyes, a raging fire lit behind them. White steam puffed from its nostrils in the morning air.

The chill emanating from the black warrior penetrated to the bone. All eyes were locked on the dark lord who had appeared below. I could feel the trembling and fear of the men along the walls. Their courage was failing them. At the sight of him, their hearts melted and they gave up hope.

I had only one thought. If I was to die, I would die for Elohim. My eyes were glued on the dark form, rearing and prancing over the field.

Crack!

The wall heaved a laborious shudder under our feet and a great splintering shook through the air. It startled us out of our awe of the powerful lord. Grabbing hold of the parapet for balance, I whirled to look at the gate a little distance from us. The massive timbers were shattered into large splinters, some still attached to the hinges, most splayed to the ground or twisted to the sides.

The cold iron head of the battering ram had struck through the central hole. Timber pieces splintered and raced towards the defenders like javelins. They had broken through the main gate. Metal encased hands grabbed at the gaping hole shattered through the heavy timber. Shreds of wood were pushed in and pulled out, making a way for them to break in. The company of soldiers, mostly composed of commoners from the city, shifted uneasily, holding out their shaking weapons. Many young faces stared wide eyed in fear at the growing breach. I was suddenly struck with compassion for them. They were so young and afraid, too young to die.

I took a quick look around me, summing things up. They didn't need me up here, not as much as they would need help down by the gate. I threw down my bow and reached for my sword. Drawing it forth, I headed towards the stairs at a run.

Breylin, who had been by me all this time, stared at me. He called after me, his voice cracking, "What are you doing?"

I didn't even look back, but yelled still racing, "They need help down there!"

"Limira! It's too dangerous!"

I didn't care. Pure determination drove me onward, I had nothing to reply to Breylin. In my mind I shouted back, "That's exactly why I need to go!" But I said nothing.

I reached the bottom of the wide stone stairs, and I raced over to join the group. The fearsome heads and upper bodies of Vaudians were visible through the hole. More boards were being torn away.

I glanced back at the stairs and saw Breylin rushing down the steps, his sword drawn as well. I smiled slightly to myself. I somehow knew that he would follow after me. He rushed up to my side, and I gave him a teasing look of questioning.

"What?" he asked, "I couldn't just let you come down here alone, now could I? Besides, now we can cover each other's backs."

Just as he finished, the last bit of timber shattered inwards under the boot of a massive Vaudian, making a large enough hole for entry. A flood of tall, large beasts charged at us.

I smiled grimly at them, daring them to come.

Chapter 39
Death Overtakes

Rushing forward a few steps, I eagerly wanted to take them on, but Breylin's strong hand grabbed my elbow, holding me back. I jerked against it just as a volley of arrows soared over our heads. The angry darts struck down the first few Vaudians to enter. I stared at the writhing wounded for only a second, thinking in shock that I might have been among them. I shot a grateful glance at Breylin as he let me go. He gave me a wink and a mischievous look that meant he wasn't about to let me forget my mistake.

Once the first of the Vaudians were downed, we rushed forward as one, racing to meet the next wave of enemies. A shout rose up among us, joining the roar of battle resounding through the air. Swords against swords, sheer force and numbers against resilience. I immediately engaged with a rather large Vaudian, while Breylin fought next to, and slightly behind me.

The Vaudian was reckless with the heat of battle upon him. He blundered clumsily to engaged with me, and I felled him within minutes. Another took his place, and he was just as reckless as the one before. I dispatched him quickly enough. I almost found them easier to fight here than on the rampart. It seemed as if the ones on the rampart were more cautious to engage, these ones simply ran into you. But these were bigger too, so their size almost made up for their lack of precision.

More Vaudians and Between burst through the rest of the gate, opening it completely. The sea outside the gate narrowed to a river flowing inside, pounding mercilessly at us. We were driven back from sheer numbers against us. Many fell on both sides. But it seemed the other side replenished the lost just as quickly as if there had been no casualties. We were not so fortunate. There was no aid, no reinforcements to send for. We were on our own.

I fought hard against them, each one proving more difficult. The rush of battle wore off and they became more cautious and intentional about their cuts. It was hardly good news for me, I was tiring quickly. The surge of initial adrenaline was wearing off. Fatigue and weariness was starting to catch up. My strokes became sloppier. Breylin covered for me more.

A particularly huge, muscular Vaudian stepped up to me, his sword raised and quickly descending down towards my head. I threw up my sword and ducked. Our swords clashed, the force of his blow pressing hard against my block. My arms were straining to hold it. Sweat pouring down my forehead, I used all the force and strength I could muster to throw off his blade. It sort of worked. His blade went sliding to the side, cutting through the air just in front of me.

He growled in anger and swung his sword for a descending blow from the left, aimed at my torso. I didn't even try blocking it. Jumping back, the tip of his sword nicked a tear in my jerkin.

Carried by the force of his cut, the Vaudian stumbled to the side, unable to fully recover. It left his side exposed long enough for me get close to him and jab my blade at his side. It disappeared between the seam of his back and breast plate. It was only a shallow cut, but he roared in pain, swinging around to find me really close to him. I was in his circle, where it would be very awkward to use his large sword.

One scarred, calloused hand went to his bleeding side. The other gripped his sword tightly. He tried an awkward downward blow, but it grazed over my head. It gave me just enough time to plunge my sword under his breastplate.

He doubled over, falling stiffly to the ground. His massive form had blocked my view of the rest of the battle outside the gate. Now I could see perfectly well, and the sight shocked me.

There, in the middle of everything, two figures of contrast fought a battle of life and death. One was the massive warrior shrouded in black, his robes fluttering with every powerful movement. The ebony winged steed beneath him moved with strength and power, as if it was only an extension of its master.

The other figure was clothed in the purest white. It was like the sun itself had been captured and now clothed this Man. He had a sword shining as if it was made of the whitest fire. It blazed with light as He masterfully wielded it against His opponent. There was this otherness about Him, this indescribable majesty. He rode upon the noblest horse I had ever seen. It was silver and shimmering, though no sun shone upon it. Its muscular limbs moved with ease and confidence. It faced the black enemy fearlessly. Authority and power swathed the steed and Rider, wreathed in the brightest light.

My mouth parted with wonder at the sight of darkness and light clashing in heated battle. I had no doubts as to who they were. They could be no other than Deceiver and Shalom Himself. None could even compare, there could be no mistake.

All I could do was stare at the splendor and majesty of my King. Everything else faded away. I was completely overwhelmed by Him. I finally managed to stutter out in an awed voice, "Breylin, look. It's... It's... Him."

"I know," came the equally awed answer in an equally awed voice. "I know."

I was smiling, pure joy overflowing inside me. New strength and hope and courage coursed through my veins. I suddenly broke out of my stupor, the feeling of awe and wonder still lingering about me.

Another Vaudian was charging at me. My smile actually widened, and I replanted my feet firmly on the stones. I was ready for anything.

Our swords struck together, a metallic ring joining the other sounds of ensuing battle. We withdrew and I arched my blade, aiming for his torso. He blocked and threw my blade to one side. I quickly pulled into a defensive stature. He rained down a succession of blows, forcing me to retreat a few steps. That ground I would never recover. I made a stand, forcing myself to stay and block his blows. He, being much taller than I, rained them down on my head. His sword kept mine busy, and I had no opportunity to get a stroke at his exposed torso.

His blows continued. I was beaten down under the weight of them. I went down on one knee, continuing to block as best I could, but his sheer strength sapped my energy. I sank lower and lower on one knee. I knew that I wouldn't last much longer. The last bit of desperate energy was expended on blocking his heavy blade. I felt my sword slipping down towards me under the weight of his massive weapon.

From the center of the battle field, where the two forces of Light and Darkness fought, a blinding flash exploded and raced through the air in all directions like a ripple in water. Bright white blew past us, knocking all the enemy to the ground.

The Vaudian fell straight over, pinning me under him. I felt a stab of sharp pain in my middle. As we went down, I saw just a glimpse of Shalom. He was on his steed of shimmering silver, standing among many fallen dark bodies. The blade of His sword was dark, and at his feet was a mass of crumpled black. The sun broke through the receding clouds, bathing the field and city in its warm light. Everything was still, paused in awe and wonder.

A gentle, warm wind blew over us, just as the light did. At the touch of the breeze, the Vaudians and the Between all crumbled, becoming nothing but ashes and dust. Everything but their cruel, blood stained weapons vanished back into the dust it was made from.

I lay on the cold stones, in complete shock. My short sword dropped from my hand. I struggled to lean forward on my elbows. A stabbing pain shot up from my stomach. Looking down, I stared at my front, blood spattered and dirty. There was the blood splotch from the Vaudian I had killed on the wall; it was dark and dry. But there was a new red mark, and this time it was my own blood. An open wound in my midsection screamed at me, the dark, wet spot growing.

When the Vaudian fell on top of me, his sword must have slipped in.

The last of my strength exhausted, I fell back on the stones. Excruciating pain emanated from my torso. Breath came in short gasps, wheezing and sticking in my throat. Every minute movement brought stabs of sickening pain. The growing blue spot of sky became blurry, and everything in my peripheral vision closed in on me as one dark mass. Numb blackness overtook me.

Part 5

Chapter 40
The Beginning

I woke up into what appeared to be a dream. Everything was bright and seemingly glowing. The light blue sky filled my vision. It seemed to grin down at me.

Then the kindest face I have ever known came into my view. He was smiling at me, His face a picture of serene love. But there was so much more about it that I could never begin to find the words to describe. Somehow, I don't think that there ever will be just the right words to describe Him fully.

Of course, I couldn't help but wonder if I had died. He seemed to know that I had thought it, and He laughed, His deep blue eyes getting brighter and merrier. He shook His head slightly at me and said in a gentle voice, "No, you're very much alive now, Limira." Then He stood up and reached a hand down to me. His smile simply glowed with warmth and love. "Will you come with Me? I have something for you to do."

I smiled with pure joy at the prospect of going with Him. I put my hand in His and replied still in awe, "Yes." Then a thought struck me as I was about to stand up. I hesitated and asked, "But...?" I moved a hand to my middle, "My...?" I frowned. There was no wound, only a scarlet stain on my jerkin was left for a reminder. I looked at Him with confusion and wonder.

He smiled all the more.

Then I realized what He had done and I returned His grin with one of my own. I stood up, His hand still in mine. The dreamlike glow faded slightly, but everything was still new and fresh looking, like the forest after a good rain. It was all washed clean and sparkling with the remnants of its Cleanser.

The sun was shining brightly on everything, steeping it in light. The streets looked swept clean, the piles of dirt gone. I could hear birds singing sweetly in the distance, and flowers were blooming again in the refreshed light.

Then I noticed the people.

I saw those whom I knew, all were safe and sound with no injuries. Breylin was standing near us, staring in humble adoration at Him. Kattim, Grenith, Findal, Nollem and Dwin were all standing on the top of the rampart, their faces wreaths of joy and awe at the sight of Shalom. There were some other citizens whom I did not know, a little distance from myself. It was clear they knew their King. I believe Mr. Helding was among them.

When I saw the rest of the soldiers and men of the city, my smiled faded slightly. They were all looking around in confusion, some of them in wonder, others with a fearful, wild look in their eye. People, mothers with their children, started coming slowly out of their houses. They had the same look of fear about them as the soldiers and men on the rampart.

I asked, confused by their responses, "Why are they still frightened?"

He replied, His expression a mix of sadness and authority, "They do not know that I have conquered Death. So they still walk in fear of its sting. Their eyes have been closed to shut out Life."

It was then that I realized they couldn't see Him. They were blinded and had no sight of the majestic splendor that surrounded them. It was right before their eyes, and they didn't see it; they didn't see Him. They didn't know Who their Savior was.

Shalom spoke again, "But, come, we will not tarry long. There is only a little to do here."

I let go of His hand, and He walked off, heading down a street. I wasn't sure what He was going to do next, but I didn't follow Him. Breylin stepped closer, and we exchanged looks of wonder and joy.

With Dwin at the lead, the rest came down the steps and joined Breylin and I. None of us had anything to say, there was nothing *to* say.

Then, from down the street, came Nettira, her children, and some of the older people from their home—which, by the way, while we were still at home, the day dragging by in anticipation of the battle, we settled on the name of Deliverance. We thought is was fitting, and Breylin approved. Mr. Helding rushed forward and embraced them all. Watching the family reunited added to our joy. To see their love for one another that could only come from Him made me smile.

Nollem slipped over to me and put his arm around my shoulders. I wrapped mine around his waist and smiled up at him. Something in that moment made me think of our own family, and the moments we wouldn't have. But somehow, it was okay. I was at peace. I still loved my parents, but I knew we could never share that same love without them finding Shalom's love first.

The moment came to an end when Shalom rounded the corner, returning from the street He had disappeared down.

Following Him was a handful of men and women, all smiling and looking wonderstruck at Him. Several horses followed them, all gently coming behind, no bridle or saddle. His own silver steed was walking right behind Him.

When the newcomers from Deliverance saw their King, the older ones fell to one knee reverently, while the young children ran up to Him unashamed. Shalom embraced them and picked them up in His arms, bestowing several smiles and embraces. Then he approached those who were kneeling. One by one, taking them each by the hand, He raised them to their feet, giving them a warm smile and a quiet word meant only for them.

There's no way to describe the looks on the faces of those who had accepted and returned the love from Him. There's nothing fitting except the purest, most enthusiastic joy and adoration ever expressed.

With the rest of us following, He led us over to the horses, and we all mounted. None of us had ever ridden a horse bareback, but we mounted fearlessly. There was no uncertainty, or fear, or sadness with Him.

We rode out under the gate and into the green field washed in sunshine. With Him in the front, we rode over the plains, on which the great battle had commenced merely hours before, and towards the pass to go over the Slaggar Mountains. The dark clouds that had formed as Deceiver paved a path of destruction from his land, dissipated, fading away into bright, warm light. Everything grew up around us, the dead things fading and replaced with bright new greenery.

Time seemed not to matter, or even exist. Minutes could have been hours, or hours could have been minutes, there was no telling. And it didn't matter, all we cared about was our King. Everything else faded.

After I don't know how long, we passed through Divel, the dilapidated small town of mud and old shacks of the same shade. As we passed through, grass and young flowers sprouted out of the mud. People came out of their houses as we went by. And there was always a horse for anyone who wanted to come. Thinking back, it seemed as if there was the exact amount of horses as there were people when we left Monare Pelm. But there was always another for anyone willing to ride with us.

I watched with joy as the Kelvin's emerged from their humble home, running with the eagerness and excitement of a child. They ran straight to their King and embraced Him without hesitation. Horses were found for them and they happily fell in next to Dwin.

When we reached the bottom of the mountains, we set our course due east, never turning to one side or the other. Our numbers grew as we went through the land. The land itself was greening and livening up as we went on. In the ashen ground of the burnt forests, little seedlings of trees sprouted, and wild flowers and grasses grew up. Squirrels, birds and other live things showed up too.

The sun never set that day, we just rode and rode. And before I knew it, we had quite the following. A large group of Lightbearers joined us in the burnt forest. There were many enthusiastic reunions, but the one I noticed was between Dwin and a young woman. After she turned from our King to find a mount, they saw each other. Dwin launched from the back of his horse. They ran towards one another and embraced for a long while. I knew exactly who she was when I saw her fiery blue eyes sparkling with joy. They returned to Dwin's horse, mounting together and riding on in blissful silence.

More pairs or lone Lightbearers seemingly appeared from nowhere to join with us.

Then we came to the border, or I should say where the border used to be. There was no shrouding fog rising from the ground to the sky, there were no clouds left over the land. The only sign that there had even been a border was a dark, burned line seared into the earth where the fog and mist used to be. All the dry, grey earth became green under our feet, young trees even sprouted. Life returned to it, all the greys became fresh greens and rich browns.

As we passed the cities, Moneth first then Birset, Lightbearers met and joined us, even though we were some distance from the cities. It was amazing to see how many Lightbearers were hidden away. And it was wonderful to see everyone meet their King. I was so glad that I had been one of the first of the party because then I got see everyone's reactions and their affections for Him. I can't even put it into words that would do it justice. It's kind of like trying to describe Him fully, I just don't have the words.

When we passed Dol Guliab, the twin mountains Deceiver once inhabited as his stronghold, I could hardly recognize them. Every shadow was dispelled, the ruins of the stone city were covered in green ivy. Life was bursting through, nothing was grey.

I was completely caught up in the sight of it and thinking all the more of Shalom.

It was shortly after then that I noticed a group of Lightbearers approaching us. All were sprinting in their joy, their expressions wreathed with smiles. Tears streamed down their faces as their King folded each one of them into His arms. Then they gladly joined our ranks.

Among them was a young woman. Her youthful face glowing with rest and peace and joy, despite its pale color. Her piercing gaze roamed over the citizens mounted and following their King. She stopped suddenly and stared with much elation in my direction. But I could tell she wasn't looking at me. Glancing over my shoulder, I checked to see if there was anyone behind me that she was staring at. I saw no one returning the gaze. Turning back, I happened to see Nollem, who was riding beside me.

He sat upon his horse, still as a blooming rose warmed in the summer sunshine. He was staring deeply into her eyes. His expression wore a funny small smile, his eyes twinkling with excitement.

Dismounting without ceasing to look at her, Nollem advanced toward her. She started to come to him as well. They met somewhere in the middle and embraced ardently. Then Nollem held her by the shoulders at arms length. Grinning, he spoke earnestly, "I knew you would be here."

She laughed, her soft voice ringing out like a melody. She nodded, her delighted expression bursting with smiles, "Yes, of course!"

Nollem beamed in return. Then they came back to where he left his horse. And somehow, another riderless horse had come up beside his. She mounted the available steed, and Nollem onto the back of his.

I knew that she must have been Arkona. They rode side by side. Nothing more was said between them, it wasn't needed. Their eyes were locked on He who was leading us. And they were filled to the fullest with adoration and affection of Him, He who took our place and gave us His.

We rode for several minutes more. It was then that I heard my name shouted from somewhere behind me. I turned slightly and scanned for the person belonging to the voice. I thought it sounded familiar, but I couldn't be sure that it was possible. It sounded like...

Haiblur!

Picking his way through the others was my old gypsy friend. His face was glowing with joy, and he made his way over to me quickly.

I smiled at the remembrance of his brave words so long ago that he would come find me again. It was thanks to him that I got away from Abburn. He rode up to me and we exchanged greetings. There was so much that we could have said, but all we could think or talk about was Shalom. And it was wonderful.

I felt right at home among all these people I had never met before. As I said, there was nothing to fear, and I knew that we were all united by our love for Him. We were complete in Him.

Before I knew it, we were past Dol Guliab, and no trace of darkness was to be seen for miles. I had never been past Dol Guliab, but I had always assumed that the land beyond was just as the rest of this land. But it wasn't anymore.

We kept going, on and on. And then I saw it for the first time. It was like we came upon it all of a sudden, because I either didn't see it or didn't notice it before it was right in front of us.

Running perpendicular to us was a sparkling river of the brightest, clearest blue. There were white and clear stones at the bottom, blinking and winking up at us from below the rippling surface. Colorful fish swam in it, and other aquatic life moved around in it. But it was only the beginning of a new land.

What was beyond the river was what really drew and held my attention. It was a beautiful land, much brighter and even more alive than the one that had just sprang up behind us. Rolling hills, bright green trees, lovely delicate flowers; not a thing was faded or dead. Everything was filled with indescribable life. Pure fluffy clouds stacked up in the sky, their edges blushed a light pink and slightly darker shades as if the sun was setting. In the center of it all was a stunning mountain that rose high. Its peak was hidden by the rosy clouds. On the slopes of that green mountain was a shining city. It shone like it was either made of glass and was reflecting the sun, or the sun was captured within it. Either way it emanated light.

It was the home of our King. And there we would live an eternity as citizens of His ultimate Kingdom. There was nothing truly important except Him, He in all His glory and majesty.

And I can truthfully say that we live happily ever after, forever in the presence of the One Who holds it all, the Lord of love, the Savior of the world.

The End

Made in the USA
Las Vegas, NV
18 February 2022

44165549R00249